Pleas
Surrer

C000068839

PRINCE'S PLEASURE

Complete your collection with
all three books!

In July: *At the Tycoon's Command*
In August: *At the Billionaire's Bidding*

AT THE
PRINCE'S
PLEASURE

JULIA   NATASHA   ROBYN
JAMES   **OAKLEY**   **DONALD**

*M&B™ and M&B™ with the Rose Device
are trademarks of the publisher.
Harlequin Mills & Boon Limited, Eton House,
18-24 Paradise Road, Richmond, Surrey TW9 1SR*

AT THE PRINCE'S PLEASURE
© by Harlequin Books S.A. 2009

Royally Bedded, Regally Wedded © Julia James 2007
Crowned: An Ordinary Girl © Natasha Oakley 2006
The Royal Baby Bargain © Robyn Donald 2005

ISBN: 978 0 263 87517 1

024-0609

*Harlequin Mills & Boon policy is to use papers that are
natural, renewable and recyclable products and made from
wood grown in sustainable forests. The logging and
manufacturing processes conform to the legal environmental
regulations of the country of origin.*

*Printed and bound in Spain
by Litografia Rosés S.A., Barcelona*

Royally Bedded, Regally Wedded

JULIA JAMES

Julia James lives in England with her family. Mills & Boon were the first 'grown up' books she read as a teenager, alongside Georgette Heyer and Daphne du Maurier, and she's been reading them ever since. Julia adores the English and Celtic countryside, in all its seasons, and is fascinated by all things historical, from castles to cottages. She also has a special love for the Mediterranean — "The most perfect landscape after England"! — and she considers both ideal settings for romance stories. In between writing she enjoys walking, gardening, needlework, baking extremely gooey cakes and trying to stay fit!

PROLOGUE

THE dark-haired figure seated at the antique desk and illuminated by an ornate, gold trimmed lamp slapped shut the leather folder, placed it on the growing pile to his right, and reached for yet another folder, opening it with an impatient flick. *Dio*, was there no end to these damned documents? How could so small a place as San Lucenzo generate so many of the things? Everything from officers' commissions to resolutions of the Great Council, all needing to be signed and sealed—by him.

Prince Rico gave a caustic twist of his well-shaped mouth. Perhaps he should be grateful the task seldom came his way. But with his older brother, the Crown Prince, in Scandinavia, representing the House of Ceraldi at a royal wedding, the temporarily indisposed Prince Regnant—their father—had for once been obliged to turn to his younger son to carry out those deputised duties he was generally excluded from.

Rico's eyes darkened for a moment with an old bitterness. Excluded from any involvement in the running of the principality—however tedious or trivial—yet his father still condemned him for the life he perforce led. The twist in his mouth deepened in cynicism. His father might deplore his younger son's well-earned reputation as the Playboy Prince, yet his exploits both in the world of expensive sports like powerboat racing, and on the glittering international social circuit—including the bedrooms of its most beautiful women—generated invaluable publicity for San Lucenzo. And, considering just how much of the principality's revenues derived from it being one of the world's most glamorous locales, his part in contributing to that glamour was not small. Not that either his father or older brother saw it that way. To them, his exploits brought the attention of the paparazzi and the constant risk of scandal—both of which were anathema to the strait-laced Ruling Prince of San Lucenzo and his upright heir.

Not, Rico grudgingly allowed, as he scanned through the document in his hand, that they were not sometimes justified in their concerns. Carina Collingham was an unfortunate instance in that respect—though how he could have been expected to know she was lying when she told him her divorce was through was beyond him.

Despite his instantly having dissociated himself from her the moment he'd discovered the unpalatable truth about the marital status of the film actress, the damage had been done, and now his father had yet another complaint to lay at his younger son's door.

His older brother, Luca, had taken him to task as well, berating him for not having had Carina security-checked adequately before bedding her. Better to exercise some self-restraint when it came to picking women out of the box like so much candy.

'There's safety in numbers,' Rico had replied acerbically. 'While I play the field, no woman thinks she has the ticket on me. Unlike you.' He'd cast a mordant look at his brother, along whose high Ceraldi cheekbones a line had been etched. 'You watch yourself, Luca,' he'd told him. 'Christabel Pasoni has plans for you.'

'Christa's perfectly content with the way things are,' Luca had responded repressively. 'And she does *not* cause a scandal in the press.'

'That's because her fond papa owns so much of it! *Dio*, Luca, can't you damn well ask her to tell *Papa* to instruct his editors to lay off me?'

But Luca had been unsympathetic.

'They wouldn't write about you if they had nothing to write. Don't you think it's time to grow up, Rico, and face your responsibilities?'

Rico's expression had hardened.

'If I had any, I might just do that,' he'd shot back, and walked away.

Well, he'd wanted responsibilities and now he'd got some—signing documents because there was no one else available to do so, and atoning for having had a misplaced affair with a still-technically-married woman.

Maybe if I sign every damn document in my best handwriting before Luca gets back I'll have earned a royal pardon…

But his caustic musing was without humour, and impatiently he scanned the document now in front of him. Something to do with a petition from a convent to be rescinded of the obligation to pay property tax on land on which a hospital had been built in the seventeenth century—a petition which, so the helpful handwritten note appended by his father's equerry reminded him, was nothing more than a *pro forma* request, made annually and granted annually since 1647, requiring nothing more than the customary royal assent. Dutifully, Rico scrawled the royal signature, put down the quill, and reached for the sealing wax, melting the required dark scarlet blob below his name, and then waiting a few moments for it to cool before impressing on it the royal seal. He was just replacing the seal when his phone went.

Not the phone on the desk, but his own mobile—to which very, very few people had the number. Frowning slightly, he slid a long fingered hand inside his jacket pocket and flicked open the handset.

'Rico?'

He recognised the voice at once, and his frown deepened. Whenever Jean-Paul phoned it was seldom good news—certainly not at this late hour of the night. The hour when, Rico knew from experience, the press went to bed. And what a certain section of the press across Europe all too often went to bed with was a story of just who *he* had gone to bed with.

Damn—had the vultures stirred yet more trouble for him over Carina Collingham? Had she been milking the situation for yet more publicity for her career?

'OK, Jean-Paul, tell me the worst,' he said, when foreboding.

The gossip-columnist, who was also the impoverished grandson of a French count, as well as a rare genuine friend in the press, started to speak. But the story that he'd heard was about to break had nothing to do with Carina Collingham. Nothing to do with any of Rico's *affaires*.

'Rico,' said Jean-Paul, and his voice was unusually grave, 'it's about Paolo.'

Rico stilled. Slowly he released his hand from the back of his neck and slipped it down on to the leather surface of the desk. It tensed, unconsciously, into a fist.

'If *anyone*—' his voice was a soft, deadly snarl '—thinks they are going to dig any dirt on him, they are—'

He could hear the wariness in the other man's voice as he interrupted.

'I wouldn't call it dirt, Rico. But I would...' he paused minutely '...call it trouble. Seriously big trouble.'

Emotion splintered through Rico.

'*Dio*, Paolo is *dead*. His broken body got pulled from the wreckage of a car over four years ago.'

Pain stabbed him. Even now he could not bear to think about, to remember, how Paolo—the golden prince, the only one of his father's three sons who had ever won his parents' indulgence—had been snuffed out before he was even twenty-two. Like a bright flame extinguished by the dark.

The news had devastated the family. Even Luca had wept openly at the funeral, where the two of them had been the chief pallbearers who had carried their young brother's black-swathed coffin into the cathedral on that unbearable day.

And now, years later, some slimeball hack *dared* to write some kind of sleaze about Paolo.

'What kind of trouble?' he demanded icily. On the desk, his hand fisted more tightly.

There was a distinct pause, as if Jean-Paul were mentally gathering courage. Then he spoke.

'It's about the girl who was in the car crash with him…'

Rico froze.

'What girl?' he asked slowly, as every drop of blood in his veins turned to ice.

Haltingly, Jean-Paul told him.

CHAPTER ONE

*'OH MY darling, oh my darling, oh my darling Benjy-mine—
You are mucky, oh, so mucky, so it's Benjy's bathy-time.'*

Lizzy chirruped away, pushing the laden buggy along the narrow country lane as dusk gathered in the hedgerows. Crows were cawing overhead in the trees near the top of the hill, and the last light of day dwindled in the west, towards the sea, half a mile back down the coombe. It was still only late spring, and primroses gleamed palely in the verges and clustered in the long grass of the lower part of the hedge. The upper part was made of stunted beech, its branches slanted by the prevailing west wind off the Atlantic, which, even now, was combing along the lane and whipping her hair into yet more of a frizz—though she'd fastened it back as tightly as she could. But what did she care about her awful hair, charity shop clothes and total lack of looks? Ben didn't, and he was all she cared about in the world.

'Not *mucky*, Mummy. *Sandy*,' Ben corrected her, craning his head round reprovingly in the buggy.

'Mucky with sand,' compromised Lizzy.

'Keep singing,' instructed Ben.

She obeyed. At least Ben was an uncritical audience. She had no singing voice at all, she knew, but for her four-year-old son that was not a problem. Nor was it a problem that everything he wore, and all his toys—such as they were—came from jumble sales or from charity shops in the local Cornish seaside town.

Nor was it a problem that he had no daddy, like most other children seemed to have.

He's got *me*, and that's all he needs, Lizzy thought fiercely, her hands gripping the buggy handles as she pushed it along up the steepening road, hastening her pace slightly. It was growing late, and therefore dark, but Ben had been enjoying himself so much on the beach, even though it was far too cold yet to swim, that she had stayed later than she had intended.

But its proximity to the beach had been the chief reason that Lizzy had bought the tiny cottage, despite its run-down condition, eleven months ago, after selling her flat in the London suburbs. It was much better to bring a child up in the country.

Her face softened.

Ben. Benedict.

Blessed.

That was what his name meant, and it was true—oh, so true! He had been blessed with life against all the odds, and *she* had been blessed with him. No mother, she knew, could love her child more than she did.

Not even a birth mother.

Grief stabbed at her with a familiar pain. Maria had been so *young*. Far too young to leave home, far too young to be a model, far too young to get pregnant and far too young to die. To be smashed to pieces in a hideous pile-up on a French motorway before she was twenty.

Lizzy's eyes were pierced with sorrow. Maria—so lovely, so pretty. The original golden girl. Her long blonde hair, her wide-set blue eyes and angelic smile. Her slender beauty had been the kind of beauty that turned heads.

And sold clothes.

Their parents had been aghast when Maria had bounded in from school, still in her uniform, and told them that she'd been spotted by a scout for a modelling agency. Lizzy had been despatched to chaperon the eighteen-year-old Maria when she went up to the West End for her try-out shoot. The two girls had reacted very differently to the experience, Lizzy recalled. Maria had been ecstatic, instantly looking completely at home in the fashionable milieu, while Lizzy couldn't have felt more out of place or more awkward—as if she were contaminated by some dreadful disease.

Lizzy knew what that disease was. She'd known it ever since her blue-eyed, golden-haired sister had been born, two years after her, when, overnight, she had become supremely unimportant to her parents. Her sole function had been to look out for Maria. And that was what she'd done. Walked Maria to school, stayed late at clubs Maria had belonged to, helped her with her homework and then, later, with exam revision. Although Maria, being naturally clever, had not, so her parents had often reminded her, needed much help from her—especially as Lizzy's own exam results had hardly been dazzling. But then, who had *expected* them to be dazzling? No one. Just as no one had expected her to make any kind of mark in the world at all. And because of that, and because going to college cost money, Lizzy had not gone to college. The pennies had been put by to see Maria through university.

But all their hopes had been ruined—Maria had been offered a modelling contract. She'd been over the moon, telling her parents that she could always go to university later, and pay for it herself out of her earnings. Her parents had not been pleased, they had looked forward to spending their money on Maria.

'Well, now you can pay for Lizzy to go to college instead,' Maria had said. 'You know she always wanted to go.'

But it had been ridiculous to think of that. At twenty, Lizzy had been too old to be a student, and not nearly bright enough. Besides, they'd needed Lizzy to work in the corner shop that her father owned, in one of London's outer suburbs.

'Lizzy, leave home,' Maria had urged, the first time she'd come back after starting her new career. 'They treat you like a drudge like some kind of lesser mortal. Come up to London and flat with me. It's a hoot, honestly. Loads of fun and parties. I'll get you glammed up, and we can—'

'No.' Lizzy's voice had been sharp.

Maria had meant it kindly. For all her parents' attention to her she had never been spoilt, and her warm, sunny nature had been as genuine as her golden looks. But what she'd suggested would have been unbearable. The thought of being the plain, lumpy older sister dumped in a flat full of teenage models who all looked as beautiful as Maria had been hideous.

But she should have gone, she knew. Had known as soon as that terrible, terrible call had come, summoning her to the hospital in France where Maria had been taken.

If she'd been living with Maria surely she'd have found out about the affair she'd started? Perhaps even been able to stop it? Guilt stabbed her. At least she'd have known who Maria was having an affair *with*.

Which would have meant—she glanced down at Ben's fair head—she would have known who had got her pregnant.

But she did not know and now she would never know.

She paused in her tuneless singing. Further back down the lane she could hear the sound of a car engine. Instinctively she tucked the buggy closer to the verge. There was a passing place further along, but she doubted she could reach it before the approaching vehicle did. Wishing it weren't quite so dusky, she paused, half lifting one set of buggy wheels on to the verge, and warning Ben that a car was coming along.

Headlights cut through the gathering gloom and swept up the lane, followed by a powerful vehicle. It slowed as the lights picked her out, and for a moment Lizzy thought it was going to stop. Then it was past them, and accelerating forward. As it did so, she frowned slightly. The lane she was walking along led inland, whereas the road back to the seaside town ran parallel to the coast. Little traffic came along this lane. Well, maybe the occupants were staying at a farm or a holiday cottage inland. Or maybe they were just lost. She went on pushing the buggy up the final part of the slope, and then around the bend to where her cottage was.

As she finally rounded the curve she saw, to her surprise, that the big four-by-four had parked outside her cottage.

A shiver of apprehension flickered through her. This was a very safe part of the world, compared to the city, but crime wasn't unknown. She slid her hand inside her jacket and flicked her mobile phone on, ready to dial 999 if she had to. As she approached her garden gate she saw two tall figures get out of the car and come towards her. She paused, right by her gate, one hand in her pocket, her finger hovering over the emergency number.

'Are you lost?' she asked politely.

They didn't answer, just closed in on her. Every nerve in her body started to fire. Then, abruptly, one of them spoke.

'Miss Mitchell?'

His voice was deep, and accented. She didn't know what accent. Something foreign, that was all. She looked at him, still with every nerve firing. His face was shadowed in the deepening dusk; she just got an impression of height, of dark eyes—and something else. Something she couldn't put a name to.

Except that it made her say slowly, 'Yes. Why do you want to know?'

Instinctively she moved closer to the buggy, putting herself between it and the strangers.

'Who are those men?' Ben piped up. His little head craned around as he tried to see, because she'd pointed the buggy straight at the gate to the garden.

She heard the man give a rasp in his throat. Then he was speaking again. 'We need to speak to you, Miss Mitchell. About the boy.' There was a frown across his brow, a deep frown, as he looked at her.

'Who are you?' Lizzy's voice was shrill suddenly, infected with fear.

Then the other man, more slightly built, and older, spoke.

'There is no cause for alarm, Miss Mitchell. I am a police officer, and you are perfectly safe. Be assured.'

A police officer? Lizzy stared at him. His voice had the

same accent as the taller, younger man, whose gaze had gone back fixedly to Ben.

'You're not English.'

The first man's eyebrows rose as he turned back to her. 'Of course not,' he said, as if that were a ridiculous observation. Then, with a note of impatience in his voice, he went on, 'Miss Mitchell, we have a great deal to discuss. Please be so good as to go inside. You have my word that you are perfectly safe.'

The other man was reaching forward, pushing open the gate and ushering her along the short path to her front door. Numbly she did as she was bade. Tension and a deep unease were still ripping through her. As she gained the tiny entrance hall of the cottage she paused to unlatch Ben from his safety harness. He struggled out immediately, and turned to survey the two tall men waiting in the doorway to gain entrance.

Lizzy straightened, and flicked on the hall light, surveying the two men herself. As her gaze rested on the younger of the two, she saw he was staring, riveted, at Ben.

There were two other things she registered about him that sent conflicting emotions shooting through her.

The first was, quite simply, that in the stark light of the electric bulb the man staring down at Ben was the most devastatingly good-looking male she'd ever seen.

The second was that he looked terrifyingly like her sister's son.

In shocked slow motion Lizzy helped Ben out of his jacket and boots, then her own, then folded up the buggy and leant it against the wall. Her stomach was tying itself into knots. Oh, God, what was happening? Fear shot through her, and convulsed in her throat.

'This is the way to the kitchen,' announced Ben, and led the way, looking with great interest at these unexpected visitors.

The warmth of the kitchen from the wood-burning range made Lizzy feel breathless, and the room seemed tiny with the two men standing in it. Instinctively she stood behind Ben as he climbed on to a chair to be higher. Both men were still regarding him intently. Fear jerked through her again.

'Look, what *is* this?' she demanded sharply. Her arm came around Ben's shoulder in a protective gesture. The man who looked like Ben turned briefly to the other man, and said something low and rapid in a foreign language.

Italian, she registered. But the recognition did nothing to help her. She didn't understand Italian, and what the man had just said to the other one she'd no idea. But she understood what he said next.

'Prego,' he murmured. 'Captain Falieri will look after the boy in another room while we…' he paused heavily '…talk.'

'No.' Her response was automatic. Panicked.

'The boy will be as safe,' said the man heavily, 'as if he had his own personal bodyguard.' He looked down at Ben. 'Have you got any toys? Captain Falieri would like to see them. Will you show them to him? Can you do that?'

'Yes,' said Ben importantly. He scrambled down. Then he glanced at Lizzy. 'May I, please?'

She nodded. Her heart was still pounding as she watched the older man accompany Ben out of the kitchen. Supposing the other man just walked out of the house with Ben. Supposing he drove off with him. Supposing…

'The boy is quite safe. I merely require to talk to you without him hearing at this stage. That much is obvious, I would have thought.'

There was reproof in the voice. As though she were making trouble. Making a nuisance of herself.

She dragged her eyes to him, away from Ben leading the other man into the chilly living room.

He was looking at her from across the table. Again, like a blow to her chest, his resemblance to Ben impacted through her. Ben was fair, and this man was dark, but the features were so similar.

Fear and shock buckled her again.

What if this was Ben's father?

Her stomach churned, his heartbeat racing. Desperately she tried to calm herself.

Even if he's Ben's father he can't take him from me—he can't!

Faintness drummed through her. Her hand clung on to the back of the kitchen chair for strength.

'You are shocked.' The deep, accented voice did not hold reproof any more, but the dark eyes were looking at her assessingly. As if he were deciding whether she really was shocked.

She threw her head back.

'What else did you expect?' she countered.

His eyes pulled away from her and swept the room. Seeing the old-fashioned range, the almost as old-fashioned electric cooker, ancient sink, worn work surfaces and the scrubbed kitchen table standing on old flagstones.

'Not this,' he murmured. Now there was disparagement clear in his voice. His face.

The face that looked so terrifyingly like Ben's.

'Why are you here?' The words burst from her.

The dark eyebrows snapped together. So dark, he was, and yet Ben so fair. And yet despite the difference in colouring, the bones were the same, the features terrifyingly similar.

'Because of the boy, obviously. He cannot remain here.'

She felt the blood drain from her.

'You can't take him. You can't swan in here five years after conceiving him and—'

'*What?*' The single word was so explosive that it stopped Lizzy dead in her tracks.

For one long, shattering moment he just stared at her with a look of total and utter stupefaction on his face. As if the world completely and absolutely did not make sense. Lizzy stared back. Why was he looking at her like that? As if she were insane. Deranged.

'*I* am not Ben's father.'

The words bit from him. Relief washed through her, knocking the wind out of her. The terror that had been dissolving her stomach—the terror that, for all her defiance, this man invading her home had the power to take Ben from her, or at the very least to demand a presence in her son's life—the fear that had gripped her since she had seen the startling resemblance in their faces, began to subside.

'I am Ben's uncle.' The words were flat. Irrefutable. 'It was my brother, Paolo, who was Ben's father. And, as you must know, Paolo—like your sister Maria, Ben's mother—is dead.' Now his voice was bleak, stark.

Lizzy waited for the flush of relief to go through her again. The man who had got her sister pregnant was dead. He could never threaten her. Could never threaten Ben. She should feel relief at that.

But no such emotion came. Instead, only a terrible empty grief filled her.

Dead. Both dead. Both parents. And suddenly it seemed just so incredibly, blindingly sad. So cruel that Ben had had ripped from him both the people who had created him.

'I'm…I'm sorry,' she heard herself saying, her throat tight suddenly.

For just a moment the expression in his eyes changed, as if just for the briefest second they were both feeling the same emotion, the same grief at such loss. Then, like a door shutting, it was gone.

'I've…I've never known who Ben's father was.' Lizzy's voice was bleak. 'My sister never regained consciousness. She stayed in a coma until Ben was full-term, and then—' She broke off. Something struck her. She looked at the man who looked so much like Ben, who was his uncle. 'Did…did you know about Ben?'

The brows snapped together. 'Of course not. His existence was entirely unknown. That might seem impossible, given the circumstances of his parents' death, which seem to have concealed even from you the identity of his father. However, thanks to the mercenary investigations of a muck-raking journalist, about which thankfully I have been recently informed, his existence is unknown no longer. Which is why—' his voice sharpened, the initial impatience and imperiousness returning '—he must immediately be removed from here.' His mouth pressed tightly a moment. 'We may have located you ahead of the press, but if we can find you, so can they. Which means that both you and the boy must leave with us immediately. A safe house has been organised.'

'What journalist? What do you mean, the press?'

A frown darkened his brow.

'Do not be obtuse. The moment the boy's location is discovered, the press will arrive like a pack of jackals. We must leave immediately.'

Lizzy stared uncomprehendingly. This was insane. What was going on?

'I don't understand. I don't understand any of this. Why would the press come here?'

'To find my nephew. What do you imagine?' Impatience and exasperation were snapping through him.

'But why? What possible interest can the press have in Ben?'

He was staring at her. Staring at her as if she were completely insane.

Across the hall, Ben's piping voice came from the living room, talking about his trainset.

'This is the level crossing, and that's the turntable.'

His voice faded again.

The man who was Ben's uncle was still staring at her. Lizzy started to feel cold seep through her.

'We haven't done anything.' Her voice was thin. 'Why would any journalist be interested in Ben? He's a four-year-old child.'

That look was still in his eye. He stood, quite motionless.

'He was born. That is quite enough. His parentage ensures that.' Exasperated anger suddenly bit through his voice. 'Surely to God you have intelligence enough to understand that?'

Slowly, Lizzy took another careful step backwards. She did

not like being so physically close to this man. It was overpowering, disturbing. Her heart was hammering in her chest.

What did he mean, Ben's parentage? She stared at him. Apart from his being so extraordinarily, devastatingly good-looking, she did not recognise him. He looked like Ben, that was all. A dark version. Very Italian. He must be quite well-off, she registered. The four-by-four was a gleaming brand-new model. And he was wearing expensive clothes; she could see that. He had the sleek, impeccably groomed appearance of someone who wore clothes which, however deceptively casual, had cost a lot of money. And he had that air about him of someone who was used to others jumping to do his bidding. So he could easily be rich.

But why would that bring the press down in droves? Rich Italians were not so unique that the press wrote stories about them.

A frown crossed her face. But what about his brother, Paolo? His dead brother who was Ben's father. Had he been someone the press would be interested in?

He'd said that surely she must know that Paolo was dead. But how should she? She knew nothing about him.

Carefully, very carefully, she spoke.

'My sister was not a supermodel, she was just starting out on her career—just making a name for herself. No journalist would be interested in her. But your brother—the man she…she had a child by. Was he—I don't know—someone well known in Italy? Was he a film star there, or on the television? Or a footballer, a racing driver? Something like that? Some kind of celebrity? Is that what you mean by Ben's parentage?'

She stared at him, a questioning look on her face. Slowly, it changed to one of bewilderment.

He was looking at her as if she were an alien. Fear stabbed her again.

'What—what is it?'

His eyes were boring into her face. As if he were trying to penetrate into her brain.

'This cannot be,' he said flatly. 'It is not possible.'

Lizzy stared. *What* was not possible?

He was holding himself in; she could see it.

'It is not possible that you have just said what you said.' His expression changed, and now he was not talking to her as if she were retarded, but as if she were—unreal. As if this entire exchange were unreal.

'My brother—' he spoke, each word falling as heavy as lead into the space between them '—was Paolo Ceraldi.'

Nothing changed in her expression. She swallowed. 'I'm sorry—the name does not mean anything to me. Perhaps in Italy it might, but—'

A muscle worked in his cheek. His eyes were like black holes.

'Do not, Miss Mitchell, play games with me. That name is *not* unknown to you. It *cannot* be. Nor can the name of San Lucenzo.'

Her face frowned slightly. San Lucenzo? Perhaps that was where Ben's father had come from. But, even if he had, why the big deal?

'That's...that's that place near Italy that's like Monaco. One of those places left over from the Middle Ages.' She spoke cautiously. 'On the Riviera or somewhere. Lots of rich people live there. But...but I'm sorry. The name Paolo Ceraldi still doesn't mean anything to me, so if he was famous there, I'm afraid I just don't—'

The flash in his eyes had come again. With cold, chilling courtesy he spoke, but it was not civil.

'The House of Ceraldi, Miss Mitchell, has ruled San Lucenzo for eight hundred years,' he said sibilantly.

There was silence. Complete silence. Some incredibly complicated arcane equation was trying to work itself out in her brain, but she couldn't do it.

Then the deep, chilling voice came again, icy with a courtesy that was not courteous at all.

'Paolo's father is the Ruling Prince.' He paused, brief and deadly, while his eyes speared hers. 'He is your nephew's grandfather.'

CHAPTER TWO

MIST was rolling in, like thick cotton wool. She felt the room start to swirl around her. Instinctively, she grabbed out with her hand and caught the edge of the kitchen table. She clung on to it.

Not true.

Not true. Not true. Not true.

If she just kept saying it, it would be true. True that it was *not* true. Not true what this man had just said. Because of course it wasn't true. It couldn't be true. It was absurd. Stupid. Impossible. A lie. Some stupid, absurd, impossible lie—or joke. Maybe it was a joke. That must be it. Just a joke. She threw her head back to suck in deep draughts of air. Then she steadied herself, forcibly, and made herself look across at the man who had just said such a stupid, absurd, impossible thing.

'This isn't true.'

Her voice was flat. As flat, she realised, with a hideous, gaping recognition in her guts, as his had been when she'd said she had no idea who…

Ben's father. Ben's father was.

'No.' She'd spoken out loud. Her legs were starting to shake. 'No. This is a joke. It's impossible. It has to be. It's just not possible. I haven't understood it properly.'

'You had better sit down.' The voice was still chill, but less so. Lizzy gazed at him with wide, shock-splintered eyes. Her eyebrows shot together in a frown.

That complicated, arcane equation was still running in her head.

He had just said that Ben's father had been the son of…she forced her mind to say it … the son of the Prince of San Lucenzo. But he had said he was Ben's uncle. His dead father's brother. Which meant that *his* father was also…

She stared. It wasn't possible. It just wasn't possible.

He let her stare. She could see it. Could see he was just standing there while she clung to the edge of the table in the kitchen in her tiny little Cornish cottage where, a few feet away, from her stood.

'I am Enrico Ceraldi,' he enlightened her.

She sat down. Collapsing on the kitchen chair with a heavy thud.

He cast a look at her.

'Did you really not know who I was?' There was almost curiosity in his voice. And something flickered in his eyes.

'Of course I bloody didn't.' The return burst from her lips without her thinking. Then, as if she'd just realised what she'd done, her face stiffened.

'I'm sorry,' she spoke abruptly. 'I didn't mean to be—' She broke off. Something changed in her face again. She lifted her chin, looking directly into his eyes. 'I didn't mean to speak rudely. But, no,' she said heavily, yet still with her chin lifted, 'I did not recognise you. I've heard of you—it would be hard not to have.' Her voice tightened with disapproval. 'But not with the surname, of course. Just your first name and…' she paused, then said it '…your title.'

She got to her feet. The room swayed, but she ignored it. A bomb had exploded in her head, ripping everything to shreds. But she had to cope with it. She straightened her spine.

'I find this very hard to deal with. I'm sure you understand. And I am also sure you understand that I have a great many questions I need to ask. But also—' she held his eyes and spoke resolutely '—I need time to come to terms with this. It is, after all, quite unbelievable.'

She looked at him directly. Refusing to look away.

Long, sooted lashes swept down over his dark eyes. Eyes, she realised, with the now familiar hollowing still going on inside her stomach, that were more used to looking out of photographs in celebrity magazines and the gossip pages of newspapers.

I didn't recognise him. I simply didn't recognise him. He's all over the press and I never recognised him.

But why should I? And why should I think that someone like him could turn up here and tell me that…that Ben is…

Shock kicked through her again.

She bowed her head. It was too much. It was all too much.

'I can't take any more.'

She must have spoken aloud, defeat in her voice.

For one long, hopeless minute she just stared blankly into the eyes of the man standing opposite her. The brother of Ben's father. Who was dead. Who had been the son of the Reigning Prince of San Lucenzo. Who was also the father of the man standing opposite her.

Who was therefore a prince.

Standing in her living room.

'I can't take any more,' she said again.

Rico shifted his head slightly, and glanced behind him as the occasional dazzle of other traffic on the motorway illuminated the interior of the vehicle.

She was asleep. So was the boy. She was holding his hand, reaching out to him in the child seat he was fastened into.

His mouth pressed together and he looked away again, back out over the glowing stream of red tail-lights ahead of him. Beside him, Falieri drove steadily and fast, the big four-by-four eating up the miles.

Rico stared out over the motorway.

Paolo's son. Paolo's son was sitting in the car. A son that none of his family had known about.

How could it have happened?

The question seared through him, as it had done so often since Jean-Paul had told him the story that was set to break in the press. It seemed impossible that Paolo's son should have disappeared, without anyone even knowing of his existence. And yet, in the nightmare of that motorway pile-up in France all those years ago, with smashed cars and smashed bodies, he could see how rescue workers, finding the female occupant of Paolo's car still alive and clearly pregnant, had cut her free first and rushed her to hospital. A different hospital from the one where Paolo's mangled body had been taken hours later, when all those still living had been dealt with.

Cold horror chilled through him. In the carnage no one had made the connection between the two—the dead Prince Paolo Ceraldi and the unknown young woman, comatose and pregnant.

Never to regain consciousness.

Never to tell who had fathered her child.

And so no one had known. No one until some get-lucky hack had decided to see if there was any mileage in a rehash of the tragedy of Paolo's death, and his investigations had turned up, against all the odds, a French fireman who'd mentioned he had freed a woman from the wreckage of the very type of sports car that the journalist knew Paolo Ceraldi had been driving. From that single item the hack had burrowed and burrowed, until he had pieced together the extraordinary, unbelievable story.

How Prince Paolo Ceraldi, dead at twenty-one, had left an orphaned son behind.

The story would blaze across the tabloids.

'Get the boy.'

Luca's urgent command echoed in Rico's head. He'd phoned Luca the moment he'd hung up on Jean-Paul.

'We have to get the boy before the press does,' Luca had said. 'Get Falieri on to it tonight. But, Rico, it's essential we look as if we don't know about the story. If they think we are trying to stop it, they'll run with it immediately. In the meantime—' his voice had hardened '—I will contact Christa. Maybe for once

I will, after all, exact a favour from her father…it won't stifle the story, but it may just delay it. Buy us some time. Enough for Falieri to get the child safely out of their reach.' He'd paused, then gone on, his voice dry. 'It seems, just for once, Rico, that your close proximity to the press has come in handy.'

'Glad to be of use,' Rico had replied, his voice even drier. 'For once.'

'Well, you can really be of use now,' Luca had cut back. 'I can't leave this wedding, if I did it would simply arouse suspicion, so I'm stuck here for the duration. I'm counting on you to hold the fort. But Rico?' His voice had held a warning note in it. 'Leave it to me to tell our father about this debacle, OK? He'll take it a lot better from me.'

Rico hadn't stuck around to find out how his father had taken the news that the Ceraldis were about to face their biggest trial by tabloid yet. He'd had only one imperative. To find Paolo's son.

Emotion buckled him. He'd been holding it back as much as he could, because there had been no time for it. No time to do anything other than get hold of Falieri and track down the child his brother had fathered.

He felt his heart squeeze tightly. It was incredible that here, now, just in the seat behind him, his brother's son was sleeping. It was almost like having Paolo back again.

Debacle, Luca had called it. And Rico knew he was right. He loathed the thought of all the tabloid coverage that was inevitably going to erupt, even with the boy safely with him now, but far more powerful was the sense of wonder and gratitude coursing through him.

He turned in his seat, his eyes resting on the sleeping form of the small boy.

His heart squeezed again. Even in the poor light he could see Paolo's features, see the resemblance. To think that his brother's blood pulsed in those delicate veins, that that small child was his own nephew.

Paolo's son. His brother's child. The brother who had been killed so senselessly, so tragically.

And yet—

He had had a son.

All these years, growing up here, in this foreign country, raised by a woman who was not even his own mother, not knowing who he was.

We didn't know. How could we not have known?

A cold, icy chill went through him.

For a long moment his eyes watched over the sleeping boy, seeing his little chest rise and fall, the long lashes folded down on his fair skin.

Then, slowly, they moved to the figure beside the child seat.

His expression changed, mouth tightening.

This was a complication they could do without.

His gaze rested on her. A frown gathered between his brows. Had she really not realised who he was? It seemed incredible, and yet her shock had been genuine. His frown deepened. He had never before encountered anyone who did not know who he was.

He dragged his mind away. It was irrelevant that his reaction to her evident complete ignorance of his identity had…had what? Irritated him? Piqued him? No, none of those, he asserted to himself. He was merely totally unaccustomed to not being recognised. He had been recognised wherever he went, all his life. Everyone always knew who he was.

So being stared at as if he were the man in the moon had simply been a new experience for him. That was all.

Dio, he dismissed impatiently. What did he care if the girl hadn't realised who he was? It was, as he had said, irrelevant. She knew now. That was all that mattered. And once she'd accepted it—not that the look of glazed shock had left her face until she'd fallen asleep in the vehicle—it had at least had the thankful effect of making her co-operate finally. Silently, numbly, but docilely.

She'd made sandwiches and drinks for herself and Ben,

telling him while he ate that they were going on an adventure, and then heading upstairs to pack. Ben had shown no anxiety, only curiosity and excitement. Rico had done his best to give him an explanation he could understand.

'I...' He had hesitated, then said it, a shaft of emotion going through him as he did so. 'I am your uncle, Ben, and I have only just found out that you live here. So I am taking you on a little holiday. We'll need to leave now, though, and drive in the night.'

It had seemed to suffice.

He had fallen asleep almost instantly, the car having only gone a few miles, and it had not taken a great deal longer for the aunt to fall asleep as well. Rico was glad. A car was not the place for the next conversation they must have.

He glanced at her now, his face tightening in automatic male distaste at the plain-faced female, with her unflattering frizzy hair and even more unflattering nondescript clothes.

She couldn't be more different from Maria Mitchell. She possessed not a scrap of her sister's looks. Maria had been one of those naturally eye-catching blondes, tall and slender, with wide-set blue eyes and a heart-shaped face. No wonder she'd become a model. The photos Falieri had dug up of her had shown exactly how she must have attracted Paolo.

They would have made a golden couple.

Pain bit at him, again. *Dio*, both of them wiped out, their young lives cut short in a crush of metal. But leaving behind a secret legacy.

Rico's eyes went back to his nephew, softening.

We'll take care of you now—don't worry. You're safe with us.

Oblivious, Ben slept on.

Lizzy stirred. Even as the first threads of consciousness returned, she reached automatically across the wide bed.

It was all right. Ben was there. For a moment she let her hand rest on the warm, pyjama-covered back of her son, still fast asleep on the far side of the huge double bed. They were in some kind of private house, at which they'd arrived in the middle of the night—specially rented, and staffed by San Lucenzans flown in from the royal palace, or so she had been told by Captain Falieri. A safe house. Safe from prying journalists.

Disbelief washed through her, as it had done over and over again since that moment when she'd stared at the man who had invaded her cottage and realised who he was.

She was still in shock, she knew. She had to be. Because why else was she so calm? Partly it was for Ben's sake. Above all he must not be upset, or distressed. For his sake she must treat this as normal.

Impossible as that was.

What's going to happen?

The question arrowed through her, bringing a churning anxiety to her stomach.

Was the Prince still here? Or had he left her with Captain Falieri. She hoped he was gone. She was not comfortable with him.

She shifted in her bed. Even had he not been royal, let alone infamous in the press—what did they call him? The Playboy Prince? Was that it?—she could never have been comfortable in his company. No man that good-looking could make her feel anything other than awkward and embarrassed.

Just as, she knew with her usual searing honesty, a man like that could never be comfortable with *her* around. Men like that wanted to be surrounded by beautiful women—women like Maria. Females who were plain and unattractive, as she was, simply didn't exist for them. Hadn't she learnt that lesson early, knowing that for men she was simply invisible? How many times had male eyes slid automatically past her to seek out Maria?

She jerked her mind away from such irrelevancies, back to what she did not want to think about. The paternity of her son.

And his uncle. Prince Enrico Ceraldi.

He won't be here still, she guessed. He'll have left—returned to his palace and his socialite chums. Why would he hang around? He probably only came to the cottage in person because he wanted to check out that Ben really did look like his brother.

She opened her eyes, looking around her. The bedroom was large, and from what she could tell the house was some kind of small, Regency period country house. Presumably sufficiently remote for the press not to find Ben. How long would they need to stay here? she wondered anxiously. The sooner the story broke, the better—because then the fuss would die down and she and Ben could go home.

She frowned. Would Ben be upset that this mysteriously arrived uncle had simply disappeared again? She would far rather he had not known who he was. Her frown etched deeper. Why had he told Ben? It seemed a pointless thing to do. The news story would just be a nine-day wonder, and, although she could understand why the Ceraldi family would want to tuck Ben out of sight while it was going on, there was no need to have told Ben anything.

She'd have to tell Ben that even though Prince Enrico was his uncle, he lived abroad, and that was why he wouldn't see him again.

Even so, it seemed cruel to have told him in the first place. Ben had asked about his father sometimes, and all Lizzy had been able to do was say that it had been someone who had loved the mummy in whose tummy he had grown, but that that mummy had been too ill to say who his daddy was.

For the hundredth time since the bombshell about Maria's lover had fallen, Lizzy felt disbelief wash through her. And a terrible chill. With all the horror of having to rush out to France, to the hospital her mortally injured sister had been taken to, the news that the pile-up had claimed the life of the youngest prince of San Lucenzo had simply passed her by. She had made no connection—how could she have?

And yet he had been Ben's father. Maria had had an affair with Prince Paolo of San Lucenzo. And nobody had known. No one at all.

It was extraordinary, unbelievable. But it was true.

I have to accept it. I have to come to terms with it.

She stared bleakly out over the room. Deliberately, she forced herself to think instead of feel.

It makes no difference. Once all the fuss in the news has died down, we can just go back home. Everything will be the same again. I just have to wait it out, that's all.

Beneath her hand, she could feel Ben start to stir and wake. A rush of emotion went through her.

Nothing would hurt Ben. Nothing. She would keep him safe always. Nothing on this earth would *ever* come between her and the son she adored with all her heart. Ever.

CHAPTER THREE

'GOOD morning.'

Rico walked into the drawing room. Ben was sitting on the floor in the middle of the room, occupied with a pile of brightly coloured building blocks. His aunt was beside him. He nodded brief acknowledgement of her, then turned his attention to Ben.

'What are you making?' he asked his nephew.

'The tallest tower in the world.' Ben announced. 'Come and see.'

Rico did not need an invitation. As his eyes had lit on his nephew, his heart had squeezed. Memories flooded back in. He could remember Paolo being that age.

A shadow fleetingly crossed his eyes. Paolo had been different from Luca and himself. As his adult self, he knew why. Luca had been born the heir. The firstborn Prince, the Crown Prince, the heir apparent, destined to rule San Lucenzo just as their father, Prince Eduardo, had been destined to inherit the throne from his own father a generation earlier. For eight hundred years the Ceraldis had ruled the tiny principality, which had escaped conquest by any of the other Italian states, or even the invading foreign powers that had plagued the Italian peninsula throughout history. Generation after generation of reigning princes had kept San Lucenzo independent—even in this age of European union the principality was still a sovereign state. Some saw it as a time-warped historical anomaly, others merely as a tax haven and a luxury playground for the very rich. But to his father and his older brother it was their inheritance, their destiny.

And it was an inheritance that would always need protection. Not, these days, against foreign powers, or any territorial interests of the Italian state—relations with Italy were excellent. What made San Lucenzo safe was continuity. The continuity of its ruling family. In many ways the principality was the personal fiefdom of the Ceraldis, and yet it was because of that that it retained its independence. Rico accepted that. Without the Ceraldis it would surely have been merged into Italy, just as all the earlier duchies and city states and papal territories had been during the great Risorgimento of the nineteenth century, that had freed Italy from foreign oppression, and united it as a nation.

The Ceraldis were essential to San Lucenzo, and for that reason, it was essential that every reigning prince had an assured heir apparent.

And—Rico's mouth tightened—that the heir apparent had a back up in case of emergency.

The traditional 'heir and a spare'—with himself as the spare.

It was what he had been all his life, growing up knowing that he was simply there in case of disaster. To assure continuity of the Ceraldi line.

But Paolo—ah, Paolo had been different. He had been special to his parents because he'd been an unexpected addition, coming several years after their two older sons. Paolo had had no dynastic function, and so he had been allowed merely to be a boy. A son. A golden boy whose sunny temper had won round even his strait-laced father and his emotionally distant mother.

Which was why his premature death had been all the more tragic, all the more bitter.

Rico hunkered down beside his nephew, taking scant notice of the way his aunt immediately shrank away. Yes, Paolo's son. No doubt about it. No DNA tests would be required; his paternity was undeniable, blazing from every feature. Perhaps there might be a little of his birth mother about him, but one look at him told the world that he was a Ceraldi.

Benedict. That was what he'd been called. And it was a true name for him.

Blessed.

His heart gave that familiar catch again. Yes, he was blessed, all right. He didn't know it yet, but he would. And he was more than blessed—he was a blessing himself.

Because, beyond all the publicity and press coverage and gossip that was going to explode at any moment now, the boy was going to be seen as the blessing he was.

The final consolation to his parents for the son they had lost so tragically.

Lizzy moved backwards across the carpet and lifted herself into a nearby armchair. She had hoped, at the fact that she and Ben had had the breakfast room to themselves, that it meant Prince Enrico had gone.

She wished he had.

She felt excruciatingly awkward with him there. She tried not to look at him, but it was hard not to feel intensely aware of his presence in the room. Even without a drop of royal blood in him he would have been impossible to ignore.

By day he seemed even taller, outlined against the light from the window behind him, and his startling good looks automatically drew her eyes. He was wearing designer jeans, immaculately cut, and an open-necked shirt, clearly handmade. Immediately she felt the full force of just how shabbily she was dressed in comparison. Her cheap chainstore skirt and top had probably cost less than his monogrammed handkerchief.

At least, apart from that brief initial nod in her direction, he wasn't paying any attention to her. It was all on Ben, or helping him build his tower.

Resentment and embarrassment warred within her.

Ben was chattering away confidently, without a trace of

shyness, his smiles sunny. He was like Maria in that, Lizzy knew. Hindsight over the years since her terrible death had made things clearer to her. It had been a miracle that Maria's sunny-tempered nature had not been warped by her upbringing. Despite the way her parents had doted on her, obsessed over her, she really had seemed to escape being spoilt. And yet, for all her sunny nature, she had known what she wanted, and what she'd wanted was to be a model, to live an exciting, glamorous life. And that was what she'd done, smiling happily, ignoring her parents' dismay, and waltzing off to the life she'd wanted.

And the man she'd wanted.

Disbelief was etched through Lizzy for the thousandth time. That Maria had actually had an affair with Prince Paolo of San Lucenzo and none of them had known. Not even his family, let alone hers.

How had they managed it? He must have been very different from his brother. Even though she hadn't recognised Enrico, she'd still heard of him—and of his reputation. The Playboy Prince. Her covert gaze rested on him a second. He certainly had the looks for it, all right. Tall, broad-shouldered, sable-haired, with strong, well-cut, aristocratic features.

And those eyes.

Dark, long-lashed, with flecks of gold in them if you looked deeply. Not that she could—or would.

She looked away. It was completely irrelevant what he looked like. It was nothing to do with her. All she had to be concerned about was how long she and Ben would have to hide here before they could go back home.

Ben had paused in his tower-building. He was looking curiously at his helper.

'Are you really my uncle?'

Immediately Lizzy stiffened.

'Yes,' he answered. He spoke in a very matter of fact way. 'You can call me Tio Rico. That means Uncle Rico. My brother was your father. But he died. It was in the car crash with your mother.'

Ben nodded. 'I was still growing in her tummy. Then I came out, and she died.'

The Prince's eyes were carefully watching his nephew. Lizzy could see as she held her breath.

Please, *please* don't say anything about the royalty stuff. Please.

There was no point Ben knowing. None at all. It wouldn't make sense to him, wouldn't mean anything. One day, when he was much older, she would have to tell him, but till then it was an irrelevance.

Then, to her relief, Ben himself changed the subject.

'We've finished the tower,' he announced. 'What shall we make next?'

He seemed to take it for granted his helper would stick around.

But the Prince got to his feet.

'I'm sorry, Ben. I don't have time. I have to leave very soon, and first I must talk with your aunt.'

He flicked his gaze across to the figure sitting tensely in the armchair. She got to her feet jerkily. Rico found himself regarding her without pleasure.

How could any female look so dire? No figure, no face, and hair like a bush. His eyes flicked away again, and he did not see her face mottle with colour.

'Please come this way,' he said, as he headed towards the door.

He went through into a room that was evidently a library, courteously holding the door open for the aunt, who walked hurriedly past him. He took up a position in front of the fireplace. She stood awkwardly in the middle of the room.

'You had better sit down.'

His voice was cool and remote. Very formal.

Lizzy tensed even more. The ease of manner he'd displayed towards Ben had disappeared completely.

What did he want to talk to her about? Hopefully it would be to tell her how long she and Ben had to stay here. She hoped it would not be long. This was so unsettling for Ben. She wanted to get him home again. Back to normal. Back to the cottage, where she could try to forget all about who Ben's father had been.

She took a seat on the long leather sofa facing the fire about ten feet away. The Prince went on standing. He seemed very tall. Lizzy wished she had remained standing too.

He started to speak.

'I hope you have begun to come to terms with what has transpired. This has been a considerable shock; I acknowledge that.'

'I still can't really believe it,' Lizzy heard herself say, giving voice to her thoughts. 'It just seems so impossible. How on earth did Maria get to meet a prince?'

Prince Enrico arched an eyebrow. 'Not as impossible as you might think. Your sister's career as a model would have taken her into the social circles frequented by my brother.'

She could read his expression quite clearly. Maria's life had been a world away from her own.

'However, now that you are aware of the situation, clearly you will appreciate that the first priority must be Ben's wellbeing.'

Lizzy's expression tightened. Did he think she didn't know that?

'How long are we going to have stay here?'

The question blurted from her.

There was a pause before the Prince answered her. Lizzy didn't care if she'd offended him, or annoyed him by asking a question of him like that. Simply being in the same room with him was just too embarrassing for her to want anything but to minimise the time she had to endure it. Besides, she didn't want to leave Ben on his own any longer than she had to.

'It is expected that the news story will break any day,' Prince Enrico informed her tersely. 'I doubt that it can be put off any longer. As for how long the story will run—' He took a sharp intake of breath. 'That depends on how much the press are fed.'

Lizzy's eyes sparked. Was that some kind of sly remark

about whether *she* would talk to any journalists when she got back home again?

But the Prince was speaking still.

'The press feed off each other, each trying to outdo the other, rehashing each other's stories, then seeking to add their own exclusive "revelation" to milk the story as much as they can, for as long as they can. It's cheap copy.'

There was a bitter note in his voice she would have had to be deaf not to hear. It was obvious he was speaking from experience. For a moment she felt a tinge of sympathy for him, then she pushed it aside. Prince Rico of San Lucenzo had not had his playboy lifestyle forced upon him, and if he didn't like being hounded by the press he shouldn't live the way he did. But Ben was innocent, a small child.

She could feel her fiercely protective maternal instincts take over. Ben was not responsible for his parentage. So Prince Paolo of San Lucenzo had taken a shine to Maria, had an affair with her, and got her pregnant—well, that was not Ben's fault.

'How long will we have to stay here?' she urged again.

'As long as is necessary. I can say no more than that.' His expression changed. 'I am returning to San Lucenzo this morning. I must report on the situation to my father. You and my nephew will stay here. You will be well looked after, naturally, but you will not be allowed to leave the house and gardens.'

Lizzy frowned. 'You don't imagine I *want* to run into any journalists, do you?'

'Nevertheless.' There was a note of implacability in the Prince's voice.

Lizzy looked at him. Did the Ceraldis think that she *wanted* this nightmare to be true? Did they really think she would do anything to make what was already a horrible situation worse by talking to the press?

Well, it didn't matter what Prince Rico or any of the Ceraldi family thought about her intentions. Right now she was in no position to do anything other than accept that she and Ben could not be at home, and she might as well be relieved—if not actually grateful—that the Ceraldis had moved so swiftly to get her and Ben away.

'However—' The Prince had started speaking again, addressing her in that same terse, impersonal tone, but he broke off abruptly. *'Si?'*

His head swivelled to the door, which had opened silently. A man stood there, quite young, but tough and muscular-looking, despite his sober dark suit. He looked like a body-guard, Lizzy realised. He said something in low, rapid Italian, and the Prince nodded curtly. Then he turned back to Lizzy.

'I am informed my plane is on standby and has air traffic clearance. Excuse me. I must leave.'

Lizzy watched him go. It was frustrating not to know how long she would have to stay here, but presumably not even the San Lucenzan royal family could know exactly what the press would do, or how long it would take for the story to die away.

Her mouth tightened. Had Prince Enrico really implied that she might try and talk to the press herself? It was the very last thing on earth she'd do.

She gave a mental shrug. There was no point her getting angry over it. Royals lived in a goldfish bowl; their wariness was understandable.

She went back to Ben, next door. He seemed to be taking all this in his stride, and she was grateful. Nor did he seem bothered by their enforced incarceration.

He seemed to take the following days in his stride too. They were left very much to themselves. Captain Falieri and the man who was probably Prince Enrico's bodyguard had disappeared as well, and she saw no sign of anyone else in the house except for the efficient Italian-speaking staff.

She was glad of the time to herself. Her mind seemed completely split in two. On the one hand she was as normal as she could be with Ben—playing with him, reading to him, taking him swimming, to his huge excitement, in the covered swimming pool built into a conservatory-style annexe off the main house—but inside her head her thoughts teemed with emotion.

She was still reeling from it all, but she did her best to hide it from Ben. He was, thank heavens, far too young to understand. He took what had happened at face value, absorbing it into his life as naturally as he had anything else, just as when they'd moved to Cornwall. The centre of his life was her, not his surroundings, and providing she was there, everything, for him, was as it should be.

It was inevitable, however, Lizzy acknowledged, that Ben would ask questions about the man who had so unnecessarily told him that he was his uncle.

'Where has he gone?' Ben asked.

'To Italy.' Lizzy told him. 'That's where he lives.'

'Will he come back?'

'I don't think so, Ben.'

Inwardly she cursed the man. Why had he gone and told Ben he was his uncle? Obviously a child would be interested—especially one who had no other relations. But what possible concern was Ben to Prince Enrico, other than being the unfortunate target of a salacious news story which threatened scandal to the San Lucenzan royal family?

Ben frowned. 'Well, what about Captain Fally-eery? Will he come back? He played trains with me.'

Lizzy shook her head. 'I don't think he'll come back either, Ben. He lives in Italy too.' Deliberately, she changed the subject. 'Now, shall we go and have our tea?'

Ben looked at her. 'Is this a hotel, Mummy, where they cook for you?'

She nodded. 'Sort of.' It seemed the easiest explanation to give.

'I like it here,' said Ben decidedly, looking around him approvingly. 'I like the swimming pool. Can we swim again after tea?'

'We'll see,' said Lizzy.

* * *

Rico stood at one of the windows of his apartments in the palace. It gave a dazzling view over the marina, with its brightly lit-up yachts, and the elegant promenade beyond. Paolo's apartments had been nearby, and had enjoyed similar views. His eyes shadowed.

To think that Paolo's young son was alive in England. That he had been there all along, brought up by a woman who did not even know who he was. It seemed incredible.

His thoughts went back to that ramshackle cottage he'd extracted his nephew from. His eyes darkened. It had shocked him to find Paolo's son living in such conditions.

Paolo's son.

He had known it the instant he had set eyes on him. And so he had told Luca.

'There won't be any need for DNA tests,' he'd told him.

'Well, they'll be done anyway. It's necessary.'

Rico had shrugged. He could understand it, but he also knew that when his family saw Ben in the flesh they would know instantly he was Paolo's child.

'And this aunt? What about her?' Luca had gone on.

'Shocked. That's understandable. She really seemed to have no idea at all.' He'd decided not to tell his brother that she'd failed to recognise him. Luca would find that darkly humorous.

'Can't believe her luck, more likely. She's got it made now.' There had been a cynical note in Luca's voice, and Rico frowned in recollection. Ben's aunt had given no indication of any emotion other than disbelief, and dread of the impending news story.

Then Luca had picked up one of the modelling shots of Maria Mitchell that was in the dossier Falieri had compiled, and glanced at it.

'Blonde bimbo like the sister?' he'd asked casually.

Rico had snorted. 'You're joking. Utterly plain.'

His brother had laughed sardonically. 'Well, at least that

should stop the press being interested in her, and that's all to the good. She won't make good copy if she's nothing to look at.'

Rico, his attention half taken by the latest version of a particular super-car that he liked to drive, which was wending its way along the edge of the marina, found himself frowning again at Luca's comment. It was a cruel way to speak about the girl, even if it was true.

He shifted his mind away from her. Ben's aunt was a complication that would be sorted out very soon now.

His father, during a brief interview with him, had made his wishes clear. And his instructions.

'I leave you to handle the matter,' his father had said.

Rico's mouth twisted. He need not take it as a compliment. As Luca had pointed out, 'It has to be you, Rico. You're the only one of us that can come and go freely. And besides—' the sardonic glint had been clear in his brother's eye '—if there's a female in the equation you're the expert—just as well she's plain, mind you. You'll be immune to her.'

He stepped away from the window. The woman who was his nephew's aunt was of no concern to him.

Only his nephew.

The news story on Paolo Ceraldi's unknown son broke the following morning. The lurid exclusive in a French tabloid was instantly picked up, and exactly the kind of media feeding frenzy ensued that his father so deplored. As Rico knew too well from personal experience, when he had been the subject of press attention.

There was nothing to be done about it except ignore it. His father ordered a policy of silence, and to carry on as if nothing had happened. The royal family's public life was not altered in any way. Rico's mother attended her usual opera, ballet and philharmonia performances, his father carried out his customary duties and Luca his. As for himself, he flew down to southern Africa to participate in a gruelling long-distance rally, as he always did at this time of year.

'No comment,' became his only words in half a dozen languages during the checkpoints, and he couldn't wait to get back into the driving seat and head out across the savannah again.

But there was something else he couldn't wait to do either. Get back to his nephew again. He was counting the days.

CHAPTER FOUR

LIZZY walked into the breakfast room and stopped dead. Prince Enrico was sitting at the table.

She'd had absolutely no idea that he was here.

At her side, Ben showed only pleasure.

'Tio Rico! You came back.'

Lizzy watched the Prince lever his long frame upright.

'Of course. Especially to see you.'

Ben's expression perked expectantly.

'Will you play with me?'

'After breakfast. Would you like to go swimming later?'

'Yes, please.'

'Good. Well, let's have breakfast first, shall we?'

He waited pointedly while Lizzy took her place, Ben beside her, before resuming his.

Lizzy watched as Ben chatted to his uncle. Tension laced through her instantly. He must have arrived back late last night. She had heard nothing.

But then she did not stay up late. In the strange, dislocated days she had spent here she had always retired with Ben, after supper, and once he was bathed and asleep she would spend the time in their room reading. The house came with a well-stocked library, and she was grateful for it. She had made a point of not watching television, quite deliberately. She had not wanted to catch anything of whatever the press might be saying by now about her sister and Ben. She didn't want to think about it.

But now, with Prince Enrico sitting at the head of the break-fast table, it all suddenly seemed horribly real again.

Her eyes had gone to him immediately as she'd entered the room—but then it would have been difficult for them to do oth-erwise, prince or no prince. He was the kind of man that drew all eyes instantly. She felt again that squirming awkwardness go through her, and wished that she and Ben had got up earlier, and so missed this ordeal.

Not that Ben thought it was an ordeal, evidently. He was chatting away with his uncle, and Lizzy felt her mouth tighten with disapproval.

'There is a problem?'

The accented voice was cool. Lizzy realised that Prince Enrico was looking at her.

'Why are you here? Has something happened? Something worse?'

Her voice was staccato, and probably sounded abrupt. She didn't care.

A frowning expression formed on his face.

'Is there more bad news?' Lizzy persisted.

'Other than what was expected? No. Did you not see any of the coverage?'

'No. It was the last thing I wanted to do. But in which case, if nothing worse has happened, why are you here?'

He looked at her. He had that closed expression on his face. Obviously he wasn't used to being spoken to like that, thought Lizzy. But she didn't care. Tension bit in her.

'I am here at the behest of my father. For reasons that must be obvious even to yourself, Miss Mitchell.'

His words were terse.

She looked blank. 'I don't understand.'

His mouth pressed together tightly, and he looked impa-tiently at her.

'We will discuss this matter later.' He turned his attention back to Ben. Shutting her out.

Dismissing her.

Anxiety and tension warred within her.

How she got through breakfast she did not know. She could not relax, and, although she deplored it, she knew she was grateful that Ben was chattering away to the Prince, making it possible for her to swallow a few morsels of food through a tight throat.

The moment Ben had finished, she got to her feet.

'Come along, Ben,' she said.

'Tio Rico said we'd go swimming,' Ben protested.

'Not straight after eating,' she said quietly. 'You'll get a sore tummy. And anyway, you need to brush your teeth,' she added, steering him out of the room.

As she gained the large hallway, she felt her stomach sink. Oh, God, now what? Why had he come back here? And why should it be *obvious* to her? Nothing was obvious to her. Nothing. Only that she was desperate for all this to be over, and for her to be able to go home with Ben.

But it seemed that she would have to get through another morning here.

After Ben had brushed his teeth they went back down to the drawing room, where Ben's toys were.

Prince Enrico was there before them. Lizzy tensed immediately.

'This is a good train track, Ben,' he said.

Ben trotted forward eagerly. 'My one at home is bigger, because we didn't bring all the pieces. And some of the engines are at home. But I will tell you who these are that I've got here.' He settled himself down by the track and started to regale the Prince, who had hunkered down.

Abruptly, Lizzy snapped her eyes away from the way the material of his immaculately cut trousers strained over powerful thighs.

Oh, God—isn't it bad enough that he's a prince?

She sat herself down on the sofa. Would the man never clear off?

It seemed not. To Lizzy's dismay, he seemed to be settling himself in. She picked up her book. Ben was happily chattering away, talking about his beloved trainset. She tried to concentrate on her book, and failed completely.

After what seemed like for ever, Ben suddenly stood up.

'Is it time to go swimming yet?'

She got to her feet, relieved. 'Good idea. Let's get your things.' She gave an awkward nod to the Prince, who had stood when she did.

She scurried off with Ben. But to her dismay, when they came back downstairs with the swimming kit and went into the pool room, there was already someone in the water.

The Prince's long, lean body cut through the water in a swift crawl, but when he reached the end of the pool he stopped.

'Ah, Ben, there you are,' he said. 'In you come.'

Lizzy stared in horrified fascination. The Prince had half levered himself out of the water, his arms folded down over the edge. She could see the water draining off his torso.

It was smooth, and perfectly muscled, honed like a sportsman.

She tore her eyes away. Ben was scrambling out of his clothes as fast as he could. With gritted teeth she inflated his armbands and slid them over his arms.

'Hurry, hurry,' said Ben, jiggling around. The moment he was fitted, he ran and jumped into the water.

Jerkily, Lizzy picked up his clothes, and went to sit on one of the padded seats that were dotted by the glass wall.

Thank God I wasn't in the water already.

That would have been the ultimate horror. She sat, feeling far too hot in what she was wearing in this sun-heated area, but there was nothing she could do about it. She felt her cheeks grow flushed as she watched Ben playing in the water.

The Prince seemed ludicrously enthusiastic about entertaining a four-year-old child. He ducked and dived and raced, and pounced on Ben like a shark, eliciting squeals of glee.

She felt resentment and anger mounting in her. What was the point? What was the *point* of Prince Enrico doing this? It would just unsettle Ben, that was all. Make him want something that he wasn't going to have.

He hasn't got a father. He hasn't got an uncle. He hasn't got anyone—he's just got me.

And it wasn't fair on him to let him get a taste of what it might be like if he had a father. A father to play with him, to pay attention to him.

Make him laugh the way he was laughing now.

I want to go home. I just want to go home. I want this over. Done with. Forgotten.

Rico helped Ben out of the pool for the last time, and glanced across at where his aunt was sitting. Her face had gone red in the heat, and she looked worse than ever. She also had a face like sour milk.

His brother's words came back to him, half-taunting, half-mocking—which was Luca's usual attitude towards him on this subject.

'If there's a female in the equation you're the expert—just as well she's plain, mind you. You'll be immune to her.'

Well, the latter was true. No doubt about that. With a dispassionate mind he could only feel sorry for any female as unattractive as this one. But as someone he actually had to deal with, however briefly, he could do without it. As for the former—well, females of this variety were definitely ones he was not expert in.

He launched himself out of the pool, effortlessly lifting himself on his arms. The boy's aunt had already busied herself wrapping Ben in a towel and getting him dry. He strolled off to get changed himself, in the cabanas provided for the purpose.

His mouth set. The sooner he'd settled the business here and was back in San Lucenzo the better.

But it had been good to start getting to know Ben.
Paolo's son.
His expression softened
I'll make sure he's OK, Paolo—I promise you.

Lunch had been just as much an ordeal as breakfast. Once again, the source of both her concern and her relief had been that Ben had dominated the proceedings, talking nineteen to the dozen to Prince Enrico. All she'd been required to do was sit there and try to eat through a throat that was getting tighter every moment.

What had happened? Why was Prince Enrico back here? He'd said he'd talk to her later—but when was later?

It was after lunch, it transpired. As they left the dining room he turned to her.

'Settle Ben with some toys, if you please. I shall await you in the library.'

'He has a nap after lunch. I'll come down when he's asleep.'

He gave a curt nod, and she took Ben upstairs, nerves jumping.

Typically, Ben took for ever to go to sleep, and her nerves were stretched thin by the time she could finally leave him, curtains closed, door ajar, and head downstairs.

He was, as he had said, in the library. A raft of daily papers, in both English and Italian, were on the low table, and he was sitting in a leather chair perusing *The Times*.

Surely such a respectable newspaper had not carried such a scurrilous story? she wondered.

But the page he was reading seemed to be about international politics. He cast the paper aside and stood up, indicating the chair opposite him, across the hearth of the unlit fire.

'Please sit down.' His voice was cool..

She sat nervously, stomach knoting.

'We must resolve, as a matter of urgency, as I am sure you will appreciate, the matter of my nephew's future.'

Lizzy stared.

'What do you mean?' she said.

A flicker of irritation showed briefly in the dark eyes, then it was suppressed.

'I appreciate,' he said carefully to her—as if, Lizzy thought, she was stupid, 'that the news of Ben's parentage has come as a profound shock to you. Nevertheless, I must ask you to focus on the implications of that discovery. Like yourself, his father's family were, unfortunately, but in the tragic circumstances understandably, equally unaware that Paolo had a son. Now that this is no longer the case, obviously steps will be taken as soon as possible to rectify the situation.'

She was still staring blankly.

'Rectify?' she echoed.

She saw him take a breath. 'Of course. Ben will now make his life in San Lucenzo.'

Cold went down Lizzy's back. She could feel it—as if her spine was turning to ice.

'No.'

The word was instinctive. Automatic.

She saw the Prince's face first tighten, then take on the same expression that it had had when she had failed to recognise him. Disbelieving.

She didn't care. Didn't care about anything. Except to refute, absolutely, what she had just heard him say.

His expression changed, as if he were making a visible effort. Again he addressed her as if she were stupid.

'Miss Mitchell, do you really not understand that your nephew's circumstances have changed now?' His tone, quite blatantly, was patronising, and Lizzy felt her hackles rise through the ice in her spine. 'It is inconceivable that my brother's orphaned son should live anywhere but in his own country.'

She stared at him.

'I can't believe you're saying that,' she cut across him. 'We're going home—back to Cornwall the moment we can. The sooner the better.'

She saw his face tighten.

'That is no longer possible.' His voice was flat. Implacable.

'What do you mean "no longer possible"?' she demanded. Her voice was rising, she could tell, and she could feel the adrenaline churning in her system. 'Ben and I are going home. That's all there is to it.'

'Ben's home will now have to be in San Lucenzo.'

The voice was still flat, still implacable.

'There's no "have to" about it. No *question* of it!'

Dark, long-lashed eyes stared at her.

'Miss Mitchell—are you being deliberately obtuse?' The question was rhetorical, for he plunged straight on. 'There is no going back. Do you not understand that? Your nephew cannot return to the life you gave him. He must come to his own country to live.'

She leant forward, tension in every line of her body.

'This is ridiculous. Absurd,' she responded vehemently. Emotion was surging through her. 'Completely out of the question. I can understand your reaction to the nightmare of this news story, and I have my sympathies for you and your family. If there is one thing I do feel sorry about for royalty, it's that their private lives are raked over by the press—even when they do not conspicuously court such publicity,' she threw in, with a glancing look in her eyes at him that drew an answering flash and a compression of his mouth. But she allowed him no time to interrupt her. 'If anything, Ben's presence in San Lucenzo could only be an further embarrassment to you. Why on earth would your family want to be landed with your late brother's illegitimate child—"love child", as I suppose the tabloids will coyly call him—as an ever-present reminder of his affair with my sister? Look,' she went on, trying to be reasonable, even with the adrenaline running in her like a river in flood, 'if you are worried that I might, God help me, be insane enough to speak to the press at any point in the future, then I'll sign any gagging papers you want. The *only* thing I want for Ben is a happy, unspoilt childhood. He can't help his parentage, and I won't let it affect him adversely.'

He was staring at her again. She wished he wouldn't do that. Not just because his eyes were the most extraordinary she'd ever seen, but because he was looking at her as if she were from another planet.

His mouth tightened. Italian broke from him, angry and incomprehensible.

Then, as if he were making a monumental effort to control his reaction, he spoke again, and she stared wildly at him, stomach churning.

'You do not seem to understand. My brother did *not* have an affair with your sister.'

'But you've just said—' she launched.

His hand shot up, silencing her.

His dark eyes were completely opaque again.

'He married her.'

Lizzy felt her mouth fall open. Her jaw drop like a stone. With numb, unconscious effort she closed it again, then spoke.

'My sister *married* your brother?' Her voice was dazed.

'Yes. The day before their fatal car crash. I have seen the marriage certificate. It is...' he paused '...quite legal. Apparently—' his voice was as dry as sand '—the name Ceraldi was also unknown to the celebrant.'

She got to her feet, staring at him blindly.

'I don't believe it.'

It was denial again. Just the same as when the man standing in front of her had told her he was a royal prince—and so had his brother been.

And if Maria had married him that meant Ben was—

No—no, it could not be. It was impossible. Ben was just... Ben, that was all.

But if her sister had been married to his father, and his father was a prince of San Lucenzo, then Ben...

She sat down. Her legs felt weightless somehow.

'It's not true.' Her voice was faint. Her eyes wide. She stared across at him. 'Please—please say it isn't true. Please.'

Rico looked at her. She could not have meant what she'd just said. No one could. Certainly no woman in her situation could mean it. She had just been told that her nephew was a royal prince. And yet she was begging him to tell her it was not true.

He inhaled sharply.

'It is hardly a subject for jest. And now that you know, you must realise why there is no question but that Ben be brought up in his own country, with his own family.'

Her eyes blazed with sudden fierce light.

'I don't care if you tell me that Ben is the King of Siam. I'm not uprooting him from his own life, from everything he knows. So *what* if he *is* legitimate? Your brother Paolo was the youngest brother, so Ben isn't going to inherit the throne or anything, is he?'

The strident voice grated on Rico's already stretched nerves. The girl's reaction was incomprehensible. Was she particularly unintelligent? It seemed he would have to spell everything out to her.

'A royal prince of the house of Ceraldi cannot be brought up as a private citizen in a foreign country.' He spoke heavily, hoping to God the damn woman would finally get through her skull what the reality of the situation was. 'He must be raised by his family—'

'*I* am his family.'

Rico's face closed.

'You are his aunt. Nothing more than that. I appreciate that you have worked very hard to raise my brother's son, and—'

Her strident voice interrupted him again. Rico felt his impatience mounting. It was not just her unbelievable pig-headedness and her exasperating lack of intelligence that got to him, but her appalling habit of cutting across him.

Her eyes were stabbing at him, and she was getting ludicrously worked up.

'I am Ben's legal guardian. He is solely my responsibility.'

Rico fought for self-control. 'Then, as his legal guardian, you will want the best for him, no? And clearly—' he tried hard to keep the withering sarcasm out of his voice '—Ben's interests will be served by his being raised by his father's family.' And now the sarcasm did creep in. He couldn't stop it, such were the emotions biting through him at the woman's incomprehensible objections. 'Or did you imagine it would be suitable for my brother's son to be raised in a semi-derelict peasant cottage?'

A line of colour leached out across her cheeks, and Rico, despite his mounting temper, felt a stab of regret. She could not help being poor, and she had, after all, done the best she could for Paolo's son, within her means.

But that was irrelevant now. Whether she liked it or not, she had to accept the truth of the matter—the Ceraldis had a new prince, and his place was with them. Swiftly, he moved on. His father had given him full authority to do whatever was necessary to ensure Ben returned to San Lucenzo as soon as possible.

He held up a hand, forestalling any further comeback from her.

'Miss Mitchell—the matter is not open for debate. I make allowances for your sense of shock, but you must face up to the necessity of the situation. My nephew must go to San Lucenzo with the minimum of delay to start his new life. You must see that.'

She shook her head wildly.

'No, I don't. I don't see anything of the sort. You can't possibly think his life should be turned upside down like that.'

Rico pressed his mouth together, willing himself to stay calm.

'And you, Miss Mitchell, cannot possibly think that Ben's life will not be immeasurably better when he is surrounded by his family. What possible justification can you have for your objection? How can you possibly not welcome this? You live in poverty—all that has changed. Changed completely. Have you not realised that?'

His eyes narrowed infinitesimally as he watched for her reaction. But her face just seemed totally blank. Obviously he would need to be blunter, distasteful though it was.

'You will not suffer by the change in Ben's life, Miss Mitchell. You will always be his aunt, and, although Ben's new life will inevitably be vastly different from what he has been used to so far, you will benefit too. It would not be appropriate for my nephew's aunt to live in poverty,' he said carefully, his eyes watching her. 'Therefore generous financial arrangements will be made in your favour, in appreciation for what you have done for my nephew. You have given up four years of your life to look after him—it is only right that your invaluable contribution should be recognised. But now you will be able to resume the life of a young woman, independent of the responsibilities you have had to assume up till now.'

His eyes rested on her as he waited for the penny to drop. But her face was still quite expressionless.

It irritated Rico. Did he have to spell *everything* out in excruciatingly vulgar detail? Evidently so. His mouth tightened. He took a controlled breath, and prepared to speak again.

But before he could say anything she got to her feet.

It was a jerky movement, like an automaton. Her eyes were pinned on his. There was something in them that took him aback. Then she spoke. Her voice was strange.

'You do not seriously think I am going to let you part me from Ben, do you?'

She was trembling like a wire strung out to breaking point. Emotion poured through her, terror and fury storming together. They spilled over into a torrent of words.

'Do you really think I would ever, *ever* allow Ben to be taken from me? Do you? How can you even imagine that for a moment? I'm his *mother*—the only mother he's ever known.'

A burning, punishing breath seared through her lungs. 'Listen to me and listen well. Because I will say this over and over again until I get you to understand it. I am Ben's mother—his guardian. And that means I guard him—I guard him from anything and everything that threatens him, threatens his happiness, his emotional and physical well-being, his long-term stability…*everything*. I love him more than my own life—I could not love him more if he were my birth child. He is all I have left of my sister, and I made a vow to her that I would keep her child safe, that I would be the mother to him that she was not allowed to be. He is my son and I am his mother. It would *devastate* him to be taken from me—how could you even *think* of doing so? Nothing will come between us. I will never let him be taken from me. *Never.*'

Her face was contorted, but she could not stop. She had to make him listen—had to make him hear.

'You must be completely insane to think of taking him from me. How do you even *begin* to think I would consent to it? Consent to Ben losing the only mother he's known. Are you mad, or just evil, even to *think* of separating us? No one takes a child from its mother. *No one.*' She shut her eyes. Her throat was burning, her breath choking. 'Oh, God, how could this nightmare ever have happened. How?'

Her anguished question rang into silence, complete silence. She stood there, shaking like a leaf.

Then, slowly, a voice spoke. Deep and resonant.

'No one will take Ben from you. You have my word.'

Rico was in his bedroom. The phone was against his ear. He stood with one arm extended, resting his hand on the folded wooden shutters that framed the sash windows. From where he stood he could see the gardens. Ben and his aunt were on the lawn, in the last of the early-evening sunshine, playing football. Two goals were roughly marked out with sticks. Ben kicked, and scored, and ran around gleefully in imitation of professional footballers. His aunt threw up her hands in exaggerated defeat, and took a goal kick. It was a very bad one, and Ben returned it instantly, scoring yet another goal. He crowed with triumph.

At the other end of the phone line, Rico's brother was speaking.

'What do you mean, she won't give him up? She's nothing more than his aunt—what claim can she have?'

'A watertight legal one,' replied Rico dryly.

There was a pause. Then Luca spoke.

'She wants more money, I take it?' His voice was sharp.

'She wants her son.' Rico realised his voice was equally sharp.

'The boy is only her *nephew*,' riposted his brother.

'She's raised him as her son, and he regards her as his mother. Which, legally, she is. She adopted him at birth. So, if she does not want to part with him, we have to accept that.'

There was a pause again.

'How much did you offer her?' Luca asked.

'Luca—this is not *about* money. She's not prepared to consider it, OK?' He paused, then spoke again. 'And neither am I any longer. The attachment between them is definitely that of mother and child. I've been with them all day—so far as Paolo's son is concerned, the woman is his mother. There's nothing we can do about that. We may not like it, but that's the way it is. Our only way forward is for her to live in San Lucenzo with the boy. I have to persuade her of that, and I will do my best to do so. But—' he took a sharp breath '—I gave her my word we would not try and take the child from her.'

There was another pause. Outside in the garden Ben was still playing football. Rico felt a sudden urge to go and join in.

Luca was speaking again. 'Rico, do and say nothing for the moment. I'll report this back to our father. He won't like it but…' Rico could almost hear Luca shrug. 'Look, I'll phone you back.'

The line went dead. Rico's gaze dropped again to the figure playing on the lawn below with Ben. She was wearing some kind of grey tracksuit, baggy and shapeless, and her frizzy hair was tied back in an unflattering bunch. She looked overweight and lumpy. She really was extraordinarily unappealing. Yet what did her appearance matter to Ben? Even as he watched, he saw Ben trip as he ran to intercept the ball, and fall sprawlingly on the grass. She was there in an instant, hugging him, inspecting his grass-stained knee, then dropping a kiss on it before resuming play again. An ordinary maternal gesture.

Memory shafted through him. Or rather, lack of it. Who had picked him up when he'd gone sprawling like that? A nanny? Whichever of the nursery floor staff was looking after him at the time? Not his mother. He'd only ever seen his mother at five in the afternoon, when she had taken tea and interviewed both himself and Luca as to their progress in lessons that day.

A frown creased his brow. Paolo had been the only one of them ever to sit beside his mother on the exquisite silk-upholstered sofa in her sitting room. The only one of them he could remember her embracing.

He felt his heart squeeze again. He would bring her Paolo's son.

He glanced at his watch. He doubted Luca would phone back within the hour. Time enough for Rico to teach his nephew some football moves. He headed downstairs.

'It's no good, Ben, it's definitely bedtime.'

'Mummy—one more goal. Just one.'

'Golden goal,' said Rico.

'All right, then,' conceded Lizzy.

She had just passed the strangest half-hour. Out of nowhere, the Prince had emerged on to the lawn and joined in their game of football. Or rather taken it over.

Ben was ecstatic.

'You can ref, Mummy,' he instructed her.

She sat in a heap at the side of the pitch area, and watched. Her emotions were still in turmoil, but at least she was calmer than she had been.

You have my word, he had said.

Did he mean it?

He had seemed different when he'd said that to her. She didn't know why, or how, but he had.

And he'd looked at her. Looked at her into her eyes.

As if she were a real person suddenly.

And something had happened in that look. Something that for the first time had made the hard, fearful knot inside her ease.

Just by a fraction.

Something had changed.

Something had changed as she'd poured out her horror and terror in front of him. Telling him—screaming at him—that she would never let Ben be taken from her, that she was his mother by everything but physical birth. That she would never, ever, let such harm come to him as to be wrested from the only person he knew to be his mother.

Who had been the only person in the world to him.

Until now.

She felt emotion move and shift within her.

A pang went through her. Yes, she was Ben's mother—she would be all her life. Nothing could ever change that.

But now he's got an uncle. Two uncles. And grandparents too.

A family.

A family to whom Ben was not just the embarrassing result of an affair—someone they would wash their hands of, hide away out of sight.

They wanted him. They wanted him because he was the son of their dead son, their dead brother.

Emotion twisted within her.

If they were anything other than what they are, I'd be over-joyed at their discovering Ben's existence.

But that was the trouble. They *were* who they were. It was unbelievable, unreal—and the truth.

Depression rolled over her. Whichever way you looked at it, the whole situation was impossible.

Anguish filled her. There could be no resolution to this. How could there be? Two worlds had collided—the normal world, and the world the Ceraldis lived in. A world that was totally unreal to everyone except themselves.

And Ben was caught in the middle. Crushed between them.

And so was she.

CHAPTER FIVE

RICO stared at his brother. He had been summoned back to San Lucenzo the following morning, and now that he was here Luca had dropped a bombshell on him.

'This is a joke, right? And, as such, it isn't funny.'

The Crown Prince of San Lucenzo looked back at him with dispassionate eyes. He was good at dispassion, thought Rico viciously. Great at dispensing insane ideas as if they were commonplace, obvious no-brainers.

'It would solve the problem we are facing.'

'Are you mad? It's not a question of solving problems—this is about my *life*. And I am *not* about to sacrifice it for the reasons you think I should.'

'It's hardly a permanent sacrifice. Besides, I thought you said you had really taken to the boy.'

Rico's eyes flashed angrily.

'That doesn't mean I have to—'

His brother held up his hand. 'Yes, I understand. But listen, Rico—what other option is there? She's the legal guardian of Paolo's son. She won't relinquish the boy. You're saying that the only way for us to have Paolo's son is to have her as well. But how? We *cannot* have an English unmarried mother, a commoner, whose father kept a shop, living here with legal responsibility for a child who just happens to be our nephew and therefore a royal prince.' His face tightened. 'It will cause serious problems of protocol and security. What I've suggested cuts those problems right out.' Both the tone of his voice and his expression changed. 'I don't have to tell you that your co-operation in this matter would be appreciated by our father.'

He pressed on.

'We're talking a year—eighteen months at the most. That's all, Rico. Enough to serve the proprieties. Make everything watertight.'

His eyes rested on his younger brother.

'You're always talking about having a more active role in affairs. Wanting to take on responsibilities. All your life you've chafed at being the "spare". Well, now you can do something about that. No one else can do this, Rico—only you. You know that. Only you.'

There was an intensity in Luca's gaze that bored into Rico. For a long, endless moment Rico met his brother's eyes. Then, with a curse, he broke away.

'Damn you for this, Luca.'

Luca raised sardonic eyebrows. 'Damn me all you like—but do this for us all,' he retorted coolly.

His brother's voice, when he replied, was even cooler. 'I'll do it for Paolo,' he said.

The sleek, powerful car ate up the miles between the airfield and the rented house. But for Rico it was still too slow. He wanted to drive faster—much faster.

And in the opposite direction.

Instead, he was heading into a cage. He was going to have to put his head into a noose and let it be pulled tight.

His mood was grim. At his side, in the passenger seat, Falieri kept silent. Rico appreciated it. Falieri had been fully briefed, he knew, either by Luca or their father, and he knew exactly what Rico was about to do.

'Tell me I'm insane,' Rico demanded.

'It makes sense, what you are going to do,' Falieri said quietly.

'Does it?' Rico retorted bitterly. 'Keep reminding me of that, will you?'

'You are doing it for the boy,' said Falieri. 'And for your late brother.'

'Keep reminding me of that too—' said Rico.

He slammed on the brakes and changed gear viciously, ready to turn off the road.

Heading into that noose.

Ben greeted him excitedly, rushing to him with a cry of pleasure. Rico scooped him up. The boy's little arms wound around his neck, his sturdy body strong against Rico's chest. The hard, tight band around his lungs seemed to lighten fractionally.

I can do this. I can do it for Paolo. I can do it for Ben.

Gently, he lowered his nephew to the ground again. His eyes slid past him to the figure standing there, looking as out of place as she always did.

Dio, she looked worse than ever. Her skin had gone mottled, and her hair seemed frizzier than ever. She was wearing faded cotton trousers and an ill fitting top.

Revulsion raced through him.

He crushed the instinctive rejection. He'd committed to this course of action and there was no way out now. It might be insane—but he'd said he'd do it.

And there was no point putting it off. He had to do it now, before his feet hardened into ice. So, as he lowered Ben to the floor, he made himself look at her again.

'How have you been?' he asked.

She gave a half-shrug and didn't quite meet his eyes. She never did, he realised. Except that time when she had laid into him about being Ben's legal guardian and never parting from him.

His expression sobered. The intensity of her reaction had shocked him. More than shocked him. It had made him realise, for the first time since discovering about Paolo's son, that it didn't matter that the girl was only Ben's biological aunt—in emotional reality she was much, much more.

And she was right. Completely and indisputably right. To take Ben from her would be an unspeakable cruelty to the child. And to her—and she did not deserve that.

It must have been hard, taking on an orphaned child all on her own, in her circumstances.

'How did your father take it?' She swallowed. 'The fact that I won't let Ben be parted from me?'

He could hear the tension in her voice, like wires around her throat.

He looked at her.

'Another way of resolving the situation has been arrived at.'

Her eyes flashed.

'Anything involving taking Ben from me is—'

He held up a hand, silencing her.

'That will not happen. However,' he spoke heavily, steeling himself to do so, 'this is not the place to discuss this matter.' He cast a speaking look at Ben, who had gone back to his trainset, to rearrange some points. 'Have you dined?'

She pressed her lips together. 'I eat with Ben,' she said. 'It saves the staff doing two meals.'

'Very considerate,' said Rico dryly. 'Well, I have not. So I suggest that I do so while Ben is in his bath and then, when he is asleep, you will appreciate that we cannot postpone any longer a discussion about his future.' He cast a look at her. 'This must be done—none of us has any choice in that.'

Her expression had become strained, and she looked away. Ben piped up, and Rico was grateful.

'I've finished the track now—come and play,' he invited him. 'Let's race engines.'

Rico grinned, his face lightening.

'A race? Then prepare to be beaten, young man.'

For his pains he got a withering look. 'Silly you. I've got the express train,' he told Rico pityingly.

Out of the corner of his eye, Rico saw Ben's aunt slip away. He settled down to play with his nephew. It was a lot easier when she wasn't around.

Then he remembered what he had committed to do, and he felt his heart sink like lead. Even for Paolo's sake, this was going to be excruciating.

Ben was asleep, drifting off even as she finished reading his bedtime story to him. Usually Lizzy just had a bath herself, then read until she fell asleep. Ben woke early, and there was no question of a lie-in. So she never minded early nights.

But tonight she had to go downstairs again.

And face the Prince.

Her stomach knotted itself. She couldn't see what his solution might be—how this nightmare could be resolved.

Round and round her tired head went the drearily familiar litany. Two worlds colliding—no way out. No way out.

She knew only one thing—whatever the Ceraldis wanted, they were not going to part Ben from her. Not while she had breath in her body.

Grimly, she left the door to the bedroom ajar, letting in light from the landing, and then headed downstairs.

She was shown into the drawing room, and the Prince was already there, standing staring out over the near-dark gardens, the curtains undrawn. He had a glass of brandy in his hand, Lizzy registered.

She also registered something else. Something she instantly did her best to suppress. And yet it was impossible.

Impossible for her and every other woman in the world. Impossible to ignore that he was the most drop-dead gorgeous male she'd ever seen.

Embarrassment flushed through her. It seemed wrong to be so aware of his ridiculous good-looks. She had no business being aware of them.

Yet with that brooding expression on his face he just looked even more compelling.

He turned as she advanced into the room, and his eyes rested on her.

Immediately she felt her face mottling, as it always did whenever she came into his eyeline. Making her horribly conscious of her grim appearance.

Yes, I know—I look awful. There's nothing I can do about it. So, please, just don't look at me.

'Won't you sit down?'

Awkwardly, Lizzy lowered herself on to the sofa. She watched the Prince walk across and take a seat opposite her, separated by a large square coffee table. He swirled the brandy slowly in his glass for a moment, staring down into it. Then his head lifted.

He started to speak.

'I know you have found it very hard to accept what has happened,' he began, his voice slow and careful, 'but I hope that the reality of the situation has now finally sunk in. And that you have begun to appreciate that Ben's life cannot continue as it was.'

She opened her mouth to speak, but he hadn't finished.

'Hear me out. Before you say anything, hear me out.' He took a breath. It rasped in his lungs. 'As I said, I understand that it's difficult to accept, but you must—you have no choice. Ben is no longer the boy you thought he was. Whether you like it or not, you cannot deny his heritage. He is my brother's son— the offspring of his marriage to your sister. The circumstances of their deaths are tragic beyond belief, but we must deal with the outcome. And the outcome is Ben—our mutual nephew and your adopted son. This is the reality. And the reality of his paternity is, therefore, that he is a prince. Nothing can change that. Not all the wishing in the world.'

His expression changed. Emotion flared in his eyes suddenly. 'And I do not wish it. I would not wish it for a fraction of a second. Ben is a blessing—a gift from God. My dead brother's son restored to us. No. Do not blanch.' His voice had changed again, become measured and formal. 'Just because he is a gift to us, to my family, it does *not* imply that he is not precious beyond price to you. Or...' He paused, then said deliberately, 'Or you to him. That is not the issue. I gave you my word I would not pursue any avenue of resolution to this situation that was premised upon Ben leaving your care. But...' He paused again, then resumed, with absolute emphasis on each word. 'You *must* accept that his old life has gone. It cannot continue. Ben is a royal prince of the House of Ceraldi. Nothing can change that. His future must be based upon that fact.' He took another sharp intake of breath. 'And that means that he cannot live an ordinary life any more. He must come to San Lucenzo. With you.'

She had gone white, he could see. Her hands were clenched in her lap, and her breathing was uneven. But at least she was not interrupting him. He took another swift mouthful of brandy, feeling the fiery liquid burning in his throat.

He started speaking again.

'There is no easy way out of this situation. But a way does exist. And that is what I am going to propose to you. We have a situation which urgently requires resolution. And there is a way to do so. A drastic way, but nevertheless, in the circumstances, the only way forward.'

He could feel cold pooling in his legs, slowly turning his feet to ice. He had to say this—he had to say this now. Before he cut and ran. Ran as if all the devils in hell were after him.

He stared blankly into the face of the woman sitting opposite him. A woman who was a complete stranger. But to whom he *had* to say the following words.

'We get married,' said Rico.

She didn't move. That was the most unnerving thing of all. She just went on sitting there, hands clenched in her lap, face white. Rico felt his guts tighten. Had he really just said what he had? Had he been *that* insane?

And yet he knew it was not insanity that had made him say the words, but something much worse.

Necessity. Because, loathe Luca as he might for what he had suggested, Rico could see the unavoidable sense of it. The *impasse* they were in was immovable. Ben and his adoptive mother came as a package—that was all there was to it. A package that had to be incorporated somehow—by whatever means, however drastic—into the fabric of the San Lucenzo royal family. Ben alone would have been no problem—but Ben with the woman who had raised him, whom he thought of as his mother and who was in the eyes of the law indeed that person, that was a whole lot more impossible to swallow.

And yet she had to be swallowed. No alternative. No choice.

And he was the one who was going to have to do it. Luca had been right, and Rico hated him for it. But it didn't stop him being right. It would solve everything.

A marriage of convenience—for everyone except himself!

He felt his jaw set even tighter, and unconsciously his hands pressed against the rounded brandy glass. He wanted to take another mouthful, but knew he should not. He'd already drunk wine with dinner, to fortify himself, and although he wanted to drink himself into oblivion he knew it was impossible.

Why wasn't she responding? She hadn't moved—not a muscle. A spurt of anger went through him. Did she imagine this was easy for him? Abruptly he found himself raising the brandy glass anyway, and taking a large mouthful.

Something moved in her eyes minutely.

Then, as if a lever had suddenly been pulled, she jerked to her feet.

'You are,' she said, and there was something wrong with her voice, 'completely mad.'

Rico's eyes darkened. He might have expected this.

'Not mad,' he said repressively, 'just facing facts. Sit down again, if you please.'

She sat. Rico got the feeling it was not to obey him, but

because her legs wouldn't hold her upright. The bones of her face were standing out, and the blood had drained from her skin, which now looked like whey.

'If you marry me,' he began, 'a great many problems simply disappear. We have already established that your old life has gone—there can be no doubt about that. Ben is a royal prince of the House of Ceraldi, and he must be raised as such, in the land of his patrimony. He cannot be raised in this country, and he cannot be raised by you alone. But…' He took an inhalation of breath. 'Were you to marry me, this problem would immediately disappear. You and Ben would be absorbed into the royal family as a unit, and Ben would make the easiest transition possible to his new life. You must see that.'

Her mouth opened, then closed, then opened again.

'No, I don't.'

Rico's mouth pressed tightly.

'I appreciate,' he began, in that same deliberate fashion, 'that you may find this hard to comprehend, let alone accept, but—'

'It's the most insane, tasteless thing I've ever heard.' The words burst from her. 'How can you say it? How can you even *say* it? You can't sit there and say something like that—you *can't*.'

Agitation shook her visibly.

Abruptly he held up a hand.

'It is a matter of expediency, that is all.'

She was staring at him as if he were speaking Chinese. He ploughed on.

'The marriage would take place for no other purpose than to regularise my nephew's existence. As my wife you will become a Ceraldi, with a due place in the royal family, a rank appropriate to the adoptive mother of the Reigning Prince's grandson. You will have a suitable place in all the events of his life. The marriage itself will be a formality, nothing more. Be assured of that.'

There was an edge in his voice, and he continued before she could interrupt him again.

'You may also be assured that the marriage will only be temporary. Once Ben is settled into his new life, and once you are settled into yours, and can move within it in an appropriate manner, then the marriage will be annulled. We will need to observe the proprieties, but my father has agreed that he will sanction a short duration—little more than a year—after which the marriage will have served its purpose and can be dissolved.'

She was still sitting there, looking as if he'd just hit her over the head with a sledgehammer. Well, that was what he *had* done, of course. He, at least, had the last forty-eight hours to accustom himself to what had been proposed as the way through the *impasse*.

'I don't believe that you are saying what I hear you to be saying,' she said very slowly, her voice hollow. 'You cannot be. It's impossible.'

Rico felt anger welling in him, and fought to subdue it.

'I appreciate,' he began again, 'that this is difficult for you to fully take on board, but—'

'Stop saying that. Stop saying I don't understand.' She jerked to her feet again. Her eyes were flaring with emotion. 'What I'm saying is that it's insane. It's *grotesque*.'

Rico's expression froze.

'Grotesque?' The word echoed from him, as though it were in a foreign language. Hauteur filled his face. 'In what way?' he bit out. He got to his feet without realising it, discarding his brandy glass on a side-table as he did so.

She was staring at him wild-eyed, her face working.

'What do you mean, "In what way?"?' she demanded. 'In *every* way. It's grotesque—absolutely grotesque—to think of me marrying you.'

Cold anger filled Rico. To use such a word about such a matter—

He had taken a great deal from this woman, made allowance after allowance for her circumstances, but for her to stand there and tell him that his offer was *grotesque*—

'Would you do me the courtesy of explaining why?' His voice was like ice.

She stared at him. For one long moment she met his gaze, and then, as if in slow motion, he saw her face seem to fracture.

'What else can it be?' she said, in a low, vehement voice.

His voice was stiff with tightly leashed anger. 'I do not see why—'

She cut across him.

'*Look at me.*'

She stood dead in front of him.

'How can you even think of it? *Look at me.*' Her voice was taut. 'It's *grotesque* to think of me...of me...marrying... marrying...you—'

She broke off. Her head dropped.

Rico stood looking at her. His anger had gone. Vanished. In its place...an emotion he was unused to feeling.

Embarrassment.

And pity.

Then, quietly, he said, 'We'll find another way to sort this out.'

Lizzy lay in bed, but she was not asleep. Beside her, on the far side of the bed, Ben's breathing rose and fell steadily, soundlessly. Lizzy stared into the darkness. Even now, if she did not steel herself, she could feel the hot tide of all-consuming mortification flooding through her. It had been one of those excruciating moments—like a dream in which she found herself walking down the street naked—that she would remember all her life.

How could he have done it? How could he have actually sat there and said that to her face? How could *anyone* in his insane family have thought of it?

She felt a cold sweat break out on her.

Grotesque, she had called it, and that was the only word for it. The very *idea* of someone who looked like her marrying someone who looked like him—for whatever reason.

As if someone were running a sadism course in her mind, she made herself think about it. Made herself see it as if it were real.

Made herself see the headlines. Forced herself to.

The Playboy Prince and the Poison Pill.

Prince Rico and his Bride of Frankenstein.

They'd have a field-day.

She gazed out, wide-eyed and unseeing. Unseeing of anything except the cruel, unforgiving reflection that greeted her every day of her life.

Then, juxtaposed beside it, the image of Prince Rico Ceraldi.

The contrast was…grotesque.

She shut her eyes, as if to banish the image in her head.

All her life she'd known that she was not just unattractive, but actively repellent. It was a harsh word, but it was true. She had proof of it, day after day. She'd learnt to see it in men's eyes—that instant dismissal and rejection.

It was the exact opposite of the reaction Maria had got. Maria, with her tall, slim figure and her lovely face, her long golden hair.

Lizzy hadn't been jealous. What would have been the point? Maria had been the beautiful sister, she the plain one. It was the way it had always been.

Maria, in her kindness, had offered to try and do something to improve her appearance, but Lizzy had never let her. It would have been too embarrassing. Even worse than looking so repellent naturally would have been trying not to, trying to do something about it—and failing.

Because of course she would have failed.

'You can't make a silk purse out of a sow's ear,' her mother would say to her, her mouth pressing tightly in displeasure as she looked over her older daughter.

So she had never tried. She had accepted herself for what she was.

Totally without the slightest attraction to the male sex.

And with Ben it just didn't matter. What did a child care if its mother was ugly? For Ben, it was her love for him that counted, her devotion to him. All he needed from her was her care and her hugs. That was all.

Ben.

Instinctively she reached out her hand and touched his folded little body, lightly brushing his hair before taking her hand away again.

Anguish filled her.

I want to go home. I want to go back home, to Cornwall—I want this nightmare never to have happened. Please, please let it not have happened. Please.

But her prayers were hopeless. The nightmare *had* happened, and she was caught in it. She would never be free of it.

Heaviness crushed her.

'We'll find another way to sort this out,' the Prince had said.

But what other way? The Ceraldis must have been desperate to even entertain what he had come up with—a temporary marriage of convenience to turn her into a princess and therefore a suitable mother for Prince Eduardo's grandson.

The weight on her chest intensified.

I'm nothing but a nuisance to them...

Then she rallied. Tough. Tough that she was nothing but a nuisance to the San Lucenzan royal family. Tough that she was a problem that had to be solved. Tough that their precious grandson just happened to come encumbered by a stand-in mother.

I don't care—I don't care about them, or what an inconvenience I am! I don't care about anything except Ben and his happiness. Ben needs me...and that's all that matters. And for him I'll do anything—anything at all.

Except marry his uncle.

Rico stood under the shower and let the stinging needles of water pound down over his head.

He should be feeling relieved. He should be feeling like a

condemned man reprieved. But he wasn't. An uncomfortable, writhing emotion twisted within him.

He kept hearing that word in his mind.

Grotesque.

How could any woman say that about herself? Feel that about herself?

OK, she was plain. But that was not her fault. So why did she seem to flay herself so for it?

A cynical voice spoke in his head.

She's just facing up to the truth, that's all. No man will ever want her, and she knows that. She knows just what an unlikely couple the two of you would make—the talking behind her back, the whispering, the scornful looks, the offers to comfort you for your affliction in having had to marry such a female.

He silenced the voice. Ruthlessly.

Instead, deliberately, he called another image to mind. The way she was with Ben. Endlessly patient, always loving and affectionate, supportive and encouraging.

She'd brought him up well.

More than well.

He frowned. It must have been hard for her.

She could have so much easier a life now. If he could just get her to see that.

He cut the water off and stepped out of the shower.

OK, so maybe it wasn't ideal having Ben's mother floating around San Lucenzo like a loose cannon. But even if she was a commoner, and an Englishwoman, so what? Something could be sorted, surely? Yes, it would make life awkward—but too bad. Wasn't Paolo's son worth some degree of inconvenience, some rearrangement of protocol and expectation?

He whipped a towel around his lean, honed body, then grabbed a hand towel to roughly pat his hair dry.

Once she and Ben were in San Lucenzo she would start to see for herself how a new life there would be possible. And he would have to make Luca and his father realise that somehow they had to set up a situation where Ben and his mother could live there.

His mind raced on. They didn't have to live in the palace, or the capital itself. The Ceraldis owned enough property in the principality—one of their numerous residences would prove suitable.

A villa by the sea—they'd like that.

He could see Ben in his mind's eye, playing on the beach—a warmer, less windy beach than the one in Cornwall.

I could visit him a lot then. Get to know him. Spend time with him.

Another thought came to him as he shrugged on a bathrobe and discarded the towels.

I'll get something done about her—for her. With good clothes, a decent haircut, make-up—surely she'd look better?

It would be a kindness to her.

He headed for bed, feeling virtuous.

And finally relieved.

CHAPTER SIX

THE jet was starting its descent. Rico could feel the alteration in pitch.

'We're starting to go down, Ben,' he announced.

Ben, captivated, stared out of the porthole, at the tiny patchwork of fields and valleys and rivers spread below. He had taken the journey in his stride so far—and so, to Rico's relief, had his mother.

'Will you at least agree to a visit?' he had asked her the next day. 'Nothing more than that. To allow my parents and brother to meet Ben.' His voice had changed. 'I do not have to tell you how much they long to meet him at last. Please do not deny them that,' he'd finished quietly. 'It will be a very emotional moment for them.'

She had nodded. Something seemed to have changed between them. He didn't know what, but somehow it was easier to talk to her. She, too, and he was sure it was not just his imagination, seemed less tense, less awkward in his presence.

Maybe, he thought sombrely, the scene that night had brought everything to a head.

Whatever it was, he was grateful. Grateful that she had agreed to move forward, even in this circumspect way, that she finally seemed to have moved beyond the stonewalling denial that had made her so difficult to deal with.

He had spoken to Luca that morning, telling him they were

going to fly out the following day. What he hadn't told him was
that it was only for a visit, not permanently. He would tell Luca
privately that there could be no question of a marriage of convenience. That the situation would have to be resolved differently, in a way that Ben's adopted mother was comfortable with.

Luca had not been communicative, had merely wanted to
know that Ben was finally on his way and when they would be
landing. He'd seemed tense, preoccupied.

Well, it had been a stressful time, Rico acknowledged. Their
father was not an easy man, and Rico had sympathy for Luca
being the one to bear the brunt of it. However much of a miracle
Ben's existence was, it had come with a price tag—one that his
father hated to pay. The focus of the world's tabloid press on
his family's private affairs.

The stewardess came forward into the cabin to request they
put their seat belts on. Rico smiled reassuringly across at Ben's
mother. She seemed outwardly calm, but he wondered how
real it was.

Ben simply seemed excited.

Ironically, thought Rico, Ben seemed a lot more excited
about flying in a plane than he did about the news, broken to
him tactfully and carefully the previous afternoon by his uncle
and his aunt, that he was, in fact, a royal prince.

'Will I have a crown?' had been his only question, and,
when a negative answer had been returned to him, had lost
interest in the matter.

His interest in royalty was revived momentarily when they
transferred to the car waiting for them at the airfield. The car
was flying a colourful standard from its bonnet, and Ben wanted
to know why.

'It's your grandfather's flag,' Rico answered. 'Because he's
the Ruler of San Lucenzo. We are going to meet him. And your
grandmother and your other uncle. The one I told you about
yesterday.'

The car glided off. Ben chattered away to Rico, asking him

question after question. Beside him, Lizzy sat, willing herself to stay calm.

But it was hard.

In England, cocooned in the safe house, it had been hard to appreciate the reality of Ben's patrimony. Now that they were here, in San Lucenzo itself, it was suddenly all too real. Fear and apprehension gouged at her, and she could feel her muscles tensing.

She was so completely out of place here. It had been bad enough in England, in that country house, but boarding a private San Lucenzan-registered jet, flying in luxury, with the stewardess saying 'Highness' to Ben's uncle every time she opened her mouth, and a uniformed airfield commander greeting them as they deplaned, and now a bodyguard, Gianni, sitting next to a peak-capped chauffeur driving them in the sleek, official-looking limo with the royal standard on it... It was all telling her that this was a world to which she did not belong.

A world as alien to her as if she'd landed on another planet.

Anxiety and nerves bit through her with merciless pincers.

'It will be all right. Trust me.'

Prince Rico had spoken in a low voice, but there was a note of consideration...kindness, even...that she was not used to. Perhaps it was simply because she was finally doing what the Ceraldis wanted her to do—bringing Ben out to San Lucenzo to meet his royal relatives.

But it seemed more than that.

And Lizzy knew why.

He's sorry for me. He's sorry for me because he knows that I know that the insane idea of a marriage of convenience was just grotesque.

His kindness should have made her feel more embarrassed than ever. And yet, strangely, it seemed to achieve the opposite.

She looked across at him, to where he was patiently answering Ben's questions. Ben was completely at ease with him now—and Rico with Ben, Lizzy could see. He was warm and affectionate, open and demonstrative with his nephew.

It brought a reassurance to her that she badly needed.

If he's like that with Ben, it means his parents and his brother will be too. OK, so they happen to be royalty—but what does that matter in the end? They want Ben to love, because they loved his father, and that's all that matters.

It would be all right—she had to believe that. It would be all right.

And if it wasn't—well. She took a heavy inhalation of breath as she reminded herself she had committed to nothing in coming out here. Ben, like her, was a British citizen, and she was his legal guardian. Nothing happened to him without her consent.

Her eyes went to Ben's uncle again.

Besides, he had given her his word.

He, a royal prince, wouldn't give that lightly or trivially. When he gave it, he would mean it.

Her reassurance deepened.

The windows of the car were tinted, so that although the occupants could see out, no one could see in.

'They are used to the cars of the royal family on the roads,' Rico remarked, as the car wound its slow way through the narrow streets of the city towards the royal palace.

'Does anyone else know we are coming here?' asked Lizzy.

Rico shook his head.

'The pavements would be mobbed with paparazzi if they knew,' he said. 'So far as the press is concerned, you and Ben are still in England. Eventually there will be an official statement from the palace, confirming both Ben's existence and yours, and also officially recognising him as Prince Paolo's son and a member of the royal family. But my father will not be hustled into making any announcements in reaction to the recent stories.'

'So no one knows we're here?' said Lizzy.

'No, you are quite safe. It will be a completely private visit.'

Her tension eased a fraction.

But not by much. The car was already approaching the wide gates of a palace, driving across its wide-paved concourse. The sugar-white, *faux*-castellated royal palace looked as if it was made out of children's candy, Lizzy thought. And the flanking guards were in picturesque antique costume and helmets as they swept past them and into the inner courtyard.

The car drew to a halt in front of a huge double door at the rear of the cobbled courtyard. As it stopped the doors were thrown open and two footmen emerged. One came to open the car door.

Prince Rico got out first, then turned to help lift Ben out and offer his hand to Lizzy. She managed to get out of the car without taking it.

As she straightened, she felt the warmth of the Mediterranean air in her lungs after the air-conditioned car.

Then they were heading indoors, and the cool of marble floors enveloped her as she walked beside Ben, his uncle on his other side, across the wide expanse of an entrance hall.

I'm in a palace, thought Lizzy, and the thought seemed bizarre and unreal.

One of the footmen was processing in front of them, the other bringing up the rear. Ben was still asking Rico questions. Lizzy glanced covertly either side of her, at the ornate walls, with alcoves inset with statuary.

Ahead was a huge flight of stairs, carpeted in royal blue. Prince Rico ascended lithely.

This is his home—he must do this every day of his life.

Her sense of unreality deepened.

So did the sense of oppression that had started to weigh her down.

How could she ever move in this world, even if only on the edges, as the legal mother of the Ruling Prince's grandson? It was impossible.

Grotesque...

The cruel word pincered at her.

They gained the top of the stairs, and a wide landing that

seemed to stretch endlessly in either direction. Off its length sets of double doors marched away.

Everywhere was marble and gilt, and there was the kind of hush that went with a deserted museum.

A man stepped forward, out of a doorway she hadn't even noticed.

The procession halted, and the man bowed briefly to Prince Rico, dismissing the footmen. The man was wearing a suit, and was clearly not a servant but one of the royal staff.

What were they called? Lizzy found herself wondering. Equerries? Was that it?

The man, who was quite young, and wearing pale spectacles which obscured his eyes, was addressing Prince Rico. His glance had gone briefly to Ben, but not to herself.

What am I? Invisible?

The caustic thought merely made her unease deepen.

Prince Rico was frowning, saying something in a sharp voice in Italian to the man. The man's expression did not change, remaining impassive. Unreadable.

Prince Rico turned towards Lizzy, shutting out the other man.

'My father and mother would like to meet Ben on his own for the first time,' he said to her. 'Please do not take offence at this. Were you to be there, they would be constrained to be formal, to behave as the protocols dictate. I hope you will understand?'

Fear flared in her eyes. Then, to her astonishment, her hand was taken.

'It will be all right. You have my word.'

His hands were warm across hers. His eyes, as he looked into hers, were rich with sympathy.

'Trust me,' he said in a low voice. 'Do not be afraid.'

Slowly, very slowly, she nodded. There seemed to be a lump in her throat.

He let go of her hand.

'You will be shown to your apartments, where you can

refresh yourself. I will bring Ben to you. In the meantime, rest and relax. Then, when I've brought Ben back, I will show you around.'

He glanced down at Ben.

'We're going to meet your grandparents now, Ben, and your other uncle. Your mother is going to have a little rest, and then we'll go exploring. There's a lot to see in this palace.' He bent forward conspiratorially. 'Even a secret passage.'

Ben's eyes widened. He slipped his hand into his uncle's, and Prince Rico started to walk off with him, still talking to him.

Lizzy watched them go.

'Signorina?'

It was the equerry, or whoever he was.

'I will show you to your new quarters,' said the man.

Numbly, Lizzy followed after him.

Tension netted her like a web.

Rico looked about him and frowned. His parents' private sitting room, which he'd just been ushered into with Ben, was deserted. Yet he'd been told to present Ben immediately. So where was everyone?

'Rico—finally.'

He turned abruptly. Luca had walked in from one of the antechambers. His brother's eyes went swiftly from himself to the small figure holding Rico's hand. For a moment he said nothing, just looked. Then he spoke.

'Yes—difficult to deny his paternity. Far too much Paolo in him.' His eyes flicked back to Rico. 'We were beginning to think you'd never get him here,' he said. 'You must be slipping.' A jibing note entered his voice. 'For a man who can charm any woman he wants into bed in the blink of an eye, it should have been a piece of cake for you to get the boy's aunt eating out of your hand.'

'Cut the sniping, Luca,' said Rico. His voice was sharper than usual. 'Where are the parents?'

His brother's eyebrows rose with a sardonic curve.

'It's Grand Council today—you know our father's never late for those sessions. And as for our fond mama, she always goes back to Andovaria for her fortnight's spa this time of year—had you forgotten?'

Rico stared. '*What?* Di Finori told me Ben had been summoned immediately.'

'Well, of course,' Luca responded impatiently. 'We've had to wait long enough to get him. But—' his mouth pressed '—at least we've got him now.' His voice changed again. 'So we can all relax finally. Especially you.' The jibing note was back in his voice. 'Poor Rico—actually reduced to offering to make the ultimate sacrifice—marriage. And to *such* a bride. I've just checked her out on the security cameras. *Dio*, if I'd known she was that bad even *I* might have thought twice before I did that number on you. Still, it did the business—as I knew it would. She must have snapped your hand off the minute you trotted out the marriage-of-convenience fairytale.'

'You never intended me to go through with it?' Rico's voice was edged like a knife.

Luca gave a laugh, abruptly cut off. 'Thump me one if you want, Rico, but you gave us no choice. I had to be convincing. I had to make sure you believed you were going to have to go through with it.' His mouth thinned. 'Why the hell you gave this Lizzy Mitchell your word that you wouldn't try and take the boy from her is beyond me. That's not something to lie about. That's why I didn't want to put you in a position where you knew you were lying about a marriage of convenience.'

The expression in Rico's eyes flickered minutely. 'I gave her my word to get her to trust me,' he said.

'Bad move.' Luca shook his head. 'You'll be glad to know I didn't mention it to our father—it wouldn't have gone down well. Still, like I said, everything's worked out finally. And now we can finally get this damn mess sorted.'

His eyes went to Ben, who had a blank, confused look on his face at all the incomprehensible Italian being spoken over his head, then to his brother again. For a moment Rico thought he saw something in Luca's eyes. Then it was gone. His voice, when he spoke next, was brisk and businesslike.

'The boy's personal household has been selected, and they're waiting to take him now. He'll have apartments here in the palace to begin with, where security is tighter. Later he'll be moved out to somewhere more remote—up in the hills, probably, to keep him out of circulation. Boarding school's a possibility when he's older, but that's a few years ahead yet. For the moment it's just a question of nannies and tutors. And keeping his profile as low as possible, of course. Everything necessary will be done to mitigate the situation and minimise his presence.' His expression changed again, and he gave a short, angry rasp. '*Dio*, what an ungodly mess! It's been hell dealing with it here, I can tell you!'

'I had the feeling,' Rico said, his eyes narrowing, 'that the idea of a grandson was welcome.'

Luca laughed shortly without humour.

'You've been reading too much of that trash in the press. Yes, of course that's the line the hacks took—they would, wouldn't they? All cloying sentimentality. You don't seriously imagine that our parents would *ever* welcome the news that Paolo had disgraced himself—and us all—by going and impregnating some two-cent bimbo and then *marrying* her?'

Rico gave a shrug. 'Could be worse—the bimbo could still be alive. As it is, it's just the frump of an aunt. What happens to *her* now, by the way?' His voice was offhand.

'Secure apartment here, in the south tower—she's being taken there now—then she'll be deported as *persona non grata* to the principality. Once outside the borders she can do what she wants. She won't get the boy back. Even if the press bankroll any counter-custody claim by her for the publicity, it will take years. While she had the boy and they were still in the

UK we were hamstrung—the law was weighted in her favour. But now it's a different story. We have possession, and that's what counts. She's finished. And you, my dear brother—' Luca clapped him on the back, his slate eyes sparking with his familiar sardonic expression '—are finally off-duty. You're free to celebrate a job well done. Mission accomplished.'

'Not quite,' said Rico.

His right hand slipped from Ben's, fisted, and landed on his brother's left temple with the full weight of his body behind the blow. Luca crumpled, unconscious, to the floor.

Ben had given a gasp, but Rico just took his hand again and started to hurry towards the door.

'Change of plan, Ben,' said Rico.

His voice was tight with fury.

The corridors seemed endless. Like a twisting maze. Numbly, Lizzy followed behind the bespectacled equerry. He said nothing to her, and walked at a pace that was slightly too fast for her. They went up stairs, and along more corridors, and then more stairs, leading upwards.

The décor was getting less palatial with every corridor. Finally he took her through a set of doors and into one more corridor. Lizzy looked about her. This wasn't just less palatial—this was…unused. It was the only word for it. A faint sheen of dust was on the floor, the skirting boards, and the air had a musty smell to it.

'*Signorina?*'

The equerry, or whoever he was, had opened a door and was waiting for her to go in. She hesitated a moment, then, not knowing what else to do, went in. It was more like a room in a budget hotel than a palace, with a plain bed and furniture, and a small and not very clean window that, Lizzy could see, overlooked some kind of delivery area.

Her suitcase was standing on a slightly frayed rug beside the bed.

It was a single bed, she noticed, frowning slightly, and she glanced around towards the door into what she presumed must be Ben's bedroom. But when she opened it it was only a small, windowless shower room, with no further door leading out of it. She turned.

'Where is my son's bedroom?' she asked. There was sharpness in her voice.

But it was wasted.

The door to the corridor was closing, and as it did she heard a distinct click.

A spurt of alarm went through her, and she hurried to the door, twisting the handle urgently.

It was locked.

The corridor was dingy, clearly disused. Emotion stabbed at Rico, and he suppressed it. There was no time for emotion now. None at all. Methodically he walked along the length of the corridor, testing each handle. Each one yielded to an empty room. They must have been servants' quarters at some point.

The fifth door refused to yield. He paused a moment, listening. There was no sound. Had she tried to scream? Or would she have realised it was bound to be pointless? No one would hear her here.

Emotion stabbed again, like a hornet stinging him. He suppressed it once more. He felt the strength of the lock with his hand, twisting the handle, then stepped back.

It hurt. In films it never looked as if it did. But the jarring pain in his shoulder as the door cracked was irrelevant.

What was not was the huddled figure on the bed. She had just launched up into a sitting position, he could tell.

Even from the shattered doorway he could see the look of terror on her face.

And the streaks of tears.

Her face contorted. Contorted into rage. Fury. Incandescent despair.

'I've got Ben—let's go.' He spoke urgently. 'We have no time—come now. *Now.*' His eyes bored at her. *'Trust me.'*

He could see the emotion in her face. An emotion that he never, ever wanted to see again on a woman's face. Then, abruptly, she hurled herself forward.

'Where is he?'

'At the end of the corridor, keeping watch. He thinks it's a game. He's not upset—he didn't realise what was happening. Don't ask questions—we've got *one* chance to get out of here, and that's all.'

How long would Luca stay out cold? He had no idea. He only knew that precious minutes were ticking by. He seemed to be divided into two people. One of them was raging with fury—the other was deadly calm. It was the latter he kept uppermost.

'Ben—' Her cry was almost a scream, but stifled in her throat.

Rico saw the child turn from his position at the end of the corridor.

'Mummy—come on.' He beckoned her furiously, his little face alight with excitement.

The palace was labyrinthine, but Rico knew it like the back of his hand. Knew exactly which levels were most likely to be deserted. He walked rapidly, blood pounding, her suitcase in one hand and Ben's hand in the other. Ben trotted beside him, his mother behind him, both instructed not to talk, not to ask questions. He mustn't think, mustn't feel. Just keep moving. Fast, urgent. Undetected. Every corner was a risk—someone, anyone, could be there.

But there was no one. No one right up to the service door to his own apartments. Ungently, he shoved Ben and his mother inside even as he yanked out his mobile phone and punched a number.

Thank God Gianni was there, in position. He'd phoned him the moment he'd left his brother out cold on the floor, to give him instructions. He snapped the phone shut and turned to Ben.

'Time for the secret passage,' he said.

Ben's mouth opened wide in wonder.

'Here it is,' said Rico. He'd crossed to the wall into which a fireplace had been set, and felt for the concealed button that operated the door mechanism. He hadn't used it in a while, but it still worked, if creakingly, revealing a narrow entrance to an even narrower staircase.

He gave a sudden grin, his mood lightening for a nanosecond.

'It's the reason I chose these apartments as a teenager. It was a great way to evade curfew. Come on.'

Ben needed no second invitation. He surged forward, his expression blissful, and Rico had to hold him while he flicked on the interior light, got them all inside, and then shut the door.

The concealed staircase opened into a side street in the palace precincts. The car was waiting, its tinted windows closed. Even so, he made his nephew and his mother lie on the floor of the back seat.

'Drive,' he instructed Gianni.

Only as he sat back in his seat, Ben excitedly clutching at his leg and asking him if it were another adventure, did the emotions start to come through.

The violence of them shook him to the core.

They made it to the border in under twenty minutes. He'd debated between speed via the coastal *autostrada* versus heading for the hills, and had gone for the former. He had to take a gamble, and it was absolutely vital they get on to Italian soil.

As they passed through the unmanned border he spoke.

'We're out,' he said. He leant down to haul up Ben, followed by his mother. She busied herself with seat-belts.

'What now?' she asked. Her voice was expressionless, but Rico heard the tremor in it. Heard the tightness of her throat. Heard the fear. The terror.

He looked at her. The chalky complexion, the bones stark

in her face. Emotion surged in him, and he clamped it down yet again.

'We get to a priest,' he said.

CHAPTER SEVEN

THE savage irony of it was that she still balked at marrying him. In the end he had to be brutal.

'It is the only way I can protect you. Protect Ben.'

She stared at him, her face a web of fear.

'It's another trick. A trap.' Her voice was hollow.

'*No*, I swear it. I swear I did not know what they were planning—I swear. If I could, I would get you back to England—but I can't. I've got you into Italy, and now you are safer, because my father will have to work through the Italian authorities and that will slow him down. But if you try and return to England you'll be taken into custody. I can't even get you into Switzerland. All the Italian borders will be watched. And don't think my father won't be able to do it—he'll have some charge against you trumped up. It doesn't matter what— it matters only to prevent you taking Ben back to the UK. You'll be separated, and there'll be some kind of court order taking him into care—something. Anything. Whatever it takes to separate you. And he'll find a way to keep you separated.'

He took a searing breath. 'The only way I can keep you safe is by doing what I've just said. Once we're married they can't touch you, and they can't touch Ben. Neither legally nor because of the publicity. They will have to accept a *fait accompli*. I know my father—he won't risk an open break with me. He won't cause that kind of scandal.'

He looked at her as she sat, her arm tight around Ben, who had lolled off to sleep with the motion of the car, steadily being driven further north towards the alpine foothills. 'I'm the only person who can protect you—keep you and Ben together.'

She stared at him.

'Why?' The question was a breath, almost inaudible. 'Why do you want to do that?'

It echoed through him, reverberating through his being.

Why? She had asked why.

'I gave you my word,' he said. 'Not to let Ben be parted from you. That's why.'

In his head he heard again Luca's voice, describing the nightmare childhood that had been planned for Ben.

Anger blinded him.

Anger at his father, his mother, his brother…the whole damn, twisted, duplicitous, hard-hearted, *callous* lot of them.

How could they do it? How could they even think it?

But he knew how. To them, the only important thing was duty and reputation, avoiding scandal, awkwardness, embarrassment.

And to achieve that they were prepared to take a four-year-old child and wrench it from its mother—trick the mother into coming here in good faith and then throw her out like a piece of rubbish.

His eyes went to her, went to her arm so tight around Ben, and to Ben, his head resting on her side, his hand lying in her lap. Mother and child.

Genetically she might only be his aunt, but to Ben she was everything—the whole world. So what if she were some ordinary member of the masses, utterly unfit to be a royal princess, the mother of a royal prince?

His lips pressed together. And so what that she was utterly unlike any woman he would have chosen for his wife? A woman who knew that brutal, cruel truth…

Grotesque.

That was what she thought a marriage between them would be. Grotesque. The word tolled through him again.

Shaming him.

Shaming him with its pitiless honesty.

Well, now it didn't matter. Didn't matter what either of them thought about such a marriage. Because neither of them was important now—only Ben.

And this was the only way to keep him safe.

Savage humour filled him. So Luca had set him up like a patsy, had he? Despatching him to mount a charm offensive on Ben's aunt that would steal her child from her, duping him into offering to marry her simply to lull her into a false sense of security. His mouth tightened.

Thanks for the idea, Luca—it's a really good one.

And it would beat his family on all points.

And keep Ben safe with his mother.

His eyes went to the boy. He was still asleep, lolling against his mother.

He met her eyes. They were huge, strained.

'Thank you,' she said, her voice low and tight.

She felt as if she was falling. Falling very far, into a deep, bottomless pit. All she had to cling to was Ben. And it was imperative she did. Imperative she keep hold of him, never, ever to loosen her hold on him—because otherwise he would fall away from her and be lost for ever.

Fear shot through her like a grid of hot wires in her veins. Over and over again the horror of what had happened in the palace, when she had realised she had been locked in that room, when she had realised that it could mean only one thing, still drenched through her.

Her eyes went to the man standing beside her in the chill, stone-built church, his expression drawn and shuttered.

Trust me, he had said.

I give you my word, he had said.

Could she trust him? Was he really rescuing her? Or simply tricking her again?

But how could he be tricking her? He was prepared to do something that would change his life for ever. Something so drastic that it made her feel faint with the enormity of it. He had disobeyed his father, knocked his own brother out cold so he could rescue her, so he could get Ben and her away to freedom…safety.

Safety with him.

He's doing it for Ben. Because he knows it would be unspeakably cruel for him to lose me. And that was why she'd do it too. For Ben.

Nothing else mattered.

The priest was starting to speak. The dimly lit, tiny whitewashed church, scarcely more than a chapel, was in a small village somewhere in the hills. She had no idea where. There had been a low-voiced, urgent conversation in the car between the Prince and his bodyguard, who was, so it seemed, not merely loyal enough to his employer to have stood by him, but also possessed of a great-uncle who was a priest.

A frail, elderly man, he stood before them now, clasping their hands together with his and intoning words she did not understand, but which, she knew, were binding her in holy matrimony to the man at her side.

She went on falling.

It was done. Ben and his mother were safe. Relief sluiced through Rico. As he thanked the priest, mentally vowing that he would take every measure to avoid the man getting into the slightest trouble over what he had done, and thanked the housekeeper who had been the witness to the ceremony along with Gianni, Rico knew that there was one more thing to be done.

He ushered Ben and his mother back into the car. Gianni slid into the driver's seat. He knew where to go, what to do.

'I'm hungry,' announced Ben. He had woken up, stood beside Gianni during the brief, hurried ceremony, passively accepting, as children did, without comprehension, what was happening to the grown-ups around him.

'We'll have some food soon—very soon, I promise,' Rico said, ruffling his hair. It was still not quite dark, but they had a way to drive. He would have preferred to fly, but that was out. There was no way he could take a helicopter up without air traffic control knowing about it. But they would head cross country, by obscure routes if they could.

This car was different anyway—a lot less conspicuous. Gianni had fixed the swap—the guy was heading for an all-time bonus. Now he came up trumps yet again.

'You like pizza?' he asked, and passed back a large, double wrapped plastic bag. 'Cold, but good. From my great-uncle's housekeeper, for the *bambino*.'

Ben's face lit.

'Yes, please,' he said.

Rico watched as his mother unwrapped the food and handed it with some paper towels to his nephew, who tucked in hungrily. As they ate, he slid his hand into his pocket and took out his phone. It took a while to be answered, but when it was, he wasted no time.

'Jean-Paul, I've got a story for you…'

The conversation was lengthy, in rapid French, and when he disconnected Rico felt another wave of relief go through him. He also felt anxious eyes on him. He turned his head.

'That was a friend of mine. The one who alerted me that there was a story building about Paolo's long-lost son. He's a good friend, and I trust him absolutely. I've told him we've just got married. That we're making a family for Ben. He'll sit on the story until I give him the word to run with it. That's the weapon I can hold over my father. I'll give him some time to come round, to accept what's happened, but if he stonewalls then Jean-Paul can run the story the way I've given it to him— without any co-operation from the palace. That's the only choice my father gets.'

His voice was grim as he finished.

He slid the phone into his jacket pocket again.

'I still cannot believe that my father did what he did. I knew he was not sentimental about Luca and myself, but Paolo—Paolo was different.' His eyes slid away into the past as he spoke, his voice low. 'Paolo was the one son my parents could treat not as a prince, but as…as a child. As someone in his own right. Someone without a royal function. Who could just be himself. That's why—' His voice halted a moment, then he went on. 'That's why I thought they really wanted Ben. Because he's Paolo's son. I thought they would…' He swallowed. 'I thought they would love him. Love him enough to know that what was important for Ben was what should be done. Love him enough to know that *you* were important to him.'

His eyes looked troubled. 'I am ashamed of them. Ashamed of what they did to you.'

Suddenly, out of nowhere, he touched her arm. Lightly. Just for a moment.

'And I am ashamed of myself as well.'

Lizzy's expression was troubled.

'You're taking the fall for this,' she said, and her voice was low and strained. 'I'm sorry—I'm really, really sorry that you had to…had to do what you've just done. I'll try…I'll try not to be—' She swallowed, then fell silent.

What could she say? *I'll try not to be too grotesque a wife to you?* She felt her throat tightening.

He was silent a moment. Then he spoke.

'It will work out. For all the reasons I told you in England, when I believed that this marriage was what my father wanted. All those reasons are still true.'

She could not reply. What could she say?

That the reason for her refusing him in England was still the same as well?

Well, it was too late for that.

The car drove on into the night. At her side, Ben finished

his pizza. She cleared away the remains, then let him cuddle against her and fall asleep. His little body was warm and sturdy, and her love for him flooded through her.

I've done the right thing. I've done the only thing. The only thing possible to keep him safe.

Her eyes met his uncle's, on the other side of Ben.

A strange emotion pricked through him.

He had done what he had had to do. No other course of action had been possible—anything else had been unthinkable.

I did what I had to do. That is all.

It was my duty.

Duty. But of a different type.

Carrying, strangely, no burden of resentment. Only relief.

Relief that he had done, if nothing else, the right thing. By Paolo, by his son, and by the girl whom he now protected. Who had no one but him to do so. The strange emotion quickened. Quite different from all the emotions that had stormed through him since Jean-Paul's first phone call to him, which seemed now to have been a long, long time ago. He tried to think what the emotion was, to identify it. Then it came to him.

It was a sense of purpose. Doing something that mattered.

A new emotion for him.

'Where are we?' Lizzy's voice sounded bleary, even to her own ears. She had been roused from heavy, uneasy sleep as the car had come to a stop. She straightened up, feeling stiff. Ben was still slouched heavily against her, fast asleep.

'Capo d'Angeli. Jean-Paul has hired a villa here for us. We can stay here as long as we want. No one will disturb us.'

She let him undo the safety catch and she scooped the sleeping Ben into her arms, while Gianni helped her out of the car. A cool breeze came in the night, and all she could make out was a house with a gravelled drive immediately beneath her feet, and a front door opening. She heard Italian spoken, and then she and Ben were being ushered inside. There were people, more Italian, but she was too tired to do anything other than carry Ben upstairs, following the tall, besuited figure ascending in front of her, blocking out of her head everything except the overriding need to get to bed. Get back to sleep.

Like a zombie, she followed him into a room—a large bedroom with a larger bed. A maid was turning it down on either side. She hurried forward to help Lizzy, and within a few minutes—blessedly so—Lizzy was laying her head down on the pillow beside her sleeping son, her eyelids closing.

She wanted to sleep for ever and never wake up. Never face up to what she had just done.

Married Prince Enrico of San Lucenzo.

Downstairs, Rico took out his mobile once more, and pressed the number he knew he had to call.

Luca answered immediately. His voice was taut with fury. Incomprehension. Rico cut him off in mid-denunciation. He called his brother a word he had never used to him before. It silenced Luca long enough for Rico to tell him the new situation. Then, slowly, in a different voice, his older brother spoke again.

'Rico—it's not too late. We'll send a helicopter, and you and the boy can be back here by morning. We'll fix an instant annulment. The girl can be taken care of—we can get her deported from Italy. We can—'

'Wrong again.' Rico's voice was a tight, vicious drawl. 'All you and our father can do is—' He gave instructions that were crude—and anatomically impossible. 'And now, if you please, you can inform my revered father that I am going to start my honeymoon, with my bride and my new son. And there is *nothing* you can do about it. Do you understand me? Nothing. They are in my care now. Mine. And if you had a shred of honour in you, you would never speak to our father again.'

He hung up.

* * *

Lizzy was dreaming. She was back in that hospital, with her sister. But her sister was not in a coma. Instead she was sitting up, cradling a baby, her golden hair like a veil. There was someone else sitting on the bed—a young man with blond hair. They were both fixated on the baby in Maria's arms. They didn't see Lizzy. Didn't even look up.

Then her parents were coming into the ward. They walked past Lizzy, their arms full of presents wrapped up in baby blue. She tried to walk forward, but she couldn't. She had a present for the baby, but there was only room to put the present on the end of the bed. It slid onto the floor. Her mother looked round sharply.

'What are you doing here?' she demanded. 'Maria doesn't need you. No one needs you. And no one wants you either.'

She reached for the curtain and drew it around Maria's bed. Shutting Lizzy out.

Lizzy woke up.

Guilt drenched through her.

She had taken something that was not hers to take. Something she'd had no right to. She turned her head. Ben was asleep on the far side of the huge double bed, his little figure swathed in the light coverlet. Ben—her sister's son. Not hers. Not hers at all.

Anguish filled her. Her hand reached to him, touching his hair. Soft and golden. Like his mother's. His father's.

Not like hers at all.

Not mine. Not mine. Not mine.

The litany rang through her head.

And now she had taken something else she'd had no right to take. Something else she didn't deserve.

And yet she knew bitterly that the theft had come with its own punishment. Heat flushed through her—the heat of mortification. *Grotesque*, she had called the very idea of a marriage between them, the two most opposite people in the world. And yet she had gone ahead with it. She had inflicted herself on him because there was no other way to keep safe the child she had taken from her sister. The child she had no right to. No right to love the way she did.

She felt Ben stir and wake. His eyes opened. Trusting. Instantly content to see her. Knowing that if she was there, then all was well.

Cold iced along her veins. It had so very nearly been different.

I could have been on my way back to England—deported. Ben imprisoned in that palace, never to see me again.

The horror of what had so nearly been consumed her.

Prince Rico had saved them.

Guilt stabbed at her again. He had saved them—and she had repaid him by chaining him to her.

'Mummy?'

Ben was sitting up.

'Is it getting-up time?' he asked brightly. 'Is Tio Rico here?' He looked around expectantly, then, in a puzzled voice, 'Where are we, Mummy? Have we gone back to the palace again?'

She shook her head. A steely hardness filled her.

'No, darling. We're not going back there.' She threw back the bedclothes. 'Come on, let's find out where breakfast is. I'm starving.'

She looked around her. The room was large and airy, and filled with sunlight diffused through bleached wood Venetian blinds. The furniture was simple, but elegant, the walls white, the floor tiled. She found her spirits lifting.

Capo d'Angeli. She had heard of it vaguely, but nothing more. A place where rich people went, but not flash or sophisticated. Discreet and classy. An exclusive, luxury resort on the Italian coast where there were no hotels, only villas, with large private grounds, each nestled into its own place on the rocky promontory overlooking the sea.

Someone had brought up her suitcase. There was not a great deal in it—even less than she'd taken from Cornwall—but there was enough to serve. Ben fell with a cry of pleasure upon his teddy bear, as well as a clutch of his favourite engines.

It did not take long to dress, and when they were both ready

Lizzy drew up the Venetian blinds. French windows were behind them, and a wide terrace, and beyond the terrace—

'Mummy—the sea! It's bluer than my paintbox. Much bluer than home.'

Lizzy opened the French windows and warm air flooded in like an embrace. Ben rushed out, clutching the stone balustrade and staring eagerly out over the tops of the pine trees set below, out to the cerulean sea beyond, sparkling in the morning light.

'Do you think there's a beach?' he asked, his voice pitched with excitement.

'Definitely a beach, Ben.'

The voice that answered him was not hers. It came from further down the terrace, where an ironwork table was set out under a large blue-striped parasol. The table was set with breakfast things, but Lizzy had no eyes for them. All she had eyes for was the man sitting in the pool of shade.

She felt her stomach clench. Oh, God, he just looked so fantastic. He was wearing a bathrobe, and its whiteness contrasted dramatically with the warm tan of his skin tones, the deep vee of the crossover revealing a smooth, hard surface that she flicked her eyes away from jerkily. Not that it did any good to look at any other part of him. His forearms were bare, too, the sleeves of the robe rolled up, and his damp hair was feathering in the warmth. As for his face—

She felt her stomach clench again. He was a ludicrously attractive male, and up to now she'd only seen him in formal attire. Seeing him like this, fresh from his shower, was…

Different.

Completely, utterly different.

And he seemed different too. The tension that had been in him throughout their time together at the safe house, culminating in the extreme emotion of their flight from the palace had gone. Disappeared.

Now he seemed…relaxed.

Carefree.

Ben was running forward. 'Tio Rico, can we go down to the beach?' he asked eagerly.

His uncle laughed. Lizzy's stomach churned yet again. The laughter lit his face, indenting lines around his mouth, lifting his eyes, showing the white of his teeth. Making him look a hundred times more gorgeous. A hundred times sexier—

Oh, God, how am I going to cope with this?

Misery filled her, and with horrible self-conscious awkwardness she walked forward. As she approached, he got to his feet.

'Buon giorno,' he said. There was still a smile in his eyes. Left over from Ben, obviously.

Lizzy swallowed, and gave a sort of half nod. She couldn't look at him—not look him in the eye and know that last night, in some unreal, disorientating, panicked ceremony, she had become this man's wife.

She pulled out a chair and sat down.

'Did you sleep well?' There seemed to be genuine enquiry in his voice.

She swallowed, and nodded again. Jerkily she reached for a jug of orange juice and began to pour herself a glass. Ben was chattering away to his uncle.

His stepfather? A stepfather who could take him away from her—

The breath tightened in Lizzy's throat as the realisation hit her. It was followed by panic. Blind, gut-wrenching panic. Was this another trick? A trap like the one that had brought her to San Lucenzo, with one object only, to take Ben from her?

'Don't look like that.' His voice was low, but it penetrated her panic. Her eyes snapped up. Locked with his. 'It will be all right. *It will be all right.* There is no need for you to fear anything now.'

She felt her throat tighten unbearably.

'Trust me,' he said.

His dark eyes were looking into hers. 'I promised you,' he said slowly, clearly, as if to a frightened child, 'that I will keep you and Ben safe, together, for as long as is necessary. I will *never* allow you to be separated from him. You have my word.'

And slowly, very slowly, Lizzy felt the panic still, the fear drain from her. He held her eyes for one moment longer, and then, with a slight, humorously resigned twist to his lips, he turned to Ben, who was tugging at his sleeve to get his attention back and find out whether he could get down to the beach right away.

'Breakfast first, young man,' he said. 'Then we'll go exploring. When I've got some clothes.' He looked across at Lizzy, who was sipping her orange juice. 'I am having some new clothes sent up to the villa. They should be here soon. The palace may send my own on; they may not. In the meantime, the on-site boutiques by the marina here can supply whatever we want.' His eyes flicked to her and Ben. 'They'll get you two sorted out as well.'

'Oh, no—please. I'm sure I can cope with what I've brought,' Lizzy said hurriedly.

'That will not be necessary.' His expression stilled a moment. 'I know this is hard for you, but everything is different. However...' his voice changed again '...today we shall spend very quietly, giving us time to get used to what has happened. I think we deserve some calm after the storm, no? So, tell me, what do you think of the villa?'

'It's unbelievably beautiful,' Lizzy said.

Rico nodded. 'I agree. Jean-Paul chose well. It's also one of the most remote villas on the Capo D'Angeli estate. Not that we need to worry. Security on the whole estate is draconian. Everyone who stays here wants privacy above all—even from each other. And by the same token,' he said reassuringly, 'you do not need to worry about the staff. They are used to all guests wanting absolute discretion. We can relax completely here—I have even sent Gianni off to take a well-deserved holiday.'

He smiled encouragingly.

On cue a manservant appeared, bearing a tray of fresh coffee and breakfast rolls. Ben needed no encouragement, and was swiftly tucking in.

'He seems to have taken it all in his stride,' said Rico contemplatively. 'I think he will like it here.' He glanced across at Lizzy. 'I think we will like it here.'

She met his eyes. It was getting easier. Not easy, but easier.

'Thank you,' she said, in a low, intense voice. 'Thank you for what you have done.'

'We did what we had to do. There was no other way. No other choice. And now—' his expression changed '—I want to hear no more on it. We have been through a great deal—we deserve a holiday. And this is a good place for one.'

He grinned suddenly, and yet again Lizzy felt that hopelessly inappropriate reaction. She crushed it as much as she could, but dread went through her. How was she going to cope? It was impossible—just impossible.

She steeled herself. Prince Rico was going to have to cope, and so was she. If he could use his upbringing to handle any situation, then she would too. She would force herself.

'What…what will happen today?' she ventured.

'Today? Today we take things easy. Ben must go down to the beach—we'll have a revolution on our hands if we don't take him. The cove at the base of the villa gardens is private to us, so we will not be disturbed. There is a swimming pool here too, of course, on the level below this one. As for toys—well, the villa comes with a fully stocked children's playroom, and for anything else the internet is a great provider. So, you see, we shall have everything we need for the perfect holiday.'

He smiled at her again, then turned his attention to Ben.

'How are you at building sandcastles?' he asked him.

'Really good,' said Ben enthusiastically. 'At home we build them when the tide comes in, and then we make big walls to stop the waves. But the waves always win in the end.'

Rico made a face. 'Alas, there is no tide here—the Mediterranean sea is too small for tides. And the waves are very small too. But the water is lovely and warm. You won't get cold. We can go on a boat, too.'

'Today?' demanded Ben.

'Not today. Perhaps tomorrow. We'll see.'

Ben's expression darkened. '"We'll see" means no,' he said gloomily.

'It means I don't know yet. This is a holiday, Ben. We're going to take it one day at a time. Isn't that right?'

Rico's eyes suddenly flicked to hers.

'One day at a time,' he repeated. 'For us too.'

For a long moment he held her eyes, then Ben reclaimed his attention with yet another question.

She needed time, Rico knew. So much had happened to her since he'd showed up at her ramshackle cottage in Cornwall. And for her, he had to appreciate, it had all been bad. The life she'd known had been ripped away from her. For her, there was no going back.

A surge of determination went through him.

I'll make that life better now. All the fear and trauma is over now.

His eyes flickered over her fleetingly, without her knowledge, as she poured herself more coffee.

I don't believe she has to look this bad. I just don't.

Covertly he studied her. It was hard to see much of her figure, as even in this warmth she was wearing a long-sleeved baggy top that seemed to flow shapelessly into long baggy cotton trousers. Both garments were cheap and worn. She dressed for comfort, not style, that much had always been apparent, but the perpetual bagginess of her clothing made it hard to judge just what her figure really was. She was no stick-thin model, that was for sure, but how overweight was she *really*? And even so, well-cut clothes could conceal a multitude of evils, surely…?

He moved on to try and evaluate her features. That was hard to do too. The unsightly frizz of her hair which, even when tied back as it was now, still seemed to straggle round her face, drew all the attention. He tried to imagine her face without it. It was difficult, he realised, to judge it accurately. The heavy eyebrows didn't help, of course, and nor did the pallid skin. But there wasn't anything actively disastrous—her nose was straight, her jaw defined, her eyes grey, her teeth not protruding or uneven. It was just that her features seemed so completely—nondescript.

Would she look better with make-up? Surely she must? Women always did, didn't they? Not that he was used to seeing women without make-up—make-up and hundreds of euros' worth of grooming, and thousands of euros' worth of clothes and accessories.

Well, now she could have that kind of money spent on *her*. Money was not going to be a problem for her from now on. He would lavish it on her.

His mouth tightened abruptly. In his head he heard Luca's sneering at the sight of her. Anger bit him. Who the hell was Luca to sneer at a woman who had taken her dead sister's child and dedicated her life to raising him? Being a single mother on little money was no ride in the park—certainly not a limo-ride. And so what if she weren't beautiful? What did Ben care?

And I don't care either. I'll get her looking the best she can—because she deserves it. She needs all the reassurance she can get. She'll feel a lot more confident, a lot more comfortable about what we've just gone and done, if she can wipe that vile word out of her mental vocabulary.

He heard it again, cruel and ugly.

Grotesque.

Well, that word was going in the trash can. And staying there. He would never let her say it again.

CHAPTER EIGHT

'WINE for you?' Rico held the bottle of chilled white wine over Lizzy's glass.

'Um—er—thank you,' she replied awkwardly, and he proceeded to fill it up.

They were back at the table on the terrace again, but over the sea the sun was sinking in a glory of red and gold.

'Mummy, I'm really hungry,' Ben said plaintively.

'Food is coming very soon,' said Rico, pouring himself a glass of wine as well.

'What are we having for tea, Mummy?'

Rico smiled. 'Pasta, Ben. All good children in Italy eat pasta. Do you like pasta?'

'I *love* pasta,' Ben exclaimed.

'In Italy you can eat pasta every day,' said Rico.

He lifted his wine glass.

'To our first day here,' he said, looking at Ben and his mother. Ben lifted his glass of orange juice. 'Have we had a good day, everyone?' he asked around.

'Yes,' said Ben.

'Yes,' said his mother. 'It's been lovely.'

It had too, and Lizzy was grateful. It was strange. She hadn't expected it to be easy. And yet it had been. They'd done nothing except spend most of the day on the beach, coming back up to the terrace for lunch, and then, after much protesting from Ben, having a brief siesta. When Ben had surfaced they'd gone down to the beach again, returning only in late afternoon for Ben to have a quick swim in the pool, before showering and getting ready for supper.

The only awkward moment had been when Ben, splashing around in the warm shallow sea with his uncle, had called out 'Mummy, aren't you going to swim?'

Lizzy had shaken her head, the thought of stripping off to a bathing costume making her cringe. It was bad enough being on a beach with a man whose honed, lean-muscled body, clad only in swimming trunks, made it impossible to let her eyes go anywhere near him.

'I'll swim another time,' she'd evaded, and gone doggedly back to her book.

Other than that it had been an extraordinarily easy day. Now, sitting watching the sun set while they shared in a nursery tea, she realised she was feeling far more relaxed than she'd thought possible. She took a sip of her chilled wine.

'Is the wine to your liking?' Ben's uncle asked.

'Um—yes, it's lovely. I—er—I don't really know anything about wine,' she answered.

'You will learn with practice.' He smiled at her. 'And another thing you will learn with practice,' he went on, taking his own mouthful of wine, 'is to call me by name.'

Lizzy stared. She couldn't do that. The whole thing about addressing him had been so awkward that she simply hadn't done it. She couldn't address him as 'Highness', and she couldn't address him as 'Prince Enrico', or even 'Prince Rico'. And she certainly couldn't address him as simply Rico.

'And I must do the same,' he continued. 'So—' He took a breath. 'Lizzy. There, I've said it. Now it's your turn.'

'I can't,' said Lizzy. Embarrassment flushed through her.

'Have some more wine—then try,' he advised.

She took another mouthful, and swallowed hard.

'Rico,' she mumbled. She couldn't quite look at him.

'*Bene,*' he said softly. 'You see—all things are possible.' For a moment he held her eyes approvingly, then, with a change of tone, he spoke again. 'Ah, supper arrives.'

'Hurrah,' said Ben.

The following days were spent very largely as the first one had been. Rico made it so quite deliberately. He was giving her the time she needed—a breathing space.

He needed one too, he knew. They all did. He'd said as much to her the next day.

'We'll take this a day at a time, like I said,' he'd told her. 'We won't think about the outside world, we won't think about anything. We'll just accept the present and relax. Get used to things—get to know each other.'

It was ironic, he realised—all his life there had been a distance between himself and the world. There had had to be. And that meant, he acknowledged, that there were very few people that he ever truly let down his guard with. Jean-Paul was one, and there were a few others. Sportsmen, mostly, to whom his birth was a complete irrelevance, and all that counted was skill and dedication.

But never women—even in the superficial intimacies of the bed.

He'd bedded a lot in his time. Taken his pick, enjoying them physically. Making sure they enjoyed him, too.

But nothing more. Safety in numbers, he'd told Luca, and it had been true.

His mouth twisted. Had he proposed marriage, any of the women he'd bedded would have, in his brother's cruel words, bitten his hand off to accept. The prospect of becoming the glittering Principessa Enrico Ceraldi would have been irresistible to them.

Yet the woman he'd actually married had been horrified at the prospect.

He knew it was because of the outward disparities between

them, which she was so hung up about. Yet her attitude towards him had, he realised slowly, had another effect on him as well.

It had made him feel safe with her.

Because it made her like no other woman he knew.

It was a strange realisation, seeping through him.

All she wants from me is protection for Ben—that's all. She wants nothing else—nothing from me.

A thought came to him—another strange, new realisation.

I don't have to be on my guard with her. I don't have to keep her at a distance. Because she doesn't want anything from me—

A sense of release came over him, as if for the first time in his life, he felt—free.

Lizzy sat in the shade of the blue and white striped awning and watched Ben and his uncle play waterpolo in the pool. Ben was shrieking with pleasure. Her heart warmed. He was just so happy—every day had been a delight for him.

And for her?

It was so strange. How could it be that, despite the huge emotional upheaval she'd gone through since that fateful evening when her world had been turned upside down and she had discovered the truth about Ben's parentage, she could now be feeling so…carefree?

So relaxed.

And yet she was.

It had seemed impossible at the outset of their panicked arrival here. The enormity of what had happened, what she had done, had been overwhelming, and yet here, in this tranquil, beautiful place—so far from the rest of the world, it seemed—she had found a peace of mind she had never thought to find.

Her eyes went to the man playing with her son, and she felt gratitude welling through her—and wonder.

He was being so kind to her. And not just because of Ben.

He had gone out of his way to be endlessly kind and patient to her, for her own sake.

It was a world away from his image as the Playboy Prince.

There's more to him than that. Much more, she thought fiercely.

She had misjudged him, she knew, seeing only the image, not the man beneath. He was a man who had defied his father, his sovereign, to defend and protect her and Ben. A man who had unhesitatingly married himself to the very last woman in the world he'd ever have chosen for a wife for the sake of a small child.

A child he really seemed to love.

She felt her heart warm as she watched Rico haul himself out of the pool. His lean body glittered with diamonds in the sun as he leant down, let Ben clutch his arm with his hands, and with effortless strength lifted him clear out of the water.

'Again!' shouted Ben, and jumped back in the water.

Rico repeated the process, swinging him high into the air with a laughing grin before lowering him gently to the paving beside the pool.

Ben rushed up to Lizzy.

'I scored *five* goals,' he exclaimed.

'Did you? How fantastic.' She smiled.

'Why don't you come in the water, Mummy?'

'Because she needs a nice new swimming costume, Ben. And lots of new clothes, like you've already had. Clothes for a princess.'

Rico had come up behind him.

Ben tilted his head to one side. 'Is Mummy a princess, then?'

'Yes,' said Rico casually, padding himself dry with a towel. 'When I married her she became a princess.'

'Has she got a crown?' Ben asked interestedly. He had a strong mental association between royalty and crowns.

'She can have a tiara. For when she goes to a ball.'

Ben's eyes lit up.

'Like Cinderella?'

'Exactly like Cinderella,' said Rico.

His eyes went to Lizzy's face, and then shadowed. There was a look in her eyes he did not want there, but he knew why it was.

Lizzy looked away. If there was any role in Cinderella she was ideally cast for, it was not the heroine. It was as an ugly sister.

It was Maria—Maria who had been Cinderella—swept off her feet by Prince Charming. But the coach had crashed.

Rico saw her look away. Read her thought. His mouth pressed tight. It was time to get this sorted. Time to put that cruel word in the trash once and for all.

She was comfortable with him now, he knew—and he with her. But that harsh word still remained between them like a poison. A poison that needed to be drawn.

And there was no point delaying it any longer. It was time, more than time, to do something about it.

It proved very easy to arrange. The shopping complex by the marina was designed to cater to the needs of those who stayed at Capo D'Angeli. And those needs included the overwhelming demand to attend to their appearance—clothes, hair, beauty treatments, manicures; whatever was required was available.

He would book the lot, and let them loose on her.

The following day, at breakfast, he made his announcement. 'I will look after Ben today. You will be too busy.'

Lizzy stared. 'Busy?' she asked. Apprehension filled her.

Rico only smiled cryptically. 'Very busy,' he said.

Within the hour, she found out just how busy.

Lizzy had her eyes shut. Over her head, it sounded as if the army of people who had invaded her bedroom were having a heated argument. They weren't, she knew—they were just discussing her. But in a very Italianate manner they were doing so vehemently, with many loud exclamations. She could understand why. They had been given an impossible brief—to spin straw into gold.

Make a silk purse out of a sow's ear.

Mortification filled her.

She'd known this moment must come. Known that, however desperate the circumstances of her sudden marriage to Rico had been, they could not hide here at the villa for ever. At some point they would have to emerge. Face the world.

The prospect appalled her.

She could wear all the designer clothes in the world, but it would still be her underneath. Nothing could change that. Maria had looked a knock-out even in rags, because she'd had a face, a body, that was a knock-out.

Guilt knifed through her. Guilt and grief. Oh, God, it should be Maria here, in this beautiful Italian villa, having her honeymoon with her golden prince. Looking forward blissfully to their happy-ever-after. Their own personal fairytale.

Her hands twisted in her lap. Grief and guilt twisted together.

And not just guilt for her sister.

I've got to go through with this. I've got to bear it. It doesn't matter how humiliating it is, how mortifying. I have to let them do what they can. Do the best they can.

But it wasn't for her. It was for the man who had married her to keep Ben safe, the man whose reward was to be saddled with a wife in a marriage that all the world would call by the only word that suited it—*grotesque*.

A man like Prince Rico, the Playboy Prince, accustomed to the most beautiful women in the world falling for him—now married to a woman like her.

She opened her eyes. The arguing stopped instantly. She looked around at the sea of faces, all watching her expectantly.

She took a deep breath.

'Please,' she said, 'just do the best you can.'

Then she shut her eyes again—and kept them shut.

'We need another tower,' Ben instructed.

Rico considered the masterwork on the terrace table. Then nodded.

'You're right,' he said. 'I'll fit one inside this corner. How's the painting coming along?'

'Good,' said Ben. He was industriously washing stone-grey paint across the expanse of large cardboard box that had been transformed into a fort to house an army of brightly coloured plastic knights in armour which had, to Ben's ecstasy, been ordered off the internet to be delivered by courier the following morning. Ben's impatience for their arrival had been such that on their return to the terrace from the beach and the pool Rico had been driven to suggest they make a fort for the knights to live in when they arrived. Its construction also helped to divert Ben from the fact he had not seen his mother all day.

Anxiety nagged at Rico.

Was she going to be all right? It was late afternoon already, but he knew that beauty treatments took for ever, and the fact that she had been incarcerated all day did not surprise him. But how was she coping with it all?

Well, it couldn't be much longer, surely?

He reached for the scissors and began the tricky business of cutting cardboard for the requisite tower. He needed divert-ing as well.

'Is Mummy *still* trying on new clothes?' Ben demanded

'It takes ladies a long time,' said Rico. 'And to do their hair and things.'

'It doesn't take Mummy long,' Ben countered. 'She's always very quick.'

'Now that she's got to be a princess it will need to take longer,' Rico answered.

Ben stared down the long terrace towards where the bedrooms opened on to it. Then, suddenly, his expression changed.

'Mummy.'

He dropped the paintbrush and pushed his chair back.

Rico looked up.

And froze.

* * *

Ben was hurtling along the terrace towards her as Lizzy stepped gingerly out through the French windows from her bedroom.

'Mummy—Mummy, you've been ages! We're making a fort, Uncle Rico and me. For the soldiers—they are knights in armour. They're coming tomorrow, in a special van, and they are a present for being good. And we're making a fort for them. Come and see—come and see.'

He seized her hand and started to pull her along. She tottered momentarily, uncertain of her balance on the sandals that, although low-heeled, seemed to consist of nothing but two minute strips of leather.

'Come on, Mummy,' Ben said, impatient at her slowness.

But the last thing on earth she wanted was to go where he was leading her.

Towards the terrace table, towards the man who sat there, quite, quite motionless.

There was no expression on his face.

Her heart started to slump heavily in her chest cavity, hollowing out a space around it. She felt sick.

Sick with dismay.

Oh, God—all that work, all that time, and it's a disaster— I can see it in his face. It's awful, awful.

It had taken so *long*—hours and hours. And so much had been done to her. All over. There had been so much chattering, and agitation, and volatility, that she had just let them get on with it. The treatments had gone on and on, one after another. Spreading stuff on her body, then wiping it off again, and on her face several more times. Then she'd had her hair washed, and more stuff had been put on it, and left in, then rinsed out, and different stuff put on. And in the meantime the tweezers had come out, and nail files and buffers and varnish and hot wax, and yet more body wraps and creams. She had had to eat lunch, served in her room, with her face and hair covered in gunk and her body swathed in some kind of thin gown. And while she'd eaten yet another one of the army of people in her room had held up one garment after another, off a trio of racks that had been wheeled in—so many garments that she'd simply lost count.

'Please,' she had murmured faintly, 'whatever you think best.'

And finally the last of the wraps had come off, and the rollers had come out of her hair, and it had been blow-dried—though heaven knew what rollers and blow-drying would do for her hopelessly frizzy hair. Then yet another beautician had gone to work on her, with a vast amount of make-up, before, at the very last, she had been lifted to her feet and one outfit after another had been whisked on to her, commented on by all in the room, then replaced with another one and the process repeated.

Until one had been left on her, her hair and make-up had been retouched one last time, and she had been gently but insistently guided towards the French windows.

She had no idea what she looked like. She could see she had nail varnish on—a soft coral-apricot colour—and her hands felt smooth and soft. Her hair felt different—lighter somehow. As if it were lifting as she walked instead of hanging in a heavy clump as it normally did. As for her clothes—she could see she was wearing a cinnamon-coloured dress, with a close-fitting bodice and cap sleeves, a narrow belt around the waist and a skirt that floated like silk around her legs.

But she hadn't seen a reflection of herself. No one had asked her whether she wanted to see in a mirror, and she had been too cowardly to want to anyway. Deferring the evil moment.

But now it had arrived, and she wanted to die.

Oh, God—what had been the point of it all?

She must look ridiculous, absurd—dressed up like this, done up to the nines. All such fine feathers could do was show just how awful she was underneath.

Hot, hopeless embarrassment flooded through her. Why had

she let them do this to her? She should have just stayed as she was—accepted what she was.

The ugly sister. Who, even when she was dressed up for the ball in gorgeous clothes, was still the ugly sister.

At her side, Ben was chattering away as she walked slowly, mortifyingly forward—towards the figure seated, motionless, under the parasol at the terrace table.

Her eyes went to him, full of dread, and as she looked at him she felt her stomach give its familiar hopeless clench.

He was wearing shorts, and a white T-shirt that strained across his torso, and he was watching her approach with absolutely no expression on his face whatsoever.

She tore her gaze away from him as she felt the hot, horrible heat of exposure rise in her. She wanted to turn and run, to bolt back to the safety of her bedroom, hide there for ever and never come out again...

She reached the table.

Say something. Anything.

She swallowed hard.

'Oh, Ben—that's a wonderful fort.' Her voice sounded high-pitched and false. And coming from a hundred miles away.

'Me and Tio Rico made it. It's got two towers, and a bridge that lifts right up, and look, Mummy, it's got a porcully that goes up and down. Tio Rico made it work. Look, I'll show you, Mummy—'

She forced herself to look as Ben tugged on the string that operated the portcullis.

'That's really good,' she said in a strangulated voice.

I've got to look at him. I must.

It was the hardest thing in the world to do, but she did it. She turned her head so that she was looking straight at him. Looking straight at that totally expressionless face.

'It's a brilliant fort,' she said to him weakly.

He answered in Italian.

'Non credo—'

She swallowed, her stomach hollowing. What didn't he believe? That so much time and effort expended on her should be so wasted?

The sickness in her stomach churned hideously.

Ben was still talking, and she tried to listen, but it was impossible. Something about where all his new knights would go—which ones would be inside the castle, and which would be attacking it. His little voice went in and out.

And opposite her, still motionless, Prince Rico of San Lucenzo just looked at her, without a shred of expression on his face.

He was in shock, he realised. Shock so profound that he was still fighting to get his brain around what his eyes were telling him.

It wasn't possible, what he was seeing. It just wasn't.

It could not be the same woman. It just couldn't.

It was impossible. Physically impossible.

She absolutely, totally, completely was *not* the woman he had last seen.

Dio—where had she *come* from? That body. That fantastic, gorgeous, *lush* body. An absolutely perfect *bella figura*. With a cinched-in waist that curved out to a pair of perfectly rounded hips, and up…he swallowed…up to a pair of breasts so ripe, so luscious, so beautifully moulded by the material swelling over them that he just wanted to…he just wanted to…

He felt his body react. He couldn't stop it. It was there—urgent, irrepressible, unstoppable. A complete, total insistence on letting him know just *exactly* what it felt about what his eyes were seeing.

With an effort he did not know he was capable of, he forced his eyes upward. But it did him no good.

The reaction was exactly the same.

The rest of her went with the figure.

It was the hair—what the *hell* had happened to her hair? The frizz had simply gone. As if it had never existed. In its place, tinted to a rich chestnut, was a smooth, glossy mane that waved back from her face, pouring down over her shoulders in a luxuriant swathe.

As for her face—

How had he not seen it? Shock punched through him again. Delicately arched eyebrows over endlessly deep, long-lashed, luminous eyes, cheekbones that arced to a perfect nose, that descended to a mouth…

He swallowed silently.

A mouth that was rich, and lush, and… *Dio*, so inviting…

Someone was talking. Tugging at his arm.

'Tio Rico. You're not listening. Is it time for tea now? Mummy's come out at last and I'm *hungry*,' he finished plaintively.

Where he found the strength of mind he didn't know. But somehow he dragged his eyes to Ben.

'Yeah—sure, right. You want to eat? OK. That's fine.' He said some more in Italian, just as incoherent.

What the hell was going on? Had the universe just stopped and restarted in a different dimension? A dimension where impossible things were totally normal?

She was saying something. Her voice was more high-pitched than usual, and she was trying to sound relaxed and casual, and failing completely.

'Has Ben been OK today? I'm sorry I…er…I took so long. I…er…'

Her voice trailed off.

He was staring at her again. He couldn't take his eyes from her. It was impossible.

For a moment Lizzy just went on standing there, while the expressionless face in front of her just looked blankly at her.

Then suddenly, totally, she couldn't cope. Just couldn't. She felt as if a stone had been punched into her solar plexus. It was almost a physical pain. She turned on her spindly heels and plunged off. She didn't know where. Just anywhere. Anywhere.

She didn't know where she was going. The terrace ended in

steps, down to the swimming pool level, and she just clattered down them, almost tripping in her desperation, past the glittering azure pool, to plunge on to the narrow stepped path that wound its way down to the sea between the vegetation and the pines. Her heart was pounding, and she could feel a sick, horrible flush in her cheeks.

She wanted to die.

Why had she let them do it? She should have known it was hopeless, useless, pointless. Hot, horrible mortification scorched through her.

I shouldn't have tried—I shouldn't have tried to make myself look better. Normal. Trying and failing is even worse than just accepting what I am—ugly, ugly, ugly…

She could hear footsteps hurrying behind her, heavy and pounding, and her name being called. She hurried faster, her heel catching in her haste, so that she had to lurch and clutch at the railing beside the pathway before trying to go on.

But her arm was being caught, held.

'Stop. What is it? What's wrong?'

She tensed in every muscle, trying to tear her arm away. His fingers pressed like steel into her bare flesh.

'Go away.'

The words burst from her. She couldn't stop them. Her head whipped round.

'Go away. Leave me alone. *Leave me alone!*'

There was shock and bewilderment in his face.

'What's happened? What's wrong?'

'What do you mean, what's wrong? Everything's wrong. *Everything*,' she gasped.

She just stood there, frozen and immobile, tugging hopelessly away from him, while he held her, feet planted on the step above, towering over her.

He was so close. Far too close. She tried to tug back again, but it was hopeless, useless. Just as everything was hopeless, useless.

For a moment he said nothing—just looked at her. A look

of complete incomprehension filled his face. Then, as he looked, the expression of shock and bewilderment began to change. She saw it happening, saw it and did not believe it.

It was something in his eyes. Something that seemed slowly to be dissolving. Dissolving not just in his eyes, but dissolving *her*. Turning her liquid, like wax left on a surface that was very slowly heating up.

The way her skin was heating. Flushing with a low, soft heat that seemed to be carried by the low, soft pulse of her blood that was creaming, like liquid sugar, like honey, through her veins.

She felt his grip on her change. Not so much halting her as…holding her. Holding her in position. Holding her just where he wanted her to be. Wanted her to be because…because…

The world had stopped moving. Everything had stopped moving. She was just there, immobile, held. And he was looking down into her face—and the expression in his eyes simply stayed the breath in her throat.

She gazed back up at him. What had happened, she didn't know. Reality wasn't there any more.

And yet it had never seemed more vivid.

'Don't look at me like that,' he said, in that low, soft voice that was curling the toes of her feet, sending liquid waves down her spine in long, honeyed undulations. 'Don't look at me like that here, now. Because if you go on looking at me like that, I'll—'

'Mum-my! *Mum-my*.'

They pulled apart, jerking away from each other. It was like surfacing from a deep, drowning sea.

'He's all right. I told him not to move.' Rico's voice sounded staccato, abstracted. He took a rapid, restoring breath.

'Mummy. Tio Rico.'

Ben's insistent call came again. Lizzy could hear alarm in it.

'I'm coming, Ben,' she called up. Her voice was shaky.

'Me too,' echoed Rico. His voice was not steady either.

He cast another look at her, then pulled his gaze away. It wasn't safe to look at her. Not here, not now.

Later…later he would look.

More than look—

Suddenly, out of nowhere, a sense of exultation crashed through him.

With light, lithe steps, he led the way up to the terrace.

Emotion was surging through Rico. Strong, overwhelming and consuming. The universe might have turned itself upside down, but right now he didn't care. How it had happened was irrelevant. Completely irrelevant. It had happened, and that was all that he was registering.

Adrenaline pumped through him. More than adrenaline. Exhilaration. Something quite incredibly amazing had happened, and he didn't want explanations—he just wanted to…to go with it.

'Here we are, Ben,' he announced as he gained the pool terrace, and he waved his hand at the little figure perched obediently on the upper level, straining his eyes downwards.

'Where is Mummy?' Ben demanded.

'Here—' said Lizzy, hurrying up the steps as fast as she could in her flimsy sandals. Her heart was racing.

It had nothing to do with her rapid ascent.

As she gained the terrace Ben stared at her, paying attention to her for the first time, instead of to his new fort.

'Is that your new dress?' he asked.

She swallowed, nodded.

He tilted his head sideways, inspecting her. Then he frowned.

'You look all pretty. Like in a magazine. But you don't look like Mummy.' He frowned, confused and bewildered.

Rico put an arm around his nephew's shoulder. He knew just how Ben was feeling.

'She's the new-look Mummy. And you're right Ben.' His voice changed. 'She does look pretty. In fact she looks…' He paused, and held her eyes. 'Breathtaking,' he finished softly. 'Quite, quite breathtaking.'

For a long, endless moment, he held her eyes.

He saw her eyes flare—uncertain briefly—and then, suddenly, it had gone again.

'It's true,' he said quietly to her. 'Quite true. I can't believe…I can't believe that all this was there, all along. Just…hidden.' He paused, and then, in a low, clear voice, said, 'And you are never—do you understand me?—*never* going to hide it again.'

For one last, lingering moment he looked at her. Sending his message loud and clear.

Then, abruptly, he turned his head.

'Right, then, Ben. Time for tea.'

CHAPTER NINE

SHE was moving in a place that was completely dissociated from what she was doing. What she was actually doing was pouring out a cup of perfectly brewed Assam tea from a silver teapot, while Ben was industriously, if inexpertly, coiling spaghetti around his fork. The DIY fort had been cleared away for the moment, and the westering sun was bathing the terrace in rich, deep golden glow.

The same glow was inside her, suffused through her, so that it seemed she was part of the warm golden light all around her. It dazed her, bemused her—and she gave herself to it because she couldn't do anything else.

As she sipped at her hot, fragrant tea her eyes slipped of their own accord to the man sitting opposite her. He lounged back, his pose so relaxed that he was like a young, lithe leopard taking its ease, taking indolent mouthfuls of espresso coffee every now and then, one arm spread out across his chair-back, one long leg casually crossed over a lean, bare thigh. He was chatting to Ben, answering the child's questions with lazy good humour, but his eyes would flicker over her as he chatted, sending tiny little shots of electricity quivering through her.

Her glow deepened.

What was happening was beyond her—completely and absolutely beyond her—and she didn't care. She didn't want to question, or analyse, or examine or understand. She just wanted to give herself to this wonderful, dazed bemusement that had taken her over, filling her with this rich, warm glow that reached through every cell of her body.

After Ben had eaten his tea, they played cards. A noisy, fast game that involved a lot of slapping down of cards and crows of triumph from both Ben and Rico. Yet even in the midst of the game Rico could still find time to glance at her, still feel the echoes of that incredible shock wave that had slammed through him as she'd approached him along the terrace, her transformation so incredible he could not, even now, fully believe it.

And yet it was there in front of him, the evidence of his own eyes. A miracle.

Her hair by itself was a miracle. The frizz had simply vanished—he hadn't known it was possible, and yet clearly it was. Her skin was clear and glowing, her make-up bringing to life features which he'd thought nondescript and unremarkable.

And now his eyes kept going back to her, time and time again.

He wanted her. He knew it, and he had no intention of denying it.

It was impossible to do so. His body had recognised it in the first moments of seeing her walk towards him, displaying that fantastic lush figure which had so incredibly been there all along—invisible under the shapeless, baggy clothes she'd worn.

How the hell had she kept it hidden?

He still couldn't get his head round it. To have such a full, lush body as that, and yet to hide it.

Well, there was no hiding it now. None at all. Never, ever again would she ever hide herself.

Especially not from him.

He felt his body react again, and had to struggle to subdue it.

He must not rush this. Dared not. She was walking a knife-edge, still in a state of shock, of disbelief about herself.

I've got to take this slowly. Very slowly.

Let her get used to it. Let her come to believe it. Take her slowly, so slowly, every step of the way.

His eyes rested on her yet again, while Ben dealt out another round, his little voice counting the cards diligently as he set them down in three piles.

He could see her awareness of him even as she oversaw Ben's dealing. Saw it in the swift, covert glance, the slight tremor of her hand as she picked up her cards.

Lizzy could see him looking at her, see it and feel it. It was tangible, like the lightest caress on her skin.

She felt her heart skip a beat, skitter inside her...

What's happening—what's happening to me?

It was a stupid, idiotic question to ask. She knew exactly what was happening to her. And she couldn't stop it. Could no more stop it than she could have stopped a whirlpool sucking her down.

She was responding to the core-deep, devastating sexuality of the man she had married to keep Ben safe with her. And how could she help it?

Ever since she had first set eyes on him, that terrible traumatic night in Cornwall, she had responded to him. She had crushed it down, embarrassed by it, knowing that she must never show the slightest sign of her response because for someone like her to do so would be...*grotesque*.

It had been easy enough to do. To him, she had simply not existed as a female. Nor did she to any man, she knew. So, although her instinctive reaction to him had been embarrassing and pointless, she had also known that it really hadn't mattered at all—it had been completely irrelevant.

All that had mattered had been Ben.

And these last few days, when he had visibly gone out of his way to try and make her feel more at ease with what had so traumatically happened to her, when he'd been kind, and nice, and nothing like the Playboy Prince of his reputation, it had still not mattered. More than not mattered.

It had allowed her to start to relax around him. Start to feel at ease around him. Start to see him not as a prince, nor as a man—but as a person.

They had talked—nothing special, nothing earth-shattering, just easy conversation. About Ben, yes, but about other things too, over meals, and on the beach, and while Ben was playing, absorbed, with his trains and all the other toys that had been delivered to the villa or which he'd discovered in the playroom.

She wasn't sure what they'd talked about—nothing much came to mind—but she knew was that it hadn't been a strain, an effort.

It had been…friendly.

Easygoing, casual, relaxed.

But now—now it felt as if tiny bubbles were fizzing through her veins. Effervescing inside her.

Every time he glanced at her.

What's happening to me?

But she knew. She knew.

'Goodnight, darling, sleep tight.'

Lizzy bent over to drop a kiss on Ben's cheek. He was asleep already, she could see. On the other side of the bed, Rico reached out and ruffled his hair gently.

He had insisted on giving Ben his bath that night.

'We don't want Mummy's new dress getting wet, do we?' he'd said.

Instead, he had been the one to get wet. Lizzy could see where the damp T-shirt clung to his torso. She averted her eyes, but not before Rico had spotted her doing so.

There was a decided glint in his eye as he spoke.

'I'll go and get myself cleaned up, then join you for dinner, OK?'

He had given instructions to the chef for a proper dinner that night. Whatever the results of Lizzy's makeover would prove, he intended to make the evening special for her.

And it would be special indeed. Another wave of disbelief went over him. They had been doing so regularly, every time he looked at her.

It was incredible, just incredible.

He frowned momentarily.

Had she actually looked at herself yet? Surely she must have? And yet that initial reaction, when she'd run from him, blurting that it had all been a disaster, argued that she surely could not have seen the transformation.

He came around the foot of the bed.

'You may need some kind of wrap,' he told her. 'The nights can still be a little chilly. Let's see what you've got.'

He opened the closet door and went in. All her new clothes hung in serried ranks, swathed in plastic protectors. He glanced at them with approval. There was a lot here, and that was good. He wanted her to have as many beautiful outfits as possible. This was just the start.

She had followed him in, just as he'd intended.

'Where would you store a wrap?' he asked.

But Lizzy didn't answer him. Could not.

The whole rear wall of the closet was a mirror, and standing in the mirror, looking back at her, was someone she had never seen before in her life.

Rico straightened and looked first at the woman in the mirror, then at the woman staring at her.

He let her look. Let the look of dazed incomprehension fill her face.

Then he spoke.

'It's you. The you that you really are. The you that was hiding all this time.'

His voice was steady, level—merely stating a fact. A fact he would no longer let her deny. Conceal.

Her eyes were wide, huge.

'It can't be me. It can't.'

Her voice was faint.

He came and stood behind her.

'Oh, it's you, all right.'

Lightly, oh so lightly, he rested his hands on her shoulders.

Her skin was like satin. He felt her tremble at his touch, but she did not move. She went on staring.

'How did they do it?' she asked faintly.

He gave a smile. 'They had good material to work with.'

She lifted her hand to her hair, then dropped it wonderingly. 'But my hair—all that frizz—'

'They fixed it. There must be chemicals they use that change the hair somehow. After that, all they had to do was...do you up.' His voice softened. 'It was always there, Lizzy. Always. And now it always will be.'

He dropped his hands away.

He didn't want to. He wanted to glide them down her arms, turn her around, lower his mouth to hers and...

But he knew he must not. Not now, not here.

Not yet.

Instead, he stepped back.

'Do you think they'd have put wraps in a drawer?' he asked. 'Let's have a look.'

Rico reached out his arm and closed his hand around the neck of the champagne bottle, drawing it up out of its bucket of ice and refilling their glasses.

They were sitting at the table on the terrace, but it had been transformed from its daytime appearance, when it was usually covered with Ben's toys and books. The parasol had disappeared, and a pristine white tablecloth had been draped crisply, laden down with silver and crystal. A beautiful floral arrangement graced the centre, and the flames of long candles in silver candlesticks flickered in the night air. Above, the stars glittered in the black velvet sky. Out to sea, the lights from fisher boats glimmered in the dark. All around, cicadas kept their soft chorus, and the scent of flowers wafted softly.

The meal had done justice to the setting. Exquisitely prepared and presented, each delicacy had been too tempting to resist. And Lizzy had not resisted—nor did she resist a second glass of the light, foaming liquid that glinted in the candlelight in its tall, elegant flute.

'To you,' said Rico, and raised his glass. 'To the new you. The real you.'

The staff had gone, leaving them to coffee, tiny crisp *biscotti*, and the rest of the champagne. It was a rare vintage, and Rico savoured it.

It was not all that he was savouring.

He took a mouthful, appreciating the dry biscuit of the champagne, and leant back. His eyes rested on the woman opposite.

She had found a wrap, a soft swathe in a subtle mix of hues that blended and complemented the cinnamon of her dress. She had draped it around her shoulders, one end scooped across her throat. It did not quite conceal the rich swell of her breasts in the beautifully cut bodice.

No, he must not let his eyes drift there. He wanted to—he badly wanted to—but he knew he must not. She could not cope with that. Not yet. He must take it slowly.

Savour it.

He took another mouthful of champagne, savouring that too.

'To you,' he said again. 'To the new, beautiful Elisabetta.'

His voice was liquid over the syllables. Then, abruptly, his brows drew together.

'How did anyone think to call you Lizzy?' He said the short form of her name disparagingly.

Lizzy's eyes flickered uncertainly. 'I've always been Lizzy,' she said.

'And yet you were also always Elizabeth—Elisabetta.' There was a sudden edge in Rico's voice, which softened as he repeated the Italian form of her name. Then his brows drew together again questioningly, frowningly. 'Was it your sister who did it to you?'

The edge was back in his voice.

'Did what?' Again her eyes flickered uncertainly.

'Was it your sister who turned you into Lizzy?'

'I don't understand,' she answered, puzzled and uncertain

'I've always been called Lizzy. Frizzy-Lizzy, because of my hair. Or Busy-Lizzy, usually.'

'Did she keep you busy, waiting on her hand and foot?' His voice was dry.

'Maria?' Lizzy's brow furrowed, confused 'Maria was the best sister anyone could ever have.' She felt her throat tighten dangerously. 'She was truly a golden girl. Everyone loved her. She was so beautiful. She was tall, and slender, and she had long, long legs, and her hair was like honey, and hung straight to her waist, and she had beautiful blue eyes, and even when she was at school the boys were all over her, and when she became a model she was even more beautiful, and no wonder a prince fell for her—' She halted abruptly.

Rico picked his words carefully.

'Maria was pretty—very pretty. But she was…' He paused. Bimbo, Luca had called her. Cruel and callous. And yet Ben's natural mother had, indeed, possessed the kind of eye-candy looks that gave rise to that harsh dismissal.

'Hers is not the only kind of beauty,' he said.

But if Maria's sister had grown up being told that only candyfloss blondeness was acceptable, that the kind of ultra-slim figure that suited models was the only ticket in town, then no wonder she'd never tried to make anything of the looks she had. No wonder she'd settled for being Busy-Lizzy, living in the shadow of her sister.

'So who called you Busy-Lizzy?' The edge was back again.

'That was Maria,' she said with a half-laugh, making herself do so. 'But she didn't mean it in a bad way. She used to say it to me in exasperation. Because I never—'

She halted, reaching for her glass of champagne and taking a deliberate sip to cover her silence.

'Never what?' probed Rico.

What had happened to her? What had made her see herself as ugly? He had thought it might be her sister, and yet she denied it. So what, then?

He wanted to know. Wanted to find out what had been done to her, and by whom.

'Because you never what?' he prompted again.

He wanted answers. Wanted to understand. So that the poison in her would come out once and for all. Never to return.

'I never stopped,' she answered.

'Stopped what?'

'Being busy, I suppose. Being useful.'

'Who to?' he asked in a low voice.

He saw her fingers tighten around the stem of her flute.

'Maria. My parents.'

'Why did they need you to be useful?'

Her eyes wouldn't meet his.

'Because—' she stopped.

'Because?' he prompted. Quietly, insistently.

Her fingers pressed on the glass. He could see her fingers whiten where they gripped.

'Because it was all I was good for. I wasn't beautiful, like Maria, and she had all the brains, not me. She was all they needed—my parents.'

Her eyes had slid past him completely now. Staring ahead of her. Something was going wrong in her face; he could see it. She jerked the champagne glass to her lips and took a gulp. Then set it down, just as jerkily.

Then deliberately, almost angrily, her eyes snapped back to his.

'When Maria was born I ceased to have a function. Apart from that of handmaid. That was all I was good for. Looking after Maria. Helping Maria. Making way for Maria. Maria, Maria, Maria! Everything revolved around Maria. Me, I was just the spare wheel—surplus to requirements. Not wanted on voyage. Existing on sufferance—justified only if I looked after Maria, and even then barely. I wanted to hate her. But I couldn't. I couldn't hate her. No one could hate her. Because there was nothing to hate. There really wasn't. She really was a golden girl. Everyone loved her. No wonder my parents adored her.

They adored her so much they forgave her everything. Even becoming a model. There was only one thing they didn't forgive her for. Only one thing.' She stilled, then spoke again.

'Dying. That's what they could not forgive her for.'

She bowed her head, as if bowing beneath a weight.

'They couldn't live without her. So they didn't. They went into the garage, locked the doors, got into the car, and turned the engine on.'

For a moment there was silence. Complete silence. Rico felt cold ice through him.

'Your parents killed themselves?' His voice was hollow. This had not been in the dossier on Maria Mitchell.

'Once they knew she would never recover. That she would be a vegetable—in a coma until....'

She halted. Her face was stark, even in the candlelight.

'She was everything to them—their whole world. They had dedicated their lives to her. And she had gone. Left them. Left them to go modeling.' She swallowed again. 'Left them to go off with some man who had, so they thought, simply "got her into trouble"—and then she left them utterly. Left them all alone.'

Slowly, still with that cold draining through him, Rico spoke.

'But they had her baby—and you.'

She looked at him. Her eyes had no expression in them.

'The baby was a bastard—fatherless, an embarrassment, a disgrace. As for me, I was…an irrelevance. I didn't count,' she said. 'I was—unnecessary—to them.'

His eyes darkened. He felt the anger rising in him like a cold tide.

Unnecessary. The word had a grim, familiar sound.

He was unnecessary too. Had been all his life. He was the spare—surplus to requirements. To be put on a shelf and left there, just in case of emergencies. But with no other purpose then simply to pass the time, fritter his life away until and in case he should ever be needed, cease to be unnecessary.

He felt the anger lash through him again. But this time it was at himself. For having accepted his parents' verdict on him. Oh, he had resented the role he'd been born to, but he'd still accepted that that was all he was. The spare to Luca's heir.

Well, that wasn't true any longer.

Emotion swept through him. He looked at the woman sitting opposite him, who had been so horrifically *unnecessary* to her parents—but who was so necessary to the one human being to whom *he*, too, had proved necessary.

He reached across the table and took her hand. He spoke with a low intensity.

'But you're necessary now—necessary and…essential. You are Ben's happiness, and I…I am his safety. And together—' his hand tightened around hers, warm, and safe and protecting '—we'll take care of him, and love him.'

Gently he drew her to her feet. Emotion filled him as he led her down the terrace to where the French windows to her room stood slightly ajar. Inside, they stood by the bed, looking down at Ben's sleeping form.

Rico's arm went around her shoulder as they stood, gazing down at the one human being on the earth to whom they were absolutely and totally necessary.

United in that.

And more, Rico knew.

'Hang on to your hats,' Rico yelled

'I'm not wearing one,' Ben yelled back, against the revving of the engine.

'Just as well,' riposted Rico, and let the throttle out.

The boat roared off, sleek and powerful, carving a foaming wake through the still blue water.

Lizzy's arm tightened around Ben automatically, but Ben was oblivious of anything except the thrill of being in a speedboat. Wind whipped at her hair, half blinding her, and she had to grip with all her might to the boat rail. The hull slapped and slammed against the water, bumping like a rollercoaster ride.

'Wheee!' yelled Ben, ecstatically.

Rico turned from the wheel and grinned.

His hair was blown off his face and he looked younger, carefree.

'Faster?' he asked.

'Yes, yes,' Ben cried.

'Here we go, then.'

He accelerated, and the boat picked up yet more speed. Exhilaration filled him. This might not be anything like the speed of a powerboat in a race, but it was still fast and furious.

When finally he slewed around in a great curve, and started heading back to land, he slackened the throttle and turned to his passengers.

'Was that fun?' he asked with a grin, his eyes dancing.

'Yes!' yelled Ben.

'You're a complete maniac,' said Lizzy.

His grin widened. 'No, just Italian.' He eased back on the throttle even more as they headed for land at a sedate pace. He patted the wheel. 'She's not bad, but she's no powerboat. They can get to speeds of over a hundred knots. Now, that's really moving. Still, we'll have some fun in this one, won't we?'

Annoyance flared in him. The boat he'd hired from the marina was ideal for cruising around, exploring the coastline. But that wasn't something they could do yet. He would be recognised, it was inevitable, and then the press would start buzzing with rumours and speculation about who he was with, and why. He didn't want that. He wanted his marriage officially announced from the palace. Not out of consideration for his father, who deserved none after his callous treatment of Ben and his mother, but for Lizzy's sake.

She'd had enough stress already. All her life, in fact. Thanks to her parents—and everything that had happened since to her.

But so far there had been nothing but silence from the palace. Well, he'd given his father time enough to climb down, to accept what he'd done—perhaps he should send him a reminder.

He'd get on to it today. Jean-Paul would oblige, he knew.

Smoothly, he brought the boat into shore, cut and trimmed the engine, and dropped anchor in the shallow water. Ben jumped out without prompting, landing with a splash to wade ashore. Lithely, Rico climbed over the side himself, then held out his arms to Lizzy. She got rather unsteadily to her feet.

'I'm sure I can manage,' she said.

He scooped her up, and she gave a gasp. He grinned down at her. She was soft in his arms. Soft and voluptuous. And in the couture beach shorts and short-sleeved matching azure top she looked fantastic. Her hair was windblown, but that only gave her a tousled, wanton look.

'I'm too heavy for you,' she gasped.

He laughed scornfully, wading ashore with her. To think he had thought that her baggy, shapeless clothes had meant she was overweight. There wasn't a kilo of flesh on her that wasn't in the right place.

'I can bench twice your weight,' he said confidently. He lowered her gently to the sand, steadying her with his hands. She looked amazing. Her bare arms were smooth and already beginning to tan, now that they were finally being exposed to the sun.

She was beginning to get used to the transformation, he could see. The look of bewildered disbelief was rarer now; she was accepting what had happened. She was out of the box her parents had locked her into—a coffin for her womanhood.

Well, that was a box she would never go back into. And soon her womanhood would blaze into the glory it deserved.

His expression changed. Patience, he was discovering, was a hard virtue.

'Tio Rico, I need a new sandcastle. Come and help—' Ben's piping treble pierced the air.

Rico was glad of the diversion.

He phoned Jean-Paul after lunch. 'How would you feel about an exclusive photo-shoot?' he asked him. 'Ready for the glossies…'

He would send the photos to the palace first. Remind his father that time was running out for him, that if he kept on stonewalling Rico would simply make the announcement of his marriage himself—and let the press go to town on why the palace had let that happen.

'Don't wait too long, Rico. Security at Capo d'Angeli might be tight, but even so—' His friend's voice held a warning. 'This is a story to kill for.'

'I hear you—so can you do the shoot tomorrow?'

'I'll be there. Would I miss the second scoop of a lifetime on you?' Jean-Paul laughed, and signed off.

Slowly, Rico slid his phone away. His eyes travelled down the terrace to the French windows, behind which Lizzy was attempting to make Ben yield to an afternoon siesta. His thoughts went to them.

Jean-Paul was coming tomorrow. To take photos of the happy couple—the happy family. A fairytale marriage that would set a glow over them all. A perfect ending to the tale—the Playboy Prince marrying the adoptive mother of his brother's child.

Who had turned out to be Cinderella indeed—not the ugly sister she had always cast herself as. A Cinderella whose transformation had taken him by storm…inflamed his senses.

Whom he longed to embrace…possess…

A troubled look entered his eyes.

Did he have the right to do it? He wanted her, badly. He wanted her because she was a beautiful, alluring woman and he was bowled over by her—because his body was telling him, every time he saw her, that she was a woman to desire. And he wanted her, too, he knew, for *her* sake—because she had made him feel free and because he had seen her turn into a swan. Yes, she had emerged from the box she'd been locked into, and he wanted to lead her out of it—lead her to where every woman should go.

But did he have the right to take her there?

She's my wife. What other woman in the world should I desire?

His expression shadowed. Became sombre.

Yes, she was his wife—but their marriage was not about them, it was about Ben. Everything about their marriage, including those fairytale photos tomorrow, would be about Ben. His safety—his future. Not theirs.

Why not about our future? Why not about us?

The words formed in his head, coming from the same place deep within him that told him that the woman he wanted so much now was his wife—a wife to desire…to possess…

He sat very still as he realised what he was thinking.

Feeling.

Wanting.

He had married her, promising her a marriage of convenience purely to protect Ben, to protect her. When that had been achieved, when it would not cause any scandal, then he would end the marriage. Set her free. Set himself free.

I don't want that—

The realisation seared through him. Burning its way through his brain.

And in its wake came another emotion. He did not know what it was. He knew only that he was yielding to it, that it was far, far too strong for him to do anything else but yield to it.

And tonight—tonight he would do just that.

Tonight he would make his marriage real.

Those photos tomorrow would be no fairytale.

CHAPTER TEN

QUIETLY, Lizzy slipped from her room out on to the terrace, carefully lifting the long rustling skirts of her gown.

Ben was asleep. Reluctantly, but finally succumbing. It was later than his usual bedtime, but then he'd been judging a fashion parade. He and Rico had sat on the bed while she'd tried on one after another of her outfits, to choose which ones to wear the following day.

Nerves clipped at her as she thought about it. A photo-shoot, Rico had said. His friend Jean-Paul, to whom he had entrusted the story of their marriage, would undertake it.

She was glad Rico had suggested trying the outfits first, even though it seemed odd to have finished with her in evening dress.

'I want a full-length portrait photo of you,' Rico had said.

Then, when he'd finally chosen which gown he thought would be best for such a photo, he'd told her to leave it on.

'It will get you used to the feel and fit,' he'd told her, before heading off to get changed himself, for dinner.

She'd complied, though the close-fitting strapless dusky-rose silk gown with its flowing skirts, gorgeous though it was, seemed to make her somewhat over-dressed for a seaside villa.

'Ah, there you are—'

Rico's voice made her head turn.

And then her breath caught, and stilled in her lungs.

He was strolling towards her in the soft light spilling out on to the terrace, and he was wearing evening dress himself.

He looked—

She swallowed.

Oh, dear God, he looks incredible.

The tailored hand-made tuxedo moulded his long, lithe form, and made her legs feel weak. His freshly washed hair feathered over his forehead, and as he approached she caught the faintest tang of aftershave from his newly-shaved jawline.

She gazed at him helplessly, incapable of tearing her eyes away from him.

He came up to her. His eyes were on her, but all she could see was him.

A half-smile played about his lips.

'Buona sera, Principessa,' he said softly, and lifted her hand with his, to raise it to his lips.

His mouth grazed at her knuckles, and she felt a thousand butterflies release inside her.

He tucked her hand over his arm, and she found herself clinging to it. Numbly, she let herself be glided along the terrace.

'We're dining indoors tonight. Some light rain is forecast.'

She glanced absently at the sky, which was clouding over from the west. Then he was leading her into the large, formal dining room where they'd never eaten before.

She could see, as she looked round, why he had decided for them to wear evening dress. Her eyes widened. She'd never been in here, and she was astonished at its opulence. The huge glass table was edged with a gold metallic border, and an ornate chandelier festooned with crystals shone above. There seemed to be mirrors everywhere, and more glass and gold all around.

'It's a little overdone,' said Rico wryly.

He led her to her place and saw her seated. Then he took his own place opposite her. Almost immediately came the soft pop of a champagne cork, and then one of the staff was filling her flute before performing a similar office for Rico.

He lifted the glass.

'To us,' he said softly, his long lashes sweeping down over his dark eyes, and yet again Lizzy felt the fluttering wings inside her taking flight.

The meal passed as if in a dream. The silent, swift staff placed dishes in front of her, then whisked them away unnoticed. One by one the array of glasses at her place were filled, and then removed. She must have eaten and drunk, she knew, and it must have been delicious. And yet food and drink were the last things on her mind.

Her eyes were held, entirely and only, by the man sitting opposite her.

She felt weak. Incapable of doing anything except drink him in. She must have talked, she must have said things, but her mind was a daze. Inside her veins, the wine creamed in her blood, infusing her with a strange wonder.

I just want to look at him.

Gaze and gaze.

She had never allowed herself to do so before. Had always dragged her eyes away from him. Never indulged herself. But tonight—tonight was different. She didn't know why, didn't question. Merely let herself do what she had wanted to do since the very first time she had ever set eyes on him, and felt the shock of her reaction go through her.

Then, it had been forbidden to her. Then, she had been someone who would never have been allowed to do what she was doing now.

But she wasn't that person any more. She had been transformed, enchanted, into someone quite, quite different.

Someone who could gaze at him to her heart's desire.

Because he was doing the same to her.

The butterflies swooped and soared. His eyes were holding hers, and she was breathless, completely breathless.

He was getting to his feet, standing up. Holding out his hand to her.

'Come.'

It was all he said.

All he had to say.

She stood up. She could feel the silk rustling around her. She gathered the skirts into her fingers, making her way around the table to him. The strapless bodice clung to her, her hair brushed over her bare shoulders, her naked back.

He led her out into the hallway to the interior of the house. Opened another door and ushered her inside.

It was a bedroom.

And it was not hers.

He caught her shoulders, and turned her to him.

For one long, endless moment Rico gazed down at her, into those wide eyes, gazing up at him as they had gazed all evening.

How he had waited this long he did not know.

She hadn't realised, he knew, that her looking at him like that had been a torment to him. That it had taken all his self-control not to push back his chair, stride around the table to her, lift her up and crush her to him.

But he had not done so. Not just because the staff had still been about their business, not just because the chef had produced a *tour de force* that evening and to abandon it halfway through would have been unthinkably inconsiderate. Not just because he had known that with the night to come both of them would require sustenance.

But because he had known that she needed time.

Time to give herself to what was happening to them.

Did she know how much he desired her? He suspected not. The ways of men were an unknown country to her.

A realisation came to him, plunging through him.

Will I be her first?

Emotion scythed through him, flaring in his eyes. .

'Elisabetta.' He spoke softly, so softly, letting his voice pour through the liquid syllables.

His hands curved around her bare shoulders. Her skin was warm to his touch. He rested his thumbs along the delicate bones that arched to her throat and let them smooth her minutely. He felt her tremble beneath his touch.

She was still gazing up at him, her eyes huge, and in them was a longing that was unconscious in its intensity. It jolted through him, tipping him over the edge.

He could resist her no longer.

Slowly, infinitely slowly, he lowered his mouth to hers.

She gave a soft, helpless sigh, her eyes fluttering shut.

He kissed her slowly, very slowly. It was a soft kiss, a caress of her lips with his, and he could feel them shape themselves to him uncertainly, exploringly.

His mouth glided over hers like silk on water.

He took his time, an infinity of time.

This must be perfect for her—perfect.

He mustn't rush this, must take it at her pace, take her with him slowly, exquisitely, on the journey.

His mouth left hers, left her lips parted as his moved on, across the line of her jaw, to the hollow beneath her ear, gliding like silk, like gossamer, to where with the lightest of touches he caressed the outline of her earlobe.

One hand had slid around the nape of her neck, fingers teasing at the fine tendrils of her hair, while his other hand spanned the arch of her throat.

He felt the low, soft gasp vibrating through his fingers, and then his mouth was on hers again, teasing and caressing, until, with a sigh, she opened to him.

His body surged at the sheer sensuality of it as his tongue glided within. He felt her still, as if with shock, and then, as he intensified his kiss, he felt that moment come again as she yielded to his desire.

His hand swept down from the nape of her neck, along the naked length of her back. His fingers sought the fastening of her dress and, with a skill honed with practice over many years, he released the hook, and slowly, very slowly, slid down the zip.

He felt the bodice loosening against his torso and his hand at her throat moved downwards.

He wanted… He wanted…

Dio, but she was exquisite. Full, and soft—and yet as he cupped the silken mound he felt it ripen at his touch. Against his palm, her nipple flowered.

He felt his body surge again, insistent and demanding. Slowly, sensuously, he palmed her fullness.

She seemed to gasp in her throat, and arched her back, pressing herself against him.

It was all he needed. Desire drove through him, and he swept her up into his arms.

The world tilted on its axis, and her eyes flew open.

Rico's eyes were blazing down at her, vivid even in the low light. Her heart was soaring like a bird in flight, which was strange, because she felt boneless, weak, helpless in his arms as he carried her the few strides to his bed.

He lowered her gently, tenderly, as if she were a delicate, precious flower.

'*Elisabetta*—'

For one long, endless moment he gazed down at her as she lay in a ruffle of silk, one breast exposed, as she looked up at him, wonder and enchantment in her eyes.

Then, with a rapid urgency that was its own message, he'd disposed of his own clothes and was lowering his long, lithe frame upon her. She felt his body crush her down into the softness of the bedding. Felt the strength, the honed, masculine beauty of his planed torso, the narrow circle of his hips, the tautness of his thighs, and the long, full shaft pressing against her.

She gasped, awareness shooting through her.

He saw her recognition.

'I have wanted you,' he breathed, 'from the first moment I saw you. Walking towards me—revealed to me—only to me—in all your beauty.'

Slowly, very slowly, he lowered his head and kissed her. Slowly, very slowly.

'Be mine,' he said to her. 'Be mine, my own Elisabetta .'

His eyes were dilated; she was drowning in their dark depths.

There was only one answer to give him. Only one answer possible.

'Rico…' She breathed his name.

Her arms came around him, closed him to her, her fingers grazing with a fierce, sweet ardour along the contours of his back.

Heat flooded through her. Her hips arched to his. A gesture old as time. The instinctive pleading of her sex. She could not speak, could not talk. She could only know that now, *now* she wanted what was the sweetest glory.

His body answered her. Sliding the silken folds of her dress from her, his hand returned, gliding along the smooth column of her leg, and then, with a touch that drew from her a breathless gasp of pleasure, he parted her.

She was lost—lost in a vortex that was taking her into another world, a world that she had never known existed, to a pleasure, a physical sensation so incredible, that her entire being was reduced to one single exquisite point. She gave herself to it, helpless to do anything but let the ravishing sensation of his skilful touch take her to the place that called to her, nearer and yet nearer, so that when the moment came it was a consummation of discovery, of such wondrous ecstasy that she cried out with it. It swept through her, overwhelming her, flooding through her to her very fingertips, wave after wave. His hand was smoothing her hair, his voice murmuring, and then, even as at last the flood began to ebb, even as she felt the pulsing of her core, he was there, seeking entrance, strong and insistent, and yet with absolute control, easing inside her.

She took him in. The pulsing of her body drew him into her,

and she felt his fullness pressing against her aroused, sensitised tissues. She gasped again, eyes flying open to see him looking down at her, his expression one of absolute focus, one of intensity.

The intensity of desire. Absolute desire.

For her.

Now. *Now.*

He moved within her, and as he did the ebbing fire in her started to lick again. Her lips parted in wonder, and he saw that wonder, and with a brief, flickering smile he moved again. And then, once more, the intensity took him over.

'Yes,' she breathed. 'Yes.' And lifted her hips to him, instinctively tilting to let him move more deeply within her, parting her straining flesh around him, moulding herself around him. He moved again, and yet again, and with each stroke she felt the bliss not just of possession, but of renewed desire.

She heard him speak again, a staccato fragment, and then an urgency took him over. Stroke after stroke, his body surging within her, he took her with him, closer and closer still, to that place where she had been.

And then she was there. Like a white heat sensation flashed through her, sweeping through her limbs. She cried out, and heard his voice too, and she was clutching him, her hands working into the smooth, heated planes of his back, her breath crying through her, her throat arching as the fire took her, took him with her.

It went on and on, until, as the final echo began to ebb, she was left with the sweet, honeyed exhaustion of fulfilment in every fibre of her being. She felt the tautness go from him, felt the full heaviness of his body on hers, and emotion flooded through her. Her arms wrapped around him, her cheek pressing against his. She wanted to hold him close, so close.

Wonder filled her, and a sweetness that was beyond comprehension. She held his warm, strong body in her arms, feeling the hectic beat of his heart gradually slow. His head was sunk against her shoulder. She felt his cheek, his soft, silky hair, the warmth of his breath. His breathing slowed, his muscles relaxing, letting go.

Languor stole through her—a peace so deep that it was like a balm, a blessing. At her hips, still conjoined, she felt his heaviness, felt the low throb within her as her body remembered the imprint of his possession, her own ecstasy. Her languor deepened as her own heart rate slowed, and sleep began to steal over her in her warm, sated drowsiness.

Her hands slackened around his back and she felt his skin begin to cool beneath her fingers. He had slipped over into sleep, she realised, and with the last of her conscious mind she pulled the dishevelled coverlet over him. Then, with a low, soft sigh, she let sleep take her.

'Principessa—je suis enchanté.'

Her hand was being taken, and kissed with courtly gallantry. Lizzy smiled uncertainly. Jean-Paul straightened and bestowed a highly appreciative look at her. He said something in French to Rico, which Lizzy did not understand.

Rico grinned.

'I am indeed,' he replied. 'Incredibly fortunate. And now, if you've finished making up to my bride, let's get on with it. Better start with Ben—before he gets bored with the proceedings.'

But Ben was on his best behaviour, and clearly determined to look angelic, which he did effortlessly, in his smart new clothes.

As for his mother.

Rico's breath caught for the hundredth time.

She sat there, on a sofa in the formal salon of the villa—a room as ornate as the dining room, but ideal for the purpose now—and looked simply—

Radiant.

It was the only word for her, and Rico could not tear his eyes from her.

As Jean-Paul took shot after shot, wonder suffused Rico.

And when it was his turn to be included—first on his own with her, then with Ben, and then with all three of them—although his pose was formal, the look in his eyes was quite different.

At the end of the session, Jean-Paul set his camera aside.

'Bon chance, mon vieux,' he said. 'And I wish you every happiness.'

He clasped Rico's hand, then let it go.

There remained only the business of downloading the digital file from the camera, and offering Jean-Paul the hospitality a friend deserved before he took his leave. And then, while Lizzy took Ben off to change them both into less formal clothes, Rico was left to e-mail Luca.

There was no text. Just a carefully selected attachment.

That would be sufficient.

For a moment after he had hit *send* he just stared at the blank screen.

Then he logged out, and went to find his wife.

She was living in the middle of a dream. A dream so wonderful she knew it could only be a dream. An enchantment. A time out of time.

The whole world seemed suffused with a glow of bliss. Every moment, every instant of every day—and, oh, every night—was filled with a happiness she had never believed possible.

How can I be so happy?

But she did not need to ask. She knew.

Rico—

She had only to breathe his name, only to look at him, hear his voice, take his hand, feel his touch upon her, to know why happiness—deep, profound, immeasurable and infinite—was in every pulse of her blood, every beat of her heart.

She did not want to think, to ask, to question. She wanted only to *be*—to be this wonderful, enchanted person, caught in her blissful, beautiful dream.

It was so strange, she mused. Outwardly, the days passed in

just the same way—easy, undemanding days, a perpetual holiday. Taking Ben down to the beach, swimming in the pool, lounging in the sun, doing everything and nothing, talking about everything and nothing.

And yet everything had changed—changed so utterly she could not believe it, could only float in her haze of wonder and bliss.

By day, the signs were subtle and unconscious—a passing caress, a physical closeness, the casual body language that was the daytime manifestation of intimacy. The hug for Ben that included a hug for her, the little touches of hands as they played with him, the warm, acknowledging glances as they talked and ate and did all the things they had already been doing since they had come to the villa.

But by night—ah, by night her heart lifted in still-incredulous wonder. By night the enchantment that suffused her with a subtle golden haze by day blazed into glory. Glory that burned like stars in its brilliance—glory that melted her body, caress by sweetest caress, touch by sensual touch, stroke by exquisite stroke, until her whole being caught flame and burned like a torch in the ecstasy of her consummation.

His consummation. Because she knew, with every cell of her being, that the strong, virile body she held in her arms, held deep within her own body, was burning too, in the same consummation. She felt his body burn with the same flame, setting him on fire as her arms wrapped him close, and closer still, their bodies fusing as one, until at last the incandescence burned away, leaving them twined about each other in sweet exhaustion.

'How…how can it be so wonderful?' she breathed at him one night, her eyes wide and bemused.

He did not answer, only smoothed her hair, lacing it with his fingers, and cradled her body against his as his hand smoothed along her back, drifting with slow, exhausted sensuousness until it slowed, and slackened, cupping the ripeness of her hip.

He murmured in Italian—words she did not understand but which flowed like honey through her. Like a balm, a blessing.

Then night folded over them and they slept, entwined, embracing. And she dreamt of heaven, because that was where she was already.

Lizzy was creaming his back. Rico lay face down on a lounger. Ben, having surfaced from his siesta, his energy levels renewed, was vigorously batting his way along the length of the pool astride a huge inflatable dolphin.

'Race me,' he called to Rico. 'You can ride the crocodile.' He pointed to a huge, inflatable crocodile with grinning jaws that was floating disconsolately in the shallows.

'Soon,' said Rico, not lifting his head. 'Very soon.'

But not that soon. It was far too good just lying here, with the sun beating down on him, the lightest of breezes playing over his skin, the drowsy sound of the cicadas, the silence of the world around him and Ben splashing happily in the pool, while warm hands glided caressingly, sensuously across his bared back, massaging sun cream deep into the muscled contours, sculpting the bones of his spine, his ribs and shoulders, with smooth, strong strokes.

Well-being, contentment—peace—filled him. He could lie here for ever.

He could be here for ever.

Life was good—so very good.

Everything—everything he wanted was here. Now. An endless now.

Time had stopped. Only day and night existed. Nothing more. There was no world beyond this.

He'd heard nothing yet from his father and Luca—and he didn't care. They belonged in a world he was not interested in right now.

Right now, all he wanted he had. He wanted nothing more.

Footsteps sounded on the shallow flight that led to the upper terrace. A shadow fell over his body. The hands at his back stopped.

He lifted his head and looked up.

Captain Falieri stood there.

Slowly, Rico levered himself up, and stood. Behind him, he could hear Lizzy doing the same. Automatically he felt for her hand and closed his fingers around hers.

'Captain Fally-eery!' Ben's piping voice called with enthusiasm. He splashed his way busily to the steps and clambered out, running up to them. 'Have you come to tea?' he asked convivially.

The Captain shook his head. 'I'm afraid not. I've come—' his eyes flicked to Rico's '—to see your uncle.'

As Falieri looked back at him, Rico could see his gaze moving past him automatically. Even so good a diplomat as he was, he could not, Rico could see, hide the flash of shock in his eyes. He knew why. The woman whose hand he was holding was all but unrecognisable. He felt her slip her hand from his and saw that she was reaching for a sarong to wind about her. Then she was holding out her hand to Ben.

'Let's go and get changed,' she said. 'Captain Falieri,' she acknowledged.

He bowed his head in return, but did not speak. He looked disbelievingly after her as she set off, hand in hand with a protesting Ben.

But Rico was not concerned that his father's chief of police was stunned by the transformation in the appearance of the woman he'd last seen looking so very different in England. He stretched out a hand and picked up his shirt, shrugging it over his shoulders.

'Well?' he asked.

Falieri's eyes snapped back to him.

'His Highness, your father, wishes to see you.'

Rico's mouth pressed together. Then, with a nod of acquiescence, he headed off after Lizzy and Ben.

'Ten minutes,' he called back to Falieri.

It was hard, punishingly hard, to take leave of Lizzy and Ben. But it had to be done. For these past days he had shut out the outside world, ignoring its existence, but that did not stop it existing. Now, he just wanted it sorted.

He took Lizzy's hands. She'd showered and changed, like him, but whereas he had put on a formal suit, knowing his father's preferences, she was wearing a simple sundress. Ben had been peeled out of his trunks and put into shorts and a T-shirt.

'What's going to happen?' He could hear the fear in her voice.

'My father has a very clear choice—he can accept our marriage with outward good grace, and keep everyone happy. Or he can have an open breach with me. I don't care which. Whichever he's chosen, it makes no difference—we're married, you're my wife, Ben is our joint legal charge, and my father *cannot* get his hands on him.' He took a breath. 'I don't want to leave you, but it's the best thing in the circumstances. I don't want you and Ben setting foot in San Lucenzo till all this is settled. I've asked Falieri to stay with you, and he's consented. I trust him. He's not my father's stoolie and he will do *nothing* illegal. He was not involved with the deception my father and brother practised on us at the palace.' His expression darkened. 'It was clever of Luca to send him to England with me—he knows I trust him, and he also knows that Falieri would have refused to be party to their despicable scheme had he been back at the palace.'

'When will you be back?' She was trying to keep her voice steady, he could tell.

'Tonight. There's a helicopter waiting for me at the marina, and the flight won't take long. Nor will whatever my father has to say to me. I'll be heading right back here.'

He gave a sudden smile, dispelling the grimness of his expression.

'Put the champagne on ice, get Ben to bed early, and…' his long lashes swept down over his eyes '…slip into something comfortable.'

For one last moment he held her gaze. Then, letting go her hands, he ruffled Ben's hair and walked out.

Lizzy watched him go. Her chest felt tight.

Ben tugged at her skirt. 'Where's Tio Rico going?' he asked.

'He'll be back later,' said Lizzy absently. She took a breath, trying to focus. 'Let's go and see if Captain Falieri would like a cup of coffee. I'm sure he would.'

'Can he stay to tea, then?' Ben asked, pleased.

'I think he can now. Yes.'

She took Ben out along the terrace. On the far side of the villa she could hear a car moving off, taking Rico down to the heliport.

Captain Falieri walked out of the house. For a moment he seemed a familiar, reassuring figure. Then he turned to look at them as they approached.

There was something in his face that made the blood freeze in her veins.

She stopped in front of him.

'What is it?' Her voice was high, and faint. The tightness in her chest was squeezing hard, so hard.

For a moment he just looked at her. His face was sombre. And in his eyes, most frightening of all, was pity.

'I have,' he said gravely, 'unwelcome news.'

CHAPTER ELEVEN

THE helicopter churned through the air, descending to the palace. Rico must have made this landing a thousand times or more—it was one of the most convenient ways of arriving and departing. He gazed down at the white towers astride the rocky promontory on which the original castle had been built. It was one of the most familiar sights in the world to him.

And yet now it seemed very alien.

He didn't want to do this. He didn't want this confrontation. But it had to be done. And the sooner it was over and done with the better.

Which way had his father chosen? Either Falieri did not know, or he was under strict instructions to give no clue. Well, the waiting would be over very soon, and then Rico would know either the best or the worst.

But it wouldn't be the worst. His father would not risk the scandal of an open breach with his son—he would accept what Rico had done. He wouldn't like it, but he would accept it. For the sake of convention, propriety. For the sake of appearances.

He felt a hardening in his guts. Appearances were all they would be. There could be no real reconciliation with his father. Not after what he had tried to do.

No one, *no one* took a child from its mother. Parted a mother from her child.

No one.

The landing pad soared up to meet them, and there was the familiar jar of impact. The noise of the rotors lessened. Rico released his seat belt, nodded his thanks to the pilot, and slid back the door. Lithely he jumped down and ducked out from under the slowing rotors, then straightened.

As he did, he saw a quartet of figures emerging from the palace. Palace guards in their duty uniforms. He paused, frowning, waiting for them to approach.

'What is it?' he demanded sharply.

The senior officer among them stared straight ahead, not looking at him. His face was expressionless.

'I regret to inform Your Highness,' he said, 'that you are under arrest.'

He was taken to his own apartments. His phone was removed from him, and he realised that all other communication devices, from PC to laptop, had been removed or disabled, including both the house phone and the phones with outside lines.

Disbelief sent shock waves through him.

What the *hell* was going on? Fury, disbelief, shock—all warred within him.

He paced, rigid with rage, across his sitting room.

The double doors opened and he snapped round. The doors had been opened by two of the guards standing outside. Through them was walking his father.

'What the *hell* is this?' Rico demanded.

His father walked in, The guards closed the doors again.

'I have placed you,' said Prince Eduardo, 'under arrest.'

'On what charge?'

Rico's voice was hollow, disbelieving.

There was a silence for a moment. His father's eyes rested on him. They were cold. Rico had never seen them look so cold.

'You have committed a crime against the principality of San Lucenzo.'

His voice was as cold as his eyes.

Rico stared.

'What?'

'It is a crime dating back to medieval times. It has little modern enforcement, with one salient exception.' His father paused again. 'Royal marriages,' he said.

'I don't understand,' Rico answered slowly. He was holding still, very still.

His father's cold eyes rested on him.

'Any member of the royal family requires the consent of the Prince before they may marry. You failed to obtain it. Therefore your marriage is void.'

Rico let the words sink in. Then he spoke.

'You can recognise it after the fact.'

'I shall not do so. The marriage is void. You have married without my consent.'

Rico looked at him.

'Why are you doing this? Does it mean nothing to you that the boy is Paolo's son?' His voice was strange, remote.

'Paolo is dead—because of this boy. Had that greedy, over-ambitious girl not sought to entrap him he would never have lost his life.'

Rico shook his head in denial.

'We know nothing of the nature of their relationship The girl might just as easily have been in love with him, and he with her.'

Something flashed in his father's eyes, and then it was gone. Before he could speak Rico continued.

'And whether or not it was love—or entrapment—Paolo did the honourable thing. He married her for the sake of his unborn child.'

His father's face was like marble. Cold and hard.

'He had no business doing so. His first duty was to his name. He was impetuous and self-indulgent.' His voice grew more heavy. 'I blame myself for that. He was indulged as a child—spoilt—and that was the consequence.'

A chill went down Rico's spine, like ice crystallising in his nerve fibres. His father was speaking again. Rico forced himself to listen.

'Nevertheless, when the existence of the boy was discovered—although I would have preferred to have ignored the matter, whatever repellent drivel the gutter press produced—I was prepared, however reluctantly, to acknowledge Paolo's brief marriage, and thereby accept his son as legitimate. Given the circumstances, it seemed the most…advisable…course of action. With the mother dead there would be no…unwelcome entanglements. The boy would be raised in an appropriate manner, without the indulgence that ruined his father, and accepted as a member of the royal family. Unfortunately the obduracy and ambition of the aunt proved a serious impediment.'

Rico's eyes hardened.

'She is more than his aunt, she is his mother—his legal guardian. I made it crystal-clear that she would not be parted from her son—and your attempt to do so was despicable.'

His father's eyes flashed coldly again.

'You will not address me in such a fashion,' he said freezingly. 'However, you will be glad to learn that the boy is no longer a requirement. I have rescinded my decision to recognise Paolo's marriage.' The cold eyes rested impassively on Rico. 'The boy is therefore illegitimate within the state of San Lucenzo. His future is of no concern to me.'

It was said with an indifference that chilled him to the core.

'He's your grandson,' said Rico. 'Does that mean *nothing* to you?'

His father's face did not change. 'Royal bastards are not acknowledged. He has no entitlements and can have no claim on Paolo's estate. Nevertheless, arrangements will be made for suitable maintenance, and an appropriate capital sum will be settled on him for his majority. The issue is now closed, and I will discuss it no further. Luca will handle the matter with the lawyers, and you will not be involved. As for yourself,' the cold voice continued, 'you will undertake to have no further contact or communication with the woman or the boy. When you have given this undertaking, the charge will be lifted.' He gave a sharp intake of breath. 'That is all I have to say to you.'

Rico looked at him. Looked at this man who was his father.

He was standing only a few metres away from him—but the distance between them was much more than that.

Then, without another word, Prince Eduardo walked from the room.

The doors shut behind him, and Rico was alone once more.

How long he stood there he did not know. He could feel his lungs breathing in, and out, he could feel the steady beat of his heart—but he could not feel anything else.

There were voices outside the doors. A sharp voice, and then a deferential one. A door swung open—only one this time.

It was Luca.

Rico looked at him. For a long moment the brothers' eyes met and held.

'Why did you do it?' There was almost resignation in his brother's voice as he put the question, Rico thought. 'Are you completely insane—or just extraordinarily stupid? Not just to do what you have, but then to think you could pressurise our father into accepting it. Good God, do you not know him well enough by now to know he would *never* back down before you?'

'I thought he would consider the scandal of an open breach with me more repugnant than forcing himself to do the decent thing by Paolo's son.'

'The decent thing?' A dam seemed to break inside Luca. 'God Almighty, Rico. You've lost us Paolo's son. His *son*. Do you know, do you have *any idea*, how hard I had to work to get our father to recognise Paolo's marriage? When I told him that there was a story brewing in the press, and what it was, his first and immediate reaction was to ignore it. He was so furious with Paolo that he couldn't think straight. But he finally agreed— after endless persuasion on my part—that the best thing to do would be to recognise the boy as legitimate. That meant he

could come here. That meant he *had* to come here. On his own,' he spelt out. 'That went without saying. Do you seriously imagine for a moment that our father would have anything to do with the family of the boy's mother?'

Luca's mouth set grimly. 'But how the hell could I have known that the girl would kick up such a fuss, and that you— *you* of all people—would let her get away with it? *Dio*, Rico— *you* were the one who was supposed to have her eating out of your hand, not the other damn way round. I never had you down for an idiot—let alone an insane one—but I do now. And now, thanks to your insane stupidity, you've gone and lost us Paolo's son. Thanks to you he's been declared a bastard. A bastard— Paolo's son. *That's* what you've achieved. And it's not something I'm going to forgive you for lightly.'

Bitter fury stung in his accusation. Then his slate eyes flashed again.

'It's time to grow up, Rico. To take some responsibility. Not to play infantile games and be led around by your damn over-active sex-drive! Because that's what's happened, obviously. That much is clear from the photos you sent. You had her done up and moved in on her. Well, I hope you've had your fill of her—because it's over now. You won't be allowed to go within a hundred miles of her. From now on she doesn't exist any more. And maybe finally you'll *learn* some responsibility, Rico. You'd better, because this really is your last chance. He's made that very clear, our father—very clear indeed. You came *this* close to stepping over the edge. This close. From now on, no more stepping out of line by you—not one more *breath* of scandal. From now on you learn to conduct yourself with some responsibility.'

He fell silent, his eyes heavy on his brother.

'Responsibility?' said Rico slowly. His eyes rested on Luca. Nothing showed in them. 'I've always had a problem with responsibility. Because I never had any. My sole responsibility was to stay alive, that was all. In case you dropped dead. Turned out gay. Refused to marry. Proved infertile. And in the meantime, until and unless any of that happened, I passed the time. Any way I could. Because that was all I *could* do. All I was allowed to do. Pass the time. However pointlessly. Until—' his voice changed '—until I found out there was something I could do, after all. Something, in fact, that only I could do— no one else could. I could save Paolo's son.'

His eyes never left Luca's, not for an instant, boring into him, burning into him. 'I could save Paolo's son from the hellish childhood that was being cooked up for him. The one you told me about when I delivered Ben and his mother into your tender hands like a fool—the fool you'd played me for. You wanted to throw his mother away like garbage and condemn Ben to a childhood that was going to be even worse than the one we had, Luca. Do you remember our childhood? Do you? Or has that just conveniently been blanked out of your memory? Because it hasn't from mine, and there was no way—no way on this earth—that I was going to let that happen to Paolo's son. There was no way that I was going to let him be taken from the woman he regards as his mother, *loves* as his mother, or let her lose her child. I could stop it happening—and I did. And I don't regret it for one second. Not one instant.' His voice was a low snarl now. 'Even though I've discovered just what kind of callous *scum* you all are.'

He took a harsh intake of breath. 'And now, if you don't want me to knock you out cold again, I suggest you get the hell out of my quarters.'

He saw his brother's lip twist.

'Thinking to use your *Boy's Own* secret passage and head for the hills again, Rico? It won't do you any good this time. It won't get you out of the hole you're in now. You've run out of options. Your marriage has been declared void, and you're under arrest.'

Rico's mouth whitened.

'I don't give a—'

'Allow me,' bit out Luca, cutting through the expletive, 'to explain to you exactly what San Lucenzan law in respect of royal marriages allows the Prince Regnant to do.'

In precise, exact and comprehensive terms, he did so.

Rico listened. And as he listened, his face slowly froze.

Lizzy was sitting very still. Very still indeed. She had sent Ben to the playroom, telling him to watch a DVD until she came for him.

'I am so very sorry,' Captain Falieri was saying, 'to be the bearer of such…unsettling…news, Miss Mitchell.'

Lizzy said nothing. What could she say? Yet she had to say something.

She swallowed. There seemed to be a stone in her throat.

'So…so what happens now? To Ben and me?'

Her voice was thin, and she was trying to stop it shaking.

Captain Falieri was being kind—so very kind. Somehow that just made it worse.

'I am to escort you both back to Cornwall. Perhaps you would instruct the staff to pack what you intend to take? Needless to say, all…' he hesitated minutely '…all personal effects purchased for your stay here will be considered yours.'

She said nothing. She would allow Ben to choose his favourites from amongst the toys that he had acquired here. As for herself…

She felt her heart crushed, as if heavy weights were squeezing it.

She would need nothing. Nothing but what she had arrived with.

She got to her feet. The motion was jerky.

'If you will excuse me—?'

'Of course. However…' The minute hesitation came again. 'Before you go, I am instructed to require you to sign a particular document.'

He drew a thick, long envelope from his inside breast

pocket and took out the folded document within. He placed it in front of her.

'Although you may wish to read it first—there is a translation attached to the original, as you can see—its content is very straightforward. His Highness, Prince Eduardo, requires you to agree to certain…restrictions. You are to make no claim either on your behalf, or that of your nephew, on the estate of his late natural father, or upon His Highness's estate. You are to have no contact with the press in any way. All approaches by any member of the press to you, you are to direct to His Highness's press secretary to deal with. You are to undertake never to agree to or participate in the publication of any book, or the broadcast of any programme, in any medium, pertaining to your nephew. When these undertakings have been agreed by yourself, a regular sum will be paid to you, for the maintenance of yourself and your nephew. When your nephew achieves his majority, a capital sum will be settled on him by His Highness, in due recognition of the financial obligation that would have devolved upon your nephew's natural father.'

He fell silent and extracted a fountain pen from his inside jacket, placing it beside the document, formally opening it to the final page, where her signature was to be appended.

'I will sign the papers,' said Lizzy. 'But I will not accept any money. Please make that very clear to His Highness.'

She put her signature to the document and waited while Captain Falieri added his own, as witness.

Then she turned away. 'I must talk to my son,' she said.

Gravely, Captain Falieri inclined his head, and watched her walk out.

Rain was falling. Heavy, relentless sheets of rain that swept in off the North Atlantic, rattling against the windowpanes, spitting down the chimney.

The cottage felt cold, so cold.

Damp and unused.

Captain Falieri's expression darkened as he brought her cases indoors.

'You cannot stay here,' he said bluntly. 'I will take you to a hotel.'

Lizzy shook her head.

'No. I would rather be here. I'll be all right.'

She turned to him and held out her hand.

'Thank you,' she said. 'For doing what you could to make this as…simple…as possible.'

He took her hand, but he did not shake it. Instead, he bowed over it.

'I wish…' he said, and he straightened and looked into her eyes. 'I wish that matters had been…otherwise.'

Her throat tightened. She could not cope with kindness.

Nor with pity.

'Thank you,' she said again. 'You had better go now. I'm sure the pilot will wish to start his return flight.'

A private plane had flown her to a military airfield further south, and then Captain Falieri had driven her and Ben to her cottage.

'If you are sure?'

She nodded. 'It would be best for Ben.' She swallowed. 'A complete break will be the easiest for him. As it was when—'

She could not continue. Memories pressed upon her, heavy and unbearable. Could it really have only been a few weeks ago that she had stood here in the hallway admitting entrance to two strangers?

She felt the vice close around her heart again.

She turned and went into the kitchen. Ben was sitting at the table, slumped over it, dejection in every line.

'Captain Falieri has to go now, Ben. Come and say goodbye.'

Ben lifted his face to her.

'Can't we go back with him, Mummy? Can't we? I don't like it here. It's cold.' There were tears in his voice. The vice inside her crushed even more tightly.

'No, my darling, we've come home now. Our holiday is over.'

Tears quivered in Ben's eyes.

'I don't want it to be over,' he said.

There was nothing she could say. Nothing at all. She wanted to sit at the table and howl with him, pour out all her grief and heartbreak. But she could not. She had to be strong for Ben.

She forced a smile to her lips.

'All holidays end, Ben. Now, come and say goodbye to Captain Falieri. He's been kind to us. Very kind.' She felt her voice crack dangerously.

She took Ben's hand and led him dejectedly out into the hallway.

'Goodbye, Ben,' said Captain Falieri gravely. He held out a hand to him.

Ben did not take it.

'Am I really not a prince any more, Captain Fally-eery?' His eyes were wide and pleading.

The Captain shook his head. 'I'm afraid not, Ben.'

'And Mummy isn't a princess?'

'No.'

'It was only for the holiday, Ben. Us being a prince and princess,' said Lizzy. It was the only way she had been able to explain it to Ben.

'What about Tio Rico? Isn't he a prince any more?'

Lizzy's hand rested on his shoulder. It tightened involuntarily.

'He will always be a prince, my darling. Nothing can change that.'

For one long, terrible moment she met Captain Falieri's eyes. Then looked away.

She waited as he took his leave, walking out into the rain. She heard the car door open, then slam shut, and the engine rev. The car drove off down the lane to the coast road, heading back to the airfield, to the waiting plane that would take him away.

She shut the door as a spatter of rain came in on the wind.

She shivered.

'Let's light a fire, Ben. That will warm things up.'

But she would never be warm again, she knew. A terrible, deathly chill embraced her.

How am I going to bear this? How?

The question rang out in her anguish, but she had no answer. There could be no answer.

She went into the kitchen. Captain Falieri had very kindly stopped at a supermarket on the way from the airfield and bought some provisions for her. They would do until she could get to the shops. Mechanically she started to unpack them, and then put some milk to heat on the electric cooker. Warm milk would be good for Ben. They had eaten on the plane; it had helped to make the journey pass. It wasn't really very late, though the rain made it seem darker. Only a few hours since they had left the villa. Only a few hours…

She stilled, unable to move. It was like a physical pain convulsing through her.

With all her strength she forced herself to continue, to make up the fire in the range, set it to draw, check the heat of the milk.

Ben sat at the table, head sunk upon his arms, a picture of misery.

I've got to keep going. It's all I can do. Just keep going. Keep going.

It became her mantra. The only thing that got her through the evening, got her through the following day. And the one after that. And it would get her through the one after that. All the days that stretched ahead of her.

For the rest of her life.

It was unbearable—yet she had to bear it.

There's nothing else. Nothing else I can do. Just keep going. It will pass. Eventually it will pass.

It had to.

Eventually it will get better. Eventually I will accept it. Accept what happened.

That for a brief golden time I was there, with him.

And that time was over. Never to return.

She looked around her, at the worn, shabby interior of the cottage. So short a time ago all she had wanted in the world was to be back here, without her life turned upside down, with Ben just an ordinary child, living a normal life with her.

She would have given anything for that.

Be careful what you pray for...

The old adage came back to haunt her.

The nights were the worst. The nights were agony. Hour after hour she stared into the dark. Remembering.

It's all I have. Memories.

Memories that were vivid, agonising. But memories that she knew, with even greater anguish, would start to fade. Like old photos, the colour seeping from them year by year. They would become blurred and lost. Gone for ever.

Just as he was gone for ever from her life.

Her thoughts reached for him, reached through the silence and the dark, reached across the sea and the land.

But where he was she did not know.

And what would it matter if you did? What would it matter if you could see him where he is? His world has taken him back—to the life he had, the life he has again. You were an...intermission...for him. He did what he did to keep Ben safe—and now Ben is safe again. Ben does not need him. He can have his own life back, as Ben has his.

As you have yours.

Without him.

Only memories. Memories to last a lifetime. Nothing more than memories.

A damp sun struggled through the clouds. After days of rain, the overcast skies were clearing. Raindrops dazzled drippingly on the branches of the trees, and a milder wind creamed up the coombe, bringing the scent of the sea.

'Come on, Ben, let's go down to the beach.'

With forced jollity she rallied him, filling her voice with an enthusiasm she did not feel. Nor did she meet with any in return.

'I don't want to,' said Ben. 'I want to go back to Tio Rico's beach.'

'Other people are having their holiday there now,' she said. 'It's like here in Cornwall. People come for a holiday, and then they go home. That's quite sad for them, isn't it? We live here all the time—so that's good.'

Ben looked at her mutinously.

'We could live in the house by Tio Rico's beach all the time,' he said.

'That house was only for a holiday for us. This is the house we live in. And we're very lucky to be here, Ben. Lots of people have to live in cities, where there isn't any beach at all.'

'I don't like the beach here. It hasn't got a swimming pool. And it hasn't got Tio Rico.' Ben's lower lip wobbled.

'The beach here has got waves,' said Lizzy, with determined cheerfulness.

'But it hasn't got Tio Rico,' Ben protested. He swallowed, and lifted his eyes to her. 'Mummy, doesn't Tio Rico want us any more?

She tried to find the words. Words that a four-year-old child could make sense of. But they were cruel words, harsh words for all that. Yet what else could she do except say them? To give Ben false hope would be the cruellest thing of all.

'Your uncle can't be with us any more, Ben,' she began carefully. 'He has duties to attend to. He has to be a prince now, not an uncle. It was just a holiday we spent with him. Just a holiday. That's all.'

Her words fell with excruciating mockery into her own ears.

A holiday. That was all it had been. A holiday of enchantment, magic, wonder, and such bliss that it made the realisation that such a time could never come again so agonising that she could hardly bear it.

But above all, above everything else, she must not say the words that ached to be said. For what was the use of saying them? What was the use, even in the dark—all alone in the bed she had once been content to lie in, solitary, celibate, untouched by the magic that he had strewn over her—what was the use, sleepless and despairing, of letting those words whisper in her mind, each one an agony of loss?

The only way she could face the rest of her life now was never, ever, to say those words. Never even to think them. Or they would destroy her.

Resolutely, she went on getting the beach things together.

Pain and memory clawing within her.

She took Ben, protesting, down to the beach. She had forgotten how chill the wind could be even at this time of year, in early summer. She made a camp in the lee of a line of rocks, sedimentary shales turned on their side by vast geological forces over vast reaches of time. So much time.

She looked out to sea.

Where was he now? she wondered. Was he in some fashionable high-society resort—Monte Carlo, the Caribbean, somewhere exotic? Mingling with fashionable high-society people? Fashionable high-society women, every one a beauty, the kind that he took his pick of—the Playboy Prince, leading the life he was born to lead?

Stop it. It doesn't matter.

It doesn't matter where he is, or who he's with, or what he's doing.

It doesn't matter.

It will never matter again, for the rest of your life.

She shook out the rug and weighted down the corners with a book, shoes and a bag.

'Who's for a paddle?' she said, forcing her voice to be cheerful.

'It's too cold,' said Ben, and sat on the rug and wrapped a towel around him.

She whisked it off.

'Then we'll make a railway track. Which engines did you bring down with you?'

'I don't want trains—I want my fort. The fort Tio Rico made with me.'

Lizzy's heart sank. Gently she said, 'We couldn't bring it back, Ben. It was too big—don't you remember? But we brought the knights, so that's good, isn't it?' she finished encouragingly.

'But it's the *fort* I want. Tio Rico and me made it. We made it together, and it had a bridge and a porcully and towers.'

She felt her heart catch with pain. Like a knife slicing into her memory stabbed her and she was there again, in the warmth and the sunshine—the ugly sister who had so miraculously been turned into Cinderella. Sleeping Beauty ready to be kissed awake by the most handsome Prince in the world.

No. Anguish crushed her. She mustn't let herself think, remember. It was gone, all gone. Like a dream. An enchantment.

A fairytale that was over now.

She took a breath.

She must not think of fairytales. They were just that. Unreal. This was real—here, now. With Ben. She chivvied him along, refusing to let him mope. What was the point of him moping? What was the point of her moping? They had to get on with things. They had to.

They had to keep going.

'Well, we haven't got the fort any more, but we have got trains. So let's start building this track,' she said, with forced resolution.

She started digging into the sand, carving out the railway tracks that Ben liked to make so that he could drive his engines along. The sand was cold beneath the surface, and wet. The sand at the villa had been warm, dry.

And Rico had helped Ben make the tracks.

'Come on, Ben, give me a hand,' she said.

Morosely he started to help, his expression unhappy. Lizzy

ignored it. She had to. She had to jolly him along, get him cheerful again, enthusiastic again. What alternative was there? She knelt down on the sand, facing out to sea, letting the wind whip her hair into unflattering frizzled wisps.

Her looks were going already, she knew. Without all the expensive attentions of stylists and beauticians she was beginning to revert. She didn't care.

What did Ben care what she looked like?

And there was no one else to care.

Never again.

'Where shall we make the train station?' she asked, kneeling back a moment, feeling the wind-blown sand stinging on her cheeks.

'Don't care,' said Ben. He sat back as well, beside her. 'It's a stupid, stupid track, and I don't care where the stupid, stupid station is. Stupid, stupid, *stupid*.' He bashed the sand with his spade, spattering it in all directions.

'Well, I'd put it just before the branch line goes off, Ben. That's the place for a station.'

The voice that spoke was deep and accented, and it came from behind them.

CHAPTER TWELVE

THE world seemed to stop. Stop completely. Except that it didn't stop. It whirled around her. Whirled with a dizzying speed that made her feel faint.

It wasn't possible. It was an illusion—an auditory illusion. They happened sometimes—you could hear people speaking who weren't there.

Who were somewhere quite different. Who were at some aristocratic house party somewhere, or on a multimillion-pound yacht, or flying in a private jet to a tropical island with a beautiful film star for company.

Who weren't on a Cornish beach, with the wind blowing off the North Atlantic. Making the wind feel as if it was being wafted there from paradise…

Her vision dimmed. She felt clouds rushing in from all around. The blood was thick in her head, bowing her down with its weight.

'Tio Rico!'

Ben's voice was alight. She could hear it, piercing through the clouds and the thickening blood.

'Tio Rico. Tio Rico!'

She bowed her head. It was impossible. Impossible.

'Hello, Ben? Have you been good without me?'

'No,' shouted Ben. Excitement overwhelmed him. 'You weren't here. Why weren't you here, Tio Rico?'

'I got delayed. I'm sorry. But I'm here now.' She felt him lower himself down on to the rug. And still she could not move. Not a muscle.

'Are you going to stay?' Ben demanded. But there was fear in his voice.

'As long as you want me to stay.' He paused. 'If your mother agrees, that is. Do you?'

His hand was on her shoulder. Warm and strong. Sending heat through her, a living warmth that she could not bear.

'Lizzy?'

She looked up. He was only a foot or two away from her, hunkered down on the rug. She saw him immediately, completely. She saw everything about him in one absolute moment. As if he had always been there.

'You shouldn't be here,' she said. Her voice was thick, as thick as the blood suffocating her veins. 'Captain Falieri explained to me. He said you would not be allowed to see Ben again.'

The expression in his eyes altered.

'Well, that depends,' he said. He was looking at her very deeply, very strangely, right into her eyes.

'No, it doesn't,' she said. 'It doesn't depend at all. He said it very clearly. He explained it very clearly. You're not allowed to see Ben any more.'

From the corner of her eye she could see Ben's face pucker.

'Why can't Tio Rico see me any more?' he said.

She saw Rico reach out and ruffle Ben's hair.

'Your mother's got it wrong. I'm here, aren't I?'

It was her turn for her face to pucker.

'But you *shouldn't* be,' she said fiercely. 'You *can't* be.'

His expression changed again. Something entered his eyes. Something she didn't want to see.

'Where else should I be,' he asked quietly, but with deadliness in his voice, 'but with my wife and my boy?'

'No,' she said. She rocked forward slightly. Denying it. Denying it completely. 'No,' she said again.

He looked at her. Looked at her with eyes that chilled her to the bone.

'Did you really think,' he asked, in that same quiet, deadly tone, 'that I would stay away?'

She snapped upright.

'You've got to go!' she shouted at him. 'You've got to go— right away. Right now. Falieri told me. He *told* me. So go—*go*.'

There was a steely glint in his eye. He reached for her hands and hauled her down again. Her eyes were wild, desperate.

'He told me,' she said, and there was despair in her voice. 'He told me everything. He told me about that law—the one that says you can't marry without the Ruling Prince's permission. He told me that it meant our marriage was null and void.'

'Our marriage is real, Lizzy. We made our vows in front of a priest. No one can overturn that.' Steel was in his voice now.

'Yes, they can. They can. Your father can overturn it—and that's what he's done.'

'All my father can do is refuse to recognise our marriage within San Lucenzo. He cannot overturn it. He has no power over our marriage, Lizzy. None.' He spoke steadily, remorselessly.

Her face contorted. 'Yes, he has. He *has*. Captain Falieri told me—he told me quite clearly. He's got absolute power over you. You've broken the law, and if you don't obey him he'll use that power. And he'll do it. Captain Falieri said he would do it.' She swallowed. The stone in her throat was agony. But she spoke, saying the words that had been burnt into her like an agonising brand.

'He'll do it, Rico—he'll strip you of your royalty. He'll disinherit you. He'll disbar you from the succession. Take you off the Civil List, freeze all your assets in San Lucenzo. He'll take everything from you—everything. He'll leave you with nothing.'

She heard Captain Falieri's voice tolling in her head. Saying the words that had taken everything from *her*. All hope. Gone for ever. They had crushed her, crushed her heart, cracking it in pieces.

There was a strange look on Rico's face. It frightened her. His expression was calm. Very calm. Far too calm.

'Falieri was wrong. There was something my father could not take from me.' He paused. Then he spoke. 'You. He could not take you from me. My wife.'

Her face contorted again.

'No. *No.*'

'You are my wife, and Ben is my adopted son, and no one—no power on earth—will take you from me.'

She twisted her hands in his grip.

'No,' she cried again. Her eyes were anguished. 'You mustn't say that. I won't let you. I won't. You've got to go now. Right now.'

He gave a sudden laugh, gripping her hands more tightly yet.

'What a venal woman you are,' he said. 'You only want me for my title, don't you?' His fingers slid into hers. 'Well, I've bad news for you, Signora Ceraldi—'

'Don't say that. Just go. It's not too late.'

He hauled her against him, crushing her against the hard wall of his chest.

'It's far too late. Far, far too late.'

He kissed her.

The kiss went on and on. And she drowned in it. Drowned in his arms. Drowned in the tears pouring from her.

'Mummy—Mummy?'

A little hand was tugging at her arm. Ben's voice was confused, bewildered. Rico half let her go. He swept Ben to him.

'Now, tell me—tell me true.' He stood him up in the crook of his arm, hugging his little body close to him. His other arm was wrapped tight around Lizzy. 'Which would you rather? Me not at all—or me not as a prince but still you and me and Mummy?'

'Would you go away again?' Ben asked.

Rico shook his head. 'Never. Unless you came with me. I might go sometimes—just to work, that sort of thing—maybe for the day or a few days. But you would live with me, and so would Mummy. Would that be any good?'

'Where would we all live?'

'Anywhere you liked. Well, except in a palace.'

'I want to live here and at the holiday house with the swimming pool,' Ben stipulated. 'With you and Mummy. For ever and ever.'

'Done,' said Rico. 'High five says yes.'

Ben gave him a high five. 'Yes,' he shouted. 'Yes, yes, *yes*.' His little face was alight—alight with joy.

Lizzy's face was wet with tears.

'You can't do this. You just *can't*,' she sobbed.

Rico's arm tightened around her shaking shoulders.

'Too late,' he told her. 'Done deal.' He kissed her forehead softly. 'Done deal, Signora Ceraldi.' His eyes gazed into hers. Deep, deep eyes. 'Now, don't go and tell me it was just the royal bit you fell for?' His voice was admonishing. 'My ego won't take it, you know. It really won't.'

She swallowed, hard. 'Ben—' her voice was shaky '—why not start on that station now? Tio Rico and I need to talk. Boring grown-up stuff.'

'OK,' said Ben.

His world was restored. Happily, he scrambled back onto the sand and started scooping it up to shape into a railway station. Carefully, very carefully, Lizzy undraped herself and pulled away, to the far edge of the rug.

'You can't do this,' she said again. She made her voice steady. Very steady. Calm and rational. 'I won't let you. I won't let you give everything up for Ben. He's young. He'll soon forget you. It will be hard at first, but in a year he'll have forgotten you. You'll just be a memory, and even that will fade.'

He was looking at her strangely. Then he spoke.

'But, you see, my memories of Ben won't fade. *I* won't forget *him*. And I won't give him up. He's my brother's son— and as clearly as if Paolo were here now I can hear him telling me to be the father to Ben that he was not allowed to be. Just as you—' he made each word telling '—are the mother to Ben that your sister was not allowed to be. And though the cruelty of their deaths can never be assuaged, we know that we can be the loving family to their son that he needs. Because we both love him—and we love each other, don't we, Lizzy?'

She opened her mouth, but no words came. He supplied them for her.

'You can't kiss a man like you just did unless you love him. You can't cry all over a man like you just did unless you love him. And you certainly can't tell a prince he's not to give up his title for the woman he loves unless you love him. I've got you on all three counts, Signora Ceraldi. And I've got you on more counts than that. An infinite number—not just every night we were together, but every moment we were together. Every look, every touch, everything we said to each other, every meal we shared—every smile we shared, everything.'

He shook his head ruminatively. 'It started right from the beginning—even though I didn't know it. Seeing you with Ben, seeing you love him and care for him. And when…' He paused, then went on, 'When you used that horrible, cruel word about yourself, describing our marriage, I wanted to do anything, *everything* I could to banish it.' His eyes softened. 'And I had my reward—oh, I did indeed. Ever since you walked towards me along that terrace, looking such a knockout, taking my breath away, I've been lost. And I know that makes me sound superficial and trivial, thinking with my Y chromosome, but you bowled me over. Blew me away. Knocked me for six. Whatever you want to call it—I went for it.' His voice changed again. 'But it isn't just because of that. It can't be—because even now, when you haven't got a scrap of make-up on, and your hair is going frizzy again, and God alone knows what rubbish dump you got that T-shirt out of, I just want to hold you and never, *never* let you go again. Why do you suppose that is?'

She fingered a corner of the rug and wouldn't look at him.

'It was just novelty. Kindness. Something like that.'

Rico said a word in Italian. She didn't know what it meant, but she could tell it wasn't one she wanted Ben to copy.

'It was love. Do you know how I know? Because when I heard my father telling me my marriage was void I wanted to hit him. Pulverise him.'

'He was trying to manipulate you. No wonder you were angry.'

'He was trying to take me away from you. And I wasn't going to let him.'

'He was trying to take you away from Ben.'

'Ben, yes—and *you*. Stop trying to tell me I don't love you, Signora Ceraldi.' He shook his head again, and only the glint in his eyes told her his jibe was not cruel. 'What a low opinion you have of me. The Playboy Prince—that's all you think of me, isn't it? Admit it.'

She could find no humour in it. 'You can't give up your birthright.' Her voice was low, and vehement. 'You can't.'

'I can and I have. Like I said, it's a done deal. It was a done deal the moment my self-righteous brother informed me what the penalty for my crime was. It took a while,' he said grimly, 'to convince Luca and my father that I was serious in the answer I gave them. That there was no way on God's earth that I would repudiate you and agree to void our marriage—and to hell with their damn laws. But finally they washed their hands of me. I've signed God knows how many documents my father had drawn up, and now, finally, I've been able to come to you.'

She shook her head urgently, violently.

'No. I won't let you. I won't let you do this, Rico. *Please* go back. Go back before it's too late. You can get your title restored, be reinstated, go back on the Civil List, unfreeze your San Lucenzan assets—'

But he only laughed, lounging back on the rug, propped up on one elbow. 'Yes, definitely a venal woman, Signora Ceraldi.' He gave an extravagant sigh. 'I'm only good enough for you when I'm a royal, and I'm only good enough for you when I've got my fingers in the San Lucenzan royal coffers.'

He shook his head sorrowfully. 'My sweet little gold-digger—don't you realise that since I turned eighteen it has been my life-long ambition never to be strung up by the family financial umbilical cord? I know you think I'm just a mindless Playboy Prince, but I haven't spent my youth simply philandering and racing powerboats and the like. I've made investments, taken financial interests in various ventures, played the stock markets. I may not be worth quite what I was before I quit San Lucenzo, but we can jog along quite comfortably, I promise you. We may even—' his eyes glinted again, making weakness wash through her '—run to buying that villa in Capo d'Angeli. Would you like that? But let's keep your cottage here. We'll do it up properly. Put central heating in. I'd like to spend time here. The surf looks good.'

Her hands twisted in her lap.

'The water's far too cold for you here.'

He took her hands and untwisted them. 'Then I look forward to you warming me up afterwards. Will you do that, hmm?' The glint turned into a gleam. The weakness washed through her again.

Then he was smoothing the fingers of her hands—softly, sensuously.

'Too many days without you,' he was murmuring. 'Too many nights. What a lot we have to make up for.'

She took a deep breath. Looked him right in the eyes. Those dark, beautiful, long-lashed eyes.

'Rico, don't do this. Please don't do this. I can't bear it.'

The long sooty lashes swept down over his eyes, then back up again.

'And I can't bear not to. It's as simple as that.'

For one long, endless moment he just looked into her eyes, her face, searching for her—finding her.

A little hand was tugging at him. With a lithe, fluid movement Rico jackknifed up to a sitting position.

'What's up, Ben?' he said smilingly.

'Tio Rico,' asked Ben speculatively, 'did you remember to bring the fort we made?'

It took Ben a long time to settle for bed that night. He bounced around in a state of over-excitement, until finally he could fight sleep no more. Carefully, Rico made his way down the narrow, creaking stairs, ducking his head under the low lintel. The door to the kitchen was open, and she was sitting there, a mug of tea in her cupped hands, staring sightlessly.

How long would it take her to believe? he wondered. Believe that he knew exactly what he was doing, regretted nothing. And would never regret.

He walked in, and her eyes flew to him instantly, unswervingly. And he saw in them such a blaze that it took his breath away.

Where had it come from, this love he felt for her? He didn't know. It had just arrived, that was all. Some time when he wasn't paying attention. When he was just being with her. With Ben.

My family, he thought. That's who they are. My wife and my boy. My son. I'll be the father he couldn't have. I'll take care of him. So simple. So easy. It had been no choice at all.

'Asleep,' he announced. 'Finally.'

'He's excited,' she said. While he'd been settling Ben she'd tried to do something with her appearance, he could tell. She'd put some make-up on, styled her hair. She looked good. Not as glossy, not as stunning as she had when she'd gone for the full works, but good. Definitely good.

The strange thing was, he didn't care.

I love her stunning, I love her plain.

Because I just love—her.

He sat himself down on the table, just by her.

'There's still time to change your mind. You could still go back.'

He smiled. It was a strange smile. Filled with humour, with resignation, with understanding.

'I'm here for good, Lizzy. You've just got to accept it.'

'I can't. That's what I can't do. Rico, it was just a dream—an enchantment. I was Cinderella at the ball, dancing with the Prince. Sleeping Beauty being woken by the Prince's kiss. Fairytales. That's all.'

He looked down at her. 'Has it never occurred to you that the Prince in the fairytale might like a fairytale of his own? One where he gets to quit being a prince all the time? Do you know—' his voice changed, his expression changed '—that you are the only person in my entire life to look at me and see me? Not a prince. Me.'

A look of confusion passed over her face. He gave a rueful smile. 'You don't remember, do you? But I do. I stood in this very cottage and told you we had to run from the paparazzi. And you kept saying why? Why did we have to run? Because you hadn't the faintest idea who I was. Not a clue. You just saw some man bossing you about for no good reason. Not a prince. Not the Playboy Prince. Not the spare Prince to understudy the Crown Prince. Just some man who was trying to boss you about. And even when you knew I was a prince you never really knew how to behave with me, did you? You never called me Highness, or Sir, or anything. The whole royalty thing just…passed you by.'

She still looked troubled, her hands tightening around her mug. 'It doesn't matter what I thought. Rico, you've been royal all your life—'

'And much good it's done me,' he interrupted her. 'Listen, Lizzy—I'm a lot like you.' His eyes were serious, holding hers intently. 'Like you, all my life I've been—unnecessary. Just as you were. To your parents, only your sister was important. To mine, only the heir was important. The spare was just that—spare. Only with Paolo did they ever seem to realise they had a son—not a ruling prince-in-waiting. They lavished on Paolo the love they weren't able to lavish on Luca and me. I don't know what screwed your parents up—because they *were* screwed up, Lizzy, badly, and they'd done an ace job of screwing you up too, until I got you out of that box they'd nailed you into—but I know what screwed mine up: being royal. I did a lot of thinking when I was put under house arrest by my own father, and it always came back to that. Maybe it's different for Luca—he has, after all, something to do, something to look forward to doing. But me—well, I never had anything useful to do. I represented my father or Luca from time to time, attended a few Great Council meetings, signed a few state papers when my father was ill and Luca abroad. But I was never really needed.'

He touched the side of her cheek with a finger.

'You and Ben are the first people that ever needed me,' he said. 'Just like Ben was the first person ever to need *you*, Lizzy. He gave your life meaning and purpose. And that's what you and he do for me. Give my life meaning and purpose. That's why,' he said very softly, his eyes darkening, 'we belong together.'

She was silent. She couldn't say anything. But her eyes slipped away from him. In her chest a hard, heavy lump was forming.

'What is it?' he asked, in that same quiet voice.

The lump hardened, and speaking over it was painful, impossible. But she made herself do it.

'You're offering me a life I can't accept.'

He frowned. 'Why can't you accept it?' he asked, his voice still low.

She swallowed. The lump did not go away.

'Because I shouldn't have it,' she said. 'Because it should be Maria's life. She was the one a prince fell in love with. She was the one who should have been a princess. She was the one Ben should have belonged to. Not me. *Not me.* I took Ben from her. I told the doctors to turn off her life support after Ben had been delivered, after he had grown to term inside a mother whose brain had died weeks earlier. I told them to kill my sister so I could have her baby for myself.'

Huge, anguished eyes looked at him. Her fingers were pressed so tight around the mug they showed white all the way through.

'I told them to do it.'

Carefully he got to his feet. Carefully he hunkered down beside her, placing a hand, warm and strong, on her thigh.

'There was no one else to tell them,' he said. 'Your parents had made their decision. They had gone, taken their way out, leaving *you* with that decision. Making *you* the scapegoat for that decision. They didn't even have the courage, the *love* to stay alive for their grandson's sake. Let alone for yours. And tell me something, Lizzy—tell me from your heart. Do you think your sister would have wanted to live on, in body only, while Paolo was already dead? Their deaths were a tragedy—each and every death that night a tragedy. But *we* are *not* responsible. All we can do is go on with our own lives—and remember theirs. So let's take Ben, you and me, and bring him up in a happy family. We can't change the past—but we can make the future. Together, Lizzy. *Together.*'

He reached and wrapped his arms around her, very close. Slowly she let go of the mug. Slowly she slid her arms around him, burying her face in his shoulder.

'Be happy, Lizzy. Let yourself be happy. With me. For now, and for all our lives together. Life isn't certain—we both know that. So more than anything we must live while we can—for Ben and for each other. And perhaps...' His hand slid across her stomach, warm and seeking. 'Perhaps for one or two more. Ben needs a family—brothers and sisters. Happy and loving, all together.'

He drew her to her feet. Kissed her softly. Then not so softly.

As he drew back she saw the glint deep in his dark, lambent eyes. She felt her heart turn over. The glint turned to a gleam. The gleam to a look that melted her bones.

'Come, Signora Ceraldi, time for bed. I want to find out whether it was just my title you fell for.'

Her arms went around him. Holding him tight, so very tight. Close against her.

'Prince of my heart,' she whispered. 'Love of my life. My adored, beloved husband.'

'Sounds good,' he said. 'Sounds very good.'
He kissed her once more, and then again.
And then he led her upstairs, to the bliss that awaited them.

EPILOGUE

THE photos that Jean-Paul had taken at the villa went round the world. So did the story of *The Playboy Prince Who Gave Up His Title For Love*.

And so, too, did the next set of photos that Jean-Paul came to take.

The ones of Signor and Signora Enrico Ceraldi, with Master Benedetto Ceraldi, posing in the gardens of their two favourite residences—the newly christened Villa Elisabetta on the exclusive Capo d'Angeli estate in Italy, and the newly restored slate-roofed Cornish cottage, against whose porch leant two surfboards. One fast and mean for Signor Ceraldi, and a junior-sized one for Master Benedetto. Signora Ceraldi's surfboard was in storage, awaiting such time as Master Benedetto's new brother or sister made his expected appearance—which, as could clearly be seen from the especially voluptuous figure of Signora Ceraldi, around which Signor Ceraldi was curving a lovingly protective hand, would not be long.

As for Master Benedetto, he was sitting cross-legged on the grass and attacking a heavily defended cardboard fort with an army of brightly coloured knights in armour. His smile was almost bigger than his face.

The smile of a happy child with a happy family.

The greatest gift of all.

Crowned: An Ordinary Girl

NATASHA OAKLEY

Natasha Oakley told everyone at her primary school she wanted to be an author when she grew up. Her plan was to stay at home and have her mum bring her coffee at regular intervals – a drink she didn't like then. The coffee addiction became reality and the love of storytelling stayed with her. A professional actress, Natasha began writing when her fifth child started to sleep through the night. Born in London, she now lives in Bedfordshire with her husband and young family. When not writing, or needed for 'crowd control', she loves to escape to antiques fairs and auctions. Find out more about Natasha and her books on her website www. natashaoakley.com

CHAPTER ONE

'You're reading Chekhov. Have you read any Tolstoy?'

Dr Marianne Chambers hesitated midway through the second paragraph of the paper she was proofreading. A small frown pulled at the centre of her forehead as she recognised the uncanny echo of a long-ago conversation.

It had to be impossible. Why would *he* be at the Cowper Hotel during an academic conference? She was being completely ridiculous.

But…

The memory of that sunny afternoon tugged at her and her frown deepened. It was the same upper-class English accent, with the same hint of something indefinably 'foreign' about it.

And *exactly* the same words.

Marianne remembered them verbatim. In fact, she remembered every single blasted thing Seb Rodier had ever said to her—from the first moment he'd seen her reading Chekhov on the steps of Amiens Cathedral.

A shadow fell across her page and the voice behind her continued. 'Or Thomas Hardy? Now, he can be really depressing, but if you like that kind of thing…'

Dear God, no.

Marianne's head whipped round to look directly up into a

calmly smiling face. Older, more determined maybe, but still the face of the man who'd completely derailed her life.

Back then he'd worn old jeans and a comfortable T-shirt, seemingly an exchange student like herself. Now he stood there in a designer suit and smelt of seriously old money.

There was no surprise in that. She must have seen several hundred newspaper photographs of Prince Sebastian II over the years, but not one of them had prepared her for the overwhelming sense of...*yearning* she felt as she met his dark eyes.

'Hello, Marianne,' he said softly.

Seb!

His name imploded in her head, while every single moment she'd spent with him all those summers before came whizzing back into high-definition clarity.

Every dream.

Every heartbreak.

In the space of a millisecond she felt as though she'd been sucked back in time. Just eighteen years old. A long way from home and living with a family she barely knew. She'd been so scared, so very scared. Waiting for him. Hoping for a telephone call...

Anything.

Wanting to understand what was happening. Wanting him. Desperately wanting *him*.

She'd wondered how this moment might feel. Not that she'd ever anticipated she'd find out. He'd left...and their paths had never crossed again.

And why would they? Lowly paid academics didn't often run into members of the aristocracy, let alone an honest-to-goodness blue blooded royal.

'Seb?' It was difficult to force the words past the blockage in her throat. 'Sh-should I call you that? Or is it Your Highness? Or...Your Royal Highness? I don't know what

I—' Marianne reached up a hand to brush at the sharp pain stabbing in her forehead.

He moved closer and spoke quietly. 'Your Serene Highness, but Seb will do. It's good to see you. How have you been?'

Somewhere in the background Marianne could hear the sound of laughter and the clink of teaspoons on china. Incongruous sounds of normality as everything around her started to spin.

'Fine. I've been fine,' she lied. 'And you?'

'Fine.' Seb moved round to stand in front of her. 'It's been a very long time.'

'Yes.'

He paused, his brown eyes seeming to melt her body from the toes up. 'You look amazing. Really amazing.'

'Th-thank you. So do you.' *Damn!* 'I mean…you look…' She trailed off, uncertain of anything—except that she really couldn't do this. Whatever *this* was.

'May I sit beside you?'

No!

What was he *doing*? They weren't merely friends who'd happened to bump into each other. Far from it. She might not have much experience of meeting 'old' lovers, but surely you didn't sit there making conversation as though you didn't know exactly what the other looked like naked?

Marianne shuffled the typed sheets back into her file. 'Can I stop you?' Her eyes flicked to the two grey-suited men standing a respectful distance away in the otherwise deserted foyer. Bodyguards, she supposed. 'I imagine Tweedle Dum and Tweedle Dee make it their business to see you get what you want.'

'Georg and Karl.'

'You give them names?'

His mouth quirked into a smile. 'Actually, no. In Andovaria

we still consider the naming of children to be entirely the prerogative of the respective parents.'

He sat beside her as blithely as if the last ten years hadn't happened. 'Unlike Denmark, where the queen needs to give permission for the use of any name not on the approved list.'

'How forward-thinking of you.'

'We like to think so.'

Marianne gave her head a little shake as though it would somehow bring the planets back into alignment. He said the name of his country as easily as if he'd never lied to her. He seemed to take it for granted she'd know it now and there was nothing to be gained by pretending she didn't.

His photograph was beamed all over the world. Every hair-dresser in the country probably had a magazine with his picture in it. She'd seen him skiing, mountain walking, standing on the steps of Poltenbrunn Castle, at assorted royal weddings…including his own.

She even remembered the name of the girl he'd married—and divorced, although they'd called it an annulment. Amelie. Amelie of Saxe-Broden. Everything about that wedding seemed to have attracted the attention of the world's media and she'd not been able to shut it out.

If she'd needed any other impetus to get on with her life, that had been it.

Marianne drew a deep breath. 'So, what brings you to England? Is there some royal event I missed hearing about?'

He shook his head. 'No, this is an entirely private visit.'

'How lovely.' The sarcastic edge to her voice shocked her. *What was happening?* She felt like a piece of fabric that had started to fray. Marianne bent to put her file into her briefcase as sudden hot tears—part anger, part sadness—stung the back of her eyes.

She *mustn't cry. Damn it!* She'd done more than enough

of that. It was as though seeing him again had pierced a hole in the dam she'd built to protect her from all the emotions of that time.

Marianne pulled her briefcase onto her knee and concentrated on fastening the clasp. 'Are you travelling incognito this time?' She spared him a glance. 'I suppose the men in grey,' she said, looking at Georg and Karl, 'might curb the possibilities a bit.'

Seb's already dark eyes took on a deeper hue. 'You're still angry with me.'

Something inside her snapped. 'Just what exactly did you think I'd be?'

'I suppose…' Seb twisted the ring on his right hand and glanced over his shoulder as though to make sure the foyer was still empty of anyone who might be listening. 'I suppose I hoped—'

'You hoped. What? That I'd somehow have forgotten you walked off into the night and didn't bother to contact me? Th-that you lied to me? Funnily enough, Seb, that kind of thing tends to stay with you.'

'I—'

She cut him off. 'Lovely though this has been, I'm afraid I've got to go. I've got an incredibly busy morning and—' she stood up and Seb stood with her '—I need to gather my thoughts.'

'Marianne, I—'

'Don't!' She adjusted her grip on the handle of her briefcase. 'D-don't you dare. It's a full decade since I've been remotely interested in anything you have to say.'

'I didn't lie to you.'

About to walk away, Marianne froze. *How dared he?* How *dared* he stand there and say that—to *her?* For a moment she was too dumbfounded to answer.

Then, on a burst of anger, 'Really? Somehow I must have misheard you telling me you were Andovarian royalty. How can I have got it that muddled? Stupid, stupid me!'

His face reacted as though she'd slapped him. Strangely that didn't feel as fantastic as she'd thought it would, but she continued relentlessly, 'And to think I've just spent years of my life thinking what a complete waster you are.'

Seb stood a little straighter. 'I admit I didn't tell you I was the crown prince—'

'No, you didn't!'

'—but there were reasons for that.'

Marianne almost snorted with contempt. It hadn't taken much introspection, even at eighteen, for her to work that out for herself. Faced with the discovery *her* Seb Rodier was about to be enthroned as his country's ruler, she'd made a good guess at what those reasons might be.

Only she didn't share his belief they were justifiable. Ever. No one had the right to treat someone as he had her. Crown prince or not.

'Rodier is my family name. I didn't lie to you about that and I—'

'Of course, that makes all the difference,' she said silkily, still keeping her voice low. 'You knew I'd no idea who you were and you deliberately omitted telling me. I didn't even know you weren't Austrian. I'd never even heard of Andovaria. *You* certainly never mentioned it and I dare say you made sure Nick didn't either.'

'I never told you I was Austrian.'

'You said you lived a short drive from Vienna.'

'Which is true. I...'

Marianne closed her eyes. This was a childish and point-less conversation—and she'd reached the end of what she could cope with. She held up her free hand as though it had the power to ward off anything else he might say. 'Honestly, I don't care any more if your real name is Ambrose Bucket and you live in the vicinity of Saturn. It wouldn't change anything. You *did* lie to me—and I *don't* forgive you.' She would *never* forgive him as long as she had breath in her body.

'Marianne—'

'No!' *No more.* Her one coherent thought was that she needed to escape. Anywhere—as long as it put enough distance between herself and His Serene *bloody* Highness.

She kept her back straight and one foot moving in front of the other. She needed air and she needed it now. Marianne headed straight for the wide double doors and practically ran down the shallow steps.

Seb. Seb Rodier. Even though she knew he was the ruling prince of a wealthy alpine principality she couldn't think of him that way. To her this Seb was merely an older version of the nineteen-year-old language student she'd met in Amiens. The one she'd eaten crêpes with, walked beside the River Seine with and, *damn it,* loved.

Marianne bit down so hard on her bottom lip she drew blood. *Oh, God.* Not swearing, praying. She just wanted the memories to stop flooding through her.

Her feet slowed because they had no choice. London traffic blocked her way and the coffee shop she wanted was on the other side of the road.

And *why* was she running anyway? Experience had taught her that there was nowhere to go that would stop the pain from jogging alongside. More slowly she crossed the road, dodging between the stationary taxis that were banked up at the junction.

Coffee. That was all she wanted right now. Coffee and a moment to gather herself together. She smiled grimly. Just enough time to place the mask firmly back in place.

Seb let out his breath in one slow, steady stream, resisting the temptation to swear long and hard, as he watched Marianne walk away.

That could have gone better. It had been a long, long time since anyone had made him look, or feel, quite so foolish. How many sentences had he managed to complete at the end there? Two? Maybe three?

For a man who was famed for his ability to say the right thing in any social situation, that was unprecedented. As unprecedented as it was for anyone to speak to him without the due deference his position demanded. Thank heaven the foyer was deserted of everyone but his own people.

Seb looked over his shoulder at his two bodyguards. 'How much of that did you hear?'

He saw Karl's lips twitch. In any other man the expression would have counted as impassive, but in Karl it was laughter.

Seb ran an exasperated hand through his closely cropped dark hair. 'Try and forget it,' he said, walking past them and further into the narrow reception area.

It was an unnecessary instruction. Karl and Georg would never divulge anything about his personal life—not to the Press, not even to other members of their team. He'd do better to direct that selfsame instruction at himself—try and forget it. Concentrate on what had brought him here.

But forget *her*?

He pulled a wry smile. Now, that was easier said than done. If merely reading the name Marianne Chambers in print had pulled him up short, it was nothing compared to how it had felt to actually see her.

Until that moment he hadn't truly believed Professor Blackwell's protégée would turn out to be the language student he'd met in France—but she'd been instantly recognisable. Casually dressed in blue jeans and white T-shirt she'd reminded him so much of the eighteen-year-old he'd known. He could never have expected that.

And she'd been reading. Something had snapped inside him when he'd seen the flash of white as she'd flicked over the page. She'd always been reading. Anything and everything. Even that first time—when Nick had tried so hard to stop him going to speak to her.

It was the only excuse he'd had for approaching her. If there'd been anyone within earshot… Seb pulled a hand through his hair. God only knew what the headlines would have looked like then.

'Your Serene Highness—'

Seb turned to see an agitated man scurrying towards him across the acres of rather dated carpet in the company of his private secretary.

'—we'd no idea you'd arrived yet. I'd intended to have someone on watch for you and—'

'It's of no consequence. Mr…?'

'Baverstock. Anthony Baverstock. I'm the manager here, Your Serene Highness.'

'Baverstock,' Seb repeated, extending his hand. 'I sincerely appreciate the thought.' He watched the pleased way Anthony Baverstock puffed out his cheeks and resigned himself to what experience had taught him would follow.

'N-not at all, Your Serene Highness. At the Cowper Hotel we pride ourselves on our service. Professor Blackwell,' the hotel manager continued with every indication that he would bore his friends and neighbours with his account of meeting royalty for the next thirty years, 'is in the Balcony Room. If, Your Serene Highness, would be so good as to follow me…'

Seb let his mind wander even while his mouth said everything that his late father would have wished. How many times had that amazing man cautioned him to remember that people who met him would remember the occasion as long as they lived?

It was true, too. The letters of condolence his mother had received had been testament to that. More than several hundred had begun with 'I met Prince Franz-Josef and he shook me by the hand…'

Even eight years and as many months into his own tenure that responsibility still sat uncomfortably with him. But training was everything—and this had been his destiny since the hour of his birth. Inescapable. Even though there'd been times when he'd have gladly passed the responsibility to someone else.

Viktoria, for example. His elder sister had always found her role in this colourful pageant easier to play. She loved the pomp and the sense of tradition. It suited her—and she was as comfortable with it as it chafed him.

The Balcony Room on the first floor was clearly labelled. A black plaque with gold lettering hung on the door. Seb stood back and allowed the hotel manager to announce portentously, 'His Serene Highness, the Prince of Andovaria.'

Inside, the man he'd come to see was on his feet immediately. 'Your Serene Highness…'

Seb extended his hand as he walked into the room. 'Professor Blackwell, I'm delighted you could spare me a moment of your time. I realise this is a busy time for you.'

The older man shook his head, a twinkle of pure enthusiasm lighting the eyes behind his glasses. 'Completely enjoyable. This conference is one of the highlights of my year.'

'May I introduce my private secretary, Alois von Dietrich? I believe you've spoken.'

The professor nodded. 'Please, come and sit down,' he said, indicating a group of four armchairs by the window, 'but I meant what I said yesterday. I'm retiring at the end of the month.'

Seb smiled. 'I'm here in person to tempt you away from that decision.'

'Don't believe I'm not tempted,' the professor said with a shake of his head, and his tone was so wistful that Seb was confident of success. 'The twelfth and thirteenth centuries are my particular passion. My wife would have it it's an unhealthy obsession.'

'Which is exactly why I want you to come to Andovaria.'

Marianne sat down in the nearest armchair and tucked her hair behind her ears in the nervous gesture she'd had since childhood.

'Why didn't you tell me?'

Professor Blackwell shook his head. 'I've scarcely had a chance,' he said, sitting opposite her, teacup in hand. 'I spoke to one of his aides late yesterday afternoon and Prince Sebastian in person this morning.

She frowned. 'And you're considering it? Going to Andovaria?'

'Who wouldn't?' The professor picked up the shortbread biscuit resting in his saucer. 'I know what you're thinking, Marianne, and you're right. Of course you're right. But it's the chance of a lifetime. If the prince's description is accurate, and there's no reason to suppose it isn't, there's not been anything like it in decades.'

Marianne sat in silence, more than a little shell-shocked, while the professor drank the last of his tea.

'Imagine for a moment what we might find there,' he said, standing up and putting his cup and saucer back on the table.

'You're weeks from retiring,' she said softly. 'You did tell him that, didn't you?'

'Eliana will understand—'

'She won't, Peter. You and I both know that if your wife had had her way you'd be retired now.'

The professor sat down again and leant forward to take hold of her hands. 'This is the "big" one, Marianne. I've waited my whole life for something like this.'

His earnest, lined face shone with the absolute certainty she'd understand, and the tragedy was, she did. Marianne understood absolutely how much he'd want this—and how completely impossible it was for him to take it.

'Have you told him about your eyesight?' she asked gently.

The professor let go of her hands and sat back in his seat.

She hated to do this to him, hated it particularly because he was the most wonderful, brilliant and caring man she'd ever met, but it was an impossible dream. He had to know that— deep down. 'You can't see well enough to do this justice and, if it's as significant as you think it is, you ought to pass it on to another expert. I can think of upward of a dozen who are eminently qualified, half a dozen I'd be happy with.'

He shook his head. 'We could do it together. I've told him I'd need to bring a colleague—'

'I'm too junior,' Marianne objected firmly. 'I've got years of study ahead of me before I'd be ready to take on something like this.'

'You could be my eyes. You've a sharp, analytical mind and we're a great team.' The professor stood up abruptly and brushed the crumbs off his tie. 'Let's not discuss it any more until after dinner tonight. There's plenty of time before I have to give him my final decision.'

After what dinner? Her mind went into spasm and the question in her head didn't make words as the professor adjusted his reactor light glasses and continued, 'You and I can talk about it after we've seen the photographs. There is a stack of them apparently and I'll need you there to take a look at them.'

'Wh-what dinner?'

'Didn't I say?' His assumed nonchalance would have been

comical if the stakes weren't so high. 'Prince Sebastian has invited us to dinner at the Randall. At eight,' he added as Marianne still hadn't spoken.

Her mind was thinking in short bursts. *Dinner with Sebastian. Tonight. At Eight.*

'Us?'

'Of course, us.' The professor sounded uncharacteristically tetchy. 'I told him I'd need to discuss the offer with my colleague and he, very graciously, extended the invitation to you.'

Marianne swallowed as a new concern slid into her befuddled mind. 'You've told him you're bringing me? B-by name? He knows it'll be me?'

The professor made a tutting sound as though he couldn't understand why her conversation had become so unintelligible. 'I can't remember what I said exactly—but why should that matter? Prince Sebastian wants me, and whatever team I care to assemble. I chose you.'

At any other time his confidence in her ability would have warmed her, but…

The professor didn't understand what he was asking—and, after ten years of keeping it a secret from him, she'd no intention of telling him now. But…

Dinner with Seb.

Who might not even know she was Professor Blackwell's colleague?

'We look at the photographs, we eat his food and then we take a taxi back here.' The Professor smiled the smile of an impish child. 'After that, we'll talk about it.'

CHAPTER TWO

THE new dress wasn't working.

Marianne stared at her reflection and at the soft folds of pink silk which draped around her curves to finish demurely in handkerchief points at her ankles. On the outside the transformation from serious academic to sophisticated lady-about-town was staggering, but on the inside, where it mattered, Marianne felt as if she was about to take a trip in a tumbrel.

What was she doing? There was no way she should have allowed Peter to talk her into this dinner. No way at all. Yet, even while every rational thought in her head had been prompting her to get herself back on the train home to Cambridge, she'd found herself in Harvey Nic's, picking out a dress.

And why? She was too honest a person not to know that on some level or other it was because she wanted Seb to take one look at her and experience a profound sense of regret.

Stupid! So stupid! What part of her brain had decreed that a bright idea? She'd squandered a good chunk of her 'kitchen fund' on a daft dress to impress a man who only had to snap his fingers to induce model-type beauties to run from all directions.

It was far, far more likely he'd take one look at her and know she'd made all this effort to impress him. And how pitiful would that look?

Marianne turned away from the mirror and walked over to the utilitarian bedside table common to all the hotel's rooms. She sat on the side of the bed and roughly pulled open the drawer, picking up the only thing inside it—a heart-shaped locket in white gold. Her hand closed round it and she took a steadying breath.

Heaven help her, she *was* going to go with Peter tonight. The decision had been made. She might as well accept that. And she was going to pretend she was fine.

More than that, she was going to pretend she'd forgotten almost everything about Seb Rodier. He'd been a minor blip in her life. Quickly recovered from…

'Marianne?'

There was a discreet knock on the door and Marianne quickly replaced the locket, shutting the drawer and moving to pick up her co-ordinating handbag and fine wool wrap from the end of the bed.

The deep pink of the wrap picked out the darkest shade in the silk of her dress, while the bag exactly matched her wickedly expensive sandals. That they also pinched the little toe on her right foot would serve as an excellent reminder of her own stupidity.

'You look very lovely,' the professor said by way of greeting. 'Not that you don't always, but I spoke to Eliana just over half an hour ago and she was worried you wouldn't have brought anything with you that would be suitable for dinner at the Randall. I said I was sure you'd manage something.'

Marianne gave a half-smile and wondered how it was possible that a fearsomely intelligent man like the professor, who'd been happily married for forty-one years, could believe she'd have a dress like this rolled up in her suitcase 'just in case'.

'I'm excited about this dinner,' he said, completely oblivious to her mood. 'Of course, what the prince is asking would mean I'd have to give up all of the projects I'm currently involved with.'

She reached out and pressed the lift button. 'You're retiring, Peter. You're supposed to be taking the opportunity to spend more time with your grandchildren...'

The professor shot her a smile and pulled out a folded piece of paper from the pocket of his dinner jacket. 'I spoke to one of Prince Sebastian's aides this afternoon about what's expected of us tonight with regard to royal protocol and the like. It all seems fairly straightforward,' he said, passing across the sheet. 'Apparently the prince is not one to stand on too much ceremony, thank God.'

A cold sensation washed over Marianne as she unfolded the paper. This was an aspect of the evening ahead of her she hadn't considered. If Seb thought she was going to curtsey he could go take a running jump.

'I think I've got it straight in my mind,' the professor continued, reaching out to hold the bar as the lift juddered to a stop. 'When we first meet him we address him as 'Your Serene Highness', but after that we can use a simple "sir".'

Marianne's eyes widened slightly. *Sir? Call Seb 'sir'?* How *exactly* did you look a man you'd slept with in the eye and call him 'sir'? Particularly when you wanted to call him a million other things that would probably have you arrested?

The doors swung open and the professor continued, 'Jolly good thing, too. Can you imagine how ridiculous it would be to have to say "Your Serene Highness" all evening? Such a mouthful.'

Her eyes skimmed the first couple of points.

—Wait for the prince to extend his hand in greeting.
—Don't initiate conversation, but wait for the prince to do so.

'It must irritate the heck out of him to have people spouting his title at him every time he steps out of doors.' The professor broke off to hail a passing black taxi. 'Not to mention having everyone you meet bob up and down in front of you like some kind of manic toy.'

Marianne's eyes searched for the word *'curtsey'*. 'Sir' she could just about cope with—particularly if she said it in a faintly mocking tone—but curtseying to him? He'd humiliated her in practically every way possible, but that would be too much to cope with. There had to be a way round it.

Hadn't she read something somewhere about Americans not having to curtsey when they met British royalty? Something about it not being their monarch that made it an unnecessary mark of respect?

The taxi swung towards the kerb.

'And an inclination of the head when I meet him is all that's required. No need for a more formal bow,' the professor continued. 'Obviously removing any hat—'

Marianne watched as he struggled with the door before holding it open for her '—but, as I'm not wearing a hat, that's not a problem.'

She gathered up the soft folds of her dress so that it wouldn't brush along the edge of the car and climbed inside. Seb wasn't *her* monarch. If he wasn't her monarch, she didn't need to curtsey...

Moments later the professor joined her. 'Of course, as a woman, you give a slight curtsey. Nothing too flourishing. Keep it simple.'

Keep it simple. The words echoed in her head. There was nothing about this situation that was simple. She was in a taxi heading towards a former lover who may or may not know she was joining him for dinner tonight. A former lover, mark you, who hadn't had the courtesy to formally end their relationship.

'Blasted seat belts,' the professor said, trying to fasten it across him. 'They make the things so darn fiddly.'

Marianne blinked hard against the prickle of tears. She wasn't sure whether they were for her and her own frustration, or for the professor and his.

The one thing she was certain of was that they shouldn't be here. Why couldn't Peter see how pointless it was? He shouldn't even be entertaining the idea of going to Andovaria. Even a simple task like fastening a seat belt was difficult for him now.

'Done it,' the professor said, sitting back in his seat more comfortably.

She turned away and looked out of the window. *Age-related macular degeneration.* It had come on so suddenly, beginning with a slight blurriness and ending with no central vision at all. Sooner or later people would notice Peter couldn't proofread his own material.

And if he couldn't cope with something in a clear typeface, how did he imagine he was going to do justice to something written in archaic German and eight hundred years old? He'd miss something vital—and the academic world he loved so much would swoop in for the kill.

It was all such a complete mess.

Familiar landmarks whizzed past as the driver unerringly took them down side-roads and round a complicated one-way system.

The taxi slowed and pulled to a stop. 'Here we are. The Randall.'

Marianne looked up at one of London's most prestigious hotels and felt…intimidated.

All she had to do was look at the photographs, eat and leave. She could do that.

Of course she could do that. This was a business meeting. There was nothing personal about it.

Marianne's eyes followed the tier upon tier of windows, familiar from the countless postcards produced for tourists.

And this was where Seb, the real Seb, stayed when he was in London. In France they'd booked a room in whatever inexpensive *chambre d'hôte* they'd happened upon and sat on grass verges to eat warm baguettes they'd bought from the local *boulangerie.* So different.

'That'll be £16.70, love,' the driver said, turning in his seat to look through the connecting glass.

Marianne jerked round and her fingers fumbled for the zip of her purse. 'P-please keep the change,' she said, pulling out a twenty-pound note.

It was only later, when she'd carefully tucked away the receipt in the side-pocket of her handbag and was standing on the pavement, that it occurred to her she should have let Peter settle the fare himself. She was so used to stepping in to do the tasks she knew he found difficult that it hadn't occurred to her that she ought to let him fail this time. Perhaps that might have shown him how impossible a proposition this was?

'This is something, isn't it?' the professor said gleefully, gesturing towards sleek BMWs that were so perfectly black they looked as if they'd been dipped in ink.

Marianne managed a smile as men in distinctive livery opened every door between the pavement and the imposing entrance hall. From there on it got worse. Enormous chandeliers hung from the high ceilings and gilt bronze garlands twisted their way along endless cream walls. It was the kind of awe-inspiring space that made you want to speak in hushed whispers.

'Professor Blackwell and Dr Chambers to see His Serene Highness the Prince of Andovaria,' the professor said, pulling out a simple white card on which Seb had written something. 'In the Oakland Suite.'

Marianne half expected the slightly superior young man to raise his eyebrows in disbelief. Her dress, which had seemed so expensive just an hour ago, now didn't seem quite expensive enough. She lifted her chin in determination not to be cowed by her surroundings. She'd enough of an ordeal ahead of her without falling apart simply by stepping through the door.

'Of course, sir. This way.'

More chandeliers. More bronze garlands twisting their way up and onwards. Marianne wasn't sure which way to look first. The cream walls were punctuated with huge gilt mirrors and original oil paintings, while the fresh roses arranged on each of the antique tables looked so soft and so perfect they could have been made of velvet.

She felt…overwhelmed. By pretty much everything. Even the lift moved as though it were floating. The doors opened and they stepped out into a space no less opulent than the one below. Marianne could feel her stomach churning as though a billion angry ants had been let loose.

Seb. His name thumped inside her brain. She had to keep focusing on the fact that this man wasn't Seb. Not her Seb. He was His Serene Highness the sovereign prince of Andovaria. He had nothing, absolutely *nothing* to do with her.

After the briefest of knocks the door to the Oakland Suite swung open and they were ushered, past the bodyguards, into what was rather like a mini-apartment. And it seemed that it had its own hotel staff member to take care of it because they were passed into the care of another uniformed man, who took her wrap.

Marianne felt disorientated and more cowed with every second that passed. Her chest felt tight and her breath seemed as though it were catching on cobwebs.

'This way. His Serene Highness is expecting you.'

Double doors opened onto a tastefully furnished sitting

room. Three sets of glass doors lined one wall, each framed by heavy curtains complete with swags and tails, while to the far end there was a baby grand piano.

'Isn't this incredible?' the professor said as soon as they were alone. He walked over to the glass doors, which had been flung open to make the most of the warm weather, and peered out. 'There's even some kind of terrace out here. Just incredible. Come and have a look.'

But Marianne couldn't move. She knew with absolute certainty that if she tried to walk anywhere her knees would buckle under her. Never, in her entire life, had she felt so...scared. But not just scared. She was also confused, angry and hurting.

There was the muffled sound of voices and the soft click that indicated a door had shut.

Seb? Her eyes stayed riveted on the connecting doorway. Any moment...

Drawing on reserves she didn't know she had, Marianne consciously relaxed her shoulders and lifted her chin. Seb mustn't see how completely overwrought she was by this whole experience.

The door opened and it crossed her mind to wonder whether she was about to faint for the first time in her life.

'Professor Blackwell,' Seb said, walking forward, hand outstretched. 'I'm delighted you could join me this evening.'

She'd never seen Seb in a dinner jacket. At least, not outside of a photograph. It was an inconsequential thought—and one she ought to be ashamed of—but nothing she'd seen in the various magazines had prepared her for the effect it was having on her.

Pure sex appeal.

Several years' experience of various university dinners had left her wondering why men bothered, particularly if they went for ruffles and an over-tight cummerbund. But Seb just looked sexy.

Seeing him this morning had been dreadful, but this felt so much worse. This time shock wasn't protecting her from anything. She felt…raw.

Vulnerable.

And after everything she'd experienced she should have been completely immune to a playboy prince who'd simply decided, long ago, he didn't want her any more.

Her eyes took in every detail…because she couldn't help it. The small indentation in the centre of his chin and the faint scar above his eyebrow she knew he'd got when he was seventeen and fallen off a scooter.

And he seemed so much broader. More powerful than she remembered. Beneath his beautifully cut black jacket was a body entirely more muscled than the one she'd known so intimately. But—if she traced a finger down his left side until she reached a point two centimetres above his hip bone she would find the small oval-shaped birthmark she'd kissed….

Marianne felt a tight pain in her chest and realised she needed to let go of the air she was holding in her lungs.

This was a mistake. She wasn't strong enough to do this. She saw the professor's slight nod of the head and heard the murmured, 'Your Serene Highness, may I introduce my colleague—'

Any moment Seb would look at her. Please, God. Marianne clutched her handbag close to her body and prayed the ground would open up and swallow her whole.

'—Dr Marianne Chambers?'

Then his dark brown eyes met hers. He had beautiful, sexy eyes. Brown with flecks of deepest orange fanning out from dark black pupils.

'Your Serene Highness.' She heard her voice. Just. It was more of a croak.

But she didn't curtsey. Not so much a conscious act of defiance as the consequence of complete paralysis. She needed to tap into some of the hate she felt for him. Remember what he'd done to her. How much he'd hurt her.

'Dr Chambers.' He extended his hand and Marianne recovered enough composure to stretch out her own. 'I understand from Professor Blackwell that you're particularly knowledgeable about the Third Crusade.'

'Y-yes.' She felt his fingers close round her hand. Warm. Confident. A man in charge. 'Yes, I am.'

'Thank you for giving up your evening at such short notice.'

Seb released her hand and turned back to the professor.

Strangers. They were meeting like strangers. Everything inside of her rebelled at that. They *weren't* strangers. She wanted to scream that at him. Shout loudly. Make herself heard.

'May I introduce Dr Max Liebnitz,' Seb said smoothly, 'the curator of the Princess Elizabeth Museum?'

Marianne had barely noticed the unassuming man standing quietly behind. He moved now and shook the professor's hand. 'Delighted to meet you,' he said in heavily accented English. 'And you, Dr Chambers. I believe I may have read something of yours on the *battle of Hattin?*'

'That's possible,' Marianne murmured, conscious that Seb was standing no more than two metres away from her and could hear everything she said and everything said to her.

It was such a surreal experience. And the temptation to look at him again was immense, but she resolutely kept her focus on the professor, who'd fallen into an easy German. Her own grasp of the spoken language was less well-developed, but she knew enough to contribute to their discussion and more than enough to know Professor Blackwell had discovered a kindred spirit in Dr Leibnitz.

Seb's well-informed observations astounded her. Once, when he referred to the siege of Acre, she was surprised into looking up at him.

He'd changed. The Seb she'd known couldn't have made a comment like that. He'd been…reckless. Irresponsible. Ready for adventure. Simply younger, she supposed with a wry smile.

She tended to forget how very young she'd been herself—and how foolishly idealistic. She'd honestly believed she'd discovered her soul mate, the man she'd spend the rest of her life with, grow old with, have children with.

How foolish was that at eighteen? Marianne lifted her chin and straightened her spine. She'd paid a heavy price for her naivety, whereas Seb had recognised their relationship for what it was and survived it unscathed.

That hurt. To know that she was the only one nursing any kind of regret.

'Marianne's recent research has been particularly focused on the role of women.' The professor turned to smile at her. 'Obviously the vast bulk of primary sources available to us have been written by men—'

'And for men,' Marianne interjected, bringing her mind back into sharp focus.

Dr Leibnitz nodded. 'It must make your research particularly painstaking.'

'But fascinating,' Marianne agreed. 'Wars have always impacted on women and the Third Crusade was no different.'

Seb stood back and listened. He wasn't sure what had surprised him most—that Marianne was fluent in German or that she was so clearly respected for her opinions. Ten years ago she'd intended to pursue an English degree. So, what had made her change direction?

And the German? It was impossible not to remember the times he'd tried to instruct her in his native tongue for no other reason than he'd loved to hear the strong English accent in her appalling pronunciation. There was no trace of that any more.

Very little trace of the girl at all. This morning he'd been struck by the similarities, but this evening her ash blonde hair was swept up in a sophisticated style and her body was much more curvaceous than the image of her he held in his memory.

Still beautiful. Undeniably. Maybe more so.

And nervous. Seb wasn't sure how he knew that, but he did. There was nothing about the way Marianne was speaking that told him that. Outwardly she seemed to be a woman in control of her destiny, comfortable wherever she found herself, but…there was something. Perhaps the grip on her handbag was a little too tight? Or her back a little too straight?

She hadn't wanted to talk to him this morning—and he'd lay money on the fact she didn't want to be here tonight. He watched the soft swing of her long earrings against the fine column of her throat and he experienced a wave of…

He wasn't sure of what. Regret that he'd hurt her? Maybe that was the ache inside of him? He'd never intended to hurt her. But then he hadn't intended to do anything more than speak to her on that first day. Not much more than that on the second.

They had all four of them been travelling through France. What was more sensible than that he and Nick should join forces with Marianne and Beth? At least, that was what he'd told his friend.

He'd been such a fool. He'd had no idea of the possible consequences. But Nick had. Seb thought of his old school friend with a familiar appreciation. Nick had tried hard to persuade him to stay longer in Amiens. Had been a constant voice in his ear reminding him of what his parents would say…

Marianne's accusation this morning that he'd lied to her had startled him—and yet the more he thought about it the more ashamed he felt.

He owed her an explanation. What he lacked was the opportunity to give it. Professor Blackwell and Dr Leibnitz might be deep in conversation, but it was pushing the bounds of possibility to imagine they wouldn't be aware of what was being said in another part of the room.

Seb nodded towards the butler, who opened the double doors into the intimate dining room. The party moved through and with great skill, he thought, he encouraged the professor and Dr Leibnitz to continue their conversation uninterrupted—and that left him next to Marianne.

The butler positioned her chair behind her and she'd no choice but to accept the place. Instinct told him that she would not have if there'd been any alternative. He watched her, surreptitiously, noticing the small curl of baby-fine blonde hair that had escaped the elegant twist and had settled at the nape of her neck.

She was a very beautiful woman. And not married. She wore no rings on her left hand. In fact, she wore no jewellery—except the long, tapering earrings that swung against her neck when she spoke.

'Your German is excellent, Dr Chambers,' Seb said, forcing her to look at him.

Her eyes turned to him, startled, and the long earrings swung softly. 'Th-thank you.'

'Where did you learn it?'

The butler stepped forward and moved to fill her wine glass.

'No. Thank you. I'd prefer water.'

Seb watched the nervous flutter of her hands. 'Your German,' he persisted, 'where did you learn it? Your pronunciation is perfect.'

He saw the slight widening of her eyes and knew she was remembering the afternoon they'd spent at Monet's garden at Giverny.

She turned her head away and her earrings swung. Marianne didn't seem to notice the way they brushed her neck. 'Eliana…' She swallowed. 'Eliana, Professor Blackwell's wife, is Austrian. From Salzburg.'

Seb frowned his confusion. He didn't immediately see the connection…

'I lived with Professor Blackwell and his family when I…was younger.'

He could have sworn she'd been about to say something different. His mind played through the options. When I…finished university? When I…started work? *When I… came back from Paris?*

He wanted to know. Certainly Marianne hadn't lived with the professor's family before France. She'd lived with her parents in a village in…Suffolk.

'Eliana and Peter are close family friends of my father's sister.'

Ah. Seb's eyes flicked across to the professor, still firmly engrossed in his conversation on the finer points of twelfth-century sword design. 'And is that why you chose to study history?'

Again her soft brown eyes turned on him with a startled expression. She gave the slightest of smiles. 'His enthusiasm is infectious.'

No doubt that was true, but Seb felt that her answer was only half the story. Ten years ago she'd had ambitions to write plays that would rival Shakespeare. She'd set herself the goal of reading her way through the entire works of

Chekhov and Ibsen by the time she started university. So, what had changed?

'I imagine it is. Professor Blackwell's reputation is second to none.' Seb paused while the butler placed the beautifully presented foie gras and wild-mushroom bourdin in front of him. 'That's why my sister is adamant I must persuade him to come to Andovaria.'

'Your sister?'

'Viktoria. My eldest sister. The Princess Elizabeth Museum is in my grandmother's memory and Vik's pet project.'

Marianne's mind felt as if it was spluttering. 'Vik' would be Her Serene Highness, Princess Viktoria? Tall, elegant, married to some equally tall and well-connected title with two young sons?

She looked down at the heavily starched tablecloth, bedecked with more cutlery choices than she'd ever faced in her life, and tried to focus on what had brought her here. 'But if much of what you have beneath the palace is connected with the Teutonic knights, then surely Professor Adler would be the obvious choice?'

Seb picked up his wine glass and took a sip. 'That's true, but we believe only a small part of what we have would be of particular interest to Professor Adler.'

The first course gave way to the second. And after the breast of guinea-fowl with asparagus and bacon came the third, an artistic arrangement of dark chocolate with a praline ice cream.

Marianne took a tiny spoonful of the ice cream. Somehow Seb managed to make it sound so *reasonable* that the professor should go to Andovaria and, if it weren't for his eyesight, he *was* the perfect choice.

Her eyes flicked to the animated, kindly face of the professor opposite. Excitement was practically radiating from him. It was a tangible thing.

He wouldn't be able to resist this opportunity. Marianne knew it with complete certainty. A lifetime devoted to uncovering the secrets of the past couldn't be pushed to one side easily.

And she couldn't, *wouldn't*, leave him to flounder alone. As much as she hated the thought of going to Andovaria, she loved Peter and Eliana more. She owed them something for what they'd done for her.

More than something. Marianne took a sip of water. They'd taken her in, pregnant and scared, when her own mother had not. She owed them everything. She took another mouthful of ice cream and let her eyes wander to Seb's handsome profile. Supremely confident, charismatic and charming. He really had no idea of the fate he'd left her to.

What would Seb say if he knew he'd left her expecting their baby?

Had he ever thought to wonder what had happened to her? Or had he really returned to Andovaria and his royal responsibilities without sparing her a moment's consideration?

What kind of conversation would they be having now if little Jessica had lived?

In many ways nature had known best. It hurt her to think it, but at eighteen she'd been hopelessly ill-prepared to take on the responsibility of a child. The logical part of her brain accepted that, even while her heart probably never would. Eliana had spent hours talking her through…everything. Patiently helping her manage emotions she'd not had the life skills to even begin to deal with.

First, there'd been the pregnancy itself and her mother's inability to cope with her 'perfect' daughter's fall from grace.

And then the stillbirth. The heartbreaking scan. The long hours of labour which had resulted in a perfectly formed baby girl—born asleep, as the euphemism went.

Marianne covertly studied His Serene Highness Prince

Sebastian II. *Their* baby. She and Seb had created a little girl—and he didn't even know.

She reached out for her water glass and took a sip, carefully placing it back down on the table. Eliana believed all men had the right to know if they were about to become a father…

Sometimes she wondered…if Jessica had lived long enough to be born safely, whether she'd ever have told him. At eighteen she'd been adamant he'd never know, but that had been her hurt talking. The first photographs of the about-to-be-enthroned Prince of Andovaria with his dark-haired fiancée had been cataclysmic. Like a switch flicking inside her—love to hate in a moment.

She sat back in her chair. But…eventually she might have told him. Perhaps. When Jessica had grown old enough to decide whether she wanted the poisoned chalice of being universally known as the illegitimate daughter of a European prince—with a mother he'd not considered worth marrying.

It was an academic question. There'd been no baby past the seventh month of her pregnancy. Marianne could feel the pain now, shooting through her—as it always did whenever she was reminded of Jessica. The sense of failure. And the emptiness that pervaded everything—and had done for practically her entire adult life.

She watched as Seb reached for his wine glass. He'd no idea. No understanding of how comprehensively he'd wrecked her life. And how she'd *never* forgive him.

CHAPTER THREE

THE photographs were fascinating. Far more so than Marianne had expected.

'This is quite remarkable. Remarkable,' the professor mumbled. 'Everything completely shut away…'

'Yes,' Seb agreed, moving to stand behind him. 'Until the renovation work began on that part of the castle, no one alive knew the rooms were even there.'

Marianne's eyes instinctively followed Seb as he walked across the room, helplessly noticing the way his jacket skimmed the powerful shoulders of a man she knew had become an Olympic skier.

It was peculiar to think that she knew so much about him, whereas he knew nothing about her since he'd left her in Paris. She forced herself to look back down at the 10" x 8" photograph of a long, narrow room with row upon row of serviceable shelving filled to capacity.

'Is nothing in here catalogued?' the professor asked, pointing at the image he was holding.

'No.'

Dr Leibnitz nodded his agreement. 'So far, all we've done is make a very cursory inventory. There's been no attempt at any sort of organisation.'

'Marianne?' The professor's voice startled her. 'What do you think?'

What did she think? Marianne looked up. 'I think it's a mammoth responsibility,' she said carefully.

He nodded. 'This needs a team.'

Seb sat down in an elegant Queen Anne armchair, his attention fixed on the professor. 'What we're hoping is you'll feel able to head up that team. Handpick the people you want to work with you.'

'Why me?'

'Because you're highly respected in your field,' Seb answered, his voice deep, sexy and tugging at all kinds of memories she didn't want to remember. Certainly not now. Not with Seb sitting so close to her. Marianne swallowed the hard lump that appeared to be wedged in her throat and deliberately looked down at the photograph in her hand.

'As are many others.'

Marianne's eyes skittered away from it as Seb leant forward on his chair. She looked back down, silently cursing. Somehow she needed to bring herself under a tighter control. Every movement he made, every blasted thing he did, she seemed to notice.

'Andovaria is a small principality. Bigger than Liechtenstein or Monaco, but nowhere near the size of Austria or Switzerland. The sheer quantity of what we've found has made us think much of it might not rightly belong in Andovaria.'

'And you have a problem with that?' the professor asked quickly.

'Not at all.'

Marianne caught the edge of Seb's smile in her peripheral vision and she felt her breath catch. For years she'd wondered why she'd talked Beth into letting the boys join them—and now she knew.

'My sister's adamant that everything is kept in the way that will best preserve it for future generations.' Seb paused. 'But my primary responsibility is to Andovaria and I intend to ensure that everything that rightfully belongs to my country stays within our boundaries.'

He stood up and Marianne noticed the powerful clench of his thigh muscle. 'And the easiest way, by far, is to put someone in charge of the project who has a neutral interest in what's found.'

'My interest is far from neutral.'

Seb smiled again and the pain in her chest intensified.

'But you're not actively seeking government funding or trying to raise the profile of any one particular museum....' Seb's words hung in the air.

The odds had always been weighted in favour of going to Andovaria, Marianne knew, but now it felt like a foregone conclusion. Peter would most definitely accept. How could he not? And how could she argue against it when it was clear his eyes wouldn't be the ones evaluating every single piece, or writing every report?

Damn it!

Marianne put the photograph back down on the table. A sharp pain burst in her temple and shot down the left side of her neck. She raised a shaky hand and rubbed gently across her forehead.

Could she honestly go to Andovaria with Peter?

Maybe this was fate's way of giving her that much talked-of 'closure'? Maybe spending time in Seb's country was exactly what she needed? And all it required was courage?

Her fingers moved in concentric circles against the pain in her temple. She was aware of Dr Leibnitz speculating about what might be found beneath Poltenbrunn Castle and the professor's comments about the Habsburg dynasty and Rudolf von der Hapichtsburg in particular.

'Marianne, are you feeling all right?' the professor asked, breaking off his conversation.

Her hand stilled and she forced a smile. 'I've a slight headache. It's nothing.'

'Perhaps some air?' Dr Liebnitz suggested. 'Shall I sit with you on the terrace for a moment, Dr Chambers?'

'N-no, thank you. I'm fine. It'll pass in a moment.'

Seb stood up and the abrupt movement startled her. 'I'll keep Dr Chambers company on the terrace while you continue your conversation, Max. It's a little stuffy in here and I'd appreciate some fresh air myself.'

Panic ripped through her. 'N-no. I—'

'The terrace is very pretty,' Seb interrupted smoothly, 'with a stunning view over Green Park. Whenever I'm in London I particularly ask for this suite for that reason.'

His arm gestured towards the open glass doors and Marianne knew she had very little choice but to acquiesce with as much dignity as she could manage. 'Thank you.'

By the time she was on her feet Seb was already standing by the doors, waiting. She didn't dare look up at him as she walked out onto the terrace. A light breeze tugged at the silk of her dress, but the evening was warm enough. Almost. She gave a slight shiver, although that might have had nothing to do with the temperature outside.

'Are you cold?' he asked quickly. 'Do you have a wrap Warner could fetch for you?'

Marianne turned. 'Warner?'

'He's the butler this evening.'

'Ah.' *Warner was the butler.* She'd forgotten—the staff had names. Although Warner, it seemed, didn't warrant the use of his Christian name. So much for the equality of mankind. Marianne shook her head. 'No. Thank you.' It was nice to feel the breeze brushing against her skin. Nice to feel something other than the tight, constrained sensation in her chest.

She looked round the terrace. It was tiny, but beautifully formed—and the view was spectacular even at night. Seb was right about that. Marianne turned round and caught him watching her. His expression made her nervous and she looked away, stumbling into speech. 'Th-this is all rather…incredible,' she said, gesturing at the display of lights below them.

Seb moved closer. She could smell the light musky scent of his aftershave. *Feel* him breathing next to her.

'The terrace?' he asked quietly. 'The view? Or us being together again?'

Marianne felt her throat constrict. Her eyes turned to look at him as though she was compelled to do so. 'All of it,' she said after a moment, her voice breathy.

Silence. Then Seb smiled and it still had the ability to seduce her. *Why* was that? Other men had smiled at her with just that look in their eyes, but they'd never made her feel so light-headed.

Marianne wrapped her arms around her waist in a movement she recognised as defensive, but she didn't move away. There was a part of her that was very proud of that. 'I didn't curtsey.'

'Pardon?'

'When I arrived. I didn't curtsey to you.' For some reason it suddenly seemed so important he knew that.

A spark of laughter lit his dark eyes and he glinted down at her. 'I think we're a little past that. Certainly in private.'

'I'm not doing it in public either,' she shot back, irritated by the suspicion he was laughing at her. Marianne nervously fingered the back hook of one of her earrings. 'Did you know I was coming with the professor tonight?'

'Yes.'

She desperately wanted to ask what he'd thought about her coming. Did he find this situation as awkward as she did? But of course, that was impossible. He'd spoken to her as though they were strangers—and that was what they were. *Strangers*.

'Peter couldn't remember exactly what he'd told you. Whether I'd been a nameless colleague...'

'No.'

No. Her eyes flicked up and away again. There was some comfort in hearing that he'd invited her to join them this evening *knowing* it was her. The hum of the traffic far below filled the awkward pause. 'Oh.' And then, 'Were you surprised when he mentioned my name?'

'Very.'

She could hear something like a smile in his voice and risked another look at him. *It was a mistake.* His eyes hadn't changed. There might be fine lines fanning out at the edges now, but they were achingly familiar.

'I knew there was a slight possibility I might see you at the conference, but that Professor Blackwell would refuse to come to Andovaria without you...' His mouth twisted and he shook his head. 'No, that part surprised me. You've done exceptionally well.'

She had, but she didn't need him to tell her that. She felt as if she'd suffered the verbal equivalent of a regal pat on the head.

'He made it very clear this morning his decision on whether he'd accept or not would be made in consultation with you. It's impressive to have achieved that level of professional respect by the age of twenty-eight.'

Seb knew how old she was. He'd remembered the fifteen-month age difference between them. Marianne swallowed—and it felt a monumentally difficult thing to do. It was as though every normal function was now something that required conscious effort.

But then, Seb was standing so close. If she stretched out her hand she could touch him… If she leant in close he could hold her… It was bound to be difficult.

'So, what do you think?'

Marianne blinked hard at the tears scratching at her eyes. 'About?'

'Coming to Andovaria? Do you have a husband to keep you in England? Family?' he added when she'd yet to answer.

'No husband.'

'Boyfriend?'

Now, that was none of his business. Marianne swivelled round and schooled her features into the expression she habitually used to quash anyone who thought to question a young blonde female's ability to have opinions that ran counter to their own. 'Andovaria is only a short flight away,' she said brusquely. 'If the professor decides to accept, I'll come with him. It's a good career opportunity for me.'

'And that's important to you?'

'Of course. It's the driving force of my life.'

There was a small beat before he asked, 'What do you think the professor's thinking?'

Marianne shook her head. 'He'll let you know when he's ready.'

'And you don't have a preference?'

His question was multi-faceted—and they both knew it. She looked down, apparently fascinated by the shades of pink that swirled together on the skirt of her dress. 'I—I didn't say that.'

'Marianne—'

Her control snapped. 'Don't!' She turned away as though to go back into the sitting room.

'We need to talk.'

'Not here,' she said in almost a whisper. 'This isn't the place.'

'It's the best we have.' And then when she didn't move

away any further, 'I get the impression that Max and Professor Blackwell will hardly miss us however long we're out here.'

He saw the faint nod of her head, her earrings swinging back and forth.

'And there's no one to hear us out here.'

Marianne stood motionless for a moment as though she was deciding what to do. The breeze caught at the light fabric of her dress. And he waited, completely uncertain whether she'd turn or walk back inside.

'I suppose that's important,' she said at last, turning back to face him.

Marianne shivered again and wrapped her arms tightly around her. It hurt him to see her looking so…strained. That wasn't the way he remembered her looking at him.

'What do you want to tell me?' She rubbed at her arms.

Another shiver. 'You're cold. If we were really on our own I'd give you my jacket.'

She seemed to uncoil and a spark of anger lit her eyes. 'Well, that's just a lovely offer, Your Serene Highness.'

It took a moment for him to remember what she was remembering. *The walk in the park. The rain. The kiss.* She'd looked so incredibly sexy in his sweatshirt, the sleeves rolled over three times…

The situation had been different then. For those brief weeks he'd been free—as he hadn't been since. That summer the embargo on reporting his private life had miraculously held. There'd been no bodyguards, no responsibilities and, amazingly, no paparazzi. He'd been free to act exactly as he wished without reference to anyone or anything.

And what he'd wanted had been Marianne.

Seb broke eye contact and crossed back to the sitting room, beckoning to the butler. 'Could you find Dr Chambers something to keep her warm?'

'Very good, sir.'

'And bring us a bottle of the dry white and a couple of glasses.'
His answer was a slight nod.

'Thank you.' He turned back to Marianne, fascinated by the
pulse beating in her neck. 'Shall we sit down?'

There was a moment's hesitation before she decided to do
just that. She sat herself facing out over the terrace, her eyes
fixed at some point out in the distance, back straight and
hands gripped in her lap.

Seb positioned himself opposite. Bizarrely, now she was
sitting there, he was in no hurry to begin. What could he say
that would begin to explain?

At nineteen he'd been so overwhelmed…by everything. All
he'd been able to do was react to whatever was happening in
that precise moment. There'd been so much to adjust to.

And somehow he'd managed to block the image of
Marianne waiting for him in Paris. Convinced himself she
wasn't his most urgent priority. For someone who lived his
entire life trying to do the right thing by everyone, it was ironic
he'd done something so spectacularly wrong.

What was it she had said? That she'd spent years of her life
thinking him a 'waster' and a 'liar'?

And yet she'd never taken her story to the Press. Never sold
the photographs she must have of their time together. There
wasn't an editor alive who'd have failed to snap them up. Her
story would have made her thousands.

But she had more dignity than that. A cool, classy lady.

'How's Nick these days?'

Her question startled him, broke into his thoughts. Seb
met her eyes and saw the steely determination. She didn't
want this, didn't want any part of this conversation, but she
was damned if she was going to let him see it. And she'd had
enough of waiting.

'Are you still in contact with him?' she prompted when he was slow to answer. 'Or was he some kind of bodyguard and you lied about that as well? He tried hard enough to keep you away from me. Was that his job?'

Seb cleared his throat, still searching for the right words. 'We're friends. Good friends. And, for what it's worth, he thought I should have told you exactly who I was—'

'Is that supposed to make me feel better?'

From the expression on her face it certainly wasn't. Seb ran a hand across his neck, easing out the tension there. 'We're still in close contact, although I see him less often since his father's death.'

'And what was *his* real name? Archduke Nikolaus?'

'Marianne…'

Her eyes widened. 'I'm sorry, am I making this difficult for you?' she asked, her rich voice distorted by sarcasm.

'As of last April Nick's the fifteenth Duke of Aylesbury.'

Marianne looked down at her fingers and concentrated on the opal colour of her nail varnish. *Nick was a duke*. Why was she surprised? *Had she honestly expected anything different?* Nick Barrington was the fifteenth Duke of Aylesbury and Seb Rodier was His Serene Highness Prince Sebastian of Andovaria. Inadvertently she must have strayed into La-La Land and nothing was as it seemed any more.

'How's Beth?' he asked, shifting in his seat.

Marianne's head came up. 'I'd love to tell you she's the Marchioness of Basingstoke, but unfortunately she isn't. You see, *we* weren't pretending. *We* were exactly what we told you we were.'

'Did she become a lawyer?'

'Y-yes. Yes, she did.'

He'd remembered. He'd remembered a single throwaway comment Beth had made on the first afternoon they'd all spent together. And somehow that made the ground shift beneath her. She didn't want to soften towards him. She wanted to keep a steel barrier between them as protection. But…

Her voice faltered. 'She's married to an anaesthetist with a baby due in a couple of months.'

'That's great.'

'She's very happy.'

The sound of footsteps brought her head round in time to see the butler walking across the rooftop courtyard with her wrap spread out over his arm. 'Your Serene Highness. Dr Chambers,' he said as he carefully placed it round her shoulders.

'Thank you,' she said awkwardly. Intellectually she knew it was his job, but she was uncomfortable with being at the receiving end of it. In her world she opened doors for herself, found the sleeves of her own coat…

Marianne looked down and pleated the tassels together. The silence was punctuated by the precise step of the butler as he crossed the terrace, returning moments later. 'Is Professor Blackwell asking for me?' she asked, looking up, hoping for an escape route.

'He's not made any comment to me, madam,' he replied, pouring the wine with easy, practised movements.

This all felt so peculiar. A balmy night in a beautiful setting…with a man she used to be in love with.

'I'm not drinking tonight,' she said as soon as the butler was out of earshot once more. 'Alcohol's not good for a woman with a headache.'

'I suppose that depends on why she has a headache,' Seb replied, his dark eyes seeming to see so much more than she was comfortable with. Then he picked up his own glass and drank. 'You should reconsider. This is considerably better than the paint stripper we drank together in France.'

It was a shared memory—and a happy one. Marianne felt

another crack in the shield. She didn't want to thaw towards him. She wanted her anger to stay at the fore... But instead she felt the first stirrings of a smile.

To hide it she picked up her glass and sipped. The chilled wine was crisp and light, with a heady scent of lemon trees. 'It's lovely.'

He smiled. 'But not as nice as our whisky?'

Something deep inside her twisted. 'No.' Nothing would ever taste as nice as the whisky they'd drunk that night. The first time she'd ever tasted whisky and the first time she'd ever made love.

'How long did you wait for me in Paris?' he asked quietly.

Marianne let her fingers curve around the glass in her hand, watching the beads of condensation. Her mind was back in the tiny bedroom they'd shared for three nights. Nothing there but a bed, a small wardrobe and the sounds of people enjoying themselves in the nearby restaurants.

'Not long,' she said, raising her eyes. 'Madame Merchand had wanted me to start earlier so I telephoned her and said I could come immediately. It seemed sensible when you didn't phone me.' She took another sip of wine.

'Were you unhappy with them?'

Marianne looked up, surprised by his question.

'I know you left early.'

He did? How? Marianne stayed watching him, her eyes wide.

His mouth twisted. 'I did contact you. Late, I admit, but Monsieur Merchand said you'd returned home weeks before.'

That was something she didn't know. Marianne felt her chest become tight. *Seb had contacted her.* Her mind felt as if it had splintered into a billion fragments. 'N-nine weeks... all but a couple of days.'

'Did you go to another family?'

His questions felt relentless—and she didn't want to answer. Marianne shook her head. 'I went home. Beth stayed in Honfleur for the full year, but I…' She trailed off. She didn't want to think about the reasons for her return home. Or what had happened when she got there.

And Seb had spoken to Monsieur Merchand. When? Why? So many questions were streaming through her brain.

'Were you homesick?'

'I—I just needed to go home,' she countered. Marianne took a deep breath and tried to re-group. The fact that Seb had eventually tried to contact her changed nothing. Nothing at all.

He'd had her address in England. He could have reached her at any time. Even when she'd gone to live with the professor and his family she hadn't been untraceable. In fact, her mother had been so desperate to know who the father of her daughter's baby was she'd happily have passed on any man's telephone number.

'Why didn't you contact me at home?'

Marianne watched the muscle pulse in his cheek before he met her eyes. Saw his unwillingness to speak and braced herself for his reply.

'I didn't want the conversation we were going to have,' he admitted, his voice more gravelly than she'd ever heard it.

He'd rung her to finish their relationship. The thought hit Marianne with a dull thud.

Seb shifted in his seat. 'I felt…grateful to have been let off the hook. The fact that you'd left France…seemed to make everything easier.'

Well, that was honest. The dispassionate part of her admired him for that even while she felt desperately hurt by what he was saying.

'I should have made more effort to speak to you.'

'It would have been nice if you'd written,' Marianne suggested in a voice that sounded small in her own ears. 'For weeks I didn't know what had happened to you. I'd no way of contacting you—'

Seb shook his head and his eyes seemed to be asking for understanding. 'I was advised against that. I was told to put nothing in writing—'

'Why?' The question was out of her mouth even as the answer flooded her mind. A frown pulled at her forehead. 'You thought I'd sell it? You...*bastard!* You pompous—'

'Marianne, they don't know you. It wasn't based on any personal evaluation—'

'You did! You knew me.' It took every ounce of control she had not to tip what was left of her wine over him. How *dared* he think that about her? 'You should have known I'd never do anything like that. I—'

'I was a coward,' Seb interrupted her. 'I should have come to England and spoken to you about what was happening in my life. If I'd been older, felt more in control of what was happening...'

He trailed off for the second time, but Marianne almost didn't notice. She was incandescently angry. It felt like a bright light burning inside her.

Everything was so much worse than she'd thought. She hadn't believed that could be possible.

But Seb had returned to Andovaria and turned their perfect, private little world into something sordid. He'd sat around with his advisers while they debated how best to 'manage' her. While she...

Dear God.

She felt hot tears prick insistently behind her eyelids and blinked furiously. She wouldn't cry. *Mustn't.* But the thought of their beautiful romance being talked over, discussed and dissected...

One single tear welled up and spilled down her cheek.

'Marianne.' Seb's voice cracked and he reached out as though to touch her.

'No!' She furiously brushed away the trail of moisture.

'I'm sorry—'

'So you say,' Marianne said, standing up abruptly. 'I think I've heard enough of your explanations now. You're sorry, I'm sorry, we're both sorry. Let's just leave it at that, shall we?'

'I haven't told you what happened when I got home. Why I—'

Marianne laughed. It wasn't a joyous sound, but hard and brittle. 'What's to understand? You forget I know practically everything about you. You're tabloid fodder. Shortly after your marriage to Amelie of Saxe-Broden, eighteen,' she said, her fingers moving to make speech marks in the air, 'you were enthroned as the Sovereign Prince of Andovaria. I've seen the pictures!'

She brushed again at another betraying tear that was making its way down her carefully made up face.

'It wasn't quite as you make that sound.'

She turned on him. 'In what way was it different, Seb?' she said in a voice laced with sarcasm. 'The Andovarian tourist industry fancied producing some memorabilia? Thought she'd look good on a stamp, perhaps?'

If he'd raised his voice or moved towards her she'd have turned and walked back into the sitting room—but he did neither. His hand rubbed at his neck and he walked over to the rail. His body language seemed to convey that she'd managed to hurt him.

Marianne felt the anger leave her like air from a balloon.

Seb didn't know anything about Jessica. However much she wanted to blame him for leaving her to deal with the consequence of their affair alone, she knew it hadn't been a conscious decision.

And she *did* want to know why he'd left her. The 'why' of it had been the thing that had prevented her from being able to truly give herself to any other relationship. The three-month cut-off, Eliana called it.

'I was called back urgently because my father was ill,' he began, his voice low and steady.

Marianne shifted her weight from one foot back to the other. 'I know.' He'd told her that at the time. She'd helped him pack. Didn't he remember?

'They'd found a tumour. In his brain.'

She knew that, too. Prince Franz-Josef's death, poignantly just weeks before his only son's marriage, had featured in glossy magazines across Europe…and probably beyond. She'd read all about it in double-page detail.

'It was inoperable and he knew he had very little time left…to make everything safe.' For the first time Seb's voice betrayed real emotion.

'Why couldn't you have rung and told me that?' she asked after a moment. 'I would have gone to Honfleur just the same and waited until—'

Seb shook his head. 'You don't understand, Marianne, it wasn't that simple.'

Why wasn't it *just* that simple? He was right. She didn't understand that. He might not have told her that he was the crown prince of Andovaria, but his identity hadn't come as a surprise to him. He'd known that when he met her. When they'd first kissed. When they'd made love…

Nothing had actually changed by his father becoming ill. Not between them.

Marianne moved closer and he must have sensed her standing there because he turned. And his eyes were…bleak. She wasn't prepared for how that would make her feel.

'God help me, I loved my father, but the months before his death were filled with far more than concern for a dying man. My life was completely turned on its head.'

'I'm sure—'

'No.' He stopped her. 'Please. Just listen.'

She nodded.

'Not just because the father I loved was dying. The Andovarian constitution…' He broke off. 'As Crown Prince, I needed to be married by my twenty-first birthday—which left me seventeen months to find a suitable bride.'

Married. To someone *suitable.* Marianne's fingers curled around the metal railing and she gripped until her knuckles showed white.

'Why…why do they have to be married?'

'Tradition.' His succinct answer came back at her like a bullet. 'If you go back far enough all Andovarian crown princes were formally engaged before they were five or six, maybe even married in their absence.'

'How ridiculous to have something like that in the constitution,' she said, her voice husky.

'Until recently Monaco made the same requirement of their ruling prince. In the last couple of hundred years it simply hasn't been an issue in Andovaria because the crown prince has always been married by the time he succeeded.'

So why didn't you marry me? The question ricocheted around her head, even though she knew the answer. Cinderella was a fantastic fairy tale, but that was exactly what it was—a fairy tale. Crown princes didn't marry lower-middle-class girls from Suffolk. She knew it. And he knew it. In fact, he must have known it from the very beginning of their relationship.

Marianne made a conscious decision to let go of the railing in front of her. Of course he wouldn't have rushed back to Paris and demanded she marry him. That didn't happen outside romance novels and Hollywood films.

'The marriage of any member of the royal family has to be approved by either the sovereign prince or, if he's under the age of twenty-one, by the regent. Any union entered into without it is deemed invalid and any children illegitimate.'

He said the words as though they were rehearsed. Marianne walked slowly back towards the table and sat back down. As a historian she knew this wasn't unusual. The English constitution required the same of its royal family—and for centuries they'd duly obliged.

How did they do that, normal, flesh and blood people... with the normal, flesh and blood desire to be loved and have someone love them? How did they make themselves marry for the good of the state?

'Suddenly the question of my marriage was the number-one priority.' He hadn't moved from the railing. 'Everything was resting on me.'

In the distance Marianne could hear the hum of traffic. She wasn't really aware of anything else. In actual fact, it really wasn't so very different from what she'd always supposed had happened. She hadn't been good enough.

Not even good enough for a phone call. Not *safe* enough for a letter.

Slowly Marianne picked up her wine glass and sipped, then carefully she placed it back down in front of her.

'And...I wouldn't have been considered suitable?' She forced herself to say the words.

The slightest pause. 'No. No, you wouldn't. Weren't,' he corrected.

CHAPTER FOUR

No. THE word echoed quietly in Marianne's head. She didn't understand why hearing Seb actually say she wasn't 'suitable' should make her feel better, but it did. Almost like a wound that had been lanced.

Years of supposition and, finally, she knew. And she'd been right all along. She was fine for a holiday romance…Fine to make love to as long as no one actually knew anything about it…

'So you married Amelie of Saxe-Broden?'

'Yes.'

'Did you love her?'

'I liked her. Still do. And I was grateful that she was prepared to take me on…but no, I didn't love her.'

Marianne swallowed hard. 'Did she know that when she married you?'

'Amelie didn't love me either. It was a marriage that made…sense,' he said, pulling that word out with difficulty. 'We'd been brought up in the same kind of circles, but she didn't stand to inherit anything herself. She was the right age.'

His was a completely different world. Hateful, actually. He'd selected Amelie as though she'd been a brood mare.

'What would have happened if you hadn't been able to find anyone *suitable* to marry you?'

'Then I would have forfeited my right to succession and my cousin Michael would be the sovereign prince of Andovaria now.'

'I see.' Marianne shivered and pulled the wrap closely about her shoulders.

'I never intended to hurt you, Marianne. And…I'm really glad your life has turned out so well…and that…you're happy and…'

Pride was an incredibly powerful thing, she thought. Marianne forced a smile. 'You know, you could have told me the truth. Even as a little girl I never thought being a princess was much of a career plan.'

Seb's dark eyes took on a sexy glint. 'Not even when you were five?'

'I think I wanted to be an astronaut when I was five—certainly not a princess. My parents are very educationally orientated and they bought me all the books…' Seb laughed and her stomach flipped over.

'I wish I could do it differently.' He walked back to the table and sat down. 'Meeting you…becoming close to you was so unexpected. I hadn't planned any of it—'

That was true for them both, then. Falling in love with him hadn't been on her agenda either. Marianne picked up her wine glass and took another sip, determined that she would keep herself under tight control.

'—and everything happened so fast between us. There was scarcely time to think. I was in too deep to do anything about it before I'd even realised I'd begun.'

Marianne let her hands curve around the ball of her wineglass. Perhaps not the correct thing to do to a crisp white wine, but she liked the feel of the cold glass against her palm.

Their relationship had *ended* as fast as it had begun. That bothered her far more than the speed of the start. One moment she'd been little more than a child on her first big adventure, and the next she'd been yanked into adulthood.

It had been different for Seb. Meeting her hadn't altered the course of his life. After he'd left her in that Paris hotel room his world had continued on its preordained trajectory.

For her nothing had ever been the same again. If it hadn't been for her Aunt Tia contacting Eliana she wouldn't have survived. She'd have been pregnant and homeless. Her relationship with her parents fractured beyond repair.

Marianne bit her lip. What would Seb have done if he'd known they'd created a baby together? No doubt his family would have been horrified if he'd presented them with a pregnant girlfriend. They'd have probably been even more convinced of her 'unsuitability' and brokered some suitable 'arrangement' to hide his 'indiscretion'.

'There's no excuse for the way I treated you. I was young, a little rebellious, but I knew what was expected of me as the crown prince. I'd always known. I probably shouldn't even have spoken to you that first day…and I certainly shouldn't have persuaded you to let Nick and me join you.'

'Why did you?'

Why? Seb sat back in his chair and watched the way the breeze caught at the single curl on her forehead. The answer was simple—because he'd wanted to.

As simple as that.

He'd wanted to be with her.

It was probably the last occasion he'd acted without any consideration of the possible consequences. He'd wanted to talk to her…. Then he'd wanted to spend time with her…. Then…

Maybe the pivotal mistake had been going to find somewhere to buy lunch that first day. He'd been blown away by her.

And it hadn't just been her beauty that had drawn him in.

He'd fallen in love with her shy smile. The way she'd blushed when he'd teased her. The way she'd laughed. Talked. Moved.

He'd never met anyone like her. That lunch had been the turning point. From that moment on everything else had been inevitable.

'I liked being with you.'

Her eyes flicked up and away again. There wasn't time to read her expression. 'Why did you agree Nick and I could join you?'

Seb watched her swallow and then search for her reply. 'I…don't know.'

'You'll have to do better than that.'

Marianne gave a slight shrug. 'Because you were so insistent? I don't know.'

There was probably more than a grain of truth in that, Seb thought. He *had* pushed hard to be allowed to join them. And Beth and Nick had followed on almost as a matter of course.

Marianne had been very young. A few weeks past her eighteenth birthday when they'd met. Innocent. And she'd made him feel important. That she seemed to like him without knowing he was a prince had done a lot for his ego too. For the first and only time in his life he'd had a taste of what it was like to be ordinary. Normal.

'Were you and Nick really on holiday?'

'Oh, yes. We'd escaped.' Seb picked up his wine and swirled it in his glass, his mind anywhere but on the liquid. 'I don't think I'd been anywhere before without some kind of protection in tow. It was a heady experience.'

'Even at school?'

'Even there. Of course, we hadn't escaped.' Seb smiled across at her. 'My parents were completely aware of where I was and what I was doing. They'd merely decided to let the leash out a little and they pulled me back in when they needed to.'

Marianne set her glass down on the table and carefully

lined up the base with the edge of her coaster. 'Did they know about me?'

'I think they probably knew your shoe size.'

Had they known she was pregnant? For a moment Marianne felt quite panicked and then she calmed down. Surely her patient notes were entirely confidential. And perhaps she'd ceased to be of much interest when she'd disappeared so quietly.

From the sitting room there was the sound of laughter. Marianne looked over her shoulder. 'We shouldn't be much longer.'

'Perhaps not. How's your headache?'

'Gone. Almost.' She took a final sip of wine. Talking *had* helped. She hadn't actually learnt anything materially different from what she'd already known, but she felt…respected by his telling her. It changed nothing. And yet it changed everything.

Perhaps the most healing thing was that he hadn't acted consciously. When she'd seen the first photographs of him with his fiancée she'd wondered whether he'd deliberately set out to have some kind of final fling. Been almost certain that he had. She looked up as a new thought burst into her head. 'You're not married now. I thought it was a requirement.' She frowned. 'Or does it all work the same way as if you were widowed?'

Seb shook his head. 'I've no heir. I needed to change the constitution.'

He changed the constitution. If it was that easy, why hadn't Seb's father changed the constitution and prevented his son being forced into a marriage he didn't want?

'It was a lengthy process, but it was necessary before Amelie and I could be granted an annulment. There hadn't been anything like it in eight hundred years of continuous rule so there were constitutional implications. It took five years of legal wrangling before everyone was satisfied.'

Which meant at some point he'd be expected to marry again. Someone *suitable*. But until then he was free to date Hollywood actresses and glamorous models. And she'd be able to read all about it.

Marianne shivered again.

Why did they settle for that? Surely the knowledge they'd slept with a prince didn't make it hurt any less to know they were only a body to him? It had hurt her.

'Still feeling cold?'

'A little.'

'Perhaps we should rejoin the others.'

Marianne nodded. She stood up and the chair grated against the paving. The comparative warmth of the sitting room hit her immediately she entered.

'How's your headache?' the professor asked.

'Much better.' Marianne smiled, though it didn't feel quite natural. Her emotions seemed balanced on a knife edge. 'The fresh air was a good idea.' She carefully unwound her wool wrap and folded it neatly on the chair.

'Excellent.'

His attention quickly returned to Dr Leibnitz. It seemed quite incredible to Marianne that it wasn't immediately obvious to the two other men she'd changed somehow.

She sat herself on the edge of the sofa and glanced over at the clock on the mantelpiece. It was late—and she wanted nothing more than to go back to the Cowper Hotel. Her feet were aching and she'd lied when she'd said her headache was better. It was sitting behind her left eyeball just waiting to explode.

How much longer was the professor going to be? Her mind seemed to be buzzing, incapable of following their conversation. Then, quite suddenly, it was over.

'I'll give you a few days to discuss everything with your

wife,' Seb said, standing up, 'and then I'll ask you for your decision.'

The professor nodded. 'Yes, indeed.'

'Perhaps you could talk directly with Johann von Renzel, my chief of court. Assuming your decision is in the positive, he'll be able to organise accommodation and your travel arrangements.'

In her heart of hearts Marianne knew there was no decision to make. And, incredibly, the thought of going to Andovaria was no longer such an ordeal. Seb hadn't set out to hurt her. She believed that—so she couldn't hate him any more.

If she ever really had. There was a part of her that would always love him. A part that was angry. And a part of her that felt sorry for him. He might live in a gilded cage, but it was a cage nevertheless. His whole life defined by an accident of birth and he hadn't had the courage to break out.

'You're very quiet,' the professor observed as he settled himself in the back of the taxi.

Marianne turned her head to look at him. 'You've already made your decision, haven't you? You've decided to accept.'

He closed his eyes, looking more tired than he'd ever admit. 'If we pick our team carefully…'

Marianne looked out of the window at the Randall before the taxi slipped out into the London traffic.

Seb shrugged off his jacket and dropped it on the nearest chair, untying his bow-tie at the same time. He walked over to the window and stood, one arm resting on the frame, looking out across the terrace.

That had been, perhaps, the hardest conversation of his entire life.

Good, though. It was as though a loose end had been finally tied.

'Will that be all, sir?'

Seb turned. 'Yes, thank you, Warner.' The butler had started to move away when Seb noticed Marianne's pink wrap lying on the chair just inside the door. 'No, wait.' He strode over and picked it up, amazed that the light rose perfume she'd worn that evening still clung to the fibres. He hadn't even been aware he'd noticed her perfume.

'Could you see that this is packaged up and delivered to Dr Chambers at the Cowper Hotel?'

'Yes, sir.'

'I believe they'll be checking out by ten o'clock tomorrow.'

'Yes, sir. I'll see that it's delivered tonight.'

The door shut behind him and Seb turned back and idly fingered the selection of books the Randall had provided. Crime, thrillers, non-fiction, classics… Nothing on the shelf grabbed his attention.

In fact, he felt…restless. Hell only knew why. The evening had gone well. He was almost certain that Professor Blackwell would accept…which was, in the main, what he'd stopped over in London for. Viktoria would be delighted. But, still…he felt dissatisfied.

It was probably remembering. Practically a full decade of royal responsibility since he'd last seen Marianne. The last time he'd acted solely in line with his own inclination.

Seb lay down on the sofa and rested his head back on the armrest. Five weeks. That was all they'd had. Five weeks before his life had been turned upside down and he'd been thrust relentlessly into the limelight.

Tabloid fodder. That's what she'd called him. For the first time he paused to wonder what she'd thought when she'd first discovered he was the crown prince of Andovaria.

It wasn't comfortable thinking.

He rubbed a hand over his tired eyes. And he *was* 'tabloid

fodder'. Every last thing he did was reported somewhere. He only had to speak to some woman for rumours of their affair to be circulating round the better part of Europe by the morning. It probably took a week for the same information to reach the States.

Seb sat up abruptly and swung his legs down to the floor. He reached out for the phone and keyed in a nine to obtain an outside line.

'Nick?' he said as soon as a sleepy voice answered. 'Have I woken you?'

'No, but I'd just about given up on you. Are you still coming over?'

He leant forward and rested his elbows on his knees. 'I'll be with you by lunchtime tomorrow. Just don't put me in the room with the leaking roof again,' he said, waiting for the crack of laughter which wasn't long in coming.

'How long are you staying this time?'

'Just the weekend. I've got to be in Vienna by Monday lunchtime for a meeting with a trade delegation and then I'm off to the States straight after that.'

'How long for?'

'Six weeks, all but a couple of days.' Seb sat back again and briefly contemplated telling Nick he'd seen Marianne. He brushed a tired hand across his face. Somehow it felt too difficult—and he wasn't ready to be questioned about her. He didn't know how he felt.

But he was fairly certain he knew how Marianne was feeling.

She'd heard him out—and, perhaps, that had been more than he'd deserved. But she still felt he'd let her down and, *damn it*, he had.

CHAPTER FIVE

SEB leant forward and tapped the driver of his car on the shoulder. 'Stefan, stop here, please. I need to stretch my legs.'

Obediently his driver brought the car to a halt, the one immediately behind doing the same, and Seb turned to Alois, sitting beside him. 'Can you take my briefcase up to my private apartment? Leave these with Liesl and I'll work on them again later.'

'Sir.'

He shuffled the papers he'd been working on back into his briefcase and handed them across with a nod of thanks. Then, leaving his jacket on the seat, he opened the door and stepped out into fresh air.

It was good to be home. Really good. Seb drew the air into his lungs. Travel might broaden the mind, but home was good for the soul. *Who'd written that?* He couldn't remember, but it was so true.

He really loved this place. It seemed to envelop him every time he stood inside its protected boundaries. Poltenbrunn Castle, with the Alps rising majestically behind it, was rather a spectacular building in a truly breathtaking setting. Most of the time he took it for granted, but sometimes, like now, after a longish absence, he was struck how incredibly fortunate he was to live the life he did in the place that he lived it.

Seb stood back and allowed the cars to snake their way up to the castle, before following on foot. Of course, six weeks of hotel suites, paparazzi with their telephoto lenses focused on every window and the constant companionship of the men assigned to protect him probably had a lot to do with his relief at being home. At least here he was afforded a modicum of privacy.

His smart leather shoes prevented him from doing anything other than sticking to the main path, but he took the longer route around the great lake. It was an incredibly beautiful vista. And one he'd loved since he was a child.

He'd spoken to people over the past couple of weeks who seemed to have no sense of place or purpose, people whose lives had been shattered through no fault of their own. And all this was his. 'In trust for future generations' —but his.

Just as he was occasionally reminded of the beauty of his home, so was he reminded of the responsibilities of his position. Few people were able to influence so much or bring about such change simply by virtue of who their ancestors were. At nineteen he'd balked at that, wished for a different life…

Seb looked across the lake towards the oldest part of the castle. *He'd wished for Marianne.* At nineteen he'd accepted he would be the next sovereign prince of Andovaria, but it had cost him. And seeing Marianne in London had reminded him how *much* it had cost him.

The sturdy grey stone of the old keep looked so permanent and dour as compared with the later more aesthetically pleasing additions. In less than a week she'd be there.

Seb paused at the brass sculpture of Maestoso Bonadea XII, his father's favourite stallion, and moved his hand down the smooth muzzle. It was going to be strange to know Marianne was at the castle…every day. Close, but not close.

Perhaps it was because their relationship hadn't been allowed to run its course that he felt…

Heck only knew what he felt.

Seb screwed his eyes up against the mid-afternoon sun. Since he'd seen her in London he'd thought about her pretty much constantly. How much worse would that be when she was actually here? Just knowing that she was a five-minute walk away from his private rooms...

He turned abruptly away and rounded the bend, his feet slowing as he saw a solitary female figure coming out of the woodland area. There was something about the way she was walking that made him stop completely and his stomach want to jump in both directions simultaneously.

It was *her*. Incredibly.

And he knew the moment Marianne had moved close enough to recognise him. Her body seemed to tense and then she resolutely carried on up the path.

Seb pulled a hand through his hair and searched his mind for something suitably casual to say. He'd spent the last six weeks thinking about her, wondering whether she'd changed her opinion of him, wondering whether she still felt anything for him...

Just wondering. Idly. And now here she was. And he wasn't prepared for how it would feel to see her against the backdrop of his home.

Marianne stopped a few feet away from him, her shoulder-length blonde hair drawn back into a casual pony-tail. She looked so absurdly young. Incredibly beautiful.

And he wanted to kiss her. He knew exactly what it felt like to slide his hands over her body and feel her lips warm and moving against his. In fact, he knew more than that. He knew what it was like to be inside her. To wake and watch her breathing. All of a sudden his skin felt several sizes too small for his body.

He drew a hand round the back of his neck to ease out the

sudden tension. Nervous as any adolescent. Unsure what he should say. What he shouldn't.

The edge of Marianne's long white cotton skirt caught in the summer breeze and her pony-tail flicked out behind her. Then she smiled.

'Y-you weren't supposed to be here until next week,' he managed in a voice that sounded hoarse.

She shook her head. 'I'm here to set up the computers before the professor arrives next week. I…came on ahead.'

'Oh,' He nodded. And now he felt foolish. *Even more foolish.* His mind was refusing to work and he didn't seem to be able to stop looking at her. She wore no make-up and he could see the pale translucency of her skin, the purple smudges beneath her dark eyes. And he remembered how those eyes had looked dilated and drowsy with passion. 'How long have you been here?'

'Ten days.'

He brushed his palms down the back of his trousers. 'I've been away—'

'I know.'

She smiled again and twisted a strand of hair behind her ears. 'Did you have a good trip?'

'Yes. Yes, I did. Thank you.'

Marianne nodded, more as though she wanted to encourage him than anything else. 'I'm glad.'

Then she moved as though she intended to continue past him and Seb felt compelled to stop her. 'D-do you have everything you need?'

'Yes.'

'Good. That's good…' His voice disappeared into a husky whisper. Seb pulled the air into his lungs. This conversation was becoming faintly ridiculous.

'I'm being really well looked after. Princess Viktoria is

very organised. She thinks of things I might need before I've thought of them.'

'That's good,' he said again, and inwardly groaned. Somewhere across the Atlantic he must have lost the ability to talk to a beautiful woman.

Or perhaps it was just the ability to talk to this one?

He'd have done better if he'd known she was already at the castle. He could have prepared himself. Steeled himself for how it would feel to see her again.

'She's very enthusiastic about the project.'

'Yes, she is.' He pulled a hand through his hair and cast her a shaky smile. 'Sorry, I'm not making much sense, I know. I'm jet-lagged. I need to get some sleep. Perhaps then I'll be able to string more than a couple of words together.'

Marianne's dark eyes lit with a glimmer of sudden laughter and he knew that whatever had been between them ten years ago was still there. For him at least. The only confusing thing was how he'd ever managed to walk away from her.

Perhaps, at nineteen, he'd not been aware how rare it was to feel such an intense connection to another person? But he knew now. In ten years he'd not come close to experiencing anything like it.

'How long was your flight?'

Even her voice was sending warm shivers through his body. Reminding him of everything his sense of duty had robbed him of. 'Eight and a half hours. Just under eleven hours door to door. And there's a six-hour time difference.'

Again her smile tugged at him and he wanted to touch her. Once he'd been allowed to do that. He could have cradled her face in his hands and kissed her.

'No wonder you're tired.'

'I'm shattered, but it's better if I can keep myself awake until evening.'

Seb knew the right thing to do was to smile and move away. Move and keep moving. But…there was something about her blonde beauty and the intelligence that shone out of her dark sexy eyes that acted like a siren's call. So difficult to resist. Almost impossible.

Smile and walk away.

As a working royal, Seb was an expert at that. He knew exactly how to finish conversations without causing offence or embarrassment. But…he seemed powerless to do what his head was telling him.

And he knew the reason why hadn't changed. *He liked being with her.* Still. She made him feel alive. Happy. As though he could do anything, achieve anything. *Be* anything he wanted.

Blood pumped through his veins and he felt acutely aware of everything around him. The trees seemed larger, the grass greener. The air felt cleaner, sharper.

The last time he'd felt like this he'd walked up to her on the steps of Amiens Cathedral. Made her talk to him, invited her to go to a coffee shop.

Seb pulled an agitated hand through his hair. 'I'd better get back or they'll be sending out a search party.'

Marianne nodded.

Walk away. The voice of caution was getting weaker and in its place was the whisper of temptation. *Where was the harm in talking to her?*

'Are you out for a walk?'

She held up the flask of coffee she'd been cradling against her. 'Having a break. Remembering it's still summer. It's cold in there,' she said, gesturing back towards the castle.

'Sorry.'

Another smile. She had the most incredible mouth. Soft and sensuous. And when she smiled it seemed to short-circuit his brain. 'It's not your fault they didn't put a good heating system in.'

Seb could feel his lips stretch into an answering smile. There was nothing he could do to stop it. 'It's not a desperately good heating system in the newer part either.'

'Isn't it?' Marianne's eyes skitted away towards the castle. It was the first indication that she might not be as comfortable as she appeared. That small movement gave him a little confidence.

'But it's nowhere near as dreadful as the heating in Nick's place. I think he should put thermal underwear as the dress code on all invitations.'

Her eyes came back, warm brown…and questioning. He still wanted to kiss her. Did she know that? Could she tell from the way his eyes hovered on her mouth despite his best intentions?

'I stayed with him for the weekend after I'd met you. He sends his regards.'

'Oh.' Her hands clasped and unclasped the flask.

Seb saw the movement and noticed the way her eyes yet again moved past him. Marianne wasn't comfortable—any more than he was. But she wasn't walking away from him either…

'Are you heading for a specific spot?'

Her eyes swung back. 'Spot? Oh…for coffee? No. I wouldn't know where to go. This is the first time I've come in this direction. I've normally walked through the parterre and up to the pavilion.'

'Do you mind if I join you?'

The slight widening of her eyes suggested that her decision might swing either way, but after a moment she shook her head. 'No. I don't mind. There's enough coffee for two. That is, if you like it white with sugar.'

He didn't. He liked it strong and black. And he didn't even

want a coffee. This was crazy. What was he doing? Exactly what he'd promised himself he wouldn't do.

'We might as well sit here,' she said, slipping the rucksack off her shoulder. 'It's an amazing view from here.'

Seb reached out for her rucksack. 'Come with me.' He turned and led the way across the grass, completely ignoring the damage he was doing to his shoes.

Marianne followed him—or followed whatever she'd put in her rucksack, he didn't really care. The sleep that had been pulling at his eyelids all the way from the airport seemed to have disappeared and he felt…reckless. Younger.

And he wanted to show her his home as it was meant to be seen. 'Here,' he said, stopping and putting her bag down on the grass. 'What do you think of this one?'

He watched as she turned to look down at Poltenbrunn Castle. From here its twelfth-century keep was entirely obscured and you were left with a fairy-tale castle.

'This looks very familiar.'

'It's the image that's most often used on postcards. All seasons. All times of day. But I've never seen a photograph yet that quite captures the essence of the place.'

'It looks like Rapunzel might appear any minute at one of those turret windows,' she said, unwrapping her jumper from around her waist and setting it out on the ground.

'Maybe that's what I ought to do with Isabelle. Lock her in the tower,' he said in answer to the slight raise of her left eyebrow.

'Your sister?'

'Younger sister,' he agreed, sitting down beside her. 'She seems to ricochet from one disaster to the next. Locking her up might be the perfect solution. I'll put it to her.'

'It didn't work for the witch who tried it.'

Seb laughed. 'I'm sure it wouldn't for us either. She'd be

bound to do something outrageous. Though it can't be much worse than disappearing for a week.'

'You disappeared for longer than that.'

True.

Seb turned and watched her as she unscrewed the top of her flask and separated the two cups. He hadn't compared himself to Isabelle before. Maybe she was that unhappy? 'Isabelle is older than I was,' he said slowly. 'She's twenty-two.'

'Not so very old.'

No, not old, but by twenty-two he'd accepted his destiny. He'd been enthroned as the sovereign prince and he'd married Amelie.

'Do you want some?' Marianne asked, holding up the flask.

He'd married Amelie when he'd been in love with Marianne. Twenty years old, with a very heavy heart, he'd done his duty. Seb swallowed. 'If there's enough. It might help keep me awake.'

She said nothing, but poured coffee in both the cups. 'What time did you leave New York?'

'About eleven. I left immediately after the charity dinner finished.'

Marianne looked up. 'Whatever time was that? Are you sure everyone else wouldn't rather have had a good night's sleep before setting off?'

'I imagine they're pleased to get back as early as possible. Most of them have families to come home to.'

Her brown eyes widened. 'But you didn't ask them?'

'It's their job—'

'To protect you and to do what you want,' she interrupted smoothly, passing him the larger of the two mugs. 'Yes, you've told me that before.' Her mouth quirked. 'You must be insufferable to be around, Your Serene Highness.'

Seb took a sip of the coffee he didn't really want and studied her. There was a new confidence about Marianne now. A quiet conviction that she had something worth saying. He liked it.

'You don't have a particularly good opinion of royalty, do you, Dr Chambers?'

Her smile broadened. 'Let's just say I had a bad introduction to the species.'

'Thanks.'

Marianne laughed. 'You're welcome.'

Seb sipped his coffee. He liked this. People rarely laughed around him, he realised, and they certainly didn't relax or treat him the way they would any other human being.

Except Nick.

But Nick was a friend from school. And Nick was someone who understood how his life worked. He was one of just a handful of people he could trust and the only person he'd ever confided in.

Which made Marianne particularly unusual. She didn't seem to see him as a ruling prince and she certainly treated him like any other human being. And she was equally trustworthy, but with far less reason.

Marianne's smile faded and she turned to grab her rucksack. He had the strongest sensation she was hiding from him and he longed to be able to reach and turn her face back so he could see her eyes. If he could see her eyes he'd know what she was thinking.

'I'm afraid I've only got one of these and it's lunch,' she said, pulling out an apple.

'Now?' He glanced down at his watch. 'You're having lunch now? I thought you said Vik had been looking after you.'

'She has,' Marianne tossed the apple in her hand, 'but not so well she forces me to come for lunch. I forgot the time. I only noticed it when I started to feel chilly.'

'That engrossed?'

She nodded, the sparkle returning to her eyes. 'You've no idea what you've got down there. It's incredible.

Yesterday I found a list of Konrad I of Thuringia's posses-
sions in 1236.'

'And he was?'

Marianne tucked a strand of hair behind her ear. 'Oh, sorry.
He was a *Hochmeister* of the Teutonic Order.'

Seb found himself smiling again as the enthusiasm rang in
her voice. It was infectious. 'You really do love what you do.'

'Of course. What's the point of doing something if you
don't love it?'

Duty. The single word slid into his mind.

'You're a long time dead. Eliana says that. She believes life
should be as fun as you can make it,' she said, taking a bite
of her apple.

When she said it like that he agreed, but it was a philoso-
phy that ran completely counter to his training. He sat silent
for a moment. Life—*his* life—wasn't about fun or enjoyment. It was about fulfilling one's duty, never losing sight of
his responsibility to his country and his family.

Marianne let the silence stretch out. Unbelievably, sitting
with Seb, talking to him, felt…all right. When she'd first seen
him as she came out of the wood she'd panicked, but it was fine.

In fact, it was better than fine. She was here on her own
merit, she was doing a good job and she was talking to Seb
as though he was an old friend. Almost comfortable.

'So why this view?' Marianne asked, staring down at the
mellow bricks. She preferred the more austere, permanent feel
of the old keep. 'I mean, it's lovely, but why do you love this
particular one?'

Seb glanced across at her. 'My father used to bring me here.'

'Just you and your dad?'

He nodded. 'From about the age of eight. During the school
holidays he made a point of it. Once, maybe twice a week.'

Marianne took another bite of apple, happy to watch him.

It was easy to see why she'd fallen so hard and so quickly. Seb, prince or not, was gorgeous.

He took a sip of his coffee. 'Other than that I never got to see him alone. There was always someone somewhere wanting a piece of him.'

'And now it's your turn.'

He looked his question.

'Someone somewhere wanting a piece of you,' she clarified with a swift smile, before taking another bite of her apple.

She couldn't even begin to imagine what his life must be like. How would it feel to be surrounded by other people—at all times—and yet be essentially alone? Set apart from birth?

Did that feel lonely?

It was easier to imagine Seb as an eight-year-old striding out with his dad. Marianne plucked at the grass beside her. 'Did your sisters mind you having their dad to yourself?'

Seb wiped a tired hand across his face and she smiled. He looked exhausted.

'Isabelle, no. She was that much younger. Viktoria might have, I think. But I was his heir. It was all part of the training regime.'

And that about said it all. Marianne looked over the top of her apple. 'Even though you're not the eldest,' she said, watching for his reaction.

It was quick to come—and she loved that about him. Loved not having to explain what she meant. 'You don't approve of male succession either? Why doesn't that surprise me? How about,' he said with a sudden glint in his eyes, 'if I tell you it's been part of our tradition since 1138?'

'So was having a married sovereign and you changed that.'

She watched him fight his laughter. 'But that was only a tradition since 1654.'

'Of course, that makes all the difference,' Marianne said,

tipping out the dregs of her coffee on the grass beside her. She looked up and smiled.

She'd missed this. Missed *him*.

What would have happened if she'd met him for the first time today? Would he have wanted to spend time with her?

Probably.

When he looked at her…

Marianne wrapped her fine cotton skirt around her bare legs. And would she have wanted to spend time with him? She glanced over as his fingers tipped his empty cup upside down on the grass.

What would Seb say if he knew that he was still the only man she'd ever made love to? That his lean hands had been the only ones ever to move across her body?

Marianne turned away and bit down on her lip. It was finished. It didn't matter how attracted she was to him—or him to her—there could never be any long-term future. She wasn't 'suitable'. He'd told her that.

'Can I ask you a question?' she said suddenly.

'Of course.'

'Wh-when you said your parents knew about me…'

'Yes?'

'Does that mean people know now?' Marianne turned her face to look at him. 'I mean…do people know that I'm the person you were with in France and—?'

'Why do you ask?'

She shrugged, trying to appear nonchalant. 'I wondered if Princess Viktoria might have…' Marianne shook her head and let her fingers stroke the grass beside her. She wasn't sure what Seb's sister had been thinking. It was just a suspicion.

'She might remember your name,' he said, handing his cup across. 'My mother certainly will. And the protection services will both remember and know absolutely that you're the same woman.'

'And be watching me?'

'They watch everyone that stands close to me. It's their—'

'Job,' Marianne finished for him. She twisted the lid back onto her flask. 'I don't like it.'

'Marianne, as soon as your life touched mine it was inevitable. You'll have been under low-level surveillance ever since we met in France.'

'Isn't that an infringement of my personal liberty or something?' she asked as she stood up. 'I thought it was illegal to keep information on people without their knowledge.'

'My safety is paramount.'

Her eyes narrowed and she swung round to look at him. 'Because you're *so* important. I keep forgetting that, don't I, Your Serene Highness?' She bent and picked up her jumper, shaking the grass and the mud off it. 'You're important and I'm not important.'

'It isn't my fault,' he said quietly. 'I was born to this.'

No, it wasn't his fault. But she didn't have to like it. It really bothered her to think that unseen people had been watching her movements—over a ten-year period. Perhaps making files on her she'd no knowledge of. Free to say anything they liked about her, make judgements, without any threat of redress.

And did 'they' know she'd been pregnant? Had 'they' decided not to tell him? Marianne rolled her jumper into a tight tube and fed it into the rucksack along with her empty flask.

It would be better if she kept angry. Kept remembering why she couldn't let herself fall under his spell for a second time.

'They only use the information if they think you're a threat.'

She swung her bag on her back. 'Can't you just tell them I'm not the bomb-planting type?'

Seb smiled and her stomach flipped over. 'They don't listen to me. I'm merely the object to be guarded.'

He was gorgeous. And what he was saying was true, she supposed. Every friend he made, all the people he met— everyone vetted for their suitability.

What a *horrible* life.

She'd thought that so many times since she'd met him again in London. It looked different in the photographs. Then you saw the beautiful surroundings, the clothes, the exotic locations you were never likely to see in person, and she'd felt…well, angry. But there was another side to it.

Even knowing that your life was at sufficient risk to warrant the level of protection Seb had must be unpleasant, let alone living with the day-to-day consequences of it. Personally she'd much rather have her life with its smaller worries about mortgage payments and lifting bamboo flooring.

'We'd better start heading back before they send out a search party. If they find me with you I'll never be able to convince them I'm not a threat to national security.'

'It's not personal.'

What a daft thing to say. It *was* personal. Of course it was personal. How could it be anything *but* personal? She'd had the temerity to fall in love with the Andovarian crown prince and been a marked woman ever since. And it was *extremely* personal not to be considered good enough.

Well, news flash, it wasn't a vacancy she wanted to fill. Maybe her guardian angel had known what she was doing when she made it impossible for her to refuse coming to Andovaria.

All she had to do was to keep focused on what had brought her here. It *was* a great career opportunity. And the professor *did* need her. And maybe, just maybe, she'd return to England and be able to get on with her life without feeling that the best part of it had already happened.

'Where are you staying?' he asked as they walked back across the grass.

Marianne looked sideways at him. She'd hoped he already knew that. 'In one of the guest suites. I thought you'd okayed it.'

'I've been in New York.'

'I know, but…' She bit her lip. That was what had worried her when Princess Viktoria had insisted. That and something indefinable in the way his sister had looked at her. 'Princess Viktoria said it would save me a great deal of time each day, not having to get through Security.'

'I'm sure it does.'

'Was that wrong of her?'

'Why would it be wrong?'

She didn't know. That was the whole point. They were on his home territory, not hers. But there'd been something about Princess Viktoria's expression that had made her wonder whether she suspected her reason for being in Andovaria was not entirely due to the discovery of twelfth-century artifacts.

Of course, she could be being over-sensitive. She was incredibly nervous about being here. Nervous about seeing Seb again. Nervous about…pretty much everything and that was bound to throw everything out of kilter.

Marianne tucked a loose strand of hair behind her ear. 'I'd booked a room in a hotel, but Princess Viktoria—'

'I'm glad she did.'

'You are?'

'Of course. There's no point running the gauntlet of the paparazzi every day when you don't need to.'

'No.' And that did make sense. She'd been shocked to see how many people seemed to be waiting at the private entrance to the castle. 'Is it always like that?'

Seb shook his head. 'They're waiting for Isabelle. She'll

be home for my mother's fiftieth birthday celebration—and they all know it.'

'And are they there day and night?'

'Only if they can't get in,' Seb said drily, 'and they do more than wait. They jump out of bushes, they try and bribe the staff here, get friends of friends to talk. Anything to make sure they get a picture no one else gets because that's the way they earn their living.'

'Does she know that that's what's in store for her?'

Seb stopped at the bronze statue of the horse and looked across at the sweeping drive which led up from to the private entrance. 'She's a fool if she doesn't. The official Press pack are hard enough to accommodate, but the paparazzi are something else altogether.'

'I'd hate that.'

Seb looked across at her. 'We all do. They're so single-minded it can be quite frightening…I'm sorry—'

'It's fine.'

'But not your problem and I shouldn't have—'

'I don't mind. It's interesting.' And she liked him talking to her. Telling her things about his life and the way he felt about it.

It was funny, but until this moment she hadn't registered how little she'd actually known about Seb while they were together in France. She'd poured out all the details of her life. Talked about her parents, her village, her school, her dreams for the future. But Seb…had said nothing. Couldn't, she now realised.

Which meant he must have been constantly editing what he was saying. Thinking of things to say and then realising he couldn't. She'd been so incredibly stupid.

'What are you thinking?'

Marianne bit back an almost hysterical laugh. There was no way she was going to tell him that. He didn't need to know she'd found a new humiliation. 'Nothing.'

'Please. I'd like to know.' His voice was deep and quiet. 'I can always tell when you're unhappy.'

Marianne looked up and the expression in his eyes made her heart beat erratically. She felt cold, frightened and incredibly small. There was something going on between them she didn't understand and couldn't seem to control. *How could she be falling for him now?*

'Marianne.' He breathed her name and it was as though it was expressing an emotion he didn't have any other way of communicating.

Slowly, giving her plenty of time to move away, Seb stretched out his hand and his knuckles brushed lightly against the side of her face. 'You're so beautiful.'

Beautiful. That single word throbbed through her body. She wanted to hear that. Needed to hear it.

His thumb moved gently against the side of her jaw, barely touching, and yet every nerve in her body had screamed to attention.

'So beautiful.' Barely a whisper. It almost seemed to hang in the air.

His eyes held hers. Dark, dark brown. His pupils wide and black. Easy to fall back in love with him. Easy to forget how alone she'd felt when he'd left her alone in Paris.

Left her.

Seb had left her. Beautiful meant nothing. It meant he wouldn't mind going to bed with her. It didn't mean he loved her. Or that he wanted to know her dreams or share them with her.

'No.' Marianne pulled away.

Seb shot a hand through his dark hair. His eyes looked bleak and, for one moment, she thought he was going to say something.

She shook her head. 'I can't,' she whispered.

Seb nodded and then he walked away.

Marianne raised one shaking hand to her lips and stood there. She felt weak…and foolish…and exposed.

He'd wanted to kiss her.

She knew it. And the truth of it was…she'd wanted to be kissed.

In the distance she saw his tall figure disappear between the archways and she knew that if she could have called him back she would have.

Marianne tightly shut her eyes against the tear that had spilled over onto her cheek. She was in one almighty mess. She wasn't over loving Seb—and she probably never would be.

So, what was she going to do now? She felt as though a fierce wind had blown through her body and had left her buffeted.

CHAPTER SIX

SEB stretched out the aching muscles in his back. He'd worked himself hard in the gym, but he knew that it was tension that was causing the problem—and that Marianne was the reason for the tension.

What had he been *thinking*? He stood under the hot jets of water and let the rivulets run down his naked body. He needed the shower to wash away more than the dirt and grime from ten hours of travelling.

The trouble was he hadn't been thinking. He'd been feeling. His hand balled into a fist, but there was nowhere to vent his frustration. *Damn it!*

'Seb?'

He leant forward and turned off the shower as Viktoria's voice penetrated the sound of the water.

'In the shower. I'll be out in a second,' he called back, reaching for a towel off the warm rail. He slung it low round his hips and then picked up another from a pile on the nearby table.

He emerged drying his hair with vigorous movements as his sister looked up from the magazine she was reading.

'I see you're featuring in this one,' she said drily, holding out the open page.

Seb spared the article a brief look and continued drying his hair. 'Liesl brought them for me to see. There's a fair bit about Isabelle in the ones below.'

'Who's the brunette?'

'The wife of someone I met in Los Angeles.' He finished drying his hair and tossed the towel across the back of a nearby chair. 'Don't worry, her husband was standing to the left of her. I'm not dragging the family into disrepute.'

'Just out of shot.' Viktoria closed the magazine disdainfully and set it down on the table. 'I hate that they can get away with that. It's completely misleading.'

'You and I both know that kind of nonsense sells magazines,' he said, walking through to his dressing room and pulling out a pair of denim jeans and a folded black T-shirt, 'and let's be grateful it's me in that one and not Isabelle.'

He heard his sister's snort of derision and smiled. Viktoria had never put a foot out of line in her life. She'd made an approved, dynastically sensible marriage and appeared reasonably content in it. If she and her two boys made increasingly lengthy stays at Poltenbrunn Castle, who was he to comment?

Seb pulled his T-shirt over his head and walked back through to see that his elegant elder sister was looking unusually pensive. And he was fairly certain he knew why—and, for the first time in a long time, it wasn't about Isabelle's exploits.

He paused in the doorway. 'Is this a conversation we ought to have over tea and cakes or is it more of a whisky and soda one?'

'I need to talk to you.'

'About?' He moved to sit down opposite her and tried to keep his body language as relaxed as possible.

'Dr Chambers.'

His sixth sense hadn't failed him. He'd known this conversation was inevitable from the moment Marianne had said his sister had placed her in one of the guest suites.

'What about her?'

'Who is she?'

'Professor Peter Blackwell's right-hand woman.'

Viktoria rubbed at her exquisitely plucked eyebrow. 'I don't doubt that, but—'

'And the grown-up version of the girl I met in France.'

At that her expressive eyes swung round to look at him. There was no surprise in them, just an incredulous disbelief. 'Why did you bring her here now?'

'I didn't; you did. You were the person who insisted on Professor Blackwell.'

Viktoria's elegant fingers nervously twisted one of her pearl earrings. 'And you didn't know your ex-lover was a close colleague?'

'No.'

Her mouth pursed. 'Somehow I find that hard to believe—'

'I don't honestly care what you believe,' Seb said, his patience exhausted. 'Vik, I'm tired. I've been travelling for something like ten hours and I don't need this. I had a relationship with Marianne Chambers ten years ago and we haven't been in contact since. What do you think is going to happen now?'

'You do know we can't afford another scandal. The annulment of your marriage rocked the monarchy…'

'I know.'

'…and with Isabelle cavorting around Europe with her skiing instructor—'

He cut her off more forcibly. 'Yes, I know.'

Viktoria made a monumental effort to smile and stood up. 'I know you'll do the right thing. You always have before.'

Yes, he always had before.

'I'll leave you to rest before dinner. You must be exhausted.' She reached for the door handle. 'But, Sebastian, please don't come down dressed like that. You'll make everyone else feel uncomfortable.' Then she hesitated. 'Incidentally, I put Dr Chambers in one of the guest suites because of the paparazzi outside…in case you were thinking—'

'She told me. She's not a fool, Vik, she had a very good idea why you'd done it.'

'How did she tell you?'

Seb pulled himself to a more upright position. 'I met Marianne outside. In the grounds. Maybe an hour ago.'

'And?'

'We spoke. I've come in for a shower. There is no "and".'

Viktoria looked at him closely. Two deep frown lines marred her otherwise smooth forehead.

He smiled and yet it was completely mirthless. 'I'm perfectly aware that you think I've brought my latest lover to the castle to rather tastelessly coincide with our mother's fiftieth birthday, but do you honestly think Dr Chambers would settle for the kind of relationship I could offer her?'

'Many do. You haven't lived like a monk since Amelie left.'

'Viktoria,' Seb took a deeply calming breath, 'Dr Chambers is here at your invitation. Whether you put her in the guest wing, a house in the grounds or a hotel in Poltenbrunn, Marianne wouldn't be interested.'

'You're sure?'

'Look at it from her point of view, Vik. She was an innocent eighteen when I met her, not some publicity-seeking starlet. What do you think she thinks of the way I treated her?'

His sister's mouth twisted in unwilling comprehension. She nodded. 'I'm glad. Not that you treated her badly, of course, but that you haven't deliberately brought her here. There are enough column inches devoted to our declining moral standards without adding anything else to the mix. And please don't forget what I said about changing for dinner,' she said before shutting the door quietly behind her.

Seb pulled himself out of the chair and walked through to his bedroom.

Damn!

He'd seriously underestimated Viktoria's ability to retain all facts pertaining to anything that threatened the stability of the Andovarian monarchy. And Marianne had certainly done that.

Seb stretched himself out on top of his bed and bent his arm over his eyes to shade them from the sun streaming through the windows. At nineteen he'd tried hard to persuade his father and uncle that he'd fallen in love and that the way he felt about Marianne was more important than anything else.

Their arguments had been strong and unequivocal. Their views on the secondary importance of love in a royal marriage fixed. Eight hundred years of tradition and history balanced against a girl he'd only just met. And he'd been young and overawed by what was immediately ahead of him.

In the end he'd allowed himself to be swayed by their experience. And, perhaps, they were right. Amelie had been desperately unhappy. She'd found royal life unbearably confining—and she'd been groomed to fill such a position.

He rubbed his fingers round his aching eye sockets. He knew what his duty required. He was acutely aware of it. At some point in the not too distant future he would need to marry again—and he couldn't afford to make a second mistake. Public sympathy would only stretch so far.

His consort would have to be someone who was comfortable with being Her Serene Highness the Princess of Andovaria. Someone who could embrace this kind of rarefied life and find it satisfying.

And that wasn't a woman who was more comfortable in

jeans and wore her hair in a casual pony-tail. Nor was it a woman who believed that enjoyment should come before duty.

It wasn't Marianne.

But, knowing all that, he had nearly kissed her. Today. Out by the statue of his father's horse. Not that the venue was important. What mattered was the overwhelming sense of compulsion.

Seb sat up abruptly and pulled a hand roughly through his hair. When he was around her he couldn't seem to stop something flaring between them. And even at nineteen he'd known that if he couldn't offer the possibility of forever, he had nothing to offer her.

Marianne woke particularly early—and she knew why that was. She lay for a moment, listening to the sound of birds outside, and then restlessly pushed back the covers. Hours of thought and she was nowhere nearer deciding what was the best thing to do.

Everything that had persuaded her to come to Andovaria was still valid. There were exciting historical discoveries to be made. Peter and Eliana were packing up their home in Cambridge and were arriving in five days. The professor was relying on her to be his support. Relying on her. And she owed him that support.

Nothing had changed.

Except…

He'd so nearly kissed her. Marianne padded over to the enormous wardrobe and pulled out her white towelling dressing gown. She wrapped it round her body and pulled the belt tight.

And she'd *wanted* him to kiss her. She didn't begin to understand how that was possible. Not when she'd spent the last ten years clawing back her self-esteem. Marianne walked through to the small kitchen area and picked up the kettle.

It was weak to want Seb to kiss her. And she didn't do weak. Not any more. She filled the kettle by aiming the water carefully into the wide spout rather than removing the lid, focusing her entire concentration on not missing a drop.

Ten years of protecting herself from being hurt again. Ten years of striving for other people's good opinion as though that would somehow make Seb's rejection of her less painful.

And in one single moment—the moment when she'd realised that if Seb kissed her she'd kiss him back—all that work had been swept away on one gigantic wave of emotion. She felt as though the foundations of her entire adult life had been shaken—and she was left desperately vulnerable.

Marianne pushed the tap lever to 'off' and carefully settled the kettle back into its cradle. She felt so sick inside, deep inside. Too hurt to cry. Too confused to think. Since meeting Seb everything had been shifting about so much she almost didn't know how she felt about anything.

But the sad truth was that no one had ever matched up to him. For ten years Seb had been the 'gold' standard by which she'd judged other men. And when they'd wanted to kiss her she'd felt entirely neutral about it.

Sometimes she'd let them and other times she hadn't. But it had never felt compelling. Or particularly sexy. Or… anything. For ten years she'd been emotionally switched off. Shut down to life.

Marianne reached across and lifted down a white china teapot and the small canister containing English tea. She'd no idea whether the tea was something Princess Viktoria had arranged especially for her because she thought she was sleeping with her brother, or whether the Blue Suite always had English guests, or whether everyone in Andovaria always drank English tea, but she was glad to find something familiar.

Because nothing else was. Seb lived in a completely different world to her. Her entire house in Cambridge would fit inside this guest suite twice over.

But what she really wanted was everything back the way they'd been in France. She wanted that magical feeling of closeness. Marianne hugged her arms around her body. It didn't matter how much she told herself that their time together had been an illusion—she still wanted that feeling of connection.

She was twenty-eight years old. *Twenty-eight*. And she'd never come close to feeling anything like it since—and deep down she was scared she never would. Perhaps she never would find someone who'd make her feel the way Seb had.

Marianne rested her hands on the edge of the sink, letting the stainless steel bite into her hands. It would probably help if she could let herself cry, but everything she felt had been buried too deep and too long for tears.

In one decisive movement she went back to her wardrobe and pulled out her navy blue suitcase. Empty now except for the red box she kept hidden in the inside zip pocket. Marianne placed the case on her bed and unzipped the side, before throwing it open.

She knew what was there. In that narrow side-pocket. It came with her everywhere she went. Always. But it felt more difficult to look at it now. Her fingers shook slightly as she pulled out the red box and pushed in the tiny catch that held it shut.

The white gold heart Seb had given her nestled against the black velvet. It was a beautiful thing but, more than that, what it represented had been beautiful. Marianne lifted it out and let the links of the chain run through her fingers.

Seb *had* loved her when he'd given her this. She honestly believed that. She might have been naïve and foolish…and young, but she was sure he had loved her. Maybe not with the depth of passion she felt for him, but there'd been something…

She had to cling to that. Because otherwise everything was a lie. The first time he'd held her hand pretending to search for her life line. The time he'd cradled her face in his hands and kissed her. When they'd nervously hired that first room and shut the door…

Marianne felt the first hot tear burn her cheek. She didn't attempt to wipe it away, but sat there letting it, and the ones that followed, scald her skin like acid.

She loved him.

She still loved him. And she loved the baby they'd made together. If Jessica had lived she would have given her entire life to make everything perfect for her.

Marianne's shaking fingers felt for the fragile catch and carefully opened the locket. Inside was a tiny photograph of a perfect little girl. Eyes shut. Looking more like a china doll than a real baby.

Her baby. Hers and Seb's.

The pain sliced through her like a chef's knife. The speed and the freshness of it always came as a surprise to her.

And she knew, looking down at the tiny picture, that the pain would never go away. Not even if she lived into very old age. Always she'd carry the grief of losing her child…

Doubly painful because she'd not even had the chance to know her. She'd held Jessica just the once. Tiny, perfect and still warm.

Just the once…

The sound of a car startled her and Marianne flicked the locket shut. She closed her hand over it protectively and went to look out of the window. It was barely six in the morning and yet there were any number of people standing in the fore-court. All in formal suits and standing beside sleek black cars with smoky windows.

Marianne turned away and went to put the locket carefully

in its case. She was no clearer now about what she should do
than before, but crying had helped a little. She had so much
to mourn. The loss of a daughter…and of a dream.

She left the suitcase open on the bed and walked over to
re-boil the kettle. If Eliana had seen her do it she'd have
objected on the grounds that it concentrated the minerals in
the water, but Marianne didn't care. Her hands went through
the practised procedure of making tea and then she stood, with
her hands cradled around its warmth, and watched the commotion outside.

Commotion was the wrong word. There was no sense of
pandemonium, just a calm sense of procedure. There were
three cars parked in an orderly row, the distance between
each of them exact. And they were flanked by riders on mo-
torbikes in a precise formation.

Marianne hid behind the window dressing and watched with
a quiet fascination. In the time she'd been at Poltenbrunn Castle
she'd not seen anything quite like this. There was a noticeable
shift in the posture of the men. They stood a little straighter,
looked a little more alert. Marianne took a sip of tea, her attention captured by what was happening outside her window.

Her breath caught in her throat as Seb stepped into the
picture frame of her window. He was dressed in a sharp black
suit and he was flanked by Alois von Dietrich on his right and
two grey-suited men either side of them both.

Marianne shrank back further into the folds of the curtain.
He looked exactly like the photographs she'd seen in so many
publications. The complete personification of what a modern
royal should look like.

He stopped and said something to Alois before ducking
down inside one of the cars. Marianne continued to watch as
the door was shut and Alois walked round to sit next to him.
Only then did everyone move. It was as though they were

working through practised procedures—which they probably were. Then the montage moved off as though it were one. Safe from detection, Marianne stepped out from behind the curtain and watched more openly as the cars and outriders snaked their way towards the private exit.

Marianne gripped her mug convulsively. She hadn't needed anything else to confirm how completely different his life was from hers, but this was a visual illustration of the gulf that separated them.

She'd hoped that coming to Andovaria would finally give her 'closure' and it seemed that someone somewhere had been listening.

CHAPTER SEVEN

THE professor pushed his glasses higher on his nose and frowned. 'Can't make this out at all. Marianne, what do you think?'

She picked up the neatly typed sheets the professor had given up on and quickly skimmed the contents. 'It's suggesting there was a second castle in Andovaria owned by Ulrich von Liechtenstein.'

'Does it pinpoint where?'

Marianne shook her head and reached for the pencil she had tucked in her pony-tail, putting a tiny note in the margin. 'Doesn't say. But, since he died in 1278, it's the right time frame.'

'Interesting.' The professor pulled off his glasses and rubbed at his eyes. 'I've had enough for today. I think I'm going to go and have supper with Eliana. How about you?'

Marianne shook her head. 'I'll finish looking over these, then I'll have a shower and head for my bed. I'm tired.'

He nodded and Marianne reached for a jumper and pulled it over her head. She liked it in the open-plan office when everyone else had gone home. She felt safer there, more cut off from what Seb was doing than when she was in the guest wing. And she found it was better if she actively tried not to know where he was.

Today there'd been the sound of a helicopter taking off and

returning and that had been bad enough. Her imagination had immediately started to picture where he'd been going.

Even the little information she'd unavoidably picked up about his life had begun to alter her perception of him. He worked hard. Long, long hours. Leaving early and returning late most days.

Marianne spotted another mistake in the translation the professor had been given so she made a small note in the margin and returned the pencil to her pony-tail for safekeeping. She kept working systematically through it, sheet after sheet, even when the last of the team had long gone.

It was all so fascinating. Names she vaguely recognised from other sources were becoming three-dimensional human beings with every paragraph. She rubbed a tired hand over her eyes and pushed herself to continue. One thing she'd learnt over the past two weeks was that it was better not to go back to the guest wing until she was ready to fall into bed. Sleep only came when she was completely exhausted.

Seb didn't feel tired. A visit to support an inter-racial community project in the north of Andovaria, followed by the royal opening of the largest neonatal unit in central Europe hadn't done anything to use up his restless energy.

He stood at the window and looked down at the guest suite. Everything was in darkness—which meant Marianne was sleeping. He glanced down at his watch. Five minutes after two in the morning. What the hell was he doing? He'd got the annual diplomatic reception in something like eighteen hours. He ought to try and get some sleep himself.

But…he knew there was little point. He simply wasn't tired.

And he'd thought about Marianne all day. He'd had a spectacular view of the keep as he'd flown out today and it had started his mind wondering, yet again, what she was doing. Whether she was still excited by what they were discovering.

And he'd wondered how long she intended to stay. Just knowing she was there was difficult. Particularly when he'd determined not to ask Viktoria anything about the project. This was her 'baby' and she would leap to a million and one conclusions if he expressed too much interest in it.

Seb opened the door of his private apartment and wandered out along the corridor, nodding at the security guard who was patrolling along it. He'd no particular destination in mind, just a desire to be doing something. The four walls of his private sitting room had begun to feel as though they were closing in on him.

He walked down the curving marble stairs and along the west gallery, past the state dining room and on into the north drawing room. Lights were low and the castle was quiet except for the ticking of clocks and the creak of old floorboards.

During the day this was a bustling hive of activity, but at night it was eerily quiet. And, perhaps, more beautiful. On the nineteenth-century walnut table was a novel by Nicholas Sparks. Seb picked it up and turned it over in his hand. Something Viktoria must have been reading and had left out.

He idly read the back cover and laid it carefully down, exactly as she'd left it. Seb glanced again at his watch. Twenty past two. It seemed as if the whole castle was sleeping except him....

Which meant it couldn't do any harm if he went to look at what was happening in the keep storerooms. He quickly walked through the interconnecting rooms that led to the panel that provided the only access to the keep's lower storage area.

Light glimmered under the almost closed doorway. He pushed it open, expecting to find someone had left the office light on—but found Marianne. Seb hesitated, his hand on the door handle.

A wise man would walk away.

She was asleep, her head resting on her arms and her drink

cold beside her. He smiled and let go of the handle. 'Marianne,' he said softly, not wanting to startle her.

The only response was a sort of snuffling sound that made his smile stretch further. He moved her coffee out of harm's way and touched her lightly on the arm. 'Marianne. Wake up. It's the middle of the night.'

She emerged rather as he'd always imagined the dormouse did in *Alice in Wonderland* but her first word wasn't 'treacle'. Marianne frowned and stared at him wide-eyed. 'Why are you here?'

'Curiosity.' He smiled because he couldn't help it. She looked so delightfully rumpled. Most of her naturally wavy hair was still pinned in its pony-tail, but there was enough that had escaped to make the look anything but tidy and she was wearing a green pencil like a stick in a cocktail drink.

'What time is it?' she asked, rubbing at her neck. 'I must have fallen asleep.'

She most certainly had fallen asleep. There were red squares across her cheek where the texture of her wool jumper had left its mark. Seb glanced down at his watch. 'Twenty-five minutes past two.'

Marianne frowned. 'Why are you here?' she asked again.

'I told you. Curiosity.'

'In the middle of the night?'

Seb fought the desire to laugh. He loved being with her. Just talking, being close to her, and he felt the pressures of his day lift away. 'It is my castle,' he protested. And then, 'I can't sleep.'

'You ought to work harder,' she said, still rubbing at her neck. 'I must have been here hours. Is it really twenty-five minutes past two?'

Seb held out his watch so she could see.

'Jeepers.'

'What's that mean?'

Marianne looked up questioningly.

'Jeepers? It's not a word I know.'

'It means… Oh, I don't know. It means it's twenty-five past two and I ought to be in bed.'

Seb smiled as she tried to ease out her body. 'Stiff?'

'Like you wouldn't believe.' She reached out for her coffee. 'This is stone cold.'

'Not incredibly surprising, is it? You probably made it hours ago.' Seb took the mug from her fingers and walked over to tip the contents away in the nearby sink. 'Why are you still here? Is Professor Blackwell a hard taskmaster?'

Marianne shook her head. 'I stayed on a bit later to finish reading this.'

'Is it that interesting?'

It was on the tip of her tongue to say that she was only reading it because the professor hadn't been able to, but she stopped herself in time. 'Possibly.'

'Noncommittal,' Seb said with a glance over his shoulder, his hand reaching for the kettle. 'Do you want another coffee?'

'You're going to make me coffee?'

His smile twisted. 'I do know how.'

'Yes, I know you do,' she began, stopping abruptly when she noticed the deep glint of amusement in his eyes. 'I suppose you'd better, since you probably don't get much practice.'

Seb laughed and it was as though someone had popped a bottle of champagne inside her stomach. She rubbed at her arms in an effort to distract herself.

'Cold?'

'Yes, I am.' Though why, she didn't know. She was wrapped up warmly in a thick hand-kitted sweater, whereas Seb was in a fine wool jumper and dark black moleskin trousers. He looked good in black. Almost Italian with his dark hair and dark eyes.

'Probably because you've not been moving around.'

'I suppose.'

'Do you still have your coffee with just the one sugar?' he asked, with a quick glance over his shoulder.

Marianne nodded. *Still.* He'd made coffee for her before.

He came over to the table and handed her a mug, before sitting down with his own. 'Tell me what you've found.'

'In this?'

He nodded.

'This is just a translation of one of the documents we found last week.' Marianne took a sip of her steaming coffee.

'And?' he prompted.

'And…' Marianne put her mug down on the table and pulled one of the sheets towards her. 'It's possible that Ulrich von Liechtenstein built a castle in Andovaria.'

Seb smiled across the top of his mug. 'Should I know his name?'

'Possibly not,' Marianne conceded, fighting the smile that was tugging at her mouth. 'Unless you've been nurturing a secret passion for knights in the thirteenth century. It's not conclusive, though, but a possibility.'

'Is he a well-known knight?'

'Not particularly,' Marianne said, tapping the papers on her desk. 'I had a pencil here somewhere—'

'It's in your hair.'

'Sorry?'

Seb leant forward and pulled the green pencil out of her pony-tail. 'In your hair.'

'Oh,' Marianne said, accepting the pencil and tapping at her head. 'I do that sometimes.'

'Yes, I know.'

And that was the trouble, he did know. Just being near him made her feel tingly and slightly edgy. He knew so much about her.

She pulled her eyes away and fiddled with the papers on the desk. 'Ulrich was born in 1200 and knighted by Duke Leopold VI of Austria in 1223. There's very little known about his life, but we do know he owned a castle in Liechtenstein—'

'Makes sense. Him being a von Liechtenstein.'

Seb's voice was teasing and Marianne ignored him as she added, 'As well as two others. One of which might have been somewhere in Andovaria.' She wrote another note in the margin.

'Stop now.' He laid his hand over hers. 'It's late.'

His hand was warm and his touch sent shivers coursing through her spine. 'You're right. I ought to go to bed.' As soon as the word 'bed' left her mouth images poured through her heightened imagination. Marianne picked up her coffee. 'I want to make an early start in the morning.'

'Why?' Seb's dark eyes were watching her, making her feel uncomfortable. Making her feel as if she were comprised of nothing but hormones.

And there was no 'why'. She'd only said it because she'd wanted to cover up the 'bed' thing. Marianne took another quick sip of coffee. 'What are you doing tomorrow?'

Seb smiled. 'Today,' he corrected.

'Today, then.'

'At ten fifteen I have a meeting with my mother—'

'With your mother?' she echoed, not quite sure he'd heard him correctly.

Seb nodded. 'The summer ball is in honour of her birthday, so I think she should have some say in what happens.'

'Yes, but…' She looked up to see his eyes laughing wickedly. Marianne gripped her mug a little tighter. 'Do you often have "meetings" with your mother?'

He grinned across at her. 'Not usually. When she's at Poltenbrunn we meet over dinner.'

Of course they did. Marianne wasn't sure how she felt about being teased by Seb. She was trying so hard to keep herself aloof, to remember all the reasons why she had to keep some distance between them. But it felt good…

Seb took a final sip of coffee and put his empty mug down on the table. 'And in the evening it's the diplomatic reception.'

'Oh.' Marianne finished her own coffee and quickly stood up. She'd absolutely no idea what a diplomatic reception was, other than it sounded as if it might be one of those state dinners she'd seen on fly-on-the-wall documentaries made about the British royal family. 'Shall I wash your mug?'

Seb hand it across to her. 'Thank you.'

'Is it fun?' she asked. 'The diplomatic reception.'

'Not often.' Seb stood up and moved closer. Marianne could feel his eyes watching her even though she had her back turned towards him. 'It's very formal. There's a guest list of around nine hundred people and I get to speak to them all.' He smiled. 'At least it feels that way.'

Marianne looked over her shoulder. 'So not fun?'

'More like an endless wedding reception. The first three hours are the worst,' he replied wickedly. 'But it's only annual, thank God.' He paused. 'Let's get out of here.'

'Pardon?'

'Leave here,' he repeated. 'You're right, it's cold. We must do something about getting some heaters in here.'

'Th-this part is fine. It's only cold now because the heating is off.' She knew she was rambling, but her stomach had started fluttering. 'Go where? It's the middle of the night.'

His smile had her blood pulsing. 'I could give you the guided tour.'

'Of the castle?'

'Well, not all of it. It's an unusually large building.'

Her eyes fell to her shoes as she wrestled with her conscience as to whether she should go with him or not. Obviously 'not' was the most sensible decision. But…to see the castle. And to see it with Seb.

Seb held out his hand. 'Coming?'

And it seemed the most natural thing in the world to put her hand inside his. 'I want to see the ballroom. Wasn't it the largest room in Europe when it was first constructed?'

He threaded his fingers through hers. 'You've been reading the guide book.'

Perhaps it was because it was the middle of the night, but Marianne felt as if she was in a bubble. It was as though this time was borrowed time. Outside of normal rules and considerations.

He led her out into the north drawing room. 'You're familiar with this room?' he said, looking down at her.

Marianne nodded.

'Well, I hope you've appreciated the stuccoed ceilings.'

She looked up. 'I'm afraid I didn't notice the ceilings.'

Seb smiled and pulled her on and out into the impressive hallway with the large curving marble staircase. Paintings of hunting and battle scenes lined the walls in big, heavy frames. Marianne hated them all. She paused at a particularly gruesome one.

'Why do you have these here?' she asked.

'Because my great-great-grandfather hung them and no one has dared move them since.'

Marianne laughed. 'Which one was he?'

'Prince Hans Adam II. He reigned from 1853 to 1917. There's a portrait of him in the long gallery, looking particularly worthy.'

'Do you know the names of all your ancestors?'

Seb released her hand and opened the doors to a room on

the left, flicking on the light switches. 'All of them. It was part of my royal training. I had a tutor who made up a tune to help them stick in my head.'

A tune. This whole night was beginning to feel rather surreal.

'So eventually someone will have to learn all about you.'

He smiled, his eyes glinting. 'Scary thought, isn't it? Now, this is the grand drawing room. And I particularly dislike the red silk-covered walls in here.'

Marianne stared past the rococo furniture and on to the huge double doors at the end of the room. 'What's through there?'

'The blue drawing room. One day I intend to paint it all green for the hell of it.'

Her breath caught on a gurgle of laughter.

'In my father's time court etiquette still demanded both parts of those doors were opened every time he wanted to go from one room to the other.'

His voice was laced with humour and Marianne turned to look at him. *Seb really loved this place.* He knew its history and secrets and he loved it. Connected to it through generations.

Not the playboy prince of the tabloid press, then. Marianne could almost hear another crack appear in the shield she'd built around herself. There wasn't a great deal of it left to protect her.

'You've been very careless with Andovarian traditions.'

'Not me. That one went when my father married my mother.'

Marianne looked up questioningly and caught the laughter in his dark eyes. 'Both sections only had to be opened when the sovereign prince walked through. Lesser mortals could manage with just the one door and, since my mother was considered a lesser mortal…'

'She didn't like it,' Marianne finished for him with a smile. 'Neither would I.'

Seb turned to look at her and it was one of those moments

where the air seemed to disappear from the room and it became, quite suddenly, difficult to breathe.

And he felt it too. 'Marianne,' he murmured, his eyes appearing almost black.

Her laughter died. *He was going to kiss her*. And she wanted him to.

'P-please,' she said on the tiny amount of air she had left in her lungs. She didn't need to say what for—which was just as well because she wasn't sure what she was asking for.

Marianne saw him swallow before he stepped back. It was the safest option, probably the right decision. Marianne opened her mouth, and then shut it again. She couldn't think of a single thing to say as regret flooded her.

'And through here is the long gallery,' he said with a swift movement towards a door to the right.

She didn't want to kiss him, didn't want to unleash all the feelings she still had for him—but she didn't want this either. It felt wrong.

Her feet moved slowly towards the long gallery. It was pretty much as she has expected. Windows to one side and portraits to the other.

Seb had switched on the lights and turned back to look for her. 'This is the way to the ballroom.'

Why was she doing this? There was no possibility of friendship with Seb. She wanted more. She wanted him to love her. To hold her, keep her safe and *love her*.

As though he knew she was deciding whether to continue with their middle-of-the-night exploration, he stayed where he was, turning to look at one of the portraits. 'This is Prince Josef Johann who by all accounts was a thoroughly unpleasant character.'

Marianne walked closer and looked up into a beautifully painted oil portrait. She couldn't resist it. She felt as if a million skeins of the finest silk were pulling her towards it. Towards Seb. Inevitable.

'He reigned from 1772 to 1781. Not particularly long, but long enough to seduce half the female population and ensure that the Rodier genes were well-established in Andovaria.'

'He's handsome,' Marianne smiled. *But not as handsome as Seb*. Not as sexy.

'And this is his son, Prince Hans Adam I.'

'The man who put the pictures along the staircase?'

Seb's dark eyes glinted down at her. 'You're not paying attention. That was Prince Hans Adam II and the paintings are far too modern. This Hans Adam ruled from 1871 to 1805 and he was a great traveller and amateur botanist.'

'And less handsome.'

'Quite. He seduced far fewer Andovarian maidens and, in fact, I think his preference lay in quite another direction.'

'Is seducing maidens part of the job description, then?' The question left her mouth before she'd realised what she was saying. Marianne bit her lip.

His voice was deep, sexy. 'No. Not since 1914.'

Marianne looked up, startled, and saw his eyes alight with laughter. She felt her skin heat.

He lifted his hand to stroke her cheek. 'You still do that?'

'What?'

'Blush.'

'Not often.'

Seb laughed. 'Only when we're discussing the seduction of maidens?'

'Something like that,' she returned, wrapping her arms protectively round her waist.

'Still cold?'

Marianne let her arms fall back down to her sides. 'No. Not

really.' And then, because he was watching her closely, 'A little. Is it peculiar to know you're related to all these people?'

'Not really. You have as many ancestors lurking behind you. I just know who mine are, that's all.'

Marianne walked on further down the long gallery. It was rather amazing to think that all these people's lives were interlinked. One life leading on to the next until they reached Seb. The latest in a long line of rulers.

She glanced up at him, searching for the distinctive Rodier family features. Dark hair, dark eyes and strong cheekbones. 'Do you have a portrait?'

'Oh, yes. Inescapable duty. I was added to the rogues' gallery when I succeeded my father.' Seb walked on a few steps. 'This is my grandfather. This is my father...and this is me.'

Marianne's shoes sounded loud on the oak floorboards of the long gallery. She gave all the portraits a cursory inspection, before stopping next to Seb. She looked briefly at him and then at the painting of him.

She wasn't sure what she'd been expecting, but this painting wasn't it. Every other portrait, it seemed, had shown grown men, confident, steely and ready to take on the challenge of their rule.

But Seb's portrait showed a boy. Tall, unmistakably a Rodier with his dark hair and dark eyes...but a boy, who was uncomfortable in his stiff uniform.

She let her eyes wander back along the corridor. So many paintings. A monarchy that stretched back hundreds of years. Then she looked at the young Seb. He'd taken his place, but he looked as if he was playing a man's role before he was ready.

Was that how it had felt? She knew he'd been young and he'd told her he hadn't felt in control of what was happening to him—and finally, seeing this, she believed him. Really believed him.

Marianne swallowed the hard lump in her throat. 'What's the blue sash and jewelled cross?'

'That's the Grand Star of the Order of Merit of the Principality of Andovaria.'

She nodded, but she scarcely heard him.

'It's very heavy. I don't think I've worn it since.'

'You look so young.'

She'd wanted to know why Seb had left her—and this was the 'why'. It was a calling—almost as sacred as one to the priesthood.

'I was young. That was painted just before Christmas the year I met you.'

Marianne swallowed again. 'Will you change it? Later, I mean?'

'No.' Seb shook his head. 'That's a moment in time. My first official portrait as the ruling prince. There are any number of other portraits.'

'Are there?'

'I sit for at least one a year.'

A different life. A very different life. Marianne pushed up the sleeves of her jumper. She wanted to run away and hide somewhere. She'd known for ten years his life was different. She'd known it when she'd first arrived at Poltenbrunn Castle. And when she'd seen him leave the castle in one of those sleek, purring cars.

But now she *felt* he was different.

'And through here,' he said, crossing to another pair of double doors, 'is the ballroom. Currently set up in readiness for the diplomatic reception.'

Light and airy because of the phenomenally high ceilings, Marianne's eyes looked upwards at the intricate mouldings. Then they travelled to the huge mirrors...

No!

She gazed at her reflection, horror-struck. She looked as if she'd been dragged through a hedge backwards. Her hair was falling out of her pony-tail and her light summer skirt looked stupid with her heavy knitted jumper.

Marianne quickly pulled the elastic band out of her hair and ran her fingers through her natural curls. And then, of course, wished she hadn't as she caught a glimpse of Seb's laughing eyes in the mirror.

'I look like the wicked witch of the west,' she said by way of an excuse.

'You look beautiful.'

Seb had said that before…in exactly the same way. And his brown eyes did that thing they did that made her feel as if she was burning up from the inside out.

And she wanted to cry. Marianne swung her head away so that her hair would give her some privacy. 'Is this where the summer ball takes place?'

'All these tables will be cleared away after tomorrow and an army of florists will set about transforming it.'

Marianne felt as if it were someone else speaking. She wanted to go back to the relative sanctuary of the guest wing. She wanted time alone to think about what she'd seen. Understand what she *felt*. 'When is Princess Isabelle arriving?'

'She spoke to Viktoria. They've agreed it would be better if she arrived at the last possible moment. There'll be so many other people arriving then…'

Marianne nodded and then she tensed as she felt Seb's hands on her arms. He spun her to face him. 'What's the matter?'

'It's nothing.' She drew in a short breath and let it out slowly. It *was* nothing. Nothing new. 'It's an amazing room,' she said on a croaky whisper. 'Thank you for showing it to me.'

His right hand slipped up to her shoulder and the other hand gently pushed back her fine blonde hair. With one thumb he brushed across her eyelids as though he could erase whatever it was that was making her look so sad.

His warm hand moved from her shoulder to tilt her chin. 'What have I done to make you sad?'

Marianne let out her breath on a broken laugh. 'Nothing. It's not you. It's me.' She tried to step away from his intense scrutiny, but he didn't release her. 'It's not your fault. It's mine. M-my fault.'

'What's your fault?'

He looked completely bemused and she couldn't really blame him. Seb didn't possess the single most significant fact about their time together. He didn't know they'd made a baby together. So for him it was all relatively simple.

Her eyes searched out his dark ones. 'I didn't understand. You told me in London, but I didn't really understand.' She tried hard to find the words that would convey what she was trying to say—without telling him about Jessica. He didn't need to know that. 'I've finally seen you as a prince. I really believe it. I don't think I did before. Not really.'

He brushed his knuckles over her cheekbones and ever so gently down her cheeks.

'This is all so impossibly big.' Marianne took another breath in on a hiccup. 'Your life is different from mine. You belong here and I d-don't.'

'Marianne.'

Her name on his lips unlocked the first tear. It carved a warm furrow down her cheek and Marianne tried to turn her head away from his incredible eyes. His thumb moved gently across it and his warm hands held her steady.

'I—I understand now what you meant in London. I needed to see this to really understand. For ten years I've been so angry at you for something you couldn't help.' She took her shaking bottom lip between small white teeth.

She wanted to die. Not really. Of course, she didn't really want to die, but she wanted him to stop looking at her that way. That mixture of compassion and tenderness. It hurt to see him look like that. It reminded her...

Another tear spilled onto her cold cheek and she felt his right hand burrow deep in her hair, moulding itself round her scalp. She should pull away, but it was what she needed. Seb was the only person who had any hope of understanding how bereft she felt. How utterly...*hopeless*.

Because, finally, she had to accept she could never have played a part in Seb's future. Whether he loved her or not—she was not part of this...however you chose to describe this.

She came from a long line of farm labourers. Their marriage certificates signed with their 'mark' rather than a signature. Only when free education had been introduced had anyone from either side of her family done anything other than live a hand-to-mouth existence in extreme poverty....

Not better. Not worse. Just *different*.

Seb kissed the teardrop away, and then her right temple, each kiss seeming to brand her as his. Warm and moist. She wanted him. Had always wanted him. But she wanted the man, not the prince.

She heard the small moan that came from deep within her throat, felt the lean muscle tone of his back as her fingers splayed out across it.

And then he kissed her lips. Soft and questioning at first. He drew back and looked deep into her eyes. He was waiting, asking for her permission. Marianne closed her eyes and leant into him.

His strong hands moved to cradle her face and his thumb moved against her softly parted mouth before he kissed her. Hard. Possessive. She opened her mouth to him the merest fraction and allowed her tongue to touch his.

She remembered this. *Exactly* this. The feel of his body pressed up against hers, the taste of him, the scent of his skin…

It was as familiar as walking from one room into another—and yet so, so sexy. Easy to forget that Seb Rodier didn't really exist. That the man she was kissing was Prince Sebastian—a man who'd left her because she wasn't 'suitable'.

She pulled back, her body suddenly tense.

'Marianne?' His dark eyes were so close to hers. She could feel his breath. 'What is it?'

'I—I can't do this.'

His thumb moved across her sensitised lips and she forced them not to open beneath it. 'What can't you do?'

'This. Us,' she whispered. 'It wouldn't work. I wouldn't be happy.'

Seb stepped back and pulled his hands through his hair. 'We need to talk—'

'We don't, Seb.' Marianne cut him off. 'There's nothing to talk about. What we had in France was special, so it's natural we should still feel something for each other, but you can never go back.' She tried to smile. 'It wouldn't be the same.'

CHAPTER EIGHT

A DOOR banged in the next room and Marianne looked round. 'What's that?'

'One of the night-time security staff, I imagine.'

Marianne drew in a shaky breath. 'He'll be wondering what we're doing here. We'd better go.'

'I imagine he knows.' Seb rubbed his hand across the back of his neck, reluctant to tell her how public their kiss had been. 'There are security cameras in all the state rooms.'

'Wh—'

'Most of the castle, in fact.'

Marianne wrapped her arms around her waist. 'We're being watched? Now?'

'As long as we're in the state rooms. Come.' He held out his hand, but she didn't move towards it. 'There are no security cameras in my private rooms.'

'What about the guest wing?'

'Not inside the suites themselves. Come with me,' he repeated. She didn't move. Her eyes were wide with shock—and he could understand that. He was used to living with people watching his every move and tended to forget it was happening. But for Marianne it was a new experience and, no doubt, unnerving. 'This way,' he said quietly.

She followed him wordlessly until they reached the grand staircase. 'I know my way from here. I can—'

'We can talk in your suite or in my rooms—I really don't care which you choose, but let's finish this. One way or another.'

Her eyes flickered with some emotion he didn't recognise and then he saw the resignation.

'This way.'

Her eyes darted around, presumably looking for security officers who might be patrolling this area of the castle, but she needn't have worried. The very fact that their kiss would most certainly have been watched on the security monitors meant they'd see no one now. The staff at Poltenbrunn were adept at not being seen.

He kept a tight hold on her until they reached the door to his private apartment. Marianne looked over her shoulder at him as he held the door open, then she walked in. Her shoulders were tense and her beautiful face as strained as he'd ever seen it.

Seb pulled his hand through his hair, unsure quite what he hoped to achieve. It was clear, though, that they couldn't continue as they were. Every time they were together something flared between them. Lust? Love? He didn't know. But he'd tried hiding from her and that hadn't worked.

He switched on a side-lamp and the warm light pooled around it. Then he moved across to dim the central lights. 'Whisky?'

'Please. A small one.'

Seb glanced over his shoulder. Marianne stood in the centre of the room, one arm clutching at the elbow of the other. *Why did she look so broken?*

'Ice?'

'Please.'

He put the ice in the bottom of the glass and then poured in the whisky. 'It's a single malt,' he said, handing it across to her.

'Thank you.'

'Make yourself comfortable,' he said, turning away to pour a second drink. There had to be an easy place to start this conversation, but he was damned if he could think of it.

What he really wanted to know was what she wanted from their relationship and, since he didn't know what he wanted from it himself, that was a difficult question to ask. They *had* options. Options that hadn't been there a decade ago.

Seb turned round to find Marianne hadn't moved. One hand was fiercely clutching the glass tumbler, the other clutching at the hand that held it. *Surely this was about more than having been caught kissing on camera?*

He walked over to her. 'Marianne...' He stopped and looked down at her hands, knuckles white with the pressure she was putting on the glass. 'We used to be able to talk to one another—'

'I talked. You didn't, Seb.' The expression in her usually soft brown eyes shocked him. It wasn't anger. It was hurt. Deep, profound hurt.

'Sit down,' he said, moving across to an attractive grouping of sofa and chairs. 'Please.'

She moved stiffly, her hands still tightly closed around her tumbler. He waited until she'd chosen her seat and then he deliberately sat opposite, where he could see her face.

Marianne took a small sip of her whisky and he could see she made a conscious decision to relax. Her hands loosened their grip and her shoulders visibly lowered. He sat, silently, waiting until she was ready to continue.

'I only realised just now how difficult it must have been for you when we were together in France. Not to be able to talk about any of the things that mattered to you.'

Seb went to speak and then realised he'd nothing to say.

'When I told you about the house I grew up in...' she stopped and took another sip of her whisky. '...you said nothing about where you'd grown up. Because you couldn't. I'd not noticed that before. I'm so stupid.'

Seb eased out the muscles in his neck.

Marianne's hair swung down in front of her face and her fingers moved against her glass. 'I feel such a fool for not noticing.'

He cleared his throat and thought of how to explain what had happened back then. He'd already tried to explain in London...

Or thought he had. Perhaps he hadn't? All he'd really done was present a calm justification of what he'd done to her ten years ago and why. He hadn't explained anything other than his reasons for leaving her.

Maybe that was where this conversation needed to begin?

'It didn't feel awkward,' he said slowly. His smile twisted as he tried to search out the words. This—being honest—was difficult. He'd deliberately not thought much about their time together. Once it was over there hadn't seemed much point. 'I liked hearing you talk.'

Marianne looked up, her hair falling back to softly frame her face. *She looked like an angel.* And he still liked hearing her talk. Liked the way she didn't simply agree with everything he said.

'I'd never met anyone who'd gone to the local non-selective school. Or who'd lived in a house that shared a wall with anyone else's.'

Her eyes flicked across to him. She was listening. And listening hard.

His fingers traced the rim of his tumbler. 'It fascinated me that if you did your piano practice before eight o'clock in the morning Mr Bayden from next door would bang on the wall.' He smiled, hoping she understood what he was trying to say. 'I didn't want to talk about me. I wasn't conscious of not being able to, just of not wanting to. Does that make any sense?'

There was a small delay before she nodded.

Seb let go of the breath he'd been holding, then continued more confidently. 'And I knew that as soon as I told you who I was…everything would change. I didn't want things to change. I liked being Seb Rodier. I liked being able to walk to the local café and find a bench by the Seine and watch the street performers…'

He heard her small sniff and saw her brush her sleeve against her nose. He'd not seen a woman do that since…she'd done it when she'd been helping him pack his bag.

Damn!

Seb put his whisky down on a side-table and ran both hands through his hair. He'd made a mess of everything. When he'd left her he'd honestly meant to contact her. More than that—his real plan had been to return to Paris. She'd known that. Forty-eight hours, he'd told her…

Only what he'd found at home had been life-changing. Very different from anything he'd expected.

'What happened to you?' he asked quietly.

Marianne's hands moved against the glass. Her shoulders moved in a defensive shrug. 'When you didn't come back?'

'Yes.'

She brushed the back of her hand across her nose again. Seb stood up and walked across to his dressing room, coming back with a starched white handkerchief.

'And?' he said, holding it out to her.

Marianne looked at it and then gave a tiny smile. 'You know, the rest of the world use paper tissues.' But she took it and held it balled against her glass.

He waited. She *would* tell him what had happened to her…if he waited. He was confident of that.

'When you didn't come back…'

'Yes.'

Her eyes flicked up to his and then away. Seb still waited, his body braced to hear whatever it was she was finding so hard to say.

She took another small sip of whisky. 'When I couldn't afford to stay at our hotel any longer I met Beth and we pooled our francs to settle the bill.'

He'd forgotten the bill. Seb pulled a hand through his hair. *Dear God, forgive him.* He'd left her to pay for their hotel room.

'Then we travelled to Honfleur together. Monsieur and Madame Merchand were lovely.' She drew a shaky breath. 'And Honfleur is a really beautiful place. Old. Lots of tall, thin houses.'

He nodded, though he'd no idea what Honfleur was like.

'And the little girl I was helping look after was sweet. I'd have been all right, I think, only my period didn't come.' She looked across at him, watching for his reaction. 'I was regular as clockwork, so it was strange, but I thought it might be because I was missing you. Sad, you know? Sometimes that messes up your cycle.' Her fingers moved against the glass. 'Anyway, that's what I thought.'

Pregnant!

Marianne had been pregnant? Seb's mind was one expletive. Of all the things he'd expected Marianne to say, this hadn't figured anywhere. 'You were pregnant?'

Marianne nodded. 'Beth and I went to buy a pregnancy test on the Monday after we got there. We were really embarrassed to ask for it.' She wiped her nose against the handkerchief. 'It was positive. Very clear. A dark blue line.' She moved her hand in a single stroke downwards.

There was probably something he should say here, but Seb couldn't think of anything. *Marianne had been pregnant.* Eighteen, pregnant and in a strange country.

'I told the Merchands I had to go home. I didn't tell them why. Just that I needed to go home.'

He nodded.

'They were very nice about it. Helped me sort out a ticket and Beth came with me to the station.'

He watched as she crumbled. First her hands twitched against the glass and then her bottom lip trembled. He saw her catch at it with her small white teeth. Then the tears started to fall in earnest.

And he sat there, powerless to do anything. He wanted to walk over and hold her, but he didn't quite dare.

'She died, Seb.' Her voice was so soft and laced with a kind of despair. 'Jessica died.'

Marianne's words hit him hard. He wasn't quite sure what to react to first. He'd left Marianne *pregnant* with no easy way of contacting him. And their baby had *died*.

She took another shaky sip of whisky, and the glass tapped against her teeth. 'Sorry. I wasn't going to tell you—'

'*You're* sorry? What have you got to be sorry about?' He moved then, coming to sit beside her on the sofa. He took the glass from her agitated fingers and placed it on the side-table, before reaching out to hold her hand. She didn't pull away. In fact, her fingers twitched inside his. 'Our baby died?'

'Jessica. I called her Jessica.' Marianne nodded and another tear welled up and slowly, so slowly, spilled onto her cheek.

Seb lifted a hand to smooth back her hair, his fingers lightly brushing across her left temple, and then he drew her back until she rested against him. He felt solid. Strong. 'Tell me.'

Marianne couldn't. Not for a minute or two. The words wouldn't come. She could hear the solid, steady beat of his heart. One hand gently stroked her hair and his fingers brushed against her neck. The other held her hand.

She felt so tired. So very tired.

'Everyone wanted to know why I'd come back early.' Her words sounded slurred and her eyelids felt heavy.

'What did your parents do?' His voice was a distant rumble.

'Cried. My mother cried a lot. She was so disappointed…and embarrassed.' Seb's fingers moved against the base of her neck.

Marianne felt a light kiss on the top of her head. So soft she might have been mistaken. She fumbled for the handkerchief and tried to sit more upright. Seb let her go and she blew her nose.

'Do you want some more whisky?' Seb asked, nodding at her empty glass.

Marianne reached out to pick it up off the table. 'Please.'

She watched him walk over to the drinks table and put in first the ice cubes and then a generous dash of the amber liquid. *What was he thinking now?* Was he angry with her? He didn't seem angry. Though why she thought he would be she didn't know. Only that so many people had been.

Marianne brushed her hair off her face and waited for him to walk back with her drink. *Two whiskies.* Her mother would be disappointed by that, too. 'Thank you.'

He smiled and sat back down beside her. His eyes were warm. 'Is that when you went to live with professor Blackwell and his family?'

Marianne nodded. 'My mother couldn't cope. She thought everyone in the village was talking.' She gave a swift, humourless smile. 'They were, too: "Pregnant without a boyfriend in sight". She thought I'd be better off in a hostel for girls in a similar position.'

She swirled the liquid round in her glass, watching it crash against the ice rocks. Funny how you could do that with words. Say one thing and mean something entirely different. Her mother had *said* that she'd be better off in a hostel, but what she'd *meant* was that it would be better for her.

And she'd been so frightened by that. She'd gone from being a 'golden' girl to being something that needed to be hidden away. She'd spoilt everything. All talk of university had been over.

'But my aunt Tia rang Eliana and I went to live with her…and her family.'

Seb pulled her in close against him. She liked that. Liked that he just held her. Ten years ago she'd ached for him to do that. When she'd been so lonely…

'How many months pregnant were you when you lost the baby?'

'Seven.' She swallowed, struggling to get the words out. 'It was late. Very late.'

Another soft kiss on her hair. She wasn't in any doubt this time. Seb's arms had tightened around her and he'd kissed her. *Which meant he didn't blame her for getting pregnant.*

Everyone else had seemed to blame her—except Eliana, who'd been kind. And they'd made plans for the future. Worked out ways she could continue to study. Talked about careers that combined well with motherhood.

The only time Eliana had been cross with her was when she'd refused to make an effort to contact the baby's father to say she was pregnant.

Marianne balled the handkerchief tightly up against the whisky tumbler. 'I'm sorry I didn't tell you.'

She took another sip of whisky. It was lovely the way it burnt a trail down her throat. Warming. Gently soothing. Like Seb's fingers moving in small circles at the nape of her neck.

'Did you try?'

She shook her head. 'At first I thought you'd come and find me. Then I imagined you'd had an accident. Amnesia maybe. You read about that sometimes. In books.'

Silence.

'Then I was too angry.'

'At what point did you find out I'd lied about who I was?'

Marianne registered his use of the word 'lie' and it was like a soothing balm.

'That was later. I didn't know for weeks.' She took another sip of whisky. 'I didn't understand why you'd left me. I was frightened by so many changes so quickly. Hurt by my mum and dad. Just taking one day at a time.'

Seb reached out and gently pushed back her hair so he could look into her eyes. 'I'm sorry.'

His own eyes were so warm. So incredibly warm. Then he kissed her forehead and tucked her close against him, his chin resting on the top of her head. She could feel him breathing.

'It didn't seem real until I could feel the baby move inside me.' She sipped her drink. 'Little kicks—sometimes she had the hiccups. When I went to my first scan I thought she looked like a kidney bean. Kind of.'

Marianne cradled the tumbler in her hand and looked down at the deep gold colour and the softly melting ice cubes. That scan had been an amazing experience.

She'd gone in a frightened girl and walked out determined to be the best mother she could, whatever the personal cost. She'd seen her baby and she'd loved her. 'Everything was going normally. She was moving about, sucking her thumb.'

Seb planted another soft kiss against her hair. 'And then she stopped moving inside me. I knew something was wrong straight away. Eliana told me not to panic, that babies were sometimes quiet for a while. But we rang the midwife anyway and she said to go to the hospital…as a precaution.'

It had been a long drive into Cambridge. They'd hit all the school traffic and it had been difficult to find a space in the hospital car park.

'They hooked me up to a monitor and tried to find a heartbeat.' Her voice became choked. Maybe this was more information than he needed. Wasn't it enough to know their baby had died?

'The midwife called a doctor and she told me that the machines sometimes played up, so they'd send me for a scan.' She dragged air into her body. 'And after that scan I had a second scan, but it was the same result: "The amniotic fluid around the baby severely reduced" and they could find "no foetal movement".'

Jessica was dead.

Marianne sat up and drank the last of her whisky. Her head felt slightly fuzzy from the alcohol, but that was good.

'They said they'd have to terminate the pregnancy.' 'Terminate'—such a neat word for what had followed. 'So they gave me a labour-inducing injection—'

'You had to give birth?'

His question seemed to have been wrenched from him. 'I was seven months pregnant. Everyone said it would be safer.'

Seb's face seemed to have become two shades paler. She passed him her empty glass to put on the table. 'They let me hold her,' she smiled tremulously, 'when she was born. She was lovely. She had little fingers with tiny, tiny nails. Completely perfect.' Marianne drew in a shuddering breath. 'But she was dead.'

Her little girl had been so beautiful…and had looked so peaceful.

'Eliana said I should give her a name. So I called her Jessica.'

'Jessica,' he repeated softly.

'It means "God is watching".' Marianne brushed a hand across her face. 'Eliana thought that was nice because God would watch over her now. Keep her safe for me.'

And that was it really. No need to tell him how it had felt to go home without her baby girl. How it had felt to look down at her stomach and not really believe it was empty.

There was no need to tell him any of that because one glance at his face told her that he knew. His eyes were bleak— as though something inside of him had died too.

'They did an autopsy and said they thought she must have been strangled by her umbilical cord because everything else was normal. Just one of those things.'

Seb reached for her and held her tight against him. His warmth wrapped about her and she lay quietly against his chest. This would have helped her. Back then. Eliana had been good, but she'd needed Seb.

She felt so tired.

'About three weeks after that I saw a photograph of you with your fiancée.'

With his arms about her that didn't seem so difficult to say. Didn't hurt so much.

'That's how you discovered who I was?' he asked, speaking into her hair.

Marianne nodded. She felt so tired and the effect of the whisky was biting. 'I hated you then,' she said, her words blurred and indistinct. 'That's why I can't do this. Can't let you hurt me again.'

Her eyelids were so heavy. And her arms and legs were heavy. Everything heavy and she was so, so sleepy.

'Marianne?'

She heard him say her name as though it was muffled.

'Sweetheart, come on.'

Marianne knew that she ought to answer. Say something to him. But she was so tired.

'Let's get you to bed.'

She felt him pull her jumper over her head and tried to be helpful. Then he picked her up and she felt as if she were flying.

* * *

Seb laid Marianne on his bed and stepped back to look at her. Her fine blonde hair was splayed out across his pillow, her fingers still loosely clutching his handkerchief. The whisky and the past had hit her with a vengeance.

He laid her jumper at the end of the bed and wondered whether he should do anything to make her more comfortable, though she looked peaceful enough. Maybe her shoes? Seb eased off both flat pumps without her stirring, then walked across to his dressing room to fetch a light duvet.

No wonder she hated him. His opinion of himself had taken a dive. She'd been eighteen and a virgin when he'd met her.

Seb walked back through to his bedroom, opened out the duvet and spread it across the top of her. Then he lightly brushed her hair off her face. Every instinct he had was urging him to lie down beside her, but he didn't have the right to do that.

She'd told him she didn't want him to kiss her. That she couldn't allow him to hurt her again. That single phrase would probably stay with him for ever. He'd never wanted to hurt her. *Never.* But what he'd done could have destroyed her.

And what if Jessica had lived? Their daughter? Seb ran a hand across his chin. He didn't honestly know the answer to that. He liked to think it would have given him the moral courage to stand his ground. Marry her anyway. However unhappy, his father would never have objected so strongly that he'd have seen the crown pass to anyone other than his son.

But…

At nineteen he hadn't had the confidence to challenge the accepted way of doing things. He'd been brought up to believe that with great blessings there came great responsibilities. Marrying someone who had the background and training to become the princess of Andovaria was his God-given responsibility.

He'd married Amelie. Because everyone around him had said it was the right thing to do. The best thing for Andovaria.

But everyone had been wrong. The constitutional crisis they'd feared would happen if he'd married Marianne had happened anyway.

Seb looked down at Marianne sleeping peacefully. He'd loved to watch her sleeping—the slow rise and fall of her breasts, her softly parted lips and the tiny murmur she made as she rolled over. He walked over to dim the lights and walked back out to the sitting room. It seemed intrusive to watch her now.

Damn, but his head ached.

On the rare occasions when he'd allowed himself to think about Marianne he'd thought about her in terms of something he'd had to give up. He'd not really thought about the consequences his decision would have had on her life. There were no acceptable excuses for that.

Seb lay down on the sofa and let his head lean back on the armrest. She'd said she'd hated him then. She must have— but *still* she hadn't sold her story to the papers. Told no one it seemed. Even though she'd hated him…

And they'd made a baby together. Seb drew his hand across his face again, feeling the stubble on his chin. *Dear God*, if he'd known about her pregnancy, would he still have let her down?

Seb pulled his hand across his face again. He'd left Marianne alone. He should have been there to comfort her when their baby died. At the very least he should have made sure she could contact him if…

He swore softly. He'd never dreamt Marianne might be pregnant. They'd been so careful. Every time. *Except the first time.*

Not that time because their hormones had overtaken them and they were lovers before they'd known it was a possibility they might be.

Seb pulled himself to his feet and paced about the room restlessly. He couldn't bear thinking of how she must have felt when she saw the pictures of his engagement to Amelie. How betrayed.

But what should he do now? What did he *want* now? By kissing her in view of the security cameras he'd forced himself to make a decision. Marianne would be looked on by his staff as either his girlfriend and their potential princess, or as his lover. There was no middle ground.

Seb walked over to the drinks table and poured himself a second whisky, much larger than the first. Things had changed in the last decade. Crown Prince Frederik of Denmark had married for love. As had Crown Prince Felipe of Spain and Crown Prince Haakon of Norway. In fact, Haakon had married a single mother called Mette-Marit and the whole country had rejoiced with them.

A relationship with Marianne *was* now possible in a way that it simply hadn't been ten years ago.

He sat back down on the sofa, elbows resting on his knees with his glass cradled between his hands. And it was his decision entirely now. No one had to sanction or ratify his marriage.

But what he couldn't do was make a second mistake. The end of his marriage was still a contentious issue with many even though it had been annulled on the grounds that it 'never was a marriage'. If there'd been children it would probably have been impossible for them to separate without doing irreparable damage to the monarchy.

He had to be sure that his next bride would be able to fulfil her role as his consort. She'd have to learn the Alemannic dialect favoured in his principality. Embrace the Lutheran religion of his country, publicly at least. Forgo the rights to her children in the event of marriage breakdown…

Difficult, very difficult things to ask of a modern career woman who hadn't been brought up to expect these demands.

But not impossible. Not if she loved him enough.

Seb stood up and pushed open the door of his bedroom and looked at Marianne. Still asleep. He didn't know whether she'd want those things. Whether he'd hurt her so deeply she'd never be able to forgive him.

He still wasn't even sure what he wanted from their relationship. People changed a lot in ten years. *He'd* changed. Marianne would have too.

But what he did know was that he didn't want her to walk out of his life.

CHAPTER NINE

MARIANNE opened her eyes and knew immediately that she wasn't where she should be. Everything about the enormous bedroom was unfamiliar and it didn't take many more moments to realise where she must be.

She groaned and put her hands over her eyes as though it would block out the reality of it. There were voices in the next-door room, too—which must have been what had woken her. Marianne lay quietly, trying to make out what was being said, scarcely daring to move in case she drew attention to herself. Being discovered in Seb's bed, albeit fully clothed, was going to be a hundred times worse than being caught on a security camera kissing him.

Because she *had* kissed him. She remembered that. And she remembered how difficult it had been to tell him she couldn't let him hurt her again. Even harder to explain the reason why.

A tiny rap on the door and Seb's voice startled her. 'Breakfast.'

Breakfast?

Marianne sat up in bed and clutched at the duvet.

'Marianne?'

It was one of those moments when she wondered whether the best course of action would be to lie back down and put a pillow over her head, but as the door began to open the ostrich manoeuvre was obviously no longer an option.

Seb stood in the doorway, still in the clothes he'd worn last night, looking completely relaxed and unbelievably sexy with the dark stubble on his chin. A real 'morning-after-the-night-before' look. 'Breakfast is on its way.'

'F-for me?'

'Of course for you. What do you want to drink? Tea or coffee?'

Marianne tried to think, but it was difficult. This whole experience had all the bizarre elements of a nightmare. She wasn't even quite sure how she came to be here. Not entirely. She remembered the whisky and the crying…and the way Seb had held her…

She brushed her hair out of her eyes.

'What time is it?'

'Eight.' He walked across and sat on the edge of her bed. *His bed.* 'How are you feeling?'

'Fine.' Marianne swallowed. Having him sit so close to her made her entire nervous system feel as if it was dancing. She tucked her hair behind her ears and struggled to appear as though unexpectedly waking in a gorgeous man's bed was something she could take in her stride. 'I'm sorry, I must have fallen asleep. Did I?'

For a moment he looked as if he might reach out and touch her and her stomach rolled over in fear and excitement. 'You went out like a light.'

'Wh-where did you sleep?'

'On the sofa.'

He'd slept on the *sofa*? Grief, but this was embarrassing. Six feet three inches of athletic male squeezed on a small sofa simply because she couldn't hold her alcohol or manage her emotions. 'I'm sorry.'

'Don't be. That was quite a conversation. Come and have some breakfast.' He stood up and walked back towards the door, stopping to ask again, 'Tea or coffee?'

Marianne was left feeling slightly open-mouthed. How could he say *'That was quite a conversation'* and *'Come and have some breakfast'* in the same breath? Last night she'd told him they'd created a baby together and that their baby had died. Didn't he have anything to say about that?

'Marianne?'

'Tea.' She blinked hard. 'I'll have tea.'

Seb nodded and shut the door. Marianne flung back the duvet, setting her bare feet down on the thick carpet. The sooner she got herself out of here and back where she ought to be the better.

She'd always be glad she'd told him about Jessica—and, in a curious way, she felt that some of the burden of it had been lifted. But she wished she hadn't cried all over him. And she really wished she hadn't fallen asleep up here. That was just embarrassing.

Marianne put a hand to her head and groaned silently as she thought a little more about it. He must have carried her into his bedroom because she sure as hell couldn't remember walking there.

She padded round the other side of the bed and swore as she banged her shin on the edge of it. If she could just find her shoes...

She'd got no recollection of having taken them off, which must mean Seb had done that too. Thank goodness he'd stopped at her shoes. If she'd woken up in nothing but her lacy knickers she'd have died of mortification.

But she still needed to ask him where he'd put them. They were nowhere she could see.

Marianne ran urgent fingers through her hair and smoothed

out her long cotton skirt, then stood with her hand on the door handle for a moment while she tried to whip up the courage to walk out there.

Just do it. How difficult could it be? Seb clearly wasn't uncomfortable with her being here, so she just had to walk out there and ask him where he'd put her shoes.

The sooner she did it, the sooner she could escape back to the guest wing—hopefully before too many of the castle security staff were out and about.

She pushed open the door.

Seb looked up from the newspaper he was reading and smiled at her.

Oh, God. Why did this feel so difficult? And why did he have to look so sexy in the morning? 'I can't seem to find my shoes,' she mumbled.

'I might have left them in the dressing room when I went to get myself a duvet last night. Come and have your tea, it's getting cold.'

Marianne looked over her shoulder in the hope she'd see where his dressing room was located. 'Sh-shouldn't I hurry away before anyone knows I'm here?'

'Why?'

Why? It all seemed perfectly clear to her. 'Because someone will see me.'

'The paparazzi have never managed to get a photograph of me here. Poltenbrunn Castle is quite private—'

'Apart from the cameras and the security guards,' she slipped in drily.

'Apart from that,' Seb agreed, a glint of humour lighting his dark eyes. 'Come and drink your tea.'

He was sitting at a small table next to open French doors. Last night she hadn't noticed either the doors or the table. She padded across the luxurious and totally impractical cream carpet. Without her shoes she felt at a complete disadvantage. 'D-do you always have breakfast here?'

'Usually.'

As she sat down he folded up his newspaper and put it to one side. And she wished he hadn't. It made this whole breakfast thing feel intimate and she didn't think she could cope with that.

She didn't want to be 'intimate'. The whole point of telling him about Jessica was to make sure he understood why she couldn't give in to…whatever it was that kept flaring between them. And to make sure he let her walk away easily, with her self-respect intact—and preferably without the entire staff of Poltenbrunn Castle whispering behind their hands.

'How are you going to get me out of here?'

He picked up his coffee. 'I was thinking we might ambush the person who delivers our breakfast and then you could escape down the trellis in her clothes.'

'Wh…'

His mouth twitched and his dark eyes were laughing over the top of his coffee-cup. 'I'm joking. I suggest we use the same way we came in.'

'But, I don't …'

Marianne stopped speaking as the door to his private rooms opened and a uniformed member of staff wheeled in a trolley. She turned back to look at him, expecting to see… Well, she wasn't sure what she was expecting, but it wasn't to see him calmly putting his coffee-cup back down on the table.

'I wasn't sure what you'd want for breakfast so I asked for a selection,' he said, exactly as if having breakfast with a women in his private rooms was a normal occurrence.

Which, of course, it might be for all she knew. Even discounting fifty per cent of what she'd read over the last few years, Seb wasn't a hermit and his opportunities were broader

than most. From her perspective that made this whole thing
so much worse. She just wanted to wake up again and find
this had been a bad dream.

She answered the woman's rapid German in a faltering
version of her own, settling on toast for no other reason than
she was too embarrassed to look properly.

Every instinct was encouraging her to bury her face in her
hands and cover her head with the starched white tablecloth.
She felt exactly as she had when her father had caught her
caught her kissing her first boyfriend after the school disco.

Seb appeared entirely comfortable with this whole situation. He made his own selection from the breakfast trays,
talked easily and oozed sophisticated charm.

'Everyone will think I've slept here,' Marianne said as
soon as the door closed behind the maid.

Seb picked up his coffee again. 'You did.'

'But I'd prefer it if everyone didn't know that. They'll
think you and I...'

Marianne trailed off helplessly. Seb knew perfectly well
what conclusions his staff would leap to. He didn't need her
to spell it out.

'Everyone who works here understands the need to be
discreet.'

Which wasn't the point! 'That doesn't mean they aren't
thinking it, only that they won't say it.'

He set his coffee-cup down. 'I think you may be surprised
what they're thinking. I've never brought any of my female
friends to Poltenbrunn.'

She looked across at him, a spark of anger in her expressive eyes. 'That's not the point. I've got my professional reputation to look after. I don't want my colleagues thinking that
you and I are...' She picked up her knife and smeared butter
across her toast.

Again that gleam of amusement. Sudden and unexpected. 'Are?'

Marianne put her knife down with a clatter. 'Lovers. All right? I've said it. Lovers. I don't want people thinking that I'm your lover.'

'Why?'

Her mouth moved wordlessly and then she said, 'Been there, done that, don't intend to do it again.' She picked up her toast as though she was going to take a bite, but then put it back down again. 'In my world, Seb, it's not about whether or not you're considered "suitable" or who your parents are—'

'I don't believe that.'

'And how would you know? Your entire experience of real life comes down to the five weeks you spent with me. That doesn't exactly make you an expert on what "normal" people do or how "normal" people plan their lives.'

Seb loved the way she did that. One moment she was delightfully confused, the next she was fiery and opinionated. 'So you're saying,' he said mildly, 'that your parents will be equally happy if you marry the drug-addict son of a convicted murderer as opposed to the lawyer son of their local doctor?'

'That's extreme and you know it.'

He shook his head. 'My life is extreme. I can't afford to act without some thought.'

'How romantic!'

Seb smiled again. She looked the way he imagined a ruffled pigeon might. 'No, it's not romantic. The only time I've been free to do exactly as I wished was when I was with you. And that's why you're here.'

As he said the words a *frisson* of awareness passed between them. It always did whenever they allowed themselves to remember what they'd once had together. Marianne's eyes fell away and she looked down, apparently fascinated by the toast on her plate.

Seb took a deep breath. This was it. This was the point at which he needed to try and put words on all the complicated thoughts he'd sat up all night thinking. And honestly, it scared the hell out of him. 'How do you feel about me?'

Her eyes flicked up. 'I don't really know you any more.'

'Perhaps not. But I still need to know how you feel about me.' He kept watching her, hoping, expecting her to say she still cared about him. 'Marianne, it's important.'

'Why?'

His mouth twisted into a wry smile. He should have known that this more mature and confident Marianne would throw his question back at him.

'Because I kissed you,' he said simply.

'I don't understand.'

Seb pushed his chair back and stood up. He'd feel better on his feet. It was how he'd done most of his thinking anyway, pacing up and down the floor. Somehow she'd managed to turn the tables on him. When he'd planned this conversation in his head it had run along completely different lines.

He wasn't good at saying how he felt. He hadn't had a great deal of practice—and he wasn't sure what words to use. Where to start. How you even began to unpack all the thought processes that had led him to this point.

'I kissed you,' he repeated, his hand rubbing the back of his neck, 'when I didn't want to.'

He knew he'd made a mistake when a frown snapped across her forehead.

'Didn't mean to,' he corrected swiftly. 'I kissed you when I didn't mean to. I spoke to you in Amiens when I didn't mean to. I travelled with you to Paris when I shouldn't have.' Seb wasn't sure this was going at all well. Marianne was still staring at him as though he'd gone completely mad.

'What I'm trying to say…is that you…affect me.' He cringed at such an out dated choice of word. It had come out of nowhere. *Affect* me. What was the matter with him? He was good with women. Spent a lot of time with lots of very beautiful women and none of them made him feel so tongue-tied and awkward.

He was trying to say that he was reaching out, for only the second time in his adult life, for what he really wanted. And both times he'd been reaching for her.

'I affect you?' she said with a slight lift of her right eyebrow.

He blew out the breath that he'd been holding in one short burst. *Yes, she affected him.* Deeply and profoundly. And she shouldn't.

Seb looked at Marianne with one bare foot crossed on top of the other, her skirt clearly showing the signs of having been slept in, no make-up on and hair that only just merited the description tousled rather than tangled.

She really *shouldn't* affect him. Only she did. He'd spent his entire life surrounded by women with easy access to haute couture and all the beauty treatments money could buy—but not one of them had made him *feel* so much.

Just looking at her made him want to re-think his day. Meetings with his mother, his head groom, the estate manager and the diplomatic reception no longer seemed particularly pressing. Marianne made him want to peel her T-shirt away from her incredible body and slip her skirt down and over her hips. He wanted to kiss a trail up the side of her neck and feel her breasts heavy in his hands.

Seb swallowed painfully. *He wanted far more than that.* He wanted her in his bed and completely certain she was going to stay there. How did you tell someone that they were filling your senses in a way that defied all logic? From the first time he'd seen her and every time since. When he was with her he forgot everything except that he wanted her.

And it wasn't merely lust. He liked her. Genuinely liked being with her. He wanted to talk to her and know all the thoughts that were going on behind her intelligent eyes.

But he couldn't ask her to be his long-term lover—because she'd already told him she wouldn't be happy. Didn't want that.

Which left marriage. And it was too soon in their relationship to make that kind of a decision. In all fairness to her, he had to make it clear what a life with him would be like….

Marianne stood up, leaving her half-eaten toast on her plate and her tea untouched. 'I think I'd better find my shoes,' she said quietly. 'I assume your dressing room is through there?'

He must have nodded because she walked through to his bedroom and disappeared out of sight. He felt as though something incredibly precious was falling through his fingers and he didn't know how to stop it.

Seb pulled a shaking hand through his hair and tried to focus on what had seemed such a sensible proposition last night. He would 'court' her, sensibly and openly. She'd have a chance to see what being royal entailed and they could monitor the public's reaction to her.

As privately as possible, with no breath of a scandal, they could see where this connection would take them. See whether she'd be a suitable princess of Andovaria. It was reasonable, balanced and adult.

But that wasn't romantic. He couldn't give her that. He couldn't simply follow his heart and propose to her now. He had a responsibility to his country….

'What I'm trying to say,' he said as soon as she reappeared with her jumper held protectively in front of her and her shoes on her feet, 'is that I'm still attracted to you.'

'I'm understanding you perfectly.' Her voice was crisp and dry, clearly misinterpreting what he was trying to say.

'Marianne—'

'Stop it! Just stop it!' Her brown eyes darted a mixture of anger and hurt. 'This might be a new experience for you, Your Serene Highness, but you've just met someone you can't buy and who's not starry-eyed that you're a prince. What I gave you was a gift. My gift to you because I loved you and I wanted to be with you.'

She shook her head in apparent disbelief and drew in one long, shaky breath. 'I'm sure you'll find someone who'll *affect* you equally and who won't mind that they're not *suitable* for anything more permanent. After all, don't want to taint the stock line, do we?'

'That's not what I meant.'

Marianne brushed past him. She felt as though she'd been violated. It hurt that someone she'd loved so deeply as Seb could treat her as a commodity. Little more than a body. How could he believe she'd settle for so little, a tiny piece of his life?

And she'd told him she couldn't become his lover. 'I know exactly what you meant.'

'No, you don't.' Seb caught her by the top of her arms, holding her with just enough strength to stop her trajectory. 'I'm trying to tell you that I want you in my life.'

'And I'm telling you I'm not interested.'

Seb's hands refused to let her go. 'You're not hearing me.' His eyes seemed to pin her to the floor. 'I'd like you to get to know me again. Think about what it would be like to be a princess.'

Marianne went limp and her eyes searched his for some explanation of what he'd said. His words pooled into silence. Unexpected. Totally, totally unexpected.

It hadn't been a question, more a statement of fact. And it made no *sense*. At least not to her.

Sure that she wasn't going anywhere Seb released her arms. He eased a hand round the back of his neck. 'That's what I want,' he said more quietly.

Seb seemed to be waiting for her reaction, but she wasn't sure what she was supposed to be reacting to. It could almost have been an academic question for the amount of emotion he'd put into it.

Not love. He hadn't said he loved her. Just that he wanted her to get to know him and *think* about how she felt about being a princess. Did that mean he wanted her to think about being *his* princess? His *wife*?

Or just to think about what it would be like and understand why she couldn't be?

Marianne started to speak and then decided she couldn't.

'What do you think?' Seb asked, watching her face closely.

She frowned. 'I think I don't understand the question. Has this got something to do with Jessica?'

'No. Yes.' He pulled a hand through his hair. 'In a way. Maybe.'

'That's clear.'

Seb reached out to take hold of her hand and she let him take it. She'd never seen him like this. Even as a teenager he'd had an aura of confidence about him. It was probably what had attracted her to him in the first place.

'I've sat up all night thinking about you.' His voice was thick and husky, laced with deep emotion. 'About Jessica. About what my life could have been like…'

'If she'd lived?'

'Not exactly, but yes.'

Marianne frowned. This felt rather like the verbal equivalent of walking through fog and, all of a sudden, she'd had enough. 'Seb, I'm not understanding any of this.' She rubbed at her arm, trying to get some life back into limbs that suddenly felt cold and heavy. 'Are you asking me to marry you because you somehow think that'll be a kind of reparation for what happened with Jessica?' It didn't matter whether she was making a complete fool of herself. She just wanted to know. 'If so, you don't have to worry. I'm doing just fine.'

Not entirely true, but true enough. She was surviving—and she'd made a fulfilling and interesting life for herself. In many ways it was good. She lifted her chin and met his dark eyes. 'I didn't tell you about her because I wanted you to feel guilty. Certainly not because I wanted you to feel sorry for me.'

His fingers moved across the back of her hand. It was an incredibly tender gesture.

She watched a muscle pulse in the side of his cheek; saw him searching for the words. 'I know that.'

'I told you about her because she was your baby, too. And because I want you to understand why I can't have another affair with you. I'm not strong enough.'

Seb shook his head. 'I'm not asking you to do that.' His smile twisted. 'Come and sit back down.'

'Seb,' she began wearily, but in the end it seemed easier to do what he wanted.

He led her back to the breakfast table and waited until she'd sat back down.

'Shall I call for some fresh tea?'

'No.' *Just tell me what you want from me.* It was a miracle she'd not said that aloud.

Seb sat himself opposite. She heard his intake of breath and waited for him to speak. It had almost reached the point where she didn't much care what he said as long as he said something. Her nerves were stretched so far she thought they might snap.

'I married Amelie—' he began slowly.

'I know. I saw your wedding pictures.'

He ignored her, focused on whatever it was he wanted to tell her. 'Because her father is the Archduke of Saxe-Broden and he was a close friend of my father. Amelie was—is,' he corrected himself, 'a very beautiful woman. She's intelligent, speaks five languages, is used to moving in royal circles and had no breath of scandal attached to her.'

'She sounds perfect.' Marianne bowed her head so Seb couldn't see how much his words were hurting her.

'That's what my parents thought. And the people of Andovaria. They loved her. It was what they wanted—the young prince in his castle bringing home his virginal princess—and our popularity soared. Which was *exactly* what my father had hoped for when he'd brokered the marriage.'

Marianne swallowed hard. She knew this. Knew all this. When she'd said she'd seen the photographs, she'd really meant she'd seen them. The horse-drawn carriage pulled by six perfectly matched white horses. The streets filled with bunting and cheering crowds.

'And, I suppose, the truth was I didn't much care who I married if I couldn't have you.'

She looked up at that. Her eyes shimmering with tears she would not let fall.

'You were young, English, with no aristocratic connections. No prince in Europe had ever had such a bride. And we were already lovers…'

'Because I loved you,' she said through a throat that felt tight and constricted. She didn't want to hear this.

'Because you loved me,' Seb repeated softly. 'But we'd only had five weeks together. So little time. And to marry you would have been to ask my parents to go against everything they knew or had any experience of.

'Everything my father did as the sovereign prince was

designed to keep Andovaria a monarchy and to keep it strong. There were voices of dissent even then—people who have a different vision for Andovaria in the twenty-first century.'

Everything Seb said seemed to have a hateful logic. Amelie had been an inspired choice. The fairy-tale princess.

'But marrying Amelie was difficult. We'd only met a handful of times before our engagement was officially announced and I scarcely knew anything about her other than that she'd been groomed to fill the kind of position I had to offer.'

Marianne nodded because she did understand. It was easy to imagine the pressure he'd been under to conform.

'But I loved you—and I should never have done it. I remember standing in here on my wedding day, dressed in my ceremonial uniform, wondering what you were doing.'

Marianne gripped her hands together in her lap. Hard.

'Hoping you were happy. Hoping I was doing the right thing, but knowing it was too late to do anything else.'

He stopped speaking. The silence sat between them.

'But Amelie is also a quiet and very private person,' Seb continued suddenly. 'She hated pretty much everything that being the Princess of Andovaria entails. She doesn't like talking to strangers, giving speeches, walking into a room and have people watch her…'

Marianne looked up.

'She found the state dinners an ordeal. She hated being photographed and having her clothes criticised. Hated having bodyguards with her whenever she left the castle.

'And she didn't love me. Between ourselves we knew very early on that our marriage wasn't going to work. We were married for five and a half years, but for five of those we were actively working towards our very amicable separation.'

He stood up abruptly and walked out onto the narrow balcony. Marianne turned in her chair so she could see him more clearly. Seb claimed not to have loved Amelie, but the failure of his marriage clearly bothered him. Offended him deeply.

'What's Amelie doing now?'

Seb turned his head slightly. 'She's living in the States. Studying for the degree she always wanted.'

'Happy?'

He nodded. 'She seems to be.'

'But you're not?' Marianne asked hesitantly.

His shoulder muscles bunched beneath the fine wool of his jumper. 'I feel I've failed. The divorce rate in Andovaria is the lowest in Europe. The people here are traditional and hold traditional family values'.

He turned. 'If I marry again—and I have to—there'll be no possibility of divorce or a second annulment. When I marry it has to be for life.'

The tell-tale muscle in the corner of his cheek pulsed. Marianne watched both it, and him.

'That's why I'm saying you need to think about what it would be like to be the Princess of Andovaria.'

Light burst in Marianne's head like fireworks.

'I want to get to know you and for you to know me, but it's not that simple. As soon as the Press get wind of the fact that we're seeing each other your life will be completely different. The paparazzi will swoop on your family and friends and their lives will change too.'

He moved back into the room. 'Whether or not we ultimately decide to marry, you'll always be known as a former girlfriend of the Prince of Andovaria. Your face will be recognised and your life interesting to people you've never met.'

Marianne swallowed. Yesterday she'd been sure where her life was going; today everything seemed to be shifting about.

'It's not easy. Isabelle was born to it and she seems to hate every moment. Amelie was hurt by it.' His smile twisted. 'I don't want you to answer me now. I want you to think about it. Really think about whether you would be happy living with cameras aimed at you all the time, knowing that video tapes can be slowed down and analysed so your words can be lip-read.

'Think about the effect it would have on your career. About never being able to express an opinion that might be construed as political.'

Marianne tucked her hair behind her ears. She was trying so hard to concentrate on what he was saying. 'So,' she said slowly, 'you're asking to *date* me?'

'With a view to marriage. Perhaps. If we feel you would…'

'Be suitable.' Marianne finished his sentence for him. She felt as if he'd reached inside her and had squeezed her heart. At eighteen that had been her dream. She'd loved him. Wanted desperately to spend her life with him…

But it hadn't been possible. In London he'd said…Marianne frowned. 'I don't understand what's changed. Why is it now possible for me to marry you when it wasn't before?'

There was a brief tap on the outside door. Seb glanced over at it. 'That'll be Alois wanting to discuss today's schedule.'

He walked over to the door and spoke quietly. Marianne didn't try to hear what he was saying. Her mind was a complete mess. She sat in stupefied silence.

Seb shut the door and smiled at her as though he could see what she was feeling. 'What's changed is that princes are now able to marry for love. Denmark, Spain, Norway…even your own country. And in each case the marriage has somehow brought the monarchy more popularity. Made it more accessible to the people. But it's a huge lifestyle change and you'd have to want to embrace those changes as much as me.'

'Wouldn't there be a scandal if it was discovered I'd been pregnant with your baby when you married Amelie?'

'Yes.' He couldn't lie to her. There would be an immense

scandal. Isabelle's behaviour was offending a huge swathe of Andovaria and he honestly doubted whether public opinion would allow him to marry a woman who'd been his lover. Particularly if they suspected his relationship with her might have been a contributory factor in the breakdown of his fledgling marriage.

Seb smiled at her. 'I think if that kind of information was out there it would have surfaced by now. Certainly when I separated from Amelie.'

He could tell she was still doubtful. Not particularly surprising since she'd grown up with salacious stories about the British royal family in the Press on a nearly daily basis.

'I would trust Nick with my life. And if Beth had wanted to sell our story she could have done it by now.'

'She wouldn't!'

'Then I think we can stop worrying about it. It's more important you take the time to think about what marriage to me would be like. Take as much time as you need to be sure. We'll spend some time together. Talk.'

But not become lovers.

'And we'll try and keep our friendship a secret from the Press. There's no point stirring up speculation unless we intend to marry in due course. And we're not going to know that for a while.'

Marianne nodded and got to her feet. 'I—I don't know. It's difficult and I…'

His hands moved to cradle her face and he looked down into her eyes. He was so close she could see the tiny flecks of amber, feel his breath on her skin. 'I need you to think about it because I think I'm falling in love with you again,' he said simply.

There was a brief moment of shivering delight when she knew he was going to kiss her, before his mouth fastened on hers. His kiss was warm, persuasive and so, so unbelievably sexy. And it was a kiss unlike any she'd ever known. It was honest and real and it touched the very essence of who she was.

Her jumper fell to the ground and she raised a shaking hand to feel the rough bristles on his chin. Seb might be falling in love with her all over again, but she'd already fallen. And she'd fallen hard—ten years ago—with no prospect of pulling back.

But what he was asking…scared her.

CHAPTER TEN

TWENTY-FOUR hours later and Marianne still wasn't sure of her decision. Every time she thought she'd decided to take a chance on what she felt for Seb she remembered how desperately hurt she'd been by him. How broken.

And he was offering no guarantees about their having a long term future together even now. Couldn't. What he was offering her was simply the *possibility* of one.

Marianne left the formal parterre and headed directly for the pavilion, loving the feel of the mid-morning sun on her skin after the chill of the keep.

She glanced down at her watch. Actually, she'd had more than twenty-four hours to make her decision. Seb's oh-so-disciplined private secretary had escorted her back to the guest wing at five minutes to nine, which meant she'd had twenty-five hours and forty-nine minutes to reach some kind of a conclusion.

What Seb was suggesting would change her life. Irrevocably. She didn't know if she was ready for what that would mean. How could she ever really know what it was like to live the life of a princess, or a potential princess, until she was actually doing it? And by then it would be too late to turn back.

Marianne tucked herself into a corner of the pavilion, slipping off her shoes and stretching her legs out along the cushioned seating. It was nice up here. It didn't have the fairy-tale grandeur of Seb's 'postcard' view, but she loved the re-volving table in the pavilion that made her think of a noisy family eating out-of-doors and the sweeping lawn that was made for children to play on.

It made her believe it might be possible to carve herself a life here with Seb. She wanted it to be possible because she loved him. Still.

But…it was difficult.

If they'd had the same conversation a decade ago she wouldn't have thought about it for a moment. She'd have jumped at the chance to be with him whatever the sacrifices involved.

Only now she was older. Had seen more, understood more. Marianne opened the flap of her small rucksack and pulled out her flask of coffee. She loved Seb and wanted to be with him, but it wasn't that simple.

It was like marrying a man who had children from a previous relationship; the children were part of the package and you couldn't ignore them. Seb was the Sovereign Prince of Andovaria and, like it or not, he came as a package. Seb *and* Andovaria.

And it wasn't even merely a question of embracing a new country; it was having to live by a completely differ-ent set of rules.

How would it feel to know you were considered important simply because you'd happened to fall in love with and marry a prince? To have people worry about whether they should call you ma'am or Serene Highness?

To have no real friends?

How did that feel? Never to be completely sure whether people genuinely liked you—or merely the status you brought them by knowing you?

What did it feel like to be hounded by the Press? To be

Princess Isabelle? To be pursued by the paparazzi—who knew that a bad photograph of you had more market value than a good one? What did that feel like, day after day?

Could she cope with a future where everything she wore, everything she said, would all be analysed and criticised…

Was she ready for that?

Honestly, she didn't think she was. The prospect terrified her. But when she thought of the alternative…leaving Seb…

Marianne unscrewed the top of her flask and carefully poured herself a coffee. She wasn't sure she could do that either. She sat back into the corner, her hands cradled round the flask-lid mug, her head whirring with all the thinking.

When she was with him she forgot he was a prince. Forgot everything except how it felt to be with him, to be able to touch him, hold him.

Have him hold her.

She wanted that.

A shadow fell across the revolving table, giving her a few seconds warning that she was about to be joined, before Seb stepped inside the pavilion. He was dressed in a sharply cut black suit, black tie and crisp white shirt. Formal. Intimidating. And spectacularly attractive.

Marianne took a moment to respond to him being there—and when she did it was with a jerk. She flicked her legs to the ground and spilt a little of her coffee on her skirt as she did so. 'I thought you'd gone,' she said, foolishly. 'I heard a helicopter.'

'Yes, I'm about to go. I told them to wait.'

'Oh.'

'I saw you walk up here.'

Unaccountably shy, Marianne looked away—using the need to place her coffee back down on the table as an excuse. Then she pulled the wrap-over on her ecru linen skirt in place and traced a finger over the coffee stain.

'Where are you going?'

'There's been a serious train crash on the border between Andovaria and Switzerland,' Seb said, sitting next to her.

'No!'

'I'm flying in to see if I can help get things moving a little quicker.'

'Are many people hurt?' she asked, shocked.

He nodded. 'The local hospitals are expecting to be over-stretched. So far thirty people are known to have been seriously injured, but they're still pulling people from the wreckage.'

'Any dead?'

'Not yet.' He looked across at her. 'I find this kind of thing difficult to deal with.'

Marianne reached out a hand and laid it across his. She did it without thinking, merely intending to comfort. His fingers closed round hers and held her hand firmly.

'What I hate the most is that when I arrive you can see people look at me and think "Great, now he'll get things sorted" and I know there's nothing I can do that isn't already being done.'

His forefinger moved against the palm of her hand. 'I feel helpless.'

Marianne said nothing. She sat and watched his finger move rhythmically over her skin.

'Five years ago there was a fairly serious train accident,' Seb continued, 'and a child was pinned in one of the carriages. I climbed in to talk to him while the rescue services were getting organised. They had to cut him out.'

'Oh, Seb.'

'I'm still haunted by his voice pleading with me not to leave him.'

'Did he survive?' she asked, her voice sounding husky.

'He lost a leg. Eight years old and he lost a leg.' Seb moved his hand and threaded his fingers through hers. 'Just doesn't seem fair, does it?'

'Better than dying.'

'Yes.' He looked out across the sweeping expanse of lawn and towards the neatly arranged parterre. 'Doesn't seem to let it stop him doing anything. He's quite inspirational. As is his mother.'

His fingers moved again against her hand. 'They'd been going to see friends. Set out that morning expecting to have a pleasant day…'

'Accidents happen,' she said. 'And, even if you can't do as much as you'd like to, at least you're trying to do something. And you can throw your weight about and demand things happen faster. That's good.'

Seb turned back to her and smiled. 'Yes, I can do that.'

The expression in his eyes stopped the air in her lungs.

The pressure on her fingers increased. 'Have you made your decision?'

Had she? She was holding his hand. Wanted to comfort him.

Marianne released her trapped breath on one shaky out-pouring. 'Yes. Yes, I have.'

'And will you?'

'Yes.' And it felt as if she'd jumped into a vast vat of fizzing lemonade.

Seb reached out and cradled one cheek in his warm hand, lightly kissing her softly parted lips. They hardly touched and yet Marianne could feel the tremor run through him and she felt a sudden surge of confidence. He might not know it, but she was sure he loved her. Just as he had before.

'You ought to go.'

'Yes.'

'I'd hoped we could have had dinner today,' Seb said, his thumb gently stroking across her cheek, 'but I don't know when I'll be back. It depends what I find when I get there.'

She shook her head. 'It doesn't matter.'

'And Saturday is the annual summer ball.' His eyes seemed to caress her. 'Come.'

'To the ball?'

Seb nodded. 'See what you think of it.'

A shiver of fear passed through her. A royal ball. At the castle. Where people would look at her and wonder who she was.

It was the point of no return—and they both knew it. *Prince Sebastian's girlfriend.*

'I'll send Alois to talk to you. Finalise the arrangements.'

Slowly Marianne nodded.

Seb's mouth curved into a sexy smile and then he leant in for another kiss. This time more certain and his tongue flicked between her lips. That still made her gasp, want more…

'See you Saturday. If not before.' His lips pressed warm against her forehead. Then he stood up and briskly walked back down towards the castle.

Marianne watched him go, uncertain whether she was relieved to have made the decision or apprehensive about what that decision would mean.

By the time Marianne returned to the guest wing that evening she'd heard more than enough about the annual summer ball. As soon as the invitations had arrived there was very little conversation in the keep office that didn't concern it.

Dr Liebnitz had received an invitation, the professor and his wife, two of the more senior historians on the team, their partners…and herself. No one had quite known what to make of it, since it was apparently unprecedented for any 'staff' member to be invited to what was, essentially, a high-society event.

She shut the door of the Blue Suite and rested her head on it, glad of the solitude. The constant speculation had made her feel awkward. Untruthful—because she'd known exactly what had prompted the Dowager Princess to send those cream invitations.

Marianne slipped her shoes off her feet and padded across to the kettle. What she was less sure of was whether the Dowager Princess knew she'd sent them. How much had Seb told his family? And how much was she allowed to confide in Peter and Eliana?

She placed the kettle in its cradle as a firm knock sounded on the outside door.

'Just coming,' Marianne called out, expecting it to be the professor…or Eliana. 'I'm…' She broke off, stunned to see Alois von Dietrich.

Seb's private secretary gave a professional smile. 'His Serene Highness asked me to run through tomorrow's arrangements with you as soon as you returned to the guest wing.'

'Oh,' Marianne managed limply. She held the door a little wider. 'You'd better come in.'

'Thank you.'

Marianne tucked her hair behind her ears. 'Would you like something to d-drink?'

'Not for me, thank you.'

She walked over to the chairs by the window and sank down because her legs had begun to feel wobbly. She'd seen Seb's helicopter take off barely twenty minutes after their conversation in the pavilion and yet he seemed to have found time to arrange so much.

'Please sit down.'

What was Alois von Dietrich thinking about her? Did he think what Seb was doing was unwise? Impossible? What did he really think about her having spent the night in his employer's private rooms? Marianne gripped her hands firmly in her lap.

Seb's private secretary took the opposite seat and pulled out his file. 'I've arranged for Gianferro DiBenedetto to bring some of his more wearable designs to the castle at nine o'clock tomorrow.' He looked up. 'Unless there's a designer whose work you prefer, Dr Chambers?'

Her mind spluttered. 'No. Gianferro DiBenedetto will be fine.'

More than fine. He was a phenomenally successful designer; his dresses were fought over by Oscar-nominated actresses. Marianne sat in stunned silence.

'I'm afraid it does need to be early to allow time for any alterations to be made before the evening.' Alois von Dietrich looked up. 'Prince Sebastian also thought that, on this occasion, you'd be more comfortable arriving with your friends, Professor and Mrs Blackwell?'

Marianne's hands clasped and unclasped in her lap. 'Yes. Yes, I would.'

'I suggest, then, that they meet you here at eight o'clock and I'll have someone sent down to escort you through the security.'

'Thank you.'

Alois shut his file. 'I will accompany Signore DiBenedetto to see you in the morning.' He stood up. 'And I wish you a very good night.'

The unmistakable sound of a helicopter flying close by had Marianne looking anxiously outside the window. 'Is that Prince Sebastian?'

'His Serene Highness doesn't anticipate returning to Poltenbrunn until the morning.'

Marianne looked round. 'Was the crash particularly bad?'

'I believe the total number of injured is now standing at sixty-five and there are three known to have died,' Alois replied. 'An even mix of Swiss and Andovarian nationals.'

It was strange that Seb's private secretary should know

more about what was happening in his life than she did. *Different rules*. Did Alois think Seb would have tried to contact her directly if she was important to him? Or did he think it was intrusive of her to want to know?

Marianne stood up. 'Thank you for everything you've done.' And then, with her hand on the door, 'Who is that arriving?'

'Prince Sebastian's youngest sister. With so many photographers outside the castle it wasn't considered safe for Princess Isabelle to arrive by car.'

It was on the tip of her tongue to ask whether Princess Isabelle had arrived alone or whether she'd brought her much older lover with her. She stopped herself just in time.

With the door shut, Marianne placed her hands against her hot cheeks. *This whole experience was so bizarre.* She was going to wear a Gianferro DiBenedetto dress. A dress that would cost more to buy than she earned in a month.

How did Seb imagine she was going to explain that to Eliana?

Perhaps it was time she took her into her confidence? Not about Seb being Jessica's father—that was too private and painful a secret. But about Prince Sebastian wanting to 'date' her. That was incredible enough.

And she needed to tell someone. Put words on what was happening to make it seem believable.

Marianne pulled a jumper from one of the drawers and quickly slipped on her shoes. She let herself out of the Blue Suite and headed out towards the Blackwells' temporary home in the castle grounds.

CHAPTER ELEVEN

IT HAD been a long time since Marianne had needed any help getting dressed, but tonight it seemed she wasn't to be trusted. An army of experts had swooped on her and she was completely transformed.

Gianferro had come especially to see that his elegant bias-cut creation was being shown to the best possible effect, a hairstylist had pulled her hair into a seemingly artless twist and a manicurist had performed a miracle on nails she'd ignored for a whole lifetime.

She looked like a princess, which must have been Seb's intention. And she felt scared. It would have felt better if she'd been able to spend some time with him, but she'd had no contact with Seb since their snatched conversation in the pavilion.

'Hurry up. It's nearly eight o'clock,' Eliana called out loudly from the next room. 'How long does it take to put on a necklace?'

Marianne drew a shaky breath. She felt exactly as she had when she'd been learning to ice skate and her teacher had told her to let go of the rail. Leaving the bedroom seemed like the hardest thing in the world.

'What do you think?' she asked, stepping into the sitting room. Eliana's face broke into a smile. 'I think you look incredible.' She walked round Marianne to study her appearance from all angles. 'Very, very beautiful. Don't you, Peter? It's just a more polished version of you, if that makes any sense.'

Marianne ran her hands over the oyster silk. 'This is the weirdest dress. It's got a kind of Lycra smoothing system built into it as part of the actual thing.'

'Is it comfortable?'

Eliana's question surprised a laugh. 'Not particularly. I'm not sure whether I can sit down.'

'Shouldn't think you'll have to.' There was a small tap on the door. 'It's time we were leaving.'

Marianne fingered the heart-shaped locket at her neck. Gianferro had been all for borrowing a diamond drop necklace, but she'd insisted on wearing her own jewellery. She needed to remember what this was all about—and Seb's gift to her was the only thing that would do that.

She was here because she loved him—and because Seb thought he might be falling in love with her. She was here because she needed him. And because she wasn't happy living her life away from him.

'Ready?' the professor asked.

Marianne didn't think she'd ever feel ready, but Alois's organisation was meticulous. His 'someone' was here promptly at eight and would, no doubt, have something scheduled for later.

She was overwhelmingly glad to have Eliana and Peter with her. Glad that they'd taken her news in their stride. Glad they didn't see anything particularly difficult or impossible about it. But *embarrassed* she couldn't confide in them completely.

It made her feel alone. Isolated.

Marianne's fingers strayed once more to the necklace she was wearing. *This mattered.* She couldn't pretend it didn't. Being with Seb mattered. Being '*suitable*' mattered.

And this was the first step. Fail here and she would be

reduced to nothing more than 'Marianne Chambers, former girlfriend of the Prince of Andovaria'.

Her chin came up and her eyes sparkled against the challenge. She *could* do this. Light strains of something classical wafted towards her. She didn't know what, but it was pleasant and…soothing.

Alois von Dietrich had worked some kind of special magic because their group of three avoided the crush of people moving inexorably towards the ballroom. They were ushered in and through and had nothing left to do but stand in rapt admiration.

The already spectacular room had been transformed into a white bower. There were flowers absolutely everywhere. Large, glossy lilies and twisting rose garlands led the eye towards the wall of open French doors and on into the rose garden beyond.

'Oh, my,' Eliana said in a soft whisper at Marianne's elbow.

Silently, Marianne echoed the sentiment. She felt her fragile confidence falter once again. This was so…*big*. Seb's life was so big.

All around her was the cream of European society. The cost of the dresses the women were wearing alone would probably cancel out Third World debt…and if you factored in their jewels…

Marianne could hear her heart beating, feel the thud as it slammed against her chest cavity. *She didn't want to fail.* She wanted him to love her.

'Their Serene Highnesses Prince Sebastian of Andovaria, the Dowager Princess Arabella…'

Marianne felt as though she'd entered that zone where everything became blurry except one central image. And for her, Seb was that image.

She'd thought she had reached a point where she understood what it meant to be royalty—but this moved her understanding up one notch more. Everyone was looking at him.

Everyone. The eyes of every man and woman, in a room holding more than a thousand people, were on him.

And Seb looked completely unconscious of it. He was used to it…because it was his birthright. Marianne hung back and watched as he led his mother towards the centre of the room. And, like some bizarre version of a Mexican wave, people bowed their heads as they moved through.

Then the entire royal party splintered and they worked the room with practised ease. It was formidable to see. At one point Princess Isabelle stood close enough to be heard and Marianne was amazed she could switch between languages without the slightest hesitation.

'Shouldn't you go and speak to him?' Eliana asked quietly.

Marianne shook her head. 'He's working.'

And that was true. It was a new perspective on what these royal occasions were about. With sudden clarity she recognised how valuable it was that so many of the world's most influential people could be gathered in one place at the same time.

'Dr Chambers?' Alois von Deitrich said quietly.

She turned at his voice.

'His Serene Highness Prince Sebastian has asked if you would come this way.'

Marianne felt her heart bounce up into her throat. 'H-has he? Yes. Yes, of course.'

Seb's private secretary seemed to have the ability to cut an effortless swathe through the massed people. Marianne simply tucked in behind him. Her stomach was churning and adrenaline was coursing through her veins.

'Dr Chambers, sir,' Alois said as they drew close enough to be heard.

Marianne managed a small curtsey and looked up into eyes that were wickedly laughing.

Seb leant forward and lightly kissed her cheek, taking the opportunity to whisper, 'I thought we'd agreed you weren't going to do that.'

'It goes against the grain, but I'm behaving well.'

His mouth pulled into a smile. 'I'll treasure the moment.' His hand reached out to take hold of hers. 'Any moment there will be dancing…and I need a partner.'

Marianne looked over her shoulder, worried by who might be watching. 'Should you be holding my hand?'

'Difficult for us to dance together if we don't.' Seb led her towards the centre of the room and then moved to hold her. One hand was pressed in the small of her back and the other kept hold of her hand.

She loved the feel of him. Marianne breathed in and filled her lungs with the smell of his tangy aftershave. 'There's no music.'

'Give them a moment.' And then, as though that had been their cue, the musicians started to play.

Marianne kept looking straight up into Seb's eyes, her feet moving effortlessly. 'What would you have done if I didn't know how to dance?'

'I knew you could,' Seb replied, his eyes alight with mischief.

'How?'

'I was sure that the Under-sixteen Eastern Counties Ballroom Champion would be able to manage a waltz.'

Marianne looked down to a point mid-chest, then back up at his eyes. 'Did I tell you that?'

'Yes.' He spun her round. 'I suddenly remembered it this evening when I was trying to work out how I could get to hold you.'

Her hand trembled. It was what she wanted to hear him say…but she was so confused. For him to dance with her like this was tantamount to making a public announcement. Surely that wasn't what they'd agreed?

'You look beautiful, by the way.'

Marianne's confused eyes flew up to his confidently smiling ones. 'What are you doing?'

'Dancing with you.'

'But why?'

Seb's fingers splayed out against the silk of her dress and she could feel the warmth of his hand on her skin. It was hard to remember how many hundreds of eyes were watching her at this moment.

'Because I want to.'

'What happened to "dating" me privately? I thought we were going to keep our…friendship a secret while we made sure it was right for both of us.'

'Yes, we were.'

'So, what changed?' Marianne asked.

Seb's hand shifted position on her lower back and she spun round, a mass of tingling sensation. Right now, right here, she didn't care who was watching. Didn't care who thought what. She just wanted to be with him, have him hold her.

He moved in closer and spoke quietly. 'Meet me outside in twenty minutes. By the third window on the left.'

Marianne nodded. She would meet him anywhere. Do anything. Her eyes scanned the side of the ballroom so she was sure where he meant.

'If I hand you over to Alois he'll take you to find your friends.' Then, as the waltz drew to a close, Seb stepped back and smiled.

She knew exactly what that smile meant. It meant 'twenty minutes'. Her stomach was a nervous knot of anticipation— but the fear had gone. There was a new expression in his eyes—one that she recognised.

A tremulous smile played across her mouth. She'd seen it

before. In France. It was that expression that had made her fall in love with him.

As Alois led her back through the clusters of people earnestly discussing issues large and small, it became clear that her status had changed. One very public dance with Prince Sebastian and she'd suddenly become interesting.

People wanted to know who she was, what her name was, how she'd met the prince... Alois began by hovering solicitously, but quickly relaxed as Marianne discovered she was quite adept at saying little while still being charming.

She even managed to switch between French, German and English with reasonable alacrity, although she didn't pretend to rival Princess Isabelle's skill. Nevertheless, Alois was impressed.

'Your knowledge of European languages is unusual for an Englishwoman,' he remarked.

Marianne smiled as she heard the grudging respect in his voice. 'It's not an inability to learn that keeps most of us only speaking English, it's merely that the rest of Europe seems to speak English so well it's difficult to see the need.'

Eliana looked up as Marianne approached. She'd found a seat and was sipping champagne.

'Dr Chambers,' Alois said in farewell, with a curious kind of bow.

'Thank you for returning me to Eliana. I wouldn't have found her without you.' Then as he turned away, Marianne pointed to the seat next to her. 'Is this taken?'

'Peter's only just vacated it,' Eliana replied, looking curiously over the top of her champagne flute.

Marianne gingerly lowered herself down and perched on the edge.

The creases at the edges of Eliana's soft blue eyes deepened. 'So you can sit in that dress,' she remarked.

'Just.'

'Nice dance.'

Marianne looked up and felt an overwhelming desire to laugh. She was happy. Really, genuinely happy. 'What time is it?'

Eliana held out her wrist.

'Oh, goodness,' Marianne said, standing up. 'I've got to go again.'

Her friend's eyes twinkled. 'I see.'

Marianne slid as unobtrusively as possible through the nearest double doors. The light was beginning to fade and the huge torches that had been lit along the length of the terrace had come into their own.

Hundreds of people, it seemed, had decided to take the opportunity to wander in the rose garden. At first Marianne felt self-conscious, as though they would all be watching her, but she seemed to have regained her anonymity.

It took a moment to realise why—they hadn't seen her dance with Prince Sebastian. She walked along the length of the terrace, trying to pinpoint which set of double doors would have been level with where they'd been dancing.

Her concentration was entirely on the ballroom inside when a hand reached out to catch hold of her arm. She looked round. 'Seb.'

'Sssh.' His eyes gleamed in the dusky light and Marianne's stomach somersaulted. He pulled her in close and kissed her. Then, 'Come with me.'

He led her round the side of the terrace and towards a high hedge.

'What's this?'

'A maze.'

The heels on Marianne's shoes sank slightly into the mud. 'I'll ruin my shoes.'

'I'll buy you some more,' he said, refusing to let go of her hand.

Marianne felt an overwhelming need to laugh. 'They're not mine.'

'Then stop worrying,' Seb said as they disappeared inside the privacy of the maze's high yew hedge. He stopped and pulled her towards him. 'I need to kiss you properly.'

She felt his eyes on her lips before his mouth closed the small distance between them. Then his hands moved up to cradle her face.

Marianne's hands pulled him in closer, loving the feel of the full length of his body against her. She know that he *needed* to kiss her, just about as much as she needed to be kissed.

As he pulled away she could feel his smile against her mouth. He was happy.

Seb's hand slid down the length of her bare arm and his fingers locked with hers. 'Come with me.'

'You do know your way through this thing, don't you?' she asked. 'It'll not be good if we have to be rescued.'

Seb laughed.

It was an incredible sound. She hadn't seen him this relaxed since…France.

Hidden at the heart of the maze was a covered seating area. The high hedge walls made it dark and private. Marianne moved a little closer. 'Why are we here?'

Seb pulled her towards the bench. 'So I can kiss you without anyone watching us. Any objections?'

She pretended to consider. 'Not really.'

His teeth gleamed in the darkness and she could see the glimmer of his sexy eyes. 'I love you.'

Marianne briefly shut her eyes against the emotion of that. He'd told her he loved her before. But this time he was doing it as a man, sure of what he wanted.

And he wasn't saying he thought he might be in love with

her. Or that he was falling in love with her. He was saying it was a done deal. He loved her. Loved.

Then he moved to kiss her. It seemed as though he was pouring all of himself into it. She could taste champagne and something that was entirely Seb.

She loved him, too.

Seb pulled back and his finger traced her collar-bone and then he picked up the locket. 'I remember this.'

Her eyes shimmered and Seb moved in to kiss her again. He didn't want her to cry. He didn't want her to remember the sad times. The ten years they'd wasted. *He'd* wasted.

If he could kiss her long enough he was sure he could erase all those memories. He was going to spend the rest of his life loving her. Making her happy.

Her hands rested on his chest and he felt her tense and hold him away. 'Seb, what's changed? This wasn't what you said you wanted.'

No, it wasn't. Seb ran a hand through his hair and brought his breathing back under control. His fingers linked with hers and he pulled her towards the seat.

'Is it clean?' she asked, still pulling back. 'I'm wearing cream.'

He gave a crack of laughter.

'What?'

Seb shook his head. He couldn't put into words what he was thinking. But…he loved that strong seam of practicality that ran through her personality. The part of her that had once told him that skinny-dipping was for people who were too dis-organised to have remembered their costumes and that bungee jumping was for people without imagination.

'You do know how to ruin a romantic moment.'

'Seb.'

He could feel her frustration and he smiled. No wonder he was confusing her. Seb pulled her onto his knee.

'I'm too heavy,' she protested.

'You're perfect.' Seb let his hand curve round the soft swell of her buttocks and pulled her in closer. 'And I really don't want you to spoil your dress.'

She gave a small gurgle of laughter. 'This is crazy.'

'I know.'

'Gianferro will be angry if I spoil his creation.'

Her neck was so near and Seb couldn't resist pressing a kiss at the base of it and then a second further up.

'Seb.' She said his name on a whisper. 'Please, tell me what's happening.'

'I love you.'

'Seb—'

He raised a hand to place his fingers over her lips. 'And I want you to marry me.' Sure that she wasn't going to speak, he let his hand fall down and he linked his fingers with hers. 'Yesterday I waited with a man while his wife was in surgery…' Seb swallowed down the painful lump in his throat as he remembered how that had felt '…not sure whether she was going to make it through the five-hour operation.'

Marianne sat so still in his arms. He could feel her concentration. 'And he talked about loving her. About knowing that he'd already had more than some people ever get a chance to experience.'

Her hand twitched inside his and he continued, 'And about not having anything to regret because they hadn't wasted a moment.'

'D-did she live?'

'Yes, she lived—and I saw his face.'

Seb turned her chin so he could see deep into her eyes. This was the woman he'd hurt so badly, the woman he'd left pregnant and alone.

The woman he loved.

They had so much to regret. *He* had regrets piled higher than the hedge walls that surrounded them. 'I don't want to waste any more time. Marry me?'

CHAPTER TWELVE

VIKTORIA paced around her mother's private sitting room, before flinging down the newspaper on a low table. 'How completely irresponsible! What were you thinking of?'

Seb glanced down at the front page. He scarcely needed to look to know what would be there.

'How did the cameras get inside the castle?' he asked calmly.

Viktoria almost snorted her rage. 'That is not the point. You assured me there was no relationship between you and Dr Chambers and you're caught on camera kissing.'

'There wasn't.' Seb stood up and walked over to the window, his eyes searching out the guest wing. 'And now there is.'

Isabelle picked up the newspaper. 'She's the woman you danced with last night.'

'Yes.'

'She's very beautiful.'

Seb smiled. 'Yes, she is.'

'Trust you to say something like that,' Viktoria said, turning on her sister. 'The papers have been full of your antics for the last two months and now Sebastian is joining in. No wonder a third of the population think we're an expensive anachronism.'

'Not a third, Viktoria,' their mother interrupted. She reached out her hand for her coffee. 'A small but vocal minority. I do think it's regrettable that this…affair has managed to push all coverage of your good work at the scene of the train crash to the third page, Sebastian, but it's not unsalvageable.'

Seb turned back from the window. 'I'm going to marry Marianne.'

'Have you asked her?' his mother asked in the small hiatus before Viktoria found her voice.

'Yes.'

Viktoria sat down in the nearest chair and covered her eyes with her hand. 'I don't believe this.'

'I fell in love with her ten years ago and I intend to marry her.'

'You're the Sovereign Prince of Andovaria. You don't "fall in love".' Viktoria's voice was laced with contempt. 'You've got a responsibility to your subjects and to your family. You can't marry some money-grabbing English girl who thinks it might be fun to be a princess on some kind of hormonal whim.'

Seb interrupted her. His eyes were fiercely angry, though his voice stayed low and even. '*Dr Chambers* is a serious academic who'll have to make real sacrifices to marry me.'

'And ten years ago she was a slutty English girl who slept with someone she hardly knew.'

'Enough.' Seb ground the single word out.

The Dowager Princess frowned her daughter down. 'It's not impossible, Viktoria. Sebastian has made countless statements over the past four years to the effect that he continues to hope that he will eventually marry for love. Not once have I read anything that suggests his popularity dipped because of it. In fact, the reverse seems to be true. People seem to feel that it puts him in touch with reality.'

Viktoria sat up. 'You're not serious.'

'Perfectly. I think there's a sufficient swell of public opinion in favour of marrying a commoner to make it possible. Even desirable.'

'Marrying the socially acceptable virgin didn't work,' Isabelle chipped in.

The Dowager Princess shot her younger daughter a look that demanded silence. 'I would very much like to meet your Dr Chambers. But, with a front page like this, you do realise you've made her position here untenable? We will have to make some kind of announcement.' There was a knock at the door. 'Come in.'

'Your Serene Highnesses,' Alois von Dietrich said as he entered. 'Prince Sebastian, if I might speak with you? Privately,' he added as Seb appeared to hesitate.

With a nod at the female members of his family Seb left the sitting room. 'You look like the world has caved in.'

'Yes, sir.' Alois pulled a file from beneath his arm. 'This has appeared in a London paper this morning. I can only assume they started looking into Dr Chambers' background when she first took up residence in the guest wing. I believe they call it investigative journalism,' he added drily.

Seb felt the first tingle of apprehension. Alois rarely showed emotion, but the other man looked as stressed as he'd ever seen him. 'What is it?'

Alois pulled out the scanned image and handed it across. Seb looked down at what had always been a poor-quality photograph of Marianne. What made it a picture that would be reproduced around the world was that she was pregnant.

'And this has already appeared in the London papers?'

'Just the one paper, sir.'

One paper, but more would follow.

Alois cleared his throat. 'I understand its publication has already prompted a radio phone-in with listeners suggesting what attributes they considered most appropriate for the wife of one of the world's most eligible princes.'

Seb swore softly. He looked back down at the image in his hand. Marianne had told him about their daughter, and he'd thought he'd understood what it must have been like for her, but seeing her pregnant with his child was painful.

Marianne looked so young. Vulnerable. And he'd left her alone. Frightened and alone.

God forgive him.

'The Press office is being besieged by reporters wanting a statement on your relationship with Dr Chambers. And there has been a significant number of comments in our own Press expressing concern that you should have brought your mistress to stay at Poltenbrunn Castle.'

Seb's mouth took on a determined line.

'We need to issue a statement, sir. The Press office have put together some suggestions and they recommend that something is said in time for the six o'clock news.'

Seb gave a brief nod in recognition that he'd heard and then he walked back into his mother's private rooms. 'The London tabloids have been busy,' he said, handing her the envelope.

She looked up questioningly before pulling out the picture of Marianne. She looked up at her son. 'She's had a baby?'

'Mine.' Seb's voice brooked no discussion.

Isabelle sat up in her chair and swore softly.

'Our baby was stillborn on 17th April—'

'Thank God for that!' Viktoria exclaimed and then backtracked when Seb looked at her. 'I don't mean that exactly, but for you to have an illegitimate child would be so difficult. Particularly if you haven't been supporting it. Very unpopular.' Her voice wavered.

The Dowager Princess stood up and picked up her cigarettes. The ones she kept especially to remind her that she no longer smoked. 'Darling.' She looked at her son. 'There's no way you can marry her now.'

Marianne shut her laptop with a fierce click. She didn't want to see any more. It was exactly what she'd feared, deep down, though where that particular photograph had surfaced from she'd no idea.

But surface it had—and her past had returned to haunt her. They'd been fooling themselves to think that it wouldn't. According to Beth, no one had yet put a date on that photograph, but they would. It was only a matter of time. And what would the headlines be then?

Marianne placed a shaking hand over her mouth. Thank God there'd been no public announcement about any engagement. Nothing done that would compound her humiliation— because she knew Seb couldn't marry her now.

It was impossible. He might love her, but he loved Andovaria more. It had the prior claim on his heart.

Perhaps she was a coward, but her instinct was to run. She didn't want to have an endless post-mortem. Didn't want to sit with Seb—loving him, aching for him—while he explained why it was no longer possible for her to be his wife.

She understood why.

With immense care Marianne packed her laptop away, twisting the leads into the narrow channel. She needed to go away. Quickly.

But where would she go? Her mind was in complete spasm. She needed to calm down and think. Going home wasn't a possibility. Her house in Cambridge would be completely besieged by reporters.

Her parents' home? Beth's? The Blackwells'? Every place she thought of was discarded for the same reason. And how did she get home anyway? She'd seen the paparazzi gathered outside the castle for Princess Isabelle, who only might be bringing her boyfriend home—what would it be like now?

Was it even going to be possible to walk into an airport and get on a scheduled flight? Marianne pulled a hand across her face as the panic inside her started to build. She didn't know how to manage this.

She would need to talk to Seb. Perhaps there was some 'safe' house she could stay at until the furor died down? Then she could quietly slip back to England.

And she would need to talk to Peter and Eliana. Perhaps she should do that first? Marianne pulled her case from out of the wardrobe, her fingers hesitating on the zip pull. *She'd let Peter down*. What would he do now? She brushed angrily at the single tear that trickled down her cheek.

She flung open the lid and filled the suitcase with her clothes. Marianne worked quickly. There was probably no need to do so, but she couldn't bear to sit still. She had to be doing something. Anything.

Eventually she squeezed the last shoe down the edge and closed her case. A mixture of shock, panic and anguish rose up inside her like a wave. Marianne placed her hand over her mouth as though that would somehow stop the dam bursting.

What was she going to do?

She went and sat down at her dressing-table stool and put in her simple studs with fingers that didn't want to co-operate. Then she picked up her heart-shaped locket, her fingers closing round it like a talisman.

For ten years she'd clung to it. Taken it with her everywhere she went. Her fingers trembled as she opened the tiny catch and let the door halves fall open to reveal the photograph of Jessica.

Their daughter.

What would have happened now if Jessica had lived? If she

were a living, breathing nine-year-old in Cambridge, going to the local school…?

Acting on a sudden impulse, Marianne laid it open on top of her pillow and then pulled her case out into the sitting room. It was time to leave. To draw one clear black line under this part of her life and reinvent herself as someone else.

But first she had to speak to Peter. Tell him that she could no longer be his eyes. Her bottom lip trembled and she caught it between her teeth. Perhaps Princess Viktoria would be so relieved she was leaving quietly that she wouldn't mind so very much?

Marianne banged a fist against her head. *Think*. She had to have options. There were *always* options.

She could dye her hair with one of Eliana's temporary rinses. She could hide in the back of Eliana's car while she drove it through the waiting photographers. Maybe travel back to England on a ticket Eliana bought? Stay with one of their friends…

Options. She just needed to keep calm—and think.

'Would you like a cup of tea?' Muriel Blackwell asked from the opposite side of her large country kitchen. 'You look like you could do with one.'

Marianne shook her head. 'I think I'd like to go for a walk.'

'Some fresh air might do you good,' the other woman said with a smile as she kneaded her bread dough.

Something needed to, Marianne thought as she stepped outside into the country lane that wound its way down to the river. Her escape from Andovaria had been successful, if not very elegant.

No doubt in twenty years she'd find things to laugh about. Being huddled on the floor of the Blackwells' car with a blanket over her, and assorted cardboard boxes on top of that, did have elements of the ridiculous.

But leaving her suitcase behind and arriving at Muriel and John Blackwell's home with not so much as a toothbrush and a clean pair of knickers was more inconvenient than ridiculous.

Marianne climbed over the stile and walked down to the single-plank bench. She liked it here. She liked the peace and the smell of warm grass. She liked to hear the sound of crickets and even the soft hum of traffic far in the distance.

Two days. And she'd deliberately not looked at a single paper since she'd arrived in Norfolk. Refused to turn on the television or listen to the radio. It was like living in a sterile environment. No contact with the outside world at all—excepting Muriel with her warm smile and fairly constant chatter.

'Marianne.'

She spun round. *Seb!*

'They told me I'd find you here.'

He looked gorgeous. Dark jeans and a slim-fitting slate-coloured T-shirt. Seeing him—here—made her want to cry because she'd missed him so much. Wanted him.

'Why are you here?'

His sensual mouth twisted into a half-smile. 'To find you.'

'Why?'

'You forgot this,' he said, holding out her locket by the chain.

She shook her head. 'I left it for you.'

Seb came to sit down beside her. 'Because I didn't have a photograph of Jessica?'

Mutely Marianne nodded. She didn't trust her voice. *Why was he here?*

'I think I'd rather see you wear it.' He placed it round her neck and fastened the clasp.

Marianne could feel his fingers as they brushed against her neck. Her head was full of the day he'd first given her the locket.

'I was thinking we might do something else to remember Jessica.' He stretched out his legs and seemed to contemplate the slow-moving river in front of them. 'I was wondering whether a statue in the formal gardens at Poltenbrunn might be nice?'

She turned to look at him, her eyes welling up.

'You didn't need to run away,' he said gently. And then, 'Don't cry, Marianne. Please don't cry.' His warm hands reached up to brush away the tears that had started to fall.

'D-did you see the photograph? Of m-me?'

Seb leant forward and kissed her trembling mouth. Marianne could taste the salt of her own tears.

'I saw it.' She started to speak, but Seb laid a finger over her mouth. 'It doesn't matter. None of that matters.'

'But you said…'

'I've said a lot of foolish things.' His eyes swept over her tear-stained face. 'What matters is that I love you and I think you love me.'

'Andovaria won't accept a princess like me.'

'Andovaria has no choice. Marianne, I love you and I want to spend the rest of my life with you. If it ever comes to a choice between that and renouncing my throne—I choose you.'

Marianne started to shake her head. 'But—'

'There is no "but". I've made my choice. If you'd stayed you'd have known I'd done it by the evening news on the day the picture of you carrying our baby was first printed in London.'

'D-did what?'

'I issued a statement to say that the baby you were carrying in that photograph was mine. That I accepted full responsibility for my actions and that I was prepared to step down from the throne if that was what the people wished, but that I loved you and hoped you'd agree to be my wife.'

He pulled a box from the pocket of his jeans and flicked it open. Inside was a platinum band set with five of the biggest diamonds Marianne had ever seen. 'You said you'd marry me.' His eyes searched out hers. 'Will you wear my ring?'

Marianne covered her face with both her hands and tried to bring in enough breath to let her brain function. She wanted to be with Seb so much, but how could she let him give up everything that mattered to him? At what point in the future would he look at her and decide she hadn't been worth the sacrifice?

'I can't let you…'

Seb flicked the ring box shut and pulled her in close. 'And I can't be without you. If you won't marry me I'll have to leave Andovaria anyway, because I'm going to have to live near where you are. I'm going to spend the rest of my life convincing you that you love me too.'

Marianne could feel her resolve weaken as the warmth of his arms began to seep into the chill of her heart. 'You'll regret it.'

'If you won't marry me, I'll regret it,' he countered. 'We can do it any way you want. I can abdicate in favour of Michael by this evening and we can plan our future in England. You can continue your career and I'll start thinking about what options are open to me. I want you.'

I want you. He sounded so sure. So certain.

'Or we can go back to Andovaria together and announce our engagement. Then we'll spend some time selecting the sculptor we want to create a statue in memory of our daughter.'

'What will people say?'

'They'll say a lot, because that's what people do. But it's not their life. Only you and I can decide what will suit us best. Make us happy. And I know I can't do another ten years without you.'

A soft sob broke from deep within her.

'I love you.'

Her fingers clutched at his T-shirt.

'We're in this together. And, honestly, I don't really mind what does happen as long as I'm with you. Whatever public opinion says or doesn't say, we're going to be happy. As happy as we would have been if I'd stood my ground at nineteen. Marianne, will you marry me? Have children with me? Spend your life with me?'

Marianne thought of all the reasons she should say no—and then she thought of the one reason she should say yes. 'I love you. I do love you. I've always loved you.'

Seb lifted her chin so she had no choice but look into his eyes. 'So which way are we going? Towards Andovaria? Or away?'

Strong, calm, loving eyes. And she'd no doubt that he meant every word. The choice was hers. If she didn't feel strong enough to face the 'slings and arrows' that would no doubt come their way, maybe even rejection by his country, he'd come with her.

'Andovaria,' she said, huskily. 'If they're prepared to give me a chance…'

Seb reached into his jeans pocket for the second time and pulled out the ring box. 'Do you like it?'

Despite everything, or perhaps because of it, Marianne felt a sudden gurgle of laughter. 'I love it.' She took the box from his fingers and opened it. 'It's beautiful.'

Seb pulled it from its slot and reached for her left hand. 'Mine,' he said, sliding it onto her third finger. 'You belong to me now. Whatever happens.'

He reached across and stroked a finger down the side of her cheek, before his hand moved to thread through her hair. Then he pulled her closer, his lips meeting hers in a kiss that seared deep into her soul.

EPILOGUE

DESPITE the snow, the crowds were at least five people deep all along the route to Poltenbrunn Cathedral. Thousands of flower arrangements had been brought in to decorate the streets and there were streamers and banners everywhere she looked.

It was the strangest sensation to know that they were there for her—her and Seb. Wishing them well.

And her tiara felt heavy. She'd spent the last two months practising walking in it and it was harder than one would imagine. As was the royal wave. Seb seemed to manage something with a flick of the wrist, but hers still needed work.

Her father smiled across at her. 'Nervous?'

'Just a little.'

He leant over to grip hold of her hand and Marianne felt a surge of love towards him and her mother. Her parents had made mistakes, but so had she. She was just grateful they were here.

The glass-topped Rolls-Royce Phantom IV stopped in front of the steps leading up to the cathedral and she was aware that millions of eyes would be watching her climb out of the car. Pencils across Europe would be poised to begin the race to see how quickly they could get a copy of her dress in the shops.

She drew a shaky breath. But none of that mattered. What mattered was the man waiting for her inside. The man who'd been prepared to give all of this up for her—because he loved her.

Marianne stood still while the dress designer moved about her, first adjusting her antique silk veil and then the five metres of train that would stretch out behind her down the aisle. The off-white silk had been covered in Andovarian embroidery, all done by hand and exquisitely beautiful.

But none of it mattered—just the man.

She gripped her bouquet of white roses and sweetly smelling lilies of the valley and walked through the doors to Poltenbrunn Cathedral. Lights were flashing everywhere in bright bursts all around her and camera crews were catching every expression she made.

Behind her she was aware of Isabelle and Beth organising the fourteen young bridesmaids chosen from old aristocratic families. Every detail had been thought about, planned with military precision.

But, none of it mattered. As the organist struck the first chord Seb turned. So far away, right down by the altar, waiting for her to walk towards him. He smiled and her nerves vanished.

Dressed in full military regalia he looked every inch the prince he was. *But it didn't matter.* She was marrying the man. For better, for worse. Whatever life threw at them, good or bad.

Seb's eyes never wavered from hers as he watched her make her way towards him. Marianne didn't notice the crowned heads of Europe and beyond, the politicians and diplomats that sat in the pews. She didn't even notice the carefully chosen white flowers and green plants that decorated an already beautiful cathedral.

Just Seb.

And then, as she came level, he reached for her hand and his smile told him how much he loved her. Would always love her.

Marianne had been nervous about so many elements of the

day, but Seb was right. In the event, she forgot the millions of people watching every move she made, all she could see was Seb.

She felt him slide the unbroken platinum band on her third finger. Her German was slightly faltering, but nothing had ever felt more right than sliding her ring on his hand. Heard the moment they were pronounced husband and wife.

Marianne moved dream-like through much of the service, but she would always remember the moment she signed the register. 'My princess now,' Seb whispered quietly.

Princess Marianne of Andovaria. Strange. A new life. New responsibilities and challenges. But whatever they were, Seb would be right alongside her.

He took hold of her hand and tucked it in the crook of his arm and led her out of the cathedral in a peel of bells. Marianne heard the cheer go up like a wall of sound and then a more distinct, 'Kiss her.'

Seb turned towards her and she could read the intention in his eyes, the deep glimmer of pride and sheer joy. 'Your mother said to wait until the balcony,' she whispered.

His smile broke forth. 'Yes, she did, didn't she?'

Marianne knew he had no intention of waiting when his eyes flicked to her lips.

'I love you.'

To the sound of cheering, Seb bent his head and kissed her.

* * * * *

The Royal
Baby Bargain

ROBYN DONALD

Robyn Donald can't remember not being able to read, and will be eternally grateful to the local farmers who carefully avoided her on a dusty country road as she read her way to and from school, transported to places and times far away from her small village in Northland, New Zealand. Growing up fed her habit; as well as training as a teacher, marrying and raising two children, she discovered the delights of romances and read them voraciously, especially enjoying the ones written by New Zealand writers. So much so, that one day she decided to write one herself. Writing soon grew to be as much of a delight as reading – although infinitely more challenging – and when eventually her first book was accepted by Mills & Boon she felt she'd arrived home. She still lives in a small town in Northland with her family close by, using the landscape as a setting for much of her work. Her life is enriched by the friends she's made among writers and readers, and complicated by a determined corgi called Buster who is convinced that blackbirds are evil entities. Her greatest hobby is still reading, with travelling a very close second.

CHAPTER ONE

ABBY stared at the list of things to do before leaving, and let out a long, slow breath, her brows drawing together as another feather of unease ghosted down her spine. Every item had a slash through it, so her unconscious wasn't trying to warn her she'd forgotten something.

It had started—oh, a couple of months ago, at first just a light tug of tension, a sensation as though she'd lost the top layer of skin, that had slowly intensified into a genuinely worrying conviction that she was being watched.

Was this how Gemma's premonitions had felt? Or had she herself finally succumbed to paranoia?

Whatever, she couldn't take any risks.

Driven into action by the nameless fear, she'd resigned from her part-time job at the doctor's surgery and made plans to disappear from the small town hard against New Zealand's Southern Alps—the town that had been her and Michael's refuge for the past three years.

The same creepy sensation tightened her already-taut nerves another notch. She put the list down on the scrubbed wooden table in the kitchen and prowled once more through the cottage, switching lights on and off as she examined each room.

Back in the inconvenient little living room, chilly now that the fire had collapsed into sullen embers, she stopped beside the bag on the sofa that held necessities for tomorrow's journey. Everything else she and Michael owned—clothes, toys, books—was already stuffed into the boot of her elderly car. Not even a scrap of paper hinted at their three years' residence.

Yet that persistent foreboding still nagged at her. All her life she'd loved to lie in bed and listen to the more-pork call, but tonight she shivered at the little owl's haunting, plaintive cry from the patch of bush on the farm next door. And when she caught herself flinching at the soft wail of the wind under the eaves, she dragged in a deep breath and glanced at her watch.

'Stop it right now!' she said sturdily. 'Nothing's going to happen.'

But the crawling, baseless unease had kept her wired and wide-eyed three hours past her normal bedtime. At this rate she wouldn't sleep a wink.

So why not leave now?

Although she'd planned to start early in the morning, Michael would sleep as well in his child seat as he did in bed. He probably wouldn't even wake when she picked him up. No one would see them go, and at this time of night the roads were empty.

The decision made, she moved quickly to collect and pack her night attire and sponge bag and the clothes she'd put out for Michael in the morning. She picked up her handbag, opened it and groped for the car keys.

Only to freeze at a faint sound—the merest scrabble, the sort of sound a small animal might make as it scuttled across the gravel outside.

A typical night noise, nothing to worry about.

Yet she strained to hear, the keys cutting into her palm as her hand clenched around them. Unfortunately her heart thudded so heavily in her ears it blocked out everything but the bleating of a sheep from the next paddock. The maternal, familiar sound should have been re-assuring; instead, it held a note of warning.

'Oh, for heaven's sake, stop being so melodramatic,' she muttered, willing her pulse to settle back into a more even rhythm. 'No one cares a bit that you're leaving Nukuroa.'

Very few people would miss her, and if they knew that she'd been driven away from their remote village by a persistent, irrational foreboding they'd think she was go-ing mad. After all, she'd scoffed at Gemma.

But if she was heading for a breakdown, who would look after Michael—?

'No!' she said firmly.

If she were losing her mind, she'd deal with it once she and Michael were safely away.

She yanked the car keys from her handbag, swearing under her breath when she accidentally dislodged an en-velope onto the sofa. It gaped open, light from the centre bulb transforming the fine wavy strands of hair inside to a tawny-gold glory.

Abby's lips tightened. She glanced at the dying fire, but before the thought had time to surface she'd pushed the envelope back into her bag and closed the catch on it.

Shivering, she took in three or four deep, grounding breaths. As soon as she got settled again she'd burn that lock of hair. It was a sentimental fetter to a past long dead; her future was devoted to Michael, which was why the miracle of modern hair colouring now dimmed her bright crown to a dull mouse-brown. A further disguise was the way she wore it, scraped back from her face in a pony-tail that straightened the naturally loose, casual waves.

She endured the change, just as she endured the cheap

clothes in unflattering shades that concealed her slender body. She'd even bought spectacles of plain glass, tinted to mute her tilted, almond-shaped eyes and green-gold irises.

Nothing could hide her mouth, wide and full and far too obvious, even when she'd toned it down with lipstick just the wrong colour. In spite of that, and the cleft in her chin, the camouflage worked.

She'd turned being inconspicuous into an art form. Anyone who took a second glance saw a single mother with no clothes sense and no money, working hard to bring up her child, refusing dates, content to lurk on the edge of life. In a year's time no one in Nukuroa would remember her.

If that thought stung, she had only to recall Michael's laughing, open face when he came running towards her each evening in the child-care centre, the warmth of his hug and kiss when she tucked him into bed, his confidence and exuberant enjoyment of life.

Nothing and nobody was more important than Michael.

And if she was going to take him away tonight, she'd better get going!

Keys dangling from her fingers, she lifted the pack and set off for the front door, only to stop, heart hammering again, when her ears picked up the faint murmur of a car on the road. After a second's hesitation, she dropped the pack and paced noiselessly across to the window. Slowly she drew back the curtain a fraction and peered into the darkness. Headlights flashed on and off like alarm beacons in the heavy darkness as the car moved past the line of trees separating the farm paddock from the road.

When the vehicle continued out of sight she let out a long, relieved breath. Her wide mouth sketched a curve at the familiar fusillade of barks from the dogs at the homestead next door, but the smile soon faded. Odd that a car should be on the road this late; in this farming district most people went to bed early.

Taut and wary, she stayed at the window for several more minutes, listening to the encompassing silence, her mind racing over her plans. First the long trip to Christchurch, where she'd sell the car for what little she could get. Tomorrow evening she and Michael would take flight to New Plymouth in the North Island—with tickets bought under a false name, of course.

And then a new safe haven, a different refuge—but the same life, she thought wearily, always checking over her shoulder, waiting for Caelan Bagaton—referred to by the media as Prince Caelan Bagaton, although he didn't use the title—to track her down.

Yet it was a life she'd willingly accepted. Straightening her shoulders, she drew the scanty curtain across and went into the narrow, old-fashioned kitchen, where her gaze fell on the list of things to do. Oh, *hell*! She'd have to get rid of that before she left. Still listening alertly, she screwed up the sheet of paper and dropped it into the waste-paper bin.

Only to give a short, silent laugh at her stupidity, snatch it out and hurry back to the living room to toss it onto the dying embers. It didn't catch immediately; some of the words stood out boldly as the paper curled and blackened, so she bent down and blew hard, and a brief spurt of flame reduced the list to dark flakes that settled anonymously onto the grate.

'Nobody,' she said on a note of steely satisfaction, 'is going to learn anything from those ashes.'

She stood up and had taken one step across the room when she heard another unknown sound. *Where?*

Twanging nerves drove her to move swiftly, noise-lessly, into the narrow hall and head for the door. Two steps away from it, she heard the snick of a key in the lock.

Fear kicked her in the stomach, locking every muscle. For a few, irretrievable seconds she couldn't obey the mindless, adrenalin-charged instinct to snatch up Michael and race wildly out of the back door.

I must be dreaming, she thought desperately. Oh God, please let me be dreaming!

But the door flew back at the noiseless thrust of an impatient hand, and every nightmare that had haunted her sleep, every fear she'd repressed, coalesced into stark panic.

Every magnificent inch an avenging prince, Caelan Bagaton came into the house in a silent, powerful rush, closing the door behind him with a deliberation that dried her mouth and sent her blood racing through her veins. He looked like some dark phantom out of her worst nightmare—tall, broad-shouldered, his hard, handsome features clamped in a mask of arrogant authority. The weak light emphasised the ruthless angle of his jaw and the hard male beauty of his mouth, picked out an auto-cratic sweep of cheekbones and black lashes that con-trasted shockingly with cold blue eyes.

Beneath the panic, a treacherous wildfire memory stirred. Horrified, Abby swallowed. Oh, she remembered that mouth—remembered the feel of it possessing hers…

'You know you should always have a chain on the door,' he said, voice cool with mockery, gaze narrowed and glinting as he scanned her white face.

Shaking but defiantly stubborn, she said, 'Get out,' only to realise that no sound came from her closed throat.

She swallowed and repeated the words in a croaking monotone. 'Get out of here.'

Even though she mightn't be able to master her body's primitive response to his vital potency, she'd stand her ground.

'Did you really think you'd get away with stealing my nephew?' Contempt blazed through every word. He advanced on her, the dominant framework of his face as implacable as the anger that beat against her.

The metallic taste of fear nauseated her; determined not to be intimidated, she fought it with every scrap of will-power. Although she knew it was futile, desperation forced her to try and sidetrack him.

'How did you get the door key?' she demanded, heart banging so noisily she was certain he could hear it.

'I'm the new tenant.' He surveyed her pinched face in a survey as cold as the lethal sheen on a knife-blade. 'And you are Abigail Moore, whose real name is Abigail Metcalfe, shortened by her friends and lovers—and my sister—to Abby.' His tone converted the sentence to an insult. 'Drab clothes and dyed hair are a pathetic attempt at disguise. You must have been desperate to be found.'

'If so, I'd have kept both my hair colour and my name,' she said through her teeth, temper flaring enough to hold the fear at bay.

His wide shoulders lifted in a dismissive shrug. 'Why didn't you move to Australia?'

'Because I couldn't afford the fare.' The words snapped out before she realised she'd been goaded into losing control. Just after she'd returned to New Zealand she'd read an article about him; he'd said that anger and fear made fools of people, and now she was proving it.

Dragging in a shallow breath, she tried again to divert him away from the child sleeping in the back bedroom.

'If you're the new tenant, you're not legally allowed in here until tomorrow. Get out before I call the police.'

He glanced ostentatiously at the sleek silver—no, probably platinum—watch on his lean wrist. 'It is tomorrow, and we both know you won't call the police. The local constable would laugh at you as he tossed you into the cells; kidnappers are despised, especially those who steal babies.'

Panic paralysed her mind until a will-power she hadn't known she possessed forced it into action again; for Michael's sake she had to keep a clear head. She said raggedly, 'I don't know what you're talking about.'

In a drawl as insulting as it was menacing, he said, 'You barely waited to bury Gemma after the cyclone before you stole her child and ran away.'

'We were air-lifted out to New Zealand.' She hid the panicky flutter in her stomach with a snap.

He ignored her feeble riposte with a contemptuous lift of one sable brow. 'I imagine the poor devils on Palaweyo were so busy cleaning up that no one had time or inclination to check any information you gave.' He paused, as though expecting an answer; when she remained stoically silent he finished, 'It was clever—although dangerous—to say he was your child.'

Abby clamped her teeth over more tumbling, desperate words, only will-power keeping her gaze away from the door to Michael's bedroom. Fear coalesced into a cold pool beneath her ribs.

What else did Gemma's brother know?

Claiming Michael as her own might have been illegal, but it had secured his future. Once the prince discovered that his sister had died in one of the Pacific Ocean's violent cyclones, he'd have flown to Palaweyo. And when he found that Gemma had given birth to a child, everything she'd feared—and made Abby promise to prevent—would have unfolded. He'd have taken Michael back to the life that Gemma dreaded—a life of privilege, bereft of love.

Abby's lie had worked a minor miracle; nobody had queried it. Instead, the overworked and pressured island authorities had immediately found her a flight to New Zealand, and once back home the authorities had fast-tracked documentation for her and Michael as mother and child.

She said stonily, 'He is mine.'

'Prove it.'

The words slashed her composure into ribbons. 'Check his birth certificate.' Trying to conceal her fear with a show of defiance, she stared at him with hostile eyes, but her glare backfired into sabotage.

She'd met the prince a few times, usually when she'd called at his opulent mansion in one of Auckland's exclusive marine suburbs to pick up Gemma for an evening out. And once, when she and Gemma were spending a weekend at the beach house on the island he owned in the exquisite Hauraki Gulf, he arrived unexpectedly.

It had been an odd, extremely tense two days; she'd been certain he disliked her, until the final night when he'd kissed her on the beach under the light of a full, voluptuous moon.

She'd gone up in flames, and it had been Caelan who'd pulled away, apologising in a cold, distant voice that had chilled her through to her bones.

Snob, she thought now, compulsively noting the subtle changes the years had made to his arrogant face—a few lines around his cold eyes, a stronger air of authority. His potent charisma still blazed forth, and beneath bronzed skin the splendid bone structure remained rock-hard and ruthless, as it would for the rest of his life.

That ruthlessness was stamped in his family tree. He looked every inch what he was—the descendant of Mediterranean princes who'd established their rule with tough, uncompromising pragmatism and enough hard tenacity to fight off pirates and corsairs and a horde of other invaders, all eager to occupy the rich little island nation of Dacia.

He could have used his social position and his astonishing good looks to lead the life of a playboy. Instead, he'd taken over his father's business in his mid-twenties and used his formidable intellect and intimidating personality to build it into a huge, world-wide organisation.

Add to that power the fact that he kissed like a fallen angel and Abby knew she had every reason to be afraid of the impact he made on her. Praying he couldn't see the mindless, bitter attraction stirring inside her, she wrenched her gaze away.

'I haven't changed as much as you,' he observed silkily. 'But then, I haven't tried to.'

A potent dose of adrenalin pounded through her veins, and, shockingly, for the first time in years she felt alive again.

He noted the heat in her cheeks with a coldly cynical smile. 'The child's birth certificate is a pack of lies,' he said with deadly precision, his hard, beautiful mouth curling.

Her heart contracted. She had to take a deep breath before she could ask, 'Can you prove that?'

'I've seen him.'

She stared at him, eyes huge and dark in her pale face. 'So?'

'He looks like Gemma,' he said flatly. 'I have a photograph of her at the same age, and, apart from the colouring, it looks like the same child.'

'You call that proof?' she asked, letting manufactured scorn ring through her voice. 'You'll need to do better than that to convince anyone.'

Caelan let the silence drag on, ratcheting up her tension until she had to stifle a small gasp when he finally drawled, 'Are you prepared to have a DNA test done?'

It was a trap, of course, and her only chance was to carry it off with a high hand.

'Of course not.' She hoped her contempt matched his.

'I could force you to.'

He meant it. Panic kicked ferociously in her stomach. 'How?'

His mouth thinned into a hard line. 'I have signed depositions from the villagers on Palaweyo—the one where you lived with Gemma—that the boy child was born to the girl with long black hair, not to the nurse who had hair like the sunrise in summer.' He studied her drab hair for a moment of exquisite torture before drawling, 'Any court would take that information as an indication that blood tests would be a good thing.'

The walls in the narrow hall pressed around Abby, robbing her of breath, clamping her heart in intolerable fear. Speared by anguish, she had to concentrate on keeping herself upright. Gemma, she thought numbly, oh Gemma, I'm so sorry…

She could still hear Gemma say, 'And I *won't* go and live with Caelan after the baby's born, so it's no use trying to make me.'

Abby had twisted in the hammock and stared at her very pregnant guest, sprawled out on the coarse white coral sand. 'Don't go all drama queen on me again! I'm not trying to *make* you do anything! All I said was that your brother seems the sort of man who'd be there for you!'

Gemma said with false heartiness, 'Oh, he is! Believe me, they don't come any more protective or autocratic or masterful than Caelan. It's in the genes—all the Bagaton men are tough and dominant. I'm not telling him about this baby because—' She stopped and sifted sand through her fingers, her expression an odd mixture of defiance and shyness. After a swift upwards glance at Abby, she began again. 'Because Caelan would step in and take us over, and for once I want to show him that I can manage.'

Doubtfully, Abby said, 'Gemma, being a single mother isn't easy.' Even when you're cushioned by money and an assured position in world society!

'I can learn. Other women do it,' Gemma said stubbornly.

'Not princesses!'

Gemma grinned. 'We don't use the title—well, not anywhere else but Dacia, where they do it automatically.' The smile faded. 'And don't try to persuade me to let my mother know either. She couldn't care less what I do. As for a grandchild—she'd kill me sooner than own to one! She never loved me, not even as a child. In fact, just before I came to stay with you she told me that she blamed me entirely for the break-up of her marriage to my father!'

'Oh, no, I'm sure she didn't…' But at Gemma's hard little laugh, her voice trailed away.

'Abby, you don't know how much I envy you those parents who loved you, and your normal happy life. I grew up in a huge house that always seemed empty and cold, with parents who fought all the time. In a way it got better after my mother left my father and I was packed off to boarding school and ignored.'

'Even by Caelan?'

Gemma shrugged, one hand stroking her thickening waistline. 'No,' she admitted. 'When he came home it was wonderful, but he was away most of the time, first at university and then overseas.'

'I still can't see why you don't tell him you're pregnant. I know he's tough, and he's obviously been a fairly difficult guardian, but even you admit he did his best for you.'

Gemma pouted. 'Well, that's part of the problem. Caelan has hugely high standards, standards I entirely failed to live up to.'

Talking to Gemma sometimes felt like trying to catch butterflies with your hands behind your back. Abby said gently, 'What's the other part of the problem?'

Gemma gave her a swift, upwards glance, then shrugged elaborately. 'You'll laugh.'

'Try me.'

For once Gemma looked self-conscious. 'Caelan says it's all hokum, but I get—premonitions. I knew when—' in a betraying gesture her hand spread out over her stomach '—when the baby's father went up to rescue those wretched climbers on Mount Everest I knew I'd never see him again. I pleaded with him to stay away, but his damned sense of responsibility drove him there. He saved them, but he died on the mountain himself.'

Abby made a soft, sympathetic noise.

Gemma looked up with tear-drenched eyes and said with sudden, passionate energy, 'OK, it sounds utterly stupid, but I think—I feel—I'm going to die soon after this baby is born.' Ignoring Abby's shocked exclamation, she hurried on, 'If I do, he'll go to live with Caelan and I couldn't bear for him to grow up like me in some huge, formal, echoing house with no parents to love him, no one to hold him when he cries except a nanny who's paid to look after him.'

'Gemma—'

'I know you don't believe me—that's all right. Only— if it happens, Abby, will you take Michael and love him and give him the sort of childhood you had?' She gave a teasing smile, and added, 'If you don't, damn it, I'll haunt you!'

Of course Abby hadn't believed that her guest's premonitions meant anything. She'd set herself to easing what she thought was maternal fear, and felt she'd managed it quite well, but Gemma had been right. Michael had only been two weeks old when one of the Pacific Ocean's vicious cyclones had changed course and smashed into Palaweyo so swiftly there had been no time to evacuate the weather coast.

They'd taken refuge in the hospital, but a beam had fallen on Gemma, breaking her spine. And before she'd died, she'd extracted a promise from Abby—one she was determined to keep.

Whatever it took.

Abby dragged in a deep breath and stared at Caelan's dark, impervious face. Attack, she thought bleakly; don't go all defensive.

'Whatever bribes you paid the villagers—and I hope they were good big ones because they need the money— he's mine.'

'I gave them a new hospital—cyclone-proof this time—and staff to run it.' Caelan's tone was dismissive, but there was nothing casual in his eyes. Icy, merciless, scathing, they raked her face. 'I know the child is Gemma's son.' Watching her with the still intentness of a hunter the moment before he launched a weapon, he finished with charged menace, 'Which makes me his uncle and you no relation at all.'

Abby's head felt woolly and disconnected. Regulating her breath into a slow, steady rhythm, she fought for composure. If the prince knew for certain she was no relation to the child he'd get rid of her so fast that Michael would wake up tomorrow without the only mother he'd ever known.

She loved Michael more than she had ever loved anything else.

Ignoring the cold hollowness inside her, she swallowed to ease her dry throat and said tonelessly, 'Michael is *my* son.'

Caelan hadn't expected to feel anything beyond justified anger and contempt for her, but her dogged stubbornness elicited an unwilling admiration.

Not that she looked anything like the radiant, fey creature who'd met his eyes with a barely hidden challenge four years previously.

In spite of that, in spite of everything she'd done, he still wanted her. He had to clench his hands to stop them from reaching out to her—to shake her? Or kiss the lie from her lips? Both, probably.

The lust should have died the moment he'd discovered she'd stolen Gemma's son.

Deriding himself, he examined her mercilessly, enjoying the colour that flared into her exquisite skin and the wariness shadowing her eyes. Even with bad hair colouring and depressing clothes, her riotous hair confined in brutal subjugation and her eyes hidden behind tinted spectacles, her sensuous allure reached out to him.

Golden as a faerie woman, as dangerous as she was treacherous, behind the almond-shaped eyes and voluptuous mouth hid a lying, scheming kidnapper.

The dossier said that the child seemed happy, but who knew what had happened to Gemma's son?

And why had she done it? Was she one of those sick creatures who yearned so strongly for a child she stole one? One glance at her glittering eyes despatched that idea. She was as sane as he was. So had she thought that possession of Gemma's child would lead to a direct line to Gemma's money?

He changed tactics. 'How much is it going to cost me?'

The last tinge of soft apricot along her astonishing cheekbones vanished, leaving her the colour of parchment. Arms swinging out to catch her, Caelan took an involuntary step forward, then let his hands fall to his sides when she didn't stagger. Sardonically, he watched her eyes close, their long lashes casting fragile shadows on her tender skin.

Oh, she knew all the tricks! He took a deliberate step backwards, removing himself, he thought with cold disgust at his body's betrayal, from danger.

Her lashes lifted and she transfixed him with eyes that usually blended green and gold; not now, though. Stripped of all emotion, enamelled and opaque, they blazed a clear, hard green, vivid in the dim light of the small, bare hall.

'How much for what?' she asked in a staccato sentence.

He didn't bother with subtlety. 'For you to give up the child.'

CHAPTER TWO

NOT a muscle moved in the delicate ivory skin, but a shadow darkened Abby's eyes. 'You disgust me,' she said woodenly. 'Get out.'

Time, Caelan decided, to use the blunt instrument; if appealing to greed wouldn't do the trick, threats usually worked. 'You're in trouble, Abby. If I decide to play it heavy, you face a conviction for kidnapping the child and giving false information to the passport authorities.'

That shocked her. She winced as though against a blow, but her soft mouth hardened. 'His name is *Michael*,' she stated fiercely, shaken by a gust of emotion he couldn't define. 'He's not some entity you can define by the term *child*; he has a personality, a place in the world.'

'A place in the world?' Caelan looked around the shabby hall, his derision plain. 'He deserves better than this.'

'*You* might have grown up in the lap of luxury, secure in the fact that you're a prince, but most children are perfectly happy with a more down-market set of relatives and much less money. He is loved and he loves. He has little friends—'

'You're taking him away from them,' he interrupted in his turn, not trying to hide the contempt in his tone.

She looked away. Whatever she'd been going to say died on her tongue; she shivered, and once more delicate colour flared along her high cheekbones. On a burst of

21

fierce, angry triumph, Caelan knew that he wasn't the only one feeling the violent pull of an old craving.

'Let's deal,' he said, forcing himself to speak judicially. Clearly, she wasn't going to be bought off, so he had no choice; she was the only mother Gemma's son had known, and, until the child could manage without her, they were both stuck with her.

Not that he was going to tell her that. No, he'd frighten her thoroughly first, and then drive as hard a bargain as he could.

With cool deliberation, he went on, 'I'm offering you a future. I want the—I want my sister's child. However, because he thinks you're his mother, I propose we bury the hatchet.'

Torn by a tumult of conflicting thoughts, she stared at him. 'How?' she said at last, her voice stiff and defensive, waiting for his next words with painful apprehension.

He said ironically, 'It's quite simple.'

'Simple?' Abby was so incensed she almost gobbled the word. 'Nothing about this is simple.'

'You should have thought of that before you decided to play with Michael's life,' the prince said grimly. 'You removed him from his family, took him away from the only people who'd know how to protect him. Have you thought of the danger you could be exposing him to?'

'Danger?' Eyes widening, she stared at him. 'What danger?'

He said coldly, 'He's a Bagaton, which makes him prime kidnap material.'

So shocked she almost fell for the trick, she had to bite back the words that trembled on her lips. Hoping he didn't notice the momentary hesitation, she said haughtily, 'He is not a Bagaton. His name is Michael Metcalfe.

And we Metcalfes are noted for our long and happy marriages, not for being kidnapped.'

A slashing jet brow rose in irony. 'A writer is sniffing around Palaweyo, researching a book on Pacific tragedies.' His hard, sensuous mouth curled. 'Any woman you can label a princess is always useful when it comes to selling books, especially if she's young and beautiful and dies in a monster cyclone after giving birth. Once the writer finds out that Michael is Gemma's child—'

Abby struggled to remain calm, but the panic beneath her ribs intensified so that she couldn't control her racing thoughts. 'I doubt whether any writer—however well his books sell!—can afford to dangle the bribe of a hospital in front of the villagers in return for the right lies,' she flashed.

'I knew that the child was Gemma's before I decided to give the villagers their hospital,' he told her casually. 'They spoke quite freely about you and her—they have no reason not to tell anyone who asks. And no writer worth his salt is going to keep it quiet.' His face hardened. 'Inevitably you will be tracked down—'

'How? It took you, with all your resources, three years to find us,' she snapped, but he could see the fear in her eyes.

'Writers have resources too.' He waited while she absorbed the impact of that before adding forcefully, 'Once he finds you, the resultant publicity will expose Michael's existence—and his lack of protection—to anyone who wants a quick fortune. Didn't you read about the de Courcy heiress?'

Colour drained from Abby's face. The fourteen-year-old daughter of a billionaire had been snatched from her exclusive school, yet although her parents had paid the huge ransom, it had been too late. She'd been killed the day after she'd disappeared.

The cold, inflexible voice of the prince battered at her composure. 'Whoever did that got away with five million euros, worth in New Zealand dollars about—'

'I know how much it's worth! You're trying to frighten me,' she said thinly, turning her head away from his intimidating gaze as though she could shut out the effect of his words.

'Damn right I am! There are people out there who'd see Michael as a passport to easy money, a soft target. Are you willing to risk that?'

She went even paler and closed her eyes. He was manipulating her, but the thought of Michael in the clutches of some cold-hearted psychopath robbed her of speech and the ability to think.

A soft noise brought her head around sharply; Michael was stirring. And the prince was walking with long, noiseless strides towards the open door of the bedroom.

Panic hit her in a howling, destructive storm, propelling her after him into the tiny room. Caelan loomed over the bed. He didn't move, didn't acknowledge her presence at all, his whole attention bent on the child as though claiming him in some primal way.

Abby pushed desperately at his hard, lean body. She might as well have tried to move a granite pillar, except that his body heat reached out and blasted through the brittle shell of her self-control.

Her hands dropped, but she didn't move. In a fierce voice pitched too low to disturb the restless child, she ordered, 'Get out of here.'

Silently Caelan turned, but he waited at the doorway, a silent, threatening figure. After straightening the bedclothes over Michael, Abby dragged in a juddering breath and left him.

'We'll go into the living room.' She pushed open the door.

Once inside Caelan Bagaton said with cold distaste, 'I don't hurt children, Abby.'

'All right, I overreacted,' she returned shakily. 'I don't think you'd be cruel to him. I know you weren't cruel to Gemma—she told me herself that she barely knew you because you were away so much. But can't you see that the last thing she wanted was for her son to be banished to a nursery like an abandoned doll stuffed in a cupboard, cared for by nannies who come and go regularly?'

Caelan's expression didn't change at her inadvertent admission that the child was Gemma's. His desire to see the boy had shattered Abby's composure; she didn't even realise she'd given herself away.

Instinct warned him to proceed with caution. He said neutrally, 'Her mother wasn't maternal, but she made sure Gemma had the best care available. And my father had duties he couldn't avoid, as well as a corporation to run. He did his best for her.'

Hands clenching into fists at her side, Abby skewered him with an outraged glance and carried on in full, indignant fervour. 'By sending her off to boarding school the minute she turned eight, where she was wretchedly, miserably unhappy? That was his *best*?' With an elaborate dismissive shrug she finished scathingly, 'In that case, I'm really, really glad to hear that he didn't dislike her!'

'That's enough!'

Caelan's harsh, deep voice drowned her in cold menace. Damn, she thought, mortified; don't let emotion get the better of you! She could see contempt in his eyes, in the hard line of his mouth, the still tautness of his powerful body. No matter how angry he was, the prince remained in full control.

'Admit that he's Gemma's child.' At her obstinate silence, he said coolly, 'You asked for proof that he's not yours. Here it is.'

He drew a sheet of paper from the pocket of his casual, superbly cut jacket. When he offered it to her she took it and tried to read, but the words danced and blurred in front of her eyes. Blinking, she forced her brain to focus.

Couched in scientist's prose, it was quite definite; there were enough points of similarity between tissue samples one and two for there to be a familial connection.

'I don't understand,' she whispered, fighting off dark dread. The paper dropped from her nerveless fingers.

Watching her with unsparing eyes, the prince made no attempt to pick it up.

When she regained enough composure to be able to speak again, she said stiffly, 'This could be anyone's samples. There's no way you could take a blood sample from Michael without my knowing, and I know you didn't get one from me.'

His beautiful mouth relaxed into a sardonic smile. 'Blood isn't necessary for DNA testing—any tissue will serve.' His inflexible tone warned her. Heart hammering, she listened as he went on. 'And I didn't need one from you. It was easy enough to send in a worker at the childcare centre; she stayed three weeks before deciding she didn't like living in the backblocks, and she came away with saliva samples and blood from a grazed knee. The results prove that you're not Michael's mother—that you're no relation to him.'

Blood roared through her head as outrage manhandled fear aside. She grabbed the back of the sofa and fought for control, finally grinding out, 'How dare you? You had no right to—'

'You had no *right* to steal my sister's child,' he cut in, his lethal tone quelling her anger as effectively as a douche of ice water. 'Why did you do it? What satisfaction did it give you?'

'Gemma asked me to take care of him.'

The strong bone structure of his face was very much in evidence. Dispassionately he said, 'If she did, it was typically dramatic and thoughtless of her to demand that you put your life on hold for Michael, but that's irrelevant now.' He paused, his hooded eyes keen and watchful. 'The next step is a court case, where the first thing any judge will do is order another DNA test. And we both know how that will turn out.'

An acceptance of defeat rose like bitter anguish inside Abby. She was going to lose Michael. But not, she thought grimly, until she'd made this arrogant prince fight to the last for his nephew.

Pride and disillusion gave her voice an acid edge when she said, 'If all you're planning for Michael is a lonely, loveless childhood like Gemma's, why on earth do you want him?'

'Because he is a Bagaton,' he said coldly.

'Gemma was a Bagaton too, but it didn't make her happy. She wanted me to look after him.' When he raised his brows she cried, 'I've got a letter to prove it.'

She stooped to her bag, holding her shoulders stiffly and her spine so rigid she thought it might splinter. With trembling fingers she unzipped an inner pocket in one suitcase and took out an envelope.

Thrusting it at the man who watched her with eyes as translucent and cold as polar ice, she said, 'Here.'

He took it, but didn't look at it. His startlingly good-looking face was set in lines of such formidable determination that she flinched, yet a melting heat in the pit of her stomach astonished and frightened her. It was one thing to acknowledge that he had a primitive physical power over her; it would be shameful to let her body's treachery weaken her.

'Read it,' she said desperately. 'It will make any judge think about his decision.'

Frowning, the prince examined the single sheet of notepaper.

Abby waited tensely, mentally going over the words she knew by heart.

Dearest Abby, If you're reading this I'm dead. See, I told you I could foretell things! Take Michael to New Zealand, but make sure neither Caelan nor my mother find you—or him. I know you love my baby, and I know you'll take care of him. And thanks for being my wise, sensible friend. Don't grieve too much. Just keep on loving Michael, and look after him.

In a voice without the slightest trace of emotion, Caelan said, 'It certainly looks as though Gemma wrote it—I recognise the aura of drama and doom.' His long fingers tightened on the sheet of paper and he looked at her from half-closed eyes, his mouth twisting. 'You're too trusting, Abby. What's to stop me tearing it to shreds and lying about seeing it?'

Oddly enough, it hadn't occurred to her. His reputation for fair dealing matched the one for ruthlessness. Her mouth tightened. 'It's a copy; the real one is in a solicitor's office,' she said steadily.

The hard, uncompromising determination stamped on

Caelan's lean, bronze face was replaced by a gleam of humour.

Her susceptible heart missed a beat. Although Gemma had told her that he despised people who used their charm to dazzle others, he possessed an inordinate amount of it himself. His smile was a weapon, a dangerously disturbing challenge that had penetrated stronger defences than hers.

Lazily he said, 'I'd have been disappointed if you hadn't made sure of that. But this means nothing; I can produce evidence to show that Gemma was a fragile, emotionally unstable woman, incapable of knowing what was best for her child.'

Abby opened her mouth, but honesty stopped the fierce words that threatened to spill out. Yes, Gemma had been fragile, as well as funny and delightful, but she'd been absolutely determined Michael wouldn't grow up without love and attention.

Caelan looked around the small room furnished with cheap, shabby cast-offs. The harsh central light turned Abby's skin sallow and robbed her hair of highlights or any depth of colour. It was, he thought with cool cynicism, a sin to hide that glorious mane of red-gold hair.

And an even greater one to cover her slender body with a loose black T-shirt and pair of dust-coloured corduroy trousers.

He banished tantalising memories of the figure beneath the shapeless clothes, sleek and lithe and strong, her exquisite skin an instant temptation...

And her mouth, soft and hot and delicious beneath his, opening to him with an eagerness that still affected him.

Abby had strayed into his life, a glowing, sensuous girl who seemed unaware of her sexual power. Not that he believed in her innocence; Gemma chose friends who tended to be sophisticated and spoilt.

Already in a very satisfying relationship with another woman, he'd put Abby resolutely from his mind. Yet he hadn't been able to prevent himself from kissing her—a kiss that had led directly to the termination of his affair. And when Gemma told him the fey, strangely tempting health worker had gone to some backwater Pacific island for a year on a volunteer basis, he'd been taken aback by an odd sense of loss.

Then all hell had broken loose in a far-flung part of the business; he'd spent months unravelling the mess while Gemma had stayed with her mother in Australia. Caelan didn't like his stepmother, but he kept in touch with his sister, and when she'd written to say she was on Palaweyo spending time with Abby, he'd decided to call in and re-acquaint himself with the alabaster-skinned girl, discover if the provocation in her inviting mouth and tilted eyes was genuine or a cynical come-on.

But the cyclone had intervened, and by the time he'd got to Palaweyo, Gemma was dead and buried and Abby had vanished with her child.

Abby swung to face him, her movements graceful in spite of her tension. 'Do you honestly believe Michael might be in danger?'

'It's always a possibility,' he said, but she broke in, colour returning in a soft flood to her skin with the heat of her response.

'I want the truth.' She paused, searching for words, then forced herself to say unevenly, 'I know that someone in your position might be seen as a target, but Michael has nothing.'

He said ironically, 'He has a very rich uncle and a large trust fund.'

Stunned, she stared at him, realising the implications of this. No wonder he was suspicious—did he believe she had her eye on that rich trust fund? 'I didn't know,' she said, knowing he wouldn't believe her.

He gave her a look that should have frozen the words on her lips. 'Come on, Abby! I'm sure Gemma spent a lot of time complaining about the cruel brother who kept such a tight grip on the purse strings, but you knew she didn't have to work.'

'I thought—I thought you made her an allowance.'

Looking down the arrogant blade of his nose, he said with forbidding restraint, 'My father made sure she was provided for.'

If anything had been needed to point up the difference between them, his casual words did it. In the prince's world children were set up with trust funds, whereas Abby had grown up on an orchard. Although her parents had worked hard, when they'd died they'd left little for her—just enough for her to pay her way for a year on Palaweyo to help the community with their health needs.

He said forcefully, 'I didn't approve of the way Gemma was relegated to the outer perimeter of her mother's life. It won't happen with her son.' His tone edged each word with satire. 'I don't intend sending Michael to boarding school until he reaches secondary school. Not even then, if he doesn't want it.' He directed an ice-laden glance around the bleak room. 'He'll be much better off with me than with a woman who's both a kidnapper and a liar, and who lives from hand to mouth in a rural slum.'

Abby forced back the bubble of hysteria that threatened to block her throat and her thought processes. 'At least I love him!'

Dark brows lifted in taunting disbelief. 'It's an odd

love that confines a child to a life in places like this. And this isn't about you or me—this is about Michael, whose rights should be paramount. After all, it's *his* future that's on the line.'

'He has all the security he needs,' she retorted, trying hard to sound sensible and confident—and failing. The thought of Michael's life at the hands of this flinty, uncompromising tyrant edged her tone with desperation. 'What can *you* offer him? I'm sure that chasing yet another million to add to the pile you've already accumulated will take precedence over spending time with a little boy.'

His white teeth snapped together. After a taut few seconds he returned caustically, 'At least he won't have to worry where his next meal is coming from.'

'He's never gone hungry.' Occasionally she had, but not Michael. 'What do you know about children? He's noisy and grubby and demanding, and he needs attention and love and the knowledge that he's hugely important to at least one person in this world. Even more, he needs to know that that person will be there whenever he wants her, not just for an hour after work. All your money and royal links and social position mean *nothing* compared to that.'

'So why did you send him to a child-care centre with constantly changing workers, most of them almost untrained?'

Goaded, she retorted, 'I needed the money, and it was only for half of each day.'

He shrugged dismissively, the swift movement reminding her of his Latin heritage. 'A nanny would provide more stability, and I can certainly make sure he never has to worry about feeling cold in winter.'

Abby stared at him, defiance crumbling under guilt and

fear. She took refuge in sarcasm. 'Of course, you know so much about small boys.'

'I was one once.'

She snorted. 'I don't believe that. You were born six feet four tall and breathing fire.'

Amazingly, his hard mouth quirked. 'If so, my mother never told me.' The momentary amusement disappeared instantly, replaced by chilling hauteur. 'Stop fencing. I asked you before—how much do you want to get out of his life?'

'And I told you that I won't sell him,' she retorted furiously.

A faint stain of colour along his high, magnificent cheekbones told her she'd hit a nerve. The raw note in his voice hardened into intimidating confidence. 'I'm not buying the child—I'm buying *you* off.'

His narrowed gaze sent shivers of sensation along every nerve in her body. Her breath stopped in her throat, and something stark and merciless and fierce linked them for a charged moment, until she saw the glint of satisfaction in his cold eyes.

He knew, she thought in wretched embarrassment. Of course he did—he'd been chased by women since his teens; what he knew about them would probably fill an encyclopaedia. He certainly realised her treacherous body had its own agenda, and it amused him to see her struggle against it.

Abby took an involuntary step backwards—a mistake, she realised instantly, and tried to cover it with a swift, proud retort. 'You don't have enough money—no one in the whole wide world has enough money—to buy Michael from me, so forget about it right now.'

His broad shoulders moved in a slight shrug that told her just how much this meant to him: nothing. 'Judging by all accounts you have done a good job with the boy. I'm offering some recompense.'

She stated, 'I'm not going to abandon him to a loveless life.' And wished she'd put it some other way because it sounded so prissy.

'I intend to love him.' His tone was glacial, as though she'd forced some shameful secret from him.

She said urgently, 'You can't fake emotion. It doesn't work like that. You, of all people, should know. Gemma said that you and she had been taught in a hard school that love is a weakness.'

'Trust Gemma to pile on the melodrama. Yes, my father was notoriously besotted with his second wife, and losing her to another man shattered him. That doesn't mean that I don't know how to love a child.'

Abby made a swift, rapidly controlled gesture, then froze as the quiet hum of an expensive engine broke into the tense silence.

The prince said crisply, 'It's a hire car. I'm going to the airport in Queenstown and my nephew is coming with me. Try to stop me, and I'll call the police.'

His tone—level, impervious, relentless—echoed in the silent room. The car drew up outside the house and the driver switched off the engine, although Abby could see the round circles of the headlights through the curtains.

Bitter pain stopped any words from escaping her lips. Wringing her hands together in futile agony, she could only look pleadingly at Caelan's inflexible face.

He glanced down at the sheet of paper in his hands and appeared to come to some decision. 'All right. I believe that it would be exceedingly bad to put him through the trauma of waking up and finding you gone.' He lifted his head to pin her with cool detachment. 'You can come with us, but on my terms.'

Elusive, defiant hope flickered like a candle in a draught. Tautly she demanded, 'Which are?'

'That you accept I've got a right to know my nephew.'

Too afraid to be cautious, she accepted bitter defeat. 'I—yes.' Indeed, it had always worried her that Michael was being deprived of what was left of his family.

Caelan nodded. 'We can negotiate everything else when you're a little less emotional,' he said, his mouth compressing into a straight line. When she didn't answer or move he said, 'Make up your mind, Abby. Are you coming with me, or staying here?'

CHAPTER THREE

NUMBLY Abby stared at Caelan, reading his ruthless will in his face, in the uncompromising authority of his tone. Anger was defeated by desolation; she didn't dare trust him, but what other choice did she have?

Impatiently the prince broke into her racing thoughts. 'I'm offering you a chance to stay in Michael's life. Turn it down and I won't give you another.'

'You can't do that,' she croaked. 'I've looked after him since he was a baby. Any court in New Zealand would grant me custody—'

'It is a remote possibility,' he conceded crisply. 'But would the justice system also protect him from any criminal who might see him as money in the bank?'

He paused to let that sink in. Her powerlessness burned like fire inside her, eating away at her will-power and courage. 'I can't believe that that sort of thing would happen here.'

'He won't always be in New Zealand. I have to travel; he'll come with me.'

'But—'

'I thought you despised my father for allowing Gemma to be banished to her nursery?'

Pain sliced through her. 'I—yes.'

With cool dispassion, Caelan inclined his black head. 'The simplest way to deal with this is for you both to come to live with me.'

Stunned, unable to believe that she'd heard him correctly, she stared at him. 'I don't want to live with

you and I'm certain you don't want me anywhere
around you.'

'True, but I'm a pragmatic man.' His voice was textured by unfaltering confidence. 'It's not negotiable,
Abby. That is, if you want to be with Michael.'

Pride brought up her chin, veiled her eyes with thick
lashes to hide the bleak shock of his blunt statement.
Fighting to salvage what she could from her surrender,
she said, 'We don't need to share a house. We—Michael
and I—could live in Auckland, and I wouldn't deny you
access to him. Michael needs a man in his life.'

The prince surveyed her with a narrow smile. 'How
do I know you won't pack your bags and sneak off?'

'If I gave you my word—'

'Why should I trust you?'

The words rang in her ears like iron on stone, cold and
hard and relentless. Thrusting his hands into his trouser
pockets he sauntered over to the window and looked out
at the night. Against the pale luminosity of starshine he
was a lean, dominant silhouette.

Abby dragged in a slow, difficult breath, aching with
a sense of loss, of defeat and pain, with the knowledge
of wasted years that were gone for ever and a future that
would never happen. She had no other choice; losing
Michael would tear her heart to shreds, and for his sake
she had to endure whatever this cold, judgmental aristo-
crat decided to dish out.

Over his shoulder, he said, 'You've got ten seconds to
make up your mind.'

Anger revived her, giving her a spurious energy that
helped her say woodenly, 'It won't work.'

'Don't look at me with those huge, horrified eyes,' he
said, his negligent tone as much an insult as his careless
survey of her. 'You'll be quite safe.'

Colour burned up through her skin. He thought she was afraid for her virtue, and his tone made it clear that she didn't attract him in the least. Humiliated, she snapped, 'I suppose if we move into your house you'll insist on a nanny, and after Michael's got accustomed to her you'll force me to leave.'

'You sound like an actor in a Victorian melodrama. There won't be a nanny unless you want one.' Mockery laced his voice as he turned and examined her, his smile as lethal as a sword-blade. When she remained silent he added, 'I assume you do want the best for Michael?'

'You know I do,' she whispered, frightened by the forbidden excitement that gripped her. 'But not if it means living in the same house as you.'

He shrugged negligently, obviously not in the least affected by her swift, harsh rejection. 'But you'll do it— for his sake.' He watched her white face with cruel detachment. 'We'll make it legal with a cast-iron contract, and if you behave yourself and concentrate on Michael's welfare, there'll even be a cut-off date—say, when he finishes secondary education. In return I'll pay an allowance that will keep you in clothes that suit you and let you grow out your hair. Dying it must have been the ultimate sacrifice.'

'It didn't worry me in the least,' she said flatly.

Clearly he didn't believe her, because her words produced another cold, enigmatic smile. 'Hard to believe, Abby. And you might as well take off those spectacles too. I know they're not necessary.'

Slowly Abby removed the rimless frames, blinking as the light burned into her eyes. She felt stripped of everything she'd tried to hide, nakedly exposed to Caelan Bagaton's hard, penetrating gaze.

He said tersely, 'Gemma might have been right when

she told you that I don't do love well, but I do understand how to protect my own. Although I failed to save Gemma, I can make sure that her son doesn't die before his time.'

Abby hesitated, but something about his tone in the final sentence made her say with quiet intensity, 'No one could have saved Gemma, not even you. The cyclone wasn't supposed to come anywhere near Palaweyo, but at the last moment it turned and roared down on us out of a cloudless sky. We didn't have time to get out—in fact, we only just had time to gather everyone in the hospital. Gemma wouldn't want you to feel that you'd failed her.'

'She died before her time; that sounds like failure to me. So what's your decision?' His voice was icily detached. 'I don't intend to spend all night in this cold, musty room while you dither. Either accept my terms and live in my house with Michael, or forget about him and get on with your life.'

In an agony of indecision, Abby bit her lip. Chilly air seeped across her skin, and the soft noises of the old cottage settling down for the night, usually familiar and comforting, had become tinged with menace.

With the prince's harsh words echoing in her ears, she accepted she had no choice. While surrender was bitter, accepting his ultimatum would afford Michael more security than she could ever offer him.

From behind her Caelan said in a voice edged with cynicism, 'After all, it's a win/win situation. I get my nephew. Michael will be with the only mother he knows. And you can emerge from the melodramatic shadows you've been skulking in, wash the dye out of your hair and buy a whole new wardrobe in the right colours. The Abby I remember dressed to play up her hair and eyes

and skin, but the outfit you're wearing now makes you
look as though you've got acute jaundice.'

That stung, even though her clothes had been carefully
selected to strip the colour from her skin. Bought from
the cheapest racks, they couldn't have been more different from the tailored trousers that showed off Caelan's
long, heavily muscled legs, or the jersey he wore, its
lustrous shine revealing that it was made from merino
wool.

'And what's in it for you?' she asked bluntly.

He gave her an ironic glance. 'The knowledge that my
nephew isn't hungry and has the position and all the advantages he deserves. Most of all, the knowledge that
he's safe.'

Nothing about love there! According to Gemma and
the newspapers, Caelan was the consummate sophisti-
cate; he'd soon get bored with the antics of a three-year-
old.

Her heart clenched painfully. Even if he couldn't be
the sort of father a child needed, she'd be there to provide
love and understanding for Michael, and to fight for him
whenever it became necessary.

Yet self-protection forced her to search for a less dangerous compromise. 'I still think it would be easier for
us all if Michael and I had our own place. You could see
him whenever you want to.'

But even as she said the words she knew they weren't
going to change Caelan's mind.

'You'll live with me, so I can keep a close watch on
you. From now on, wherever Michael goes, either I—or
someone I employ—will be half a step behind.' He spoke
with the cold, raw impact of a punch in the face, his tone
implacable.

'All right,' she said at last, the acrid taste of defeat in

her mouth. She had no room to manoeuvre, and he knew it. Apprehension shivered through her, setting her nerves jumping.

'Then let's go,' he said without expression. 'Do you want me to carry the child out to the car?'

'No,' she said too quickly.

Ignoring her, he strode out of the room and opened the front door, giving crisp, low-voiced orders to whoever had driven the car up to the cottage.

Abby walked back into Michael's room, but once there she fixed her gaze painfully on his beloved face. Even when Caelan came back in she didn't move.

He interrupted her darting thoughts with an impatient command. 'Forget the past—it's not relevant—and think of Michael's well-being; at the moment he needs both of us—me for the security which, believe it or not, Gemma would have considered to be just as important as the love you dispense.' After a tense pause he drawled, 'Or is it too big a sacrifice for you to make for him?'

'Damn you,' she whispered, torn on the rack of her ambivalence, disillusion and pain warring with the ignominy of her own helplessness.

A sobbing sigh from the bed broke the thick web of tension between them. Nerves taut and brittle as spun toffee, she sat down on the edge when Michael rubbed his eyes and began to hiccup.

'Hush, darling, it's all right,' she crooned, lifting his solid, warm body against her. 'Did you have a bad dream?'

He murmured something and clung, cuddling into her, so utterly dear that her heart clenched in a tight, hard ball.

Abby kissed his tousled hair and pressed her cheek against it, looking across to where Caelan stood.

Michael must have sensed that someone else was in the room too; he turned his head, his eyes growing larger as he examined Caelan. Sobs dying, he said, 'Abby?'

'Hello, Michael, I'm your Uncle Caelan, and you're coming to live with me.' Caelan's voice was deep and cool and utterly confident.

His nephew stared at him, clutching Abby tighter. 'And Abby too?' he said uncertainly.

Caelan looked at Abby. 'Tell him,' he commanded.

She dragged in a deep breath, praying fiercely that this was the right thing for Michael. 'Of course, darling,' she said simply. 'You know I'll always be with you.'

Michael looked up at her, brows drawing together in a frown that reminded her eerily of the man with them.

'Give him to me,' Caelan ordered.

When she hesitated, he said curtly, 'I'm not a monster, Abby.'

But she handed Michael over with huge reluctance. Carrying the small boy easily, his uncle strode out of the room; swiftly Abby scooped up blankets and Michael's stuffed elephant and the fire engine she'd made of wooden blocks and followed, panting slightly by the time she reached the big, waiting car.

Caelan was stooping, his voice level and reassuring as he lowered Michael into a child seat in the back. Another man stood some distance away—possibly the one who'd kept her under surveillance. A sudden shiver of foreboding tightened her skin.

She didn't understand power at all, whereas Caelan Bagaton reeked of it. Very little of that inherent authority came from the title he rarely used and his heritage; if he'd been born plain Caelan Smith he'd have made his way in the world. He was a winner.

As soon as the restraints on the car seat were clipped

home Michael peered anxiously at Abby, who hovered
in the crisp air.

'Sit beside him,' Caelan ordered, straightening up so
that she could drape the blankets around the child. 'Give
me your car keys first—'

'Why?'

'I assume the bag on the sofa isn't the sum total of
your belongings?'

'No, but—'

He frowned, explaining with surprising patience,
'We'll transfer the rest of your luggage from your car to
this one. Then someone will drive yours to Auckland.'

Feeling foolish, she muttered, 'I was going to sell it in
Christchurch,' and rooted for the keys in her bag. She
dropped them into his outstretched hand, noting that he
wasn't looking at her; his gaze was fixed on Michael.

She took Michael's warm little hand and coaxed, 'Go
back to sleep, darling.'

Caelan stepped back and turned away. As she got in
beside Michael and tucked the blankets around him more
securely she was aware of the prince's deep voice giving
concise orders. The boot was opened, the bags put in and
it slammed shut again, before the silence was punctuated
by the sound of her car door closing. Its engine coughed
into life and headlights probed the darkness as it turned
down the drive in front of them.

Caelan slid in behind the wheel of the hire car. Turning
so that he could see her, he said negligently, 'Try to stay
awake until we get to Queenstown. You can sleep on the
plane; there's a bed in it as well as a cot for Michael.'

In the dark cocoon that was the interior of the car she
thought his eyes lingered on her face for a second before
he turned back and the engine purred into life.

Hot blood stung her skin. What had she done, letting

herself be ambushed and captured like this? The prince took no prisoners; what did he have in mind for her?

A tiredness more than physical, a weariness of the spirit, chilled her from the bones out. While Michael slid back into the sleep of the very young and secure, she stayed wide-eyed and tense until the luxurious car drove into the airport at Queenstown.

But he didn't drive towards the darkened terminal building. 'Where are we going?' she asked.

'There's a private plane waiting on the runway.'

Well, of course, she thought wearily. As well as being cousin to the ruler of a principality, Caelan Bagaton was a tycoon, a billionaire, rich enough to afford his own country as well as a private jet.

Oh, you fool, she thought painfully, you're so far out of your depth here you might as well drown now and get it over and done with.

They'd met when Gemma had almost run her over in one of Auckland's summer storms, and, although her car was a miracle of design that Abby knew she'd never be able to aspire to, Gemma had insisted on taking her home.

Their friendship had ripened rapidly; they'd gone clubbing together and spent other nights talking and listening to music; Gemma had invited her up to the beach house, although she had said, 'But Caelan won't be there.'

Abby's brows shot up. 'So?'

'Oh, just that quite a few of the girls I know try to use me to get to him. And even my friends fall in love with him and then get their hearts broken. He's a big, bad wolf, my brother.'

Well, he'd turned up at the beach, and Abby had found out for herself the truth of that assessment! Fortunately her year abroad working for a volunteer organisation was due to start the week after, so she hadn't had time to brood about Gemma's fabulous, arrogant, incredibly sexy brother.

When she'd left for the Pacific Gemma had wept a little and promised to visit. Abby hadn't expected her to; Palaweyo was a poor atoll, only the bounty of its huge lagoon saving it from third-world status, and few tourists came within a thousand miles. But months later Gemma had arrived, tense and oddly desperate, and during the long hot nights she'd confided a few details of her passionate affair with a gangly, laconic Australian mountain-climber, and his heroic death. Before she'd had time to grieve, she'd discovered that she was pregnant.

Eerily, as though he could read her thoughts, Caelan said, 'I believe Michael's father was another Michael—Moncrieff, the mountaineer who died rescuing stranded climbers on Mount Everest.'

Stunned, Abby swallowed. 'Yes,' she said thinly.

'A decent man, but not her usual sort. Didn't it occur to you that his relatives might have wanted to have contact with their grandchild?'

'Gemma said he had none; he'd grown up in care.'

Something about Caelan's nod made her realise that he knew this. Of course he'd have had Gemma's lover investigated. Suddenly loathing him and everything he stood for, she finished curtly, 'Gemma said he was genuine gold all through.'

Surprisingly Caelan didn't dig further. 'Why does Michael call you Abby? It would have been less obvious if he'd called you his mother.'

'But I'm not his mother,' she said quietly. 'He knows his parents are dead. He doesn't know what that means, of course, but he's entitled to know who he is.'

'But not about his mother's family.'

The lash of his sarcasm flicked across her skin like a whip; she was glad when he eased the car to a stop beside the sleek executive plane.

Once in the aircraft, with Michael asleep in the luxurious bedroom, and the prince going through papers in a leather-upholstered armchair that somehow didn't look incongruous with a seat belt, Abby stared through a window until the sky began to turn grey towards the east. Thoughts churned in her mind, going over and over old ground while she tried to work out how she could have avoided this.

In the end she gave up; against the prince's iron-clad determination she had no defence.

The stark volcanic landscape of the central North Island unrolled beneath the plane as the sun tinted the distant clouds a radiant pink that swiftly turned to gold.

Foolish to let an everyday miracle lift her heart, yet she wondered if the sunrise was some sort of omen, a pointer of hope. Perhaps she and the prince could work together for Michael's sake; perhaps Caelan could find it in his cold heart to learn to love a small child.

And perhaps not, she thought grimly, but staying with Michael was all she asked at the moment.

As though her thoughts had woken him, she saw Michael peep cautiously through the door of the bedroom. He beamed at her before turning to examine his uncle.

Caelan had noticed, of course; he put his papers down and said, 'Good morning, Michael.'

For a moment Michael looked apprehensive, but he was a friendly child and he essayed a tentative grin. Abby's breath locked in her throat; she watched the formidable assurance of Caelan's expression relax into a rare, compelling smile.

Deep inside her something twisted, and a pang of excitement—hot and feverish and piercing—seized her so fiercely she almost gasped under its impact.

'Do you want to go to the bathroom?' his uncle asked.

Michael thought for a moment, then nodded. 'Yes. With Abby.'

'Of course.' An ice-blue, enigmatic gaze roamed Abby's face. 'When you've finished, breakfast will be ready.'

Eyes wide and incredulous, Michael stared around the plane and demanded, 'Where are we, Abby?'

'We're in an aeroplane, darling, up in the sky.' Warily conscious of Caelan's presence, Abby tried to resurrect her brisk common sense. 'When you've been to the bathroom you can look out of the window and you'll see the sea a long way underneath us.'

Bubbling with excitement, Michael shot questions at her on the way to the bathroom and all the way back, falling silent only when he at last saw the sea, a gleaming bow against the craggy bulk of the land.

Caelan said, 'Everything you packed into your car is on the plane; I thought it best for him to have as many familiar things around him as possible.'

'Thank you,' she said in a stilted voice.

'It was nothing.'

And indeed, for him, it wasn't. All he had to do was command, and people hurried to do his bidding. Travelling with the prince was nothing like the normal hassle; leg-room wasn't a problem and luggage didn't need to be monitored. Money made things easy in so many ways, and of course his heritage meant that he took such things for granted.

But he had considered Michael's feelings; it seemed a good omen. Fortified by that hopeful thought, Abby leaned back in the seat, remembering how startled she'd been when she'd discovered that he and Gemma were distant cousins of the ruler of Dacia.

Gemma had said, 'One of these days I'll take you to see the crown jewels there. They're a magnificent collection of the world's most perfect emeralds.' She'd peered into Abby's face and then sat back, pronouncing, 'In fact, some are exactly the same colour as your eyes. And you'd like the Bagaton cousins. The men are totally, over-the-top gorgeous, and there's a Kiwi connection too. Several—including Prince Luka, the reigning monarch— have married New Zealanders.'

Don't go there! Abby commanded, relieved when Caelan interrupted her memories.

'If you agree, your car can be sold today.'

Her lips tightened. Resentment at being taken over, forced into a situation she couldn't escape, scraped across her nerves. 'I suppose so,' she said colourlessly.

'Yes or no?'

'Yes,' she said between her teeth, and leaned away to point out another, smaller plane beneath them to Michael.

Who crowed with delight before turning a radiant face to the prince to shout, 'Uncle Caelan, look!'

Caelan got to his feet and bent over them to look through the window; Abby caught a faint, masculine scent, and a merciless sexual awareness dazzled her. Her body tightened and her head swam.

Fortunately he straightened up almost immediately, looking down at her with burnished silver-blue eyes, unreadable and hard. 'Breakfast should be ready. I'll go and see.'

Her breath hissed out as he walked to the back of the

plane, his lithe gait a challenge in itself. No wonder he turned up frequently in the gossip columns; he packed a powerful physical charge that overrode all the cautious warnings of her mind.

But at least Gemma had told her what he was—utterly intolerant, quick to judge and incapable of trust. And she'd found out for herself that he was able to effortlessly control his sexual appetite.

It took all of her powers of persuasion to coax Michael back into his seat and buckle him in; his vigorous objections were only halted by the appearance of a middle-aged stewardess carrying a tray. Entranced by this, and the promise of fruit to follow, he settled down to demolish a boiled egg with his usual gusto.

Too strung-up to eat, Abby refused anything apart from a cup of coffee. But it arrived accompanied by thin, crisp toast and several little pots containing a variety of spreads.

'Mr Bagaton said you should have something,' the stewardess explained with a smile.

Abby quelled a frisson of foolish pleasure. His thoughtfulness warmed some small part of her she'd thought permanently frozen.

She looked up as he came back down the aisle, an inchoate smile freezing on her lips when she met a long, watchful inspection that made her acutely aware of the signs of her sleepless night in her face—shadowed eyes, pale skin, and hair like string. Even after combing, it looked the way she'd wanted it to—dull, mousy, boring.

And she didn't—couldn't—allow herself to care what Caelan Bagaton thought of her. Her lips straightened and defiance glittered beneath her lashes as she lifted the coffee-cup to her lips.

No matter what it took, she had to kill this painful

awareness, so intense it had only taken one glance at him to roar into life. In spite of its power and primal force it was meaningless.

Yet, oh, so dangerous.

Caelan transferred his attention to Michael, his mouth curving. 'Are you enjoying your breakfast?'

Trying to ignore the painful twist to her heart, Abby thought cynically that that smile had to be one of the world's great weapons. Michael was no more able to resist it than she was.

A wide grin split Michael's face. 'I had a negg.'

'Was it good?' Caelan lowered his big frame to his seat.

'Yes. And some peaches,' Michael informed him gleefully, and went back to emptying his plate.

But once the tray had been cleared, he began to find the confinement of the seat belt irritating. Abby changed places with him so he could again see out of the window. Obediently he gazed at the lush green countryside that had replaced the stark central plateau beneath, but his interest didn't last long.

Caelan got to his feet, opened the overhead locker and took down the bag she'd packed for just such a moment, but Michael resisted all his favourites with every appearance of loathing.

Not now, she thought wearily. It was too much to expect him to accept the huge change of circumstances without any response, but it would be so much easier if he'd kept the inevitable reaction for later.

Preferably after she'd had a good night's sleep, and with the prince well out of the way!

CHAPTER FOUR

ABBY glanced across the aisle, straight into Caelan's cool, guarded eyes. Hiding her trepidation, she met them with all the composure she could summon, and asked, 'How much longer?'

'About half an hour. Why?'

She inclined her head slightly sideways. 'Energy needs to be expended.'

'He'll have to wait.' Even as she bristled he reached into his narrow leather briefcase and drew out a book she recognised. 'Does he know this?'

'Yes,' she said, truly grateful. 'But we've always had to get it from the library so he'll be more than happy to hear it now.'

How did Caelan know that Michael adored the iconic adventures of a small New Zealand dog? Surely, she thought, going cold, he couldn't have had them investigated that intensively?

Of course he had; a man who thought nothing of infiltrating a child-care centre with an operative to get DNA samples would have insisted on a complete dossier. How else would the stewardess have known that Michael loved peaches?

The thought of such close surveillance sent chills down her spine. Hastily, she opened the book and began to read to an enthralled Michael.

Although the witty, clever exploits of Hairy Maclary and his canine friends did the trick, Abby gave a silent sigh of relief when they finally touched down at the airport in Auckland.

As they made their way to the car park the crowds and the noise and the unfamiliar bustle silenced Michael; wide-eyed, he trailed along between her and the prince, clinging to her hand while he gazed around.

Abby saw a middle-aged woman watching them. Heat stung her skin; she knew what the woman was thinking, just as she recognised the barely concealed interest in other women's eyes when they'd noticed the man beside her. His powerful physical presence demanded instant respect.

Then their eyes swung to her, and envy was replaced by astonishment. They were wondering what on earth a woman like her was doing with a man like Caelan Bagaton.

She wanted to say out loud, 'We're not a family! This is just a sham.' A tormenting sham, one she'd been forced into by the man who'd ruthlessly shattered her life.

Instead, she gave the woman a half-smile and walked on by, her heart contracting into a solid ball in her chest.

'The car's over here,' the prince said brusquely.

The big vehicle had a child's car seat already installed in the rear seat. Naturally, she thought, bristling. Caelan didn't accept defeat.

Stop going over and over and over this, she commanded herself. It's finished—dead as a doornail, or a dodo, or the Dead Sea. All of them, actually.

At first Michael was too interested in the traffic—especially, Abby noted with wry amusement, extremely large trucks—to get bored. However, by the time the car left the motorway for inner-city streets he demanded in a voice that came too close to a whine, 'Where we going, Abby? Are we nearly there?'

'Five minutes,' Caelan said calmly.

So he wasn't taking them to the beach house, where he'd kissed her.

She fought a humiliating let-down; he probably didn't even remember that kiss. After all, he'd had at least one long-term relationship since he'd broken up with the then-current lover. And Gemma had told her of the constant stream of hopefuls he fended off. The kiss they'd shared probably no longer registered on his radar—if it ever had.

Pinning a steady smile to her lips, she said to Michael, 'There you go—we're almost at Uncle Caelan's house.'

'It's an apartment,' Caelan informed her.

'An apartment?' Abby shot a swift glance at his unyielding profile. In a neutral voice she said, 'Children need easy access to grass and trees, and a place where they can run and jump and roll.'

'All highly desirable, but not as necessary as decent food and clothes and security,' Caelan returned, his urbane tone not hiding the whiplash of scorn in his words. 'The apartment is central and convenient, but if it doesn't work out we'll move to somewhere more suitable for a family.' Skilfully he eased the car past a courier van.

She frowned to hide a suddenly thudding heartbeat. A family...

In spite of her effort to be reasonable, anticipation warmed her from the inside, curling through her like warm honey shot with fire. To quell it she asked more aggressively than she intended, 'But you told Michael on the flight that you have a pool.' And then she remembered an article she'd seen about a very up-market apartment complex in Auckland. 'Oh, is there a gym there?'

'There's a lap pool on the terrace.'

She flushed. His casual words underlined again the

huge difference between growing up on a Northland citrus orchard, and amongst the ranks of the hugely rich.

Expertly Caelan avoided three laughing teenagers who chose to dash across the road as the lights turned green. 'And of course there's the one at the beach.'

So he did still own it.

A wild, foolish second of elation was rapidly smothered by another cold splash of common sense. How pathetic was that—thinking that one kiss might have meant anything to him? Turning to Michael, she infused enthusiasm into her voice. 'Just about there, darling.'

Very much there, in fact; the car stopped outside a gate that led to a basement car park. Absently Abby read a notice on the wall, then stiffened.

'This is a hotel,' she accused.

The gate rattled back and Caelan put the car into gear, easing it down into the well-lit basement. 'An apartment hotel. I live in the penthouse.'

Michael asked with eager anticipation, 'Can I go for a swim, Abby? Now?'

He adored the water; the day-care centre had a small paddling pool, but Abby had never been able to afford lessons for him in the school pool.

'Sweetheart, I think it would be better if you left it until it's warmer,' she told him. Although nowhere near as cold as Nukuroa, Auckland's spring wasn't exactly balmy, and at the airport she'd noticed a brisk, cool wind.

His lower lip jutted, but Caelan cut short his objections. 'The pool is heated, and sheltered from the wind. I'll go in with him if you don't want to.'

Well, yes, she thought cynically, of course it would be heated. Standard tycoon equipment!

The car came to a halt in a reserved slot. Abby tamped down a flare of anger; she'd been making decisions for

Michael for three years, and Caelan had no right to query them.

In a toneless voice she answered, 'If it's heated, that's fine. Unfortunately he's absolutely fearless in the water, although he hasn't got beyond the fundamentals yet. He needs careful supervision.'

'Point taken. He'd better learn to swim as soon as possible.' Caelan switched off the engine.

Abby examined the autocratic lines and curves of his profile as he said, 'The pool is fenced off from the apartment, so he'll be safe enough.'

Physically, yes. Emotionally? Ignoring a cold little worm of fear, she told herself sturdily that all she could hope to extract from this tensely disturbing situation was Michael's happiness.

Inside the hotel lift, a warm little hand clutching hers, Abby stared blindly at the carpet, alienated by the atmosphere of sleek, elegant luxury. A faint scent permeated the air—a very exclusive, very expensive perfume; disliking its cloying sensuousness, Abby wrinkled her nose and tried to ignore an alarming needle of jealousy.

The atmosphere was compounded inside the penthouse apartment. Of course it was elegant and large, filled with reflected light from the harbour and the sky, and superbly decorated by a professional who hadn't surrendered comfort for style.

The prince took them into a large, informal sitting room with a dining table and chairs at one end. It opened out onto a wide, partly covered terrace where potted plants flourished around a narrow swimming pool.

'There's another, more formal sitting room through that door, but I use it mainly for entertaining,' he told her. 'This one is more suitable for a child.'

'It's lovely,' she murmured, walking across to a row

of windows at the end. Startled, she looked straight into the harbour, as though they were on the bow of an ocean liner.

From behind Caelan said, 'The hotel is built on one of the wharves.'

A fat ferry bumbled purposefully towards the North Shore; it reminded Abby of a beetle and she smiled involuntarily.

'The kitchen is through that door,' he said crisply. 'Do you want a drink? No? Then I'll show you your rooms.'

Michael's was the first. Abby had expected an exercise in sleek minimalism, but this was a young boy's dream, a circus fantasy with a tasselled tent top and a frieze of prancing animals.

Oh, Caelan had been utterly and completely confident that he'd be bringing Michael back with him! And why not? He held all the cards.

'Your room is next door, you share a bathroom,' he told Abby, indicating a door. He glanced at his watch and frowned. 'I have to check out a few things, so I'll leave you to explore by yourselves for ten minutes or so. Your luggage has arrived, so you'll be able to change into your togs, Michael.'

Left alone with a silent, fascinated Michael, Abby admired a magnificently prancing rocking-horse. At the back of her mind she wondered how many women had come to this penthouse and been swept off their feet by their host's potent sexuality.

Droves, she thought savagely. A small voice insisting on being taken to the bathroom put a welcome end to her thoughts. She gave Michael a swift hug and showed him where it was.

Then they explored the room next door, furnished in restful, sophisticated shades of sand with a throw rug of deep rust lending richness to the neutral scheme. A chair and a desk against one wall were set out for writing; a daybed in the window suggested long afternoons of reading. Abby's gaze lingered on a vase of orchids, exquisite fly-away things in shades of caramel, rust and golden-green.

Had Caelan chosen them? Highly unlikely, she decided. No doubt a florist kept each of the rooms in this luxurious place filled with blooms that matched the décor as perfectly as those orchids did.

Well, she'd far rather have a handful of dandelions picked from the paddock and given to her in a chubby little hand.

'Where does Uncle Caelan sleep?' Michael asked, looking around.

'I don't know,' Abby said crisply. Not at this end of the penthouse, anyway. Possibly he had a suite well away from his guest rooms. 'Come on, we'd better find your swimming togs.'

Ten minutes later, Caelan knocked on the door. Made exuberant by excitement, Michael rushed across to open it.

Abby's stomach lurched and that treacherous flow of anticipation turned into sharp, painful awareness. In swimming shorts, a large towel draped over one copper-bronze, sleekly muscled shoulder, Caelan's compelling physicality cut through centuries of civilised conditioning. In spite of every barrier she'd constructed, the primitive instinct to mate with the most alpha male flamed into life within her.

'Do you have a towel?' he asked, smiling as his nephew jumped around him like a puppy.

Michael grabbed it up from the bed and went off without a backwards glance, chattering and animated. Feeling resentfully like an unwanted extra, Abby followed them out onto a wide terrace overlooking the harbour and the North Shore.

She sat down in a lounger beneath a sail that kept the hot northern sun from her head, and watched intently as the two men now in her life stopped by the gate into the pool enclosure. The light in this sub-tropical part of New Zealand was softer, more humid than in the south, smoothing over Caelan's torso to delineate every coiled muscle as he stooped to speak to his nephew. Broad-shouldered, narrow-hipped and with the innate grace of a leopard, he looked dangerous and dynamic and fascinating.

Furious at the slow burn of desire in the pit of her stomach, she thought acidly that Mediterranean heritage had a lot to answer for. No doubt the splash of Celtic blood that had given him his name and his ice-blue eyes had provided the long, powerful legs, but his formidable confidence and authority were his own.

She must never allow herself to forget that Caelan used his tough tenacity and ruthless intelligence—and his charisma—like weapons. He was a warrior, gathering the fruits of war.

In which quest it probably helped that he didn't have a heart. In fact, it surprised her that he had enough glimmerings of conscience to feel responsible for Gemma's son.

No, that was unfair; even Gemma had admitted that her half-brother was meticulous in fulfilling his obligations. In fact, it had been one of the reasons she'd demanded Abby's promise.

'I don't want Michael to be a duty like I was,' she'd said flatly. 'He'd be just another project to see through to completion. Oh, Caelan would do his best for him, but it's not enough to know you're no more than a responsibility.'

The early death of his father had pitched Caelan into the cut-throat arena of international business in his mid-twenties, and, to most people's astonishment, he'd succeeded wildly. At the same time he'd taken charge of his impulsive, wilful sister.

His best hadn't been good enough for Gemma; she'd make sure he dealt better with Michael, Abby decided, her gaze following them into the pool enclosure. Excitement raised Michael's voice higher than usual against his uncle's deeper tones. The elusive resemblance between them tugged at her heartstrings.

Oh, Gemma, she thought forlornly, I'll look after him whatever happens, but I feel very outgunned right now!

And then she stiffened her spine in a determination that masked a deep, abiding dread. There was much more than her happiness at stake; weigh her wary, reluctant attraction against a child's future, and that feverish tug at her senses meant very little.

And as she clearly wasn't necessary here, she should really go and unpack Michael's clothes.

Instead, she leaned back into the sleek, luxuriously comfortable lounger to watch. Against the shimmer of the water in the bright spring sun, Caelan crouched by his nephew and began to talk. Abby watched Michael's face, solemn and intent as he nodded.

Straining her ears, she heard Caelan say, 'And no jumping in.'

'No jumping,' Michael repeated, a little disappointed but resigned.

'Only if I'm there to catch you. Wait until I'm in the water, and I'll tell you when to jump.'

After another serious nod Michael gave a great beaming smile, twisting Abby's heart. Both were feeling their way; Michael was prepared to like the man who'd appeared out of the darkness, and so far Caelan had settled for treating his nephew like a small adult.

An attitude that made Michael blossom, she noted with another despicable stab of jealousy.

Glass panels sheltered both pool and terrace from the cool breeze that trailed in off the harbour. When the two swimmers got into the water her heart—foolish organ!—contracted even more tightly as Michael imitated everything the prince did. She kept a close eye on them, only relaxing when she saw that Caelan was always near enough to rescue his nephew from any risky exploits.

Their laughter blended, and a great weariness weighed down her eyelids. She'd cope, but first she had to accept that her life had changed irrevocably. From now on it wouldn't be just her and Michael against the world; Caelan had altered the balance, and nothing would ever be the same.

Michael had someone else to rely on, and she'd just have to accept it.

Too soon, so swiftly she wasn't aware of what was happening, Abby's wakeful night caught up with her and she slid into darkness.

Michael's voice woke her, soft and urgent in her ear. 'Abby, Abby, wake up now.'

After a prodigious yawn, she said, 'What's the time, darling—?'

And remembered where she was.

Her eyelids jerked up, but she was no longer lying in the lounger by the pool; instead, she was curled up on the bed in the room Caelan had given her, the rust-red wrap covering her.

Fully dressed in T-shirt and shorts, his hair dry, Michael stood beside it, and behind him loomed Caelan—who must have carried her in and put her there. She could see the knowledge in his expression, a subtle tension and awareness that stoked her own mindless response to him.

Head whirling, she got up on her elbow and swung her legs onto the floor. 'What time is it?' she asked thinly.

She sounded slack, almost drugged. Caelan scrutinised her face, but the colour flooded back into her skin as she straightened. He tried to ignore the sensuous memory of her sleek body in his arms, her breathing when she'd snuggled her cheek against his chest. Yet other images prowled his brain, images snatched from barely remembered dreams in which she'd lain beneath him, soft and warm and silken, of little gasping cries as she climaxed around him, the scent of her skin and the perfumed cloud of her hair, the way her voice changed from crisp confidence to an enchanting husky shyness when he'd made love to her, the way she laughed—

How the hell could one kiss four years ago light the need and hunger that still burned like a fire underground?

He'd never stopped wanting her, he admitted, and never stopped resenting the power she wielded over him.

So he should do something about sating this damned inconvenient desire.

She was watching him, her face guarded and stubborn, but in spite of her prickly demeanour he was too experienced not to recognise the unwanted tug of attraction. Everything pointed to it—her careful avoidance of his touch, the soft flutter of her pulse at the base of her throat whenever he came near her, and the colour that came and went in her silky, seductive skin.

A plan that had occurred to him as they'd flown up solidified in his mind.

In spite of his best attempt at control, his voice was rough when he told her, 'Almost one o'clock. I wouldn't have woken you, but I have an appointment shortly.'

'One o'clock?' She pushed back a tumbling lock of hair and asked swiftly, 'Has Michael had his lunch?'

'Yes. Peanut butter sandwiches,' Caelan returned with a faint smile.

She hid another yawn behind her hand. 'His staple food,' she said in a wry voice.

'He also had half an orange and a glass of milk.'

Abby nodded. 'Give me five minutes. I need to wash my face.'

It took a little longer than that, because she had a rapid shower in the sybaritic bathroom, all glass and tiled walls with equipment that looked as though it fitted out a spaceship. Spirits marginally boosted by a change of clothes, she closed the bedroom door behind her and followed the sound of voices to the living room off the kitchen.

She'd almost got there when Caelan laughed, for once without the undernote of cynicism she'd always heard.

But when she came into the room all humour vanished from his strong face. He said aloofly, 'I'll be back around six this evening. Don't worry about dinner; we can order from the hotel menu.'

'What about Michael?' she said steadily. 'I don't imagine the hotel kitchen caters to children his age.'

'It can, but check out the fridge.' He ruffled Michael's hair, smiled down into his face and looked up to assess Abby with hard blue eyes. Very casually, he finished, 'Don't try leaving the apartment.'

'Why?'

'You both need time to get your bearings.' He paused before saying deliberately, 'It would be inconvenient if I had to go out looking for you.'

The warning was no less intimidating for being implied rather than stated forcefully. Her stomach a tight, apprehensive knot, she watched him leave, grateful when a question from Michael broke into her thoughts.

'Abby, can we swim again now?'

'After you've had your nap,' she said automatically, and concealed her furious resentment by opening the refrigerator.

Of course it was filled with eminently suitable food for a hungry three-year-old. After a molten survey of the interior, Abby almost slammed the enormous door shut. Whatever else he was—or wasn't—Caelan was a superb organiser. No doubt if she tried to leave the apartment someone would stop her, or accompany her.

She didn't need the humiliation.

Still fuming, she spent the hour of Michael's nap unpacking, grimacing at the pathetic show her few dreary clothes made in a wardrobe almost as big as Michael's bedroom in the cottage. They were so out of context they looked ludicrous.

Growing up she'd known comfort and security, but the luxury Caelan took for granted was completely alien to her.

'That's what you get for getting in the way of a dominant alpha male,' she told herself. Money and power had helped forge his intimidating inner confidence, but mix with a brilliant mind and loads of disturbing male magnetism, spice the whole mix with a soupçon of princely blood, season with a hint of Latin—and you had Caelan Bagaton, one on his own.

Once Michael woke, they explored his room, discovering a box of toys to go with the rocking-horse, and a whole new library of books. Abby thought of the tattered, much-read volumes she'd packed, and wondered whether Michael would want to read them again.

They spent the rest of the lazy afternoon out on the terrace with books, blocks and crayons until, when the sun began its slow slide down towards the west, she braved the unknown terrors of the impressive stove in the kitchen.

She was bathing Michael when Caelan arrived. To her astonishment he came into the bathroom as though he were accustomed to such familiar rituals, not even grimacing when Michael slipped as he was getting out and sent a tidal wave of water onto his uncle's superbly cut shirt and trousers.

'Careful,' Abby said, more sharply than she'd intended.

Horrified, Michael flushed and screwed up his face. 'I'm sorry, I didn't mean to.'

Caelan said mildly, 'I know that.' And was rewarded with a shy smile.

A pang of dislocation and guilt hit Abby. She dried Michael down, stuffed him into his pyjamas and tried hard not to feel left out when Michael asked that Caelan read his bedtime story. At least he'd chosen one of his old favourites, not the glossy new ones Caelan had provided. As she heard Caelan provide a spirited rendition of an old fairy tale she decided that he must have been practising…

Then he bent his head for Michael's goodnight kiss as though he'd been doing it all his life.

At last, leaving Michael safely tucked up in bed and supervised by a brand new state-of-the-art monitor, Caelan escorted her into the living room.

'I'll get you a drink,' he said. 'Is it still white wine?'

She nodded, although it had been four years since she'd tasted any.

As he poured he said levelly, 'You look triste. What is it?'

She shut down her emotions, hoping her face was a composed mask. 'Just thinking.'

Apart from the child sleeping in his bed, they were alone in the apartment. That dangerous, mindless excitement was stirring in her body, basic and inescapable as the breath in her lungs and the blood that raced through her veins.

Handing her the glass, Caelan said, 'I've already ordered dinner; it arrives in half an hour. Until then, try to relax.'

Relax? He had to be mad! She looked up, but his expression was coolly noncommittal, his eyes transparent and slightly amused.

Baffled and angry, she evaded the hidden tension by walking through the long glass doors onto the terrace.

The swift northern dusk had turned into night; beyond the safety-glass balustrade the harbour gleamed like black satin, and the North Shore suburbs sparkled against the bulk of Rangitoto, Auckland's iconic island volcano. A small breeze carried the scent of the sea to her, ghosting over her sensitised skin. Feeling utterly forlorn, she shivered.

She didn't belong to Caelan's world of privilege and sophistication and wealth, of ancient aristocratic bloodlines and power. Responding to him in any way was not only stupid, it was humiliating and pathetic and embarrassing.

Her lips widened in a bleak, mirthless smile and she

swung around to look at the Harbour Bridge, a shallow arc of lights reflected in the water.

She sipped some of the exquisitely fragrant wine. Just when she sensed that Caelan had followed her out she had no idea; the knowledge of his presence came as a feather of response down her spine, a slow conviction that escalated the turmoil inside her.

Heart jumping, tense as a stretched wire, she hurried into speech, choosing the most innocuous subject that came to mind. 'What made you decide to live here?'

'I travel a lot, so the chopper pad at Mechanic's Bay is handy for quick trips to the airport.'

Moving slowly, she turned her head a few degrees to see him. Unwanted, unbidden, a memory surfaced. Once—in another lifetime—she'd ruffled his black hair, fascinated by its silken warmth. Her fingers tingled as though they'd been deprived, and her heart jolted in her breast. Breath came fast through her lips, and she shuddered at the seductive impact of the forgotten sensation.

And then she met his eyes, and every languorous memory disappeared; nothing could survive in the frigid wasteland of his gaze.

Angry with herself for her chagrin, she said, 'Michael loved the toys and the books. Thank you.' Even though she suspected that Caelan had consulted an expert, it had to be said.

'And the horse?'

She said, 'He's most impressed, and is taking his time to get to know it.'

His broad shoulders lifted negligently. 'It's the one I had as a child. I had a craftsman in Northland repair and refurbish it. I'm glad another child will ride it.'

He was pointing out the difference between what she had given Michael, and what he could give. Meeting the subtle implication head-on, she said clearly, 'Too many toys aren't good for children. Michael hasn't missed anything in his life except parents.'

He said coolly, 'And his uncle. Why did you decide to leave Nukuroa?'

The eerie wail of a siren somewhere close by cut into the tense pause that followed Caelan's words. Abby covered an uneasy movement with another sip of her drink.

In the end she admitted, 'I felt—stalked. And I've learned to trust my instincts. How did you find us?'

'I've had an investigator looking for you ever since you arrived in New Zealand with Michael,' he said, adding abruptly, 'He seems a happy, secure child, and for that I thank you.'

Made more uncomfortable by his rare softening than by his open contempt, she muttered, 'You don't need to thank me.' And because she wanted to get things settled, she went on abruptly, 'You said yesterday—was it yesterday?—that we'd work out some sort of arrangement for this situation when I was less emotional. Exactly what do you have in mind for this—for our lives?'

He set his glass down on a nearby table and examined her face, remote in the darkness, with eyes she couldn't see. 'Have you decided to stop resisting the inevitable?'

'I—yes, I have.' Although she was quaking inside, pride steadied her voice and gave an edge to her words. 'As you pointed out so cogently, I don't have any choice. You have power and money and I have none. And you could send me to prison if you press charges against me for claiming Michael as my son.'

He accepted that as the simple statement of fact it was. 'You have power too. You're the only mother Michael's ever known. For his sake, I suggest we try to make this as normal a relationship as possible.'

What did he mean by that? A kind of panicky anticipation set her nerves sizzling. Avoiding his eyes, she said, 'Explain normal.'

And relationship!

His mouth twisted mockingly. 'It's quite simple. We marry.'

CHAPTER FIVE

ABBY'S jaw dropped. 'We—*what*?' she said faintly, her brain empty of anything but shock. Blinking fiercely to stop Caelan's dark, sardonic face wavering in front of her dazed eyes, she croaked, 'What did you say?'

'You heard.' The cynical amusement in his tone rubbed her nerves raw. 'It's the most sensible thing to do.'

Stunned, Abby stared at him, her emotions spinning in endless free fall. 'The most sensible thing to do?' she parroted, sounding both feeble and incredulous, heart thudding sickly as though she stood on the brink of a precipice.

'For Michael,' Caelan agreed courteously, although the amusement in his voice rubbed her pride raw. 'For everyone, in fact.'

Her teeth snapped shut on an unwise retort. Disgusted with the treacherous heat that surged through her, she dragged in a jagged breath. 'I'd sacrifice a lot for Michael,' she said, her voice a brittle thread in the silence, 'but I won't marry you for him. The idea is outrageous.'

'Only if you view it emotionally.' His deep voice was so completely empty of feeling that she shivered.

'*Any* way you view it.'

He shrugged, every angle and plane of his hard face radiating tough self-assurance. 'Michael is a Bagaton. I want his status regularised. Gemma was proud of her heritage—she'd want it too.'

69

Abby bit her lip. Oh, he knew where to aim his arrows!

Before she could formulate the objections buzzing around her brain Caelan said, 'I've taken legal opinion on this. The simplest way to achieve his correct surname is for us to marry.'

Suspiciously she asked, 'That's all?'

'Not quite. We then apply to adopt him.'

'Surely you do the applying,' she returned swiftly, her suspicion growing. 'He's already registered as my son.'

'That doesn't count. As the law in New Zealand stands, both of us need to adopt him.' When she was silent he said indifferently, 'I'll find a decent lawyer for you to consult if you don't believe me.'

Almost she said that it didn't matter, but perhaps that was the reaction he was hoping for. 'That's an excellent idea,' she said tonelessly.

'We'll need to convince the welfare authorities that we'll be good parents, but I doubt there'll be any difficulty about that. Naturally the main criterion will be a solid, loving home life for him.' He paused, before adding deliberately, 'Once the adoptions are formalised, you won't have to face the prospect of losing him, and I won't worry about him ending up in the clutches of the social welfare system.'

Abby flashed a swift, startled glance at him. 'Why would he do that?'

'There's the small matter of you claiming him as your child. As you acknowledged, forging documents can earn you a prison offence.'

She went white. 'Are you threatening me?'

'No.' He went on in a pragmatic tone that iced her blood. 'But any writer ferreting around in Palaweyo is almost certain to discover that Michael is Gemma's child, so your actions could come to the notice of the authorities in New Zealand. The sooner we get married and set the wheels in motion for adoption, the better, because an adoption can't be negated.'

Trying to think clearly, Abby said numbly, 'I—yes, I see.' Shattered, she dragged breath into her compressed lungs. 'You're sure of all this?'

His eyes met hers, cold, completely level, utterly convincing. 'Yes.'

Oddly enough she believed him. She pushed a shaky hand through her hair and wondered how he could sound so casual when he was suggesting such a complete disruption to his life. And hers.

The thought of being married to him made her quake inside. She'd tried so hard to do what Gemma had asked, and it seemed it was all for nothing—but at least this way she'd be there to look after Michael.

If she didn't end up in prison.

Even if that happened, she thought painfully, there were worse things than being looked after by a nanny—being lost in the welfare system, for one, as Caelan had pointed out.

The silence grew, backgrounded by the slow hum of traffic and music drifting up from somewhere in the hotel. Slow, moody, erotically charged, it brushed across her skin, tightening it and alerting her senses to the overpoweringly male presence of the man watching her.

In the end she said wearily, 'If it safeguards Michael then I'll—I'll marry you.'

The prince didn't gloat. Instead he said, 'I'll ring my cousin tonight.'

She stared blankly at him. 'What?'

One black brow rose. 'My cousin Luka rules Dacia. We'll be married there.'

'In Dacia?' she said foolishly, panic surging up to kick

her in the stomach. 'Surely a quiet private wedding here…' Her voice trailed away.

'We'll do that before we leave for Dacia so that we can set the adoption in motion immediately.'

She pushed a shaking hand across her forehead. 'Two marriages?' she said thinly. 'It seems overkill.'

'For Michael's sake we need to make a statement to the world.' His face hardened when her lips formed a silent negative. Ruthlessly overriding her objections he stated, 'It's a family tradition to marry in Dacia, and, looked at from a purely practical point of view, my cousin can control the media there. My family will want to meet you, and there will be a series of celebrations. The Dacians are a warm-hearted people, and they enjoy weddings.'

Desperately she broke in. 'I can cope with this—with anything—in New Zealand, but I'm not the sort of person you should marry, and you know it. I'd be out of my element with your relatives, and they'd have every right to wonder what on earth you're doing bringing me into the family.'

'They wouldn't dare,' he said forcefully. 'Anyway, that's not their style. You're not out of your element with me, are you?'

Oh, if only he knew! She flung the truth at him. 'Of course I am!'

His eyes gleamed with amusement. 'Rubbish. And you dealt with Gemma. If you can cope with us, you can cope with anyone else you might meet.'

Abby picked up her glass and took a large sip of wine. 'This is just a nightmare, right?' she said hopefully when she could speak again. 'We're really going to get married quietly at the beach house with two witnesses, and I'll never have to meet any of your family.'

He gave a swift mirthless smile. 'The beach house part, yes—three days from now, in fact. The family—you don't know the Bagatons if you think they'll be content to ignore my marriage.'

Turmoil churned inside her, a mixture of scared apprehension salted with a hot excitement she despised. She swivelled away and stared out across the harbour. High above them a thin moon curled against the depthless sky; Rangitoto loomed to the east, still and dark and silent, as though it had never filled the sky with fire. If she turned her head she could see a number of other small dark hills, their conical shapes all proclaiming their violent origins.

She said on a long, harsh sigh, 'That's the point, surely? I *don't* know the Bagatons—in fact, apart from you and Gemma, I've never met anyone with a drop of royal blood.'

'You're almost certainly wrong there,' he said, more cool amusement grating across her nerves like emery paper. 'It's far more common than you think. You probably have more than a drop yourself.'

'If so, it's from the wrong side of the blanket.' She muttered hopelessly, 'I don't believe this.'

His voice hardened. 'Believe it. And just to make sure that no rumours reach the welfare agencies here, we need to convince everyone we meet that this is a love match.'

By now too numb to react, she asked, 'Why?'

He shrugged, broad shoulders cutting out the lights of Harbour Bridge. 'We're sacrificing our freedom to provide Michael with the stability and love he needs. I don't see us being able to reassure a social worker that we've got a good marriage while you and I are circling each other like wolves on the prowl.'

Heart jolting, Abby took a step backwards, but Caelan's lean fingers snaked around her wrist, pulling her towards him with a smile that blended desire and calculation.

Abby's senses rioted, savouring his unique aroma, an erotic mixture of heat and masculinity. She searched his face, eyes widening at the glitter of desire firing ice-blue eyes, the predatory curve of his bold mouth. Oh, God, he was going to kiss her, and if he did—what hope did she have of standing against him?

A wild mixture of searing anticipation and terror almost silenced her, but she managed to protest, 'No!'

'Then we might as well call a halt to this right now.'

His aloof, studied tone set her stomach roiling, almost banishing the excitement of his nearness. He had to feel the betraying turmoil in her pulse, because one lean, tanned finger was stroking across the fine blue veins in her wrist. Her will-power wavered and dissolved under a wave of desire so intense she could feel it scorching away every sensible thought.

But she had to corral the thoughts blundering around her brain. He had money and influence, and she had none. He was offering a settled life for Michael, his rightful place in the world and security.

And parents, a family...

Nevertheless, she pushed a lock of hair back from her forehead and said hoarsely, 'Caelan, it won't work.'

He looked at her with a cool irony that hurt far more than his contempt. 'Frustration makes people unreasonable and stupid. You want me, as I want you. Whatever else has changed, that hasn't. Four years ago the kiss we exchanged told me we'd be good together.' His voice deepened, a raw note appearing beneath the words. 'And you knew it too. It's still there, so why should we deny ourselves?'

And then he pulled her into his arms and his mouth

came down on hers in a kiss that was more than erotic; it registered a primal claim, fundamental and exhilarating and utterly compelling.

Abby melted, wild hunger shutting down everything but the delight of Caelan's mouth on hers, effortlessly working a dark enchantment that fogged her brain and loosened the reins of her will-power.

When her mouth opened to his demand he took instant possession of its depths, exploring with a carnal, leisurely expertise that sent a current of delicious hunger through every cell. He tasted so good, she thought exultantly, a slow, dangerous pulse flowering deep in her pelvis. After the long, empty years she was where she belonged, with Caelan.

Without volition, her free hand lifted, coming to rest over his heart; it beat heavily, unsteadily, driving into her palm with a clamorous force. Sensation stormed through her, sweet as honey, potent as wine, fierce as a bushfire.

But apart from his lips and the loop of fingers around her wrist he wasn't touching her. Desperately she jerked her head free and stared up into his eyes, and the heat in her body congealed into chilly emptiness. Silence stretched between them, jagged with unspoken thoughts and emotions.

'No,' she grated, scarcely aware of what she was refusing.

He'd set out to prove that he wielded a sorcerer's power over her, and she'd just delivered the proof, signed, sealed and gift-wrapped. Despising herself, she twisted away, humiliated afresh when he let her go as though it had meant nothing to him.

His next words astonished her. 'Still the same flash-fire of passion,' he said in a voice that couldn't hide the intensity of the words. 'Sex has a lot to answer for. Did I hurt your wrist?'

'What?' She looked down, flushing when she realised she was massaging the fragile skin there. Dropping both hands to her sides, she said through lips that were tender and full, branded by his kiss, 'No, it's all right.' Pride drove her to articulate the next words with cold clarity in spite of the bitter turmoil inside her. 'I'm not in the market for an exorcism, Caelan.'

The heat in his eyes was swallowed by darkness. 'Is that what it would be?' he said. 'Somehow I don't believe it's going to be that easy. Or even necessary.'

With the flimsy safety of a few feet between them, Abby closed her eyes and took a deep breath, calling on anger to replace the sensual chains of desire.

'I refuse to be your legal mistress.' Everything that made marriage special—love, trust, determination to make it work, emotional commitment—would be absent, and all they'd have in common was that flash-fire of passion, as he'd called it. But really it was lust.

'That's a different way of looking at marriage.' His voice deepened into a sexy rumble. 'I can promise you that any pleasure will be mutual.'

Oh, God, she was so tempted to give into desire, to forget everything but this need pulsing through her, a wanton hunger that sliced through the fabric of her fragile composure, highlighting promised sexual delights with the emphasis of memory...

You're forgetting Michael, her mind prompted her.

She had to clamp her mouth shut to keep the words of surrender unsaid. When her lashes lifted she saw Caelan smile—all hard derision, but the blue heat she remembered so well still gleamed in the depths of his eyes.

'Mutual pleasure?' She managed to produce some sort of scorn in her tone.

'However much you despise yourself for wanting that pleasure, it means that with our common concern for Michael we can build some sort of life together.'

Bitterly, she answered, 'There's a lot more to marriage than sex. What about trust?'

His lashes hooded his eyes. 'Trust is an entirely different thing,' he said indifferently. 'It has to be earned.'

Temper, hot and reviving, flared into action, temporarily masking the dangerous flare of passion. 'So I'm on probation? For the rest of my life, I suppose.'

He shrugged negligently. 'Once Michael's grown up you can do what you like.' But there was nothing negligent about his next words. They echoed with cold menace. 'Keep in mind that I don't share. If you stray, I'll make your life so unpleasant that you'll beg to be free of me—even if it means leaving Michael.'

White-lipped, she flung back, 'You just don't understand, do you? Nothing would make me abandon him—*nothing*.' Sheer temper spurred her on. 'When I make promises I keep them. And while we're living together, I'll expect you to be faithful too. When you kissed me at the beach you were another woman's lover.'

Colour burned along his magnificent cheekbones. 'I broke it off the next day,' he grated. 'I intend to remain faithful.'

'Why should I believe you?' She whirled around and stalked across to the balustrade, staring down at the lights shimmering across the water for taut seconds before turning to say defiantly, 'I don't want to make love with you. Not now, not at some later date—not ever.'

'You do, but you're not ready to admit it yet,' he said

with an unruffled detachment that made her feel over-emotional and foolish.

At her disbelieving snort he said flatly, 'I feel that way too—like a lesser person because I seem to be unable to control this hunger.' His voice turned flinty. 'I'm no monster, Abby. I can wait until you're ready.'

Until you surrender, he meant.

Aching as though she'd been defeated in a physical fight, she said numbly, 'I don't want any dinner. I'll go to bed.'

Caelan glanced at his watch. 'Run away by all means—but your meal will be here in ten minutes. I'll bring it to your room. And you'd better eat it—starving yourself won't win you any sympathy from me.'

He waited until she got to the door before saying, 'Before you go—'

Abby paused, but fixed her gaze on the door handle.

'Two things—wash that damned dye out of your hair.'

Rebellion churned through her, but she asked distantly, 'And the second order?'

'Don't try to leave,' he advised. 'You won't get far. And if you do, all bargains are off.'

'As you've pointed out, I don't have any choice, do I?' she said starkly, burning with resentment.

He waited long enough to tighten her every nerve with unbearable tension before saying with an indifference that cut her as much as his contempt, 'No. Everyone has to live with the results of the choices they've made.'

Silently she walked out and closed the door behind her.

But once inside her alien, luxurious room her shoulders slumped. Tears aching behind her eyes, she wondered why she felt so desolated.

Why had she flung down that ridiculous gauntlet about

not wanting to make love with him? He must know she had no defences against her overwhelming need for him.

Four years ago, dazzled and unwary, she'd been intrigued by him. Only too aware of his reputation, she'd fought her craving.

At least his kiss had jolted her out of that! Terrified by her capacity for feeling, she'd panicked, but for months on Palaweyo she'd dreamed that he'd followed her. Fortunately—and inevitably—he hadn't. Instead, he'd found a new love—an enormously talented writer notorious for her fascinating, sensual poetry and unrestrained enjoyment of life.

Mouth turned down at the corners, Abby strode into the bathroom. How stupidly innocent she'd been. And how ridiculous she was being now!

OK, so she'd been sure she was over him. Naturally, when she discovered that in less than twenty-four hours that violent, mindless attraction had rekindled, she was concerned.

Stopping in front of the mirror she stared at her reflection with smoky, dazed eyes. Unwittingly she touched her lips, soft and red and still trembling from Caelan's kiss.

Concerned, she taunted silently—what sort of word was that? She wasn't concerned—she was *terrified*. How could he shatter her defences with just one kiss?

If she married him, inevitably she'd give in to that wildfire hunger. What then? Did he want children from her, or would Michael be enough? The thought of bearing Caelan's child produced an odd pang somewhere in the region of her heart. Then there was the social thing— their marriage would stun his rarefied world of aristocrats and magnates, causing a firestorm of gossip.

She'd be the maverick in his select retinue of sophisticated, experienced, beautiful women, all of whom had been sensible enough not to expect love from him. Not that he was a playboy; in spite of her accusation, he'd been faithful to each of his mistresses—a serial monogamist, she thought, trying to soothe her jangling nerves with common sense.

'What am I going to do?' she whispered, seeking counsel from her reflection.

The woman in the mirror stared wildly, helplessly back until a firm tap on the bathroom door stopped the breath in her throat.

'Your meal's waiting,' Caelan said. 'Eat it.'

Battered by emotion, as though his kiss had stripped a protective skin away to leave her defenceless and naked, she swung around and waited until she was sure he'd left the room. Even then, she eased the door open.

Of course he'd gone.

After eating as much as she could of food that tasted like ashes, she had to force herself to take the tray into the kitchen. There was no sign of Caelan, although she could hear him speaking, his deep voice articulating with swift firmness. He was on the telephone, she realised, and thrust the remainders of the food into the fridge so she could flee back to her room before he finished the call.

Once in its sanctuary, she washed her hair, watching colour stream down the plug until the golden-amber of her own colouring shone through. Even wet, her hair still looked dull, its vibrant gloss banished by the dye. She picked up the conditioner in the shower, nodding when she saw the name.

Only the best for Prince Caelan Bagaton, she thought sardonically, and slathered the liquid on, letting hot, slow tears run down her cheeks.

Then she tried to shower the effects of his kiss from

her sensitised body, staying in so long her fingers wrinkled.

Once out and in the oversized T-shirt she wore to bed, she checked Michael, blissfully asleep. She lingered a few moments, watching him before bending to kiss his cheek and heading back into her own room.

Exhausted, she wanted nothing more than to crawl beneath the covers and fall headlong into sleep, but she sat down on the side of the bed and stared sightlessly around the stylish, expensive room while memories replayed in her head and her body ached for a banished ecstasy.

So now Caelan knew—they both knew—that the sexual link between them was as compelling and intense as it had been four years before.

Abby straightened her shoulders. Obsessively going over and over what had happened years ago solved nothing; she had something much more contemporary to deal with.

Caelan had re-ignited a fire deep inside her, a fire she'd thought long dead, but the real danger wasn't the untamed, elemental hunger in his eyes, the raw urgency of his kiss. No, the true peril lay in her fierce response.

She had so pathetically few defences against his passion.

'So,' she said aloud, trying to convince herself, 'it must never happen again.'

The practical part of her mind scoffed.

Whatever price she had to pay, she thought defiantly, was worth it to keep Michael safe. Shivering, she crawled into bed, trying to empty her mind.

Eventually, after hours of listening to the night sounds of the city, devouring sleep replaced her darting, frightened thoughts with dreams.

* * *

Night should have brought some ease of mind. It didn't; when she woke she felt as though her life had been dumped into a blender.

Until an eager little voice from the door asked interestedly, 'You 'wake, Abby?'

And she was right side up again, because the only important thing in this huge mess was Michael. 'Yes, darling, I'm awake! What time is it?'

'Ha'-pas' four,' he said promptly and inaccurately, and ran across the room to give her a hug and good-morning kiss. Newly minted as the dawn, he was dressed in his favourite jeans and the sweatshirt with the dog on the front. 'Uncle Caelan says you can have breakfast in bed if you like.'

She most emphatically did *not* like. 'Tell him to give me ten minutes to wash my face and I'll join you both.'

Giggling, and clearly on the best of terms with the world, he left on a shout of, 'Uncle Caelan, Uncle Caelan, she's getting up!'

Exactly ten minutes later Abby walked into the room off the kitchen, to find Michael perched on a cushion on one of the dining chairs, his shiny face eager as he watched his uncle approach with a packet of cereal.

Caelan glanced at her astonished face. 'I found this in your emergency pack,' he said drily. 'Do you eat it too?'

Abby shook her head. Emotions tumbled around her mind in chaotic disarray, but of course Caelan was in full control. 'Toast, thank you,' she said.

He nodded at a bowl on the table, saying laconically, 'Stewed tamarillos. Help yourself,' as he poured cereal into the bowl in front of Michael.

Who warmed her heart by politely thanking his uncle as he picked up his spoon. Abby sat down, wondering if

Caelan had made sure there were tamarillos because his investigator had found out they were her favourite fruit.

Stop that right now, she commanded. Possibly she *had* told someone in Nukuroa that she loved tamarillos, but it meant nothing; part of the reason for Caelan's formidable success was a brain like a calculator.

He sat down and shot her an assessing look, his brows drawing together. 'I hope you slept well.'

Once she got to sleep she had, although she recalled waking several times in turmoil, her mind filled with images that brought sudden, shameful heat to her skin. 'Very well, thank you,' she told him, hoping that her tone was steady enough to hide her jumping pulse.

At least her hand didn't tremble when she helped herself to the ruby-coloured fruit.

'Coffee?' His voice was courteous.

A touch of hysteria tightened her nerves. He was being the perfect host, she thought feverishly, but at least he wasn't freezing the air around him with his special brand of killer contempt.

She responded in kind, and with Michael as buffer breakfast proceeded in a state of apparent civility, neither adult acknowledging the fierce undercurrents that ran through the calm, civilised, idiotic conversation.

Caelan said, 'This morning I'll lodge a notice of intended marriage with the registrar. I'll need some information from you.'

Panic clutched her throat, but some time during the long night she'd accepted that this was going to happen. Stiffly she gave him the data he needed, watching as he wrote it down with swift, slashing strokes of his pen.

'I'll organise the wedding,' he said, 'but you'll need to do some shopping. I'll pick you up at two this afternoon.' He made another note. 'I'll also organise an appointment with a solicitor so that you can go over a pre-nuptial agreement and the necessity for the adoption process.'

Astonished, she met his keen, impervious gaze. He waited, and when she said nothing he added quietly, 'Be here.'

Abby's head came up. She met his eyes with unflinching dignity. 'We both know,' she said, choosing her words with extreme care, 'that sooner or later there will be an opportunity for your—new housemates—to leave. Imprisonment isn't possible.'

His brows snapped together in a forbidding frown. 'Your point is?'

Abby quelled a nervous flutter. 'I've agreed to marry you. I won't go back on my word.'

Caelan's silence was a tangible force in the room, predatory, intimidating. He glanced at Michael, who was applying himself with gusto to the bowl of cereal.

His hard smile sent shivers of foreboding down her spine. 'Very well,' he said, and held out his hand. 'Shall we shake on it?'

Reluctantly she extended hers. 'Why would you trust a handshake?'

'I trust it about as much as I trust you, but it's the recognised thing,' he said.

His grip was firm and impersonal, but she shivered when she looked into his narrowed analytical eyes. She knew what he was doing—proving to her again that the raw physical magic was as strong as ever, that her body sang when she saw him because every cell in it recognised him.

White-lipped, she jerked her hand free.

And then Michael slipped down from his chair and stuck out his hand. Abby said nothing, watching as

Caelan stooped and took the small paw and shook it gently. Michael grinned. When Caelan smiled back something tight and hard and fiercely defended shattered inside Abby's heart.

'Very well,' Caelan said. 'It's a deal.'

With a final keen look, he turned and the door closed behind him. Abby drew a deep breath, feeling as though she'd just come battered and bloody through a battle.

'Come on, Michael,' she said cheerfully. 'Finish your breakfast. We've got things to do.'

In spite of the changes in their lives, she was going to make some sort of routine for him. And if she clung to the idea because she needed the reassurance of normality, then that was all right too.

CHAPTER SIX

ABBY had washed the dishes and made their beds when two women from the hotel housekeeping staff arrived to circumvent any further attempts at housekeeping. She and Michael unpacked his books and arranged them on the shelves in his bedroom. Later, she coaxed him into the saddle of the rocking-horse.

It didn't take him long to decide that this was a wonderful experience. Half an hour of vigorous riding followed by a running game on the terrace before lunch used up some of his boundless energy, but he needed more space. Tropically exuberant though the penthouse terrace was with its lush plants in huge pots and the view of the harbour—today a shimmering silver-blue expanse beneath a benign spring sky—he was accustomed to an expanse of lawn with trees to climb.

Shortly after midday the housekeeping staff departed, leaving the apartment immaculate. Abby made lunch, Michael demolished it with gusto, then yawned widely.

'I'm not tired,' he maintained stoutly.

'Of course you are,' Abby said, scooping him up and hugging him. 'And the sooner you have your nap, the sooner Uncle Caelan will be here!'

Much struck by this, he went to bed with an eagerness that roused a simmer of jealousy in her.

She bent to kiss him softly on his cheek, but outside his room she hesitated, wondering how to fill in the next hour. Since she'd brought Michael to New Zealand, she'd been so busy she'd had little time for introspection; work and caring for him had taken every ounce of energy she possessed.

She'd longed for time to read, to garden, to go to a movie.

Now she had no work and too much time to think— thoughts she didn't want to face, intensified by long-repressed emotions.

Tensely she walked out into the warm, fresh air. The penthouse unnerved her, so superbly decorated she didn't dare let Michael go anywhere but the casual dining and living area off the kitchen. How on earth were they going to deal with a palace, if that was what they were going to stay in on Dacia?

Bumble-bees colliding in her stomach, she recalled the rented house in Nukuroa, sparse and bare, its bedrooms faintly smelling of mould in spite of everything she could do, the elderly stove with chipped enamel and electric elements that wobbled whenever she put a saucepan on them...

She'd worried about Michael's health in that house, longed for the money to rent somewhere better. Yet now, lapped in luxury, she thought with a wry, painful grimace that if she could click her heels together and find herself back there she'd never ask for anything again.

And if the apartment intimidated her, how was she going to cope with Dacia and its royal family?

Or—the big one—with life as Caelan's wife?

Heat flared suddenly inside her, sweet and fierce and heady. He meant to have her, and she, pitifully weak where he was concerned, would fight him as best she could, but in the end she'd give in.

How could she bear that—to give everything she had and always be aware that it meant nothing to him beyond the transient satisfaction of an animal appetite?

Caelan strode silently out through the glass doors. His hooded gaze sought Abby, and found her, slender—too slender, he thought on a spurt of irrational anger—examining one of the large potted palms.

She had her back to him, a T-shirt in just the wrong shade of green skimming trousers cut for a more matronly figure than hers. Only her feet, slimly elegant in a pair of cheap sandals, reminded him of the woman he'd once kissed because he couldn't help himself.

But nothing could take away from her natural grace. Or his reaction to it; at the sight of her his body sprang to life, desire summoned by a primal hunger he'd never experienced with any other woman.

What was it about her that snapped the leash on his control? He'd always enjoyed sophisticated, intelligent lovers, women who were self-sufficient and confident. Although Abby was intelligent, her actions spoke of a life ruled by impulse and emotions—the sort of woman he'd consciously avoided because they'd have demanded too much from him.

No wonder she and Gemma had become friends.

Grief caught him unawares, mingled as always with anger and a gnawing conviction of failure. If he'd been available to his sister when she'd discovered her pregnancy he'd have been able to keep her safe.

But she'd gone to Abby, and to a death that need never have happened.

Abby stirred, the sun lighting up her hair in a tongue of fire. Ignoring a fierce jab of satisfaction because she'd washed most of that damned colouring out of it, he started towards her.

He hadn't taken more than a couple of steps when her spine stiffened. She didn't move, didn't turn her head, but he knew she'd sensed his presence.

Damn her, he thought with unusual anger, for once she could acknowledge him! He stopped behind her, waiting until she turned her head.

'Oh, hello,' she said warily, her features so composed he knew she'd been practising. 'Did you have a good morning?'

'You sound very wifely,' he said, not hiding the irony in his tone. 'Yes, the morning went well. How was yours?'

'So far, so good.' But a little frown furrowed her delicate brows and she returned her gaze to the feathery fronds of the palm tree as though finding enlightenment there. 'Michael's still asleep. I hope you're not planning to wake him up.'

'Why would I do that?'

She gave a short shrug. 'To fit him into your busy schedule.'

He said coolly, 'I plan to be around for Michael whenever he needs me.' And before she had a chance to say anything he added, 'We'll buy clothes for him this afternoon.' He scrutinised her with a cool smile before adding, 'One of Auckland's best salons is holding a showing for you tomorrow morning. The wedding's organised for three days' time, and we fly out to Dacia immediately afterwards.'

She opened her mouth to reply somewhat heatedly to his high-handed authority, only to be cut off by the imperative summons of a telephone.

'I'm sorry,' he said abruptly, taking a small mobile phone from his pocket. 'This must be important.' He walked away, not speaking until he was out of hearing range.

Jealousy, bitter and dark, sliced through her. Although she couldn't hear what he said a subliminal instinct told her he was talking to a woman. Outrage clawed across her heart; she swung abruptly around and started for her bedroom.

'Abby,' Michael announced accusingly from his doorway, 'I'm awake. You said Uncle Caelan would be here soon!'

She forced a tender smile; his sunny nature took a few minutes to reassert itself after sleep. 'He's talking on his phone out on the terrace. Let's go and wash your face.'

How could she expect Caelan to trust her if she didn't extend him the same courtesy? He'd told her he intended being faithful; for her own peace of mind, she had to believe him. So she plucked the poisoned dart of jealousy from her mind and tried not to wonder if this promised faithfulness started on the wedding day or before…

Michael looked past her, his face lighting up. 'I want Uncle Caelan to wash my face,' he announced.

'Then you'd better ask him politely,' Abby suggested.

He thrust out his lower lip and looked sideways at her. 'You ask him, Abby.'

'Ask him what?' Caelan said from behind her.

Michael, stumbling a little, lifted his face and asked him.

Struck again by that fleeting resemblance between them, Abby drew in a sharp breath. Except for his brilliant eyes Caelan was a study in darkness— Mediterranean black hair, midnight brows and lashes, warm olive-bronze skin—while Michael's colouring bathed him in sunlight, yet they shared the same strong bone structure and arrogant nose.

Caelan's deep voice broke into her thoughts. 'Anything you need to tell me about this face-washing?'

She forced a smile and a light tone. 'Michael knows what to do.'

They came back five minutes later, Michael damp around the hairline and excited. 'Abby, Uncle Caelan says when I can swim properly he'll take me out in his boat!'

'Then you'll have to try really hard, won't you?' Abby said cheerfully. Was Caelan making sure she realised the difference his presence in Michael's life would make?

Caelan said, 'He already has the basics, and there's an excellent swimming school for pre-schoolers in Auckland.'

She nodded. Swimming, rocking horses, new clothes and new books were important, she decided sombrely as they went down in the lift, but more was needed to make a happy child. Although Gemma had grown up in a home where wealth was taken for granted, it hadn't brought her serenity or confidence. The only way Caelan could become important to Gemma's son was to give him time and affection.

It did seem that he was prepared to do that for Michael, but time would tell. Parenting success depended on the long haul, not short sprints.

Michael chattered non-stop about swimming all the way to one of the northern suburbs. Inside the shop however, he fell silent, gazing around with awed delight.

After a startled survey, Abby said wryly, 'This looks more like a coral reef than a children's clothes shop—sheer tots' heaven. How did you find out about this place?'

Caelan looked down at her with sardonic eyes. 'The owner contacted me for help; she had a vision, but couldn't get anyone to back her in it.'

One of his lovers? 'I'll bet it's doing well,' Abby observed tightly.

'She's worked hard; she deserves her success.' He

changed the subject without finesse. 'I suggest you choose clothes suitable for travelling. It will still be warm in Dacia when we arrive, so he'll need gear for playing outdoors and going to the beach, as well as some more formal outfits for meeting the relatives.'

For once, Michael didn't wriggle when it came to trying on clothes, and, with the help of a young assistant who knew exactly how to head off imminent boredom, they managed to acquire a wardrobe for him with the minimum amount of fuss.

What surprised Abby most was Caelan's attitude. It should have warmed her heart that, sophisticated and cynical though he was, he seemed to enjoy Michael's company. Instead, she felt as though she were on a slippery slope to some menace she couldn't discern.

And even relief at not being forced to squeeze every cent until it shrieked didn't overcome that unease.

Outside the shop Caelan said calmly, 'I'll take Michael home while you see the solicitor.'

His unreadable gaze lingered a moment on her bright hair. A shock of excitement sizzled through her like electricity.

But beneath that purely physical reaction lurked the formless fear that he might whisk Michael away so she'd never see him again. She looked up, flushing when she saw his mocking smile. He knew what she was thinking.

It was ridiculous to let the same old fears surface over and over again. Caelan had made it clear that he saw her and Michael as a package, and she suspected that he was learning to like his nephew. He must realise that Michael needed her.

'All right,' she said distantly, irritated because he was taking over again.

Middle-aged and efficient, the solicitor talked over the

pre-nuptial agreement that set out what Caelan expected of her as Michael's mother and his wife. She pointed out several areas that Abby should consider before she signed it, while saying that it seemed to protect both her and Michael's rights as well as the legal system could.

'Of course, the simplest way to safeguard the child's future,' she said, 'is for you both to adopt him. Has the prince—Mr Bagaton—discussed this with you?'

'Yes. It seems a good idea.'

'It will certainly give him legal standing as your child.'

Abby asked tightly, 'I assume that a stable marriage is important in the adoption process.'

After a keen glance, the solicitor said simply, 'Very.'

Back in the penthouse Michael was bursting with excitement; while they'd been away a splendid children's gym had been delivered and assembled on the terrace. 'Look at me, look at me, Abby,' he shouted, hanging by his knees from a bar. 'There's a slide here too!'

Acutely aware of Caelan's scrutiny, she exclaimed over its beauty and multitude of features. Finally she said, 'Did you thank Uncle Caelan for buying it for you?'

Michael scrambled off and stared at him. 'He didn't say,' he muttered. He gave his uncle a charming, lopsided grin. 'Thank you, Uncle Caelan!'

'I'm glad you like it,' Caelan told him. But when Michael had run back to his new toy, he said, 'I don't want his thanks.'

Abby turned baffled eyes onto his hard face. 'Why?'

He gave her a long, measuring look, then shrugged. 'Gemma once said that I tried to buy her affection. It wasn't true, but I don't think it would be good for Michael to feel that all good things come from me.'

Surprised, she said, 'That's—very thoughtful of you.

But saying thank you is a necessary part of bringing up a child.'

Something happened between them, some sort of communication deeper than words. She felt her skin tighten and swallowed to ease a dry throat. 'I'd better unpack his new clothes.'

Caelan stopped her with a hand on her arm. She froze, and humiliating excitement leapt into full life.

Dropping his hand, he said, 'What did you think of the pre-nuptial agreement?'

'It seemed very fair.'

He was watching her too closely. Something swift and impetuous scudded the length of her spine, and her breath came too fast.

'In that case we can sign it tomorrow morning before we go shopping. I've opened a bank account for you.'

When she opened her mouth to protest he put a lean forefinger over her lips. Her mouth dried and she stared into eyes as cool and enigmatic as the sea, the blue irises edged by a silver-grey band that gave them their distinctive translucence.

Coolly unyielding, he said, 'I don't want to hear any futile objections. You read the agreement—the allowance is specified there. If it's not enough, we can adjust it later.'

He removed his finger and Abby could breathe again. Feeling in some obscure way as though she was compromising her integrity, she said colourlessly, 'All right.' And vowed to spend as little of his money as she could.

Amusement gleamed in the depths of his eyes. 'I suggest that instead of looking for an excuse to fight—or kiss—we consider Michael's welfare and keep our more volatile reactions under strict discipline.'

Skin heating, Abby ignored the beginning of that sentence. 'Yes,' she returned with spurious sweetness, 'let's just do that.'

That night after dinner Caelan said abruptly, 'Tell me about Gemma.'

Abby put her cup of coffee onto the table beside her chair. Feeling her way cautiously, she asked, 'What about her?'

'Why did she leave her mother's house to go to Palaweyo? She must have known it was no place for her to have a child.'

Abby chose her words carefully. 'She didn't know she was pregnant when she arrived; she'd come to think things over, she said.'

'What things?'

'Whether or not to marry Mike.'

He looked surprised. 'I didn't realise it had gone so far.'

Abby said quietly, 'She'd only been there a week when Mike called, telling her about the rescue. She pleaded with him not to do it, but he told her he had to and that he loved her. Then we heard of his death. I was so worried—she went all silent and distant, as though to get the courage to keep going she had to call on all her reserves.'

He said harshly, 'You should have got in touch with me.'

'I wanted her to call you.' Abby couldn't look at him; guilt still cast its dark pall over her. If she'd given in to the temptation to go behind Gemma's back and call Caelan, his sister would still be alive. 'She said she'd run to you for every little thing in her life, and that now she had to deal with this by herself.'

He said something under his breath and she flinched.

'Caelan, I'm so sorry.'

'It wasn't your fault,' he said evenly. 'Yes, I'd have liked you to contact me, but she was an adult and your friend. It would have been a betrayal.'

Incredibly relieved, Abby swallowed to ease a dry throat. 'When she found out she was pregnant it seemed to give her the courage to keep going. I insisted she get the doctor at the hospital to check her out. He said she was fine, so I thought it was safe to let her stay.'

Caelan said harshly, 'I wish I'd known.'

'Gemma said you were under tremendous pressure with a really bad problem in some part of the corporation.'

Abby thought she'd strained every bit of condemnation from her voice, but he glanced at her as though she'd directly accused him. 'A rogue manager in South America was siphoning off funds to acquire his own cocaine enterprise; he had links to a terrorist cell. Several of my people were kidnapped by them, a couple killed. It took time and effort to lure them out of the jungle and into custody, but if I'd known Gemma needed me I'd have been there for her.'

Abby believed him. 'She knew that. And she achieved some sort of peace in Palaweyo, even while she grieved for Mike. I wouldn't say she was happy, but she managed a sort of quiet contentment. And when his son was born she was—awed, and stunned at how much she loved him, how hugely important he was to her, how he changed everything. She'd started talking about taking him back to New Zealand when the cyclone struck.'

'I'm glad of that,' he said, his voice cold and detached.

But something glittered in his pale eyes, and Abby's heart was wrung. Without thinking she got up and went over, putting her hand on his arm and looking up into a face as cold as flint. Urgently, wanting only to offer comfort, she said, 'She didn't die in pain, Caelan. She said that Mike was waiting for her, and she kissed Michael goodbye and she was smiling when she died—so peacefully.'

With an odd raw sound deep in his throat, Caelan pulled her into his arms. They contracted around her and his mouth came down on hers, famished and avid.

Although Abby fought the surge of passionate abandon, trying to force her body into passive stillness, it was no use. A tide of white-hot sensation swamped caution, washing it away into regions beyond recovery, along with her will-power and her common sense.

She swayed and linked her hands around Caelan's neck, fingertips thrilling to the texture of his dark hair, warm from his powerful body.

Their hungry kisses—deep as those of lovers reunited after an eternity of loneliness—broke down every barrier. And when he said her name against her lips, the primal note of possession in his voice released the shackles around her heart.

She wanted Caelan; she had to accept that she always would. And he wanted her. That elemental sorcery still linked them with chains of desire and need.

Elation and despair melded in bittersweet response; in his arms, with his kisses on her lips, she felt reborn, even though nothing had changed.

But when he cupped the soft curve of her breast, she froze, jerked back into reality by the keen, exquisite pang of delight that arrowed from his hand to the place that longed to welcome him in the most intimate of all embraces.

If she let this happen, she'd not only experience the glory of sexual awakening but the pain and the eventual despair. This man, she thought desperately, is forcing you into a marriage you don't want.

The only barrier left was her self-respect.

'No!' The word was torn from her, guttural with intense emotion. She couldn't let this go further; it would kill her to become his toy, his mistress-wife.

Cold satisfaction glittered in Caelan's hooded eyes.

'Why not?' His voice came deep and raw and demanding through lips that barely moved. Warm and sure and confident, his thumb moved back and forth across the pleading tip of her breast.

Despising herself for the rills of unbearable pleasure coursing through her, she said aggressively, 'Because I don't want it.'

The perfect opening, she realised the moment the words left her mouth, and cursed herself for handing it to him.

His mouth hardened into a mirthless smile. 'When your actions speak as loudly as your words, I might believe you.'

'Believe me now,' she said bleakly, adding with stark, sharp honesty, 'My body appears to be beyond my control, but my head and my heart don't want it.'

He looked into her eyes with piercing intentness; she held her breath and met that probing stare with defiance.

Finally, he let her go.

Shivering, her mind so tumultuous she didn't know what she was thinking, she watched him walk across to the balustrade. That long, silent stride, his lethal male grace, the sheer masculine presence of the man summoned a vivid, blinding image from out of nowhere.

Caelan with his knees clamped around the barrel of a rearing horse, long hair flying in some long-dead wind, a sword in his hand, eyes gleaming with cold determi-

nation and a ferocious battle cry on his lips as he reached down for her...

Blinking, she swallowed and the swift vision snapped out, banished by the taunt in his voice when he swung around and said, 'Want it or not, Abby—and you can't despise this embarrassing hunger more than I do—it's not going to go away.'

'We don't have to act on it,' she returned with curt emphasis. 'It's only lust—and lust dies if it's not satisfied.'

He lifted a satirical eyebrow. 'Four years without satisfaction doesn't seem to have quenched it.'

Did he mean that he'd—? No!

One glance at his lean, arrogant face scotched that thought. Of course he hadn't been celibate since that first kiss! She knew of at least two lovers in the intervening years.

Those kisses had been a test. If she'd given in he'd have taken her, without emotion, without compassion.

Her emotions churned in wild disarray, while her body simmered with resentful disappointment at being deprived of his love-making. Abruptly, unable to bear being in the same room as him, she said, 'I meant what I said.'

Handsome face cast from bronze, he said mockingly, 'Ah, yes, but how long do you think you can fight it?'

Willing her composure to hold for a few minutes longer, she retorted with passion, 'I won't be a convenient outlet to be used whenever it suits you. This isn't going to work unless you understand that.' His cynical smile goaded her over the edge. Rashly she finished, 'If you can't keep your hands to yourself, then I'll leave and take Michael with me.'

He leaned back against the balustrade, narrow hips emphasising his long legs and wide shoulders. 'Do that,' he said, his gaze burning like ice and a white line around his mouth, 'and I'll hunt you down—right across the world if I have to.'

He paused a taut, terrifying second before adding with silky precision, 'And when I find you, you'll wish I hadn't.'

She hoped her involuntary shudder didn't register with him. 'I don't mean that I'd run away again.'

'Then what *did* you mean?' He didn't wait for an answer. 'Forget this idea of living somewhere in Auckland and granting me visitation rights. I won't be a part-time presence in Michael's life. He's had too many of those already. And I don't trust you. You kidnapped him once.'

Heatedly she returned, 'Only because I knew you'd take him away from me. You would have, wouldn't you?'

He didn't answer straight away. The silence loomed, almost threatening, until he said, 'Surely Gemma must have known that I'd do my best for him.'

Was there a note of pain beneath the level words? Abby said quietly, 'Of course she did.'

Caelan swung on his heel to stare out across the lights and the harbour. Something about the stiffness of his shoulders persuaded her to continue tentatively. 'She loved you, Caelan, and respected you, but she knew how busy you were. And you've already admitted that her childhood was lonely.'

He shrugged, dismissing the subject. 'This isn't getting us anywhere, and we've got no time to hash over things we can't change. My cousin Luka has suggested that you might like to choose an emerald from the Dacian collection for an engagement ring, but if you'd rather have anything else we can organise that.'

Engagement ring? Her stomach contracted as though warding off a blow. 'I haven't thought of it.'

'You'll need one. A notice announcing our engagement will be issued once we're in Dacia, and official photographs will be released. I'd prefer it if you don't mention the first ceremony, as it's just to set the wheels of the social welfare system on track here. Any indication could attract media attention.'

'I see,' she said colourlessly, inwardly appalled at the prospect of reporters and photographers lurking in ambush. 'I don't know about the ring—what do you think would be best?'

He shrugged. 'We'll take Luka up on his offer. There's bound to be an emerald in the treasury that matches your eyes. I have an early appointment tomorrow, but I'll pick you up around ten.'

'What for?'

'You're buying clothes.'

Abby had forgotten completely about the private showing at the salon. She opened her mouth to protest, then closed it. Although she was intensely reluctant to admit it, she craved the armour of clothes that at least fitted her, in colours that suited her.

'All right,' she said reluctantly.

He smiled and came across the room to stand in front of her. He startled her by touching the soft crease where her lips curved. 'I like your smile,' he said softly, and before she could stop him he kissed the corner of her mouth.

Traitor that it was, her body responded with blatant delight. She had to clench her fists to stop herself from inhaling his scent, faint and entirely male, so erotic it melted her bones and sent her blood racing through her body.

'Dream of that,' he said, his voice rough and urgent, 'For whatever satisfaction dreams give you.'

CHAPTER SEVEN

THREE days later at the beach house, Abby sucked in her breath and stared at herself in a mirror. A woman she didn't recognise gazed back at her from wide, glittery green eyes. She looked feverish—the glow in her skin so hectic that her brand-new, expensive cosmetics barely toned it down, and lips riper and fuller and more obvious than ever.

The tawny gold of the slender silk suit only added to that betraying air of lush anticipation. In the frighteningly exclusive salon in Auckland it had looked restrained and sophisticated, the short sleeves and wide, scooped neckline vaguely bridal without implying that sort of hopeful, happy delight that should be symbolic of marriage.

Not this marriage; it was a mockery, and she didn't want Caelan to think she was going into it with expectations he couldn't fulfil.

She adjusted the top, moving slightly so that sunlight angled golden in the crystal embroidery of the jacket, beneath which she wore a bra made of satin and lace and a whisper-soft camisole the same colour as the suit.

Caelan—or his PA—had organised a trip to an incredibly chic salon where her hair had been washed, conditioned and styled into a sleek cut that restored the sheen.

Despairing, because the loose waves added to that eagerly expectant look, she picked up a comb and ruthlessly pulled it into a knot behind her head.

'I should have bought a veil to hide behind,' she muttered when it was done.

Of course she wore no engagement ring, and had no idea what wedding rings Caelan had chosen.

In fact, she thought bleakly, she didn't even know who the witnesses were! The helicopter pilot and the house keeper, probably, or the hotel nanny who'd agreed to spend the weekend looking after Michael at one end of the beach house, while Abby and her new husband supposedly enjoyed a one-night honeymoon in the owner's suite at the other end.

Except that after the deed was done Abby would be spending the night in this guest bedroom, close enough to Caelan's to quieten any gossip. An aching sorrow welled up inside her and to her horror she had to blink back stinging tears.

It was no use crying for the moon; not in a million years would he have fallen in love with her.

This was for Michael, she reminded herself stringently

She swung around at a knock on the door. 'Come in,' she called, her heart hammering madly against her ribs.

Neither the nanny nor the housekeeper came in. Tall slim and darkly elegant, with a serene, aristocratic beauty, the woman who entered was a complete stranger although her face seemed familiar. Her superb clothes indicated that she was also a wedding guest.

Feeling an utter fool, Abby stared blankly at her.

'I've just found out from Caelan that he didn't tell you we were coming,' the newcomer said severely. 'I love him very much, so I hate to think that he's too ashamed of us to even mention us! I am Lucia Radcliffe, his cousin, and my husband Hunt is busy pouring him a pre wedding drink.'

Abby found her voice and said with banal formality 'I—how do you do? I'm so glad you've come.'

And if Caelan was ashamed, it certainly wasn't of his lovely cousin!

Princess Lucia—whose name and face she recognised because they'd been scattered through magazines since her marriage a couple of years previously—smiled and closed the door behind her.

'And I am very glad to be here. You look absolutely exquisite, Abby.' She gave a mischievous smile. 'I always knew there was someone like you in Caelan's past.'

Abby swallowed. 'I'm not sure what you mean.'

The gleam of mischief deepened. 'I've never seen my darling cousin stressed enough to rely on whisky to restore his famous composure! He's the most maddening man—he knows exactly what he wants, and he's always so sure he'll get it. I used to long for the day when he'd meet someone who turned him inside out. And now I can see that he has. Ah, here comes the champagne!'

The housekeeper, looking flustered, entered carrying a tray with two crystal flutes and a bottle of what, Abby realised, was vintage wine.

'It'll steady your nerves,' the amazingly obtuse Princess Lucia said. 'Just take a couple of mouthfuls. Now, where are the flowers? Ah, yes, there they are.' She picked up the three magnificent tawny roses, and sniffed pleasurably. 'Gorgeous, aren't they? Little Michael is almost beside himself with anticipation, so take a second sip of wine and then let's go.'

Filling the silence with a stream of comforting chatter that somehow calmed Abby's fears, she got them out of the sanctuary of the bedroom and onto a wide terrace overlooking the white beach and the blue-green sea. Heavily wooded headlands sheltered the house and the bay from the ocean.

Closer at hand a temporary altar had been erected at

one end of the terrace, shaded from the bright sun by a white awning.

More stupid, swift tears stung Abby's eyes; she'd had no idea that Caelan had planned to go to such lengths— even to choosing roses that matched the ones she held.

Her eyes flew to him, tall and superbly confident by the altar. He dwarfed the glorious scenery and the superb house, dominating it more with his powerful personal magnetism than his impressive height. The exquisite tailoring of his business suit couldn't conceal the raw, primal power of the man; he looked exactly what he was, she thought with a swift skip of her heart—the leading male in the pride, the alpha lion.

Whenever she was with Caelan the world seemed a richer, more vibrant place.

Beside him stood another man, every bit as tall, the sun picking up highlights in his dark hair, his face lean and tough. Hunt Radcliffe, no doubt.

Michael was standing on Caelan's other side, one small hand clasped in his, his face serious.

The celebrant looked up as she and the princess came out, and everyone turned. Abby's heart jumped; Caelan smiled, and for a second she thought she saw something more than swift lust in his eyes.

Desire is a drug, she told herself sturdily. She'd always hoped that one day she'd find a man to love, yet, although she'd met some nice men over the past years, not one had stirred her blood.

In a sudden, unwilling leap of insight, she acknowledged that Caelan was the man who gave her life savour and meaning, the only man she'd ever really wanted— the only she'd ever want.

Enter heartbreak, stage left, she thought with bleak desperation.

She met his eyes with a hint of defiance, stunned when he smiled at her, a lazy movement of his mouth that reminded her too vividly of his kisses.

'Abby,' he said deeply, and strode to meet her as though she was the most precious thing in his life.

He didn't touch her, but he didn't need to; he'd stamped his possession of her as clearly as if he'd swept her off her feet and kissed her.

And some primitive part of her rejoiced, even though it was a bitter farce played for the benefit of anyone who happened to be watching.

Michael said in an awestruck voice, 'Abby, you look jus' like the princess in my book!'

And everyone smiled. Swallowing, Abby went with Caelan up to the table that served as an altar. Lucia Radcliffe moved to stand by her husband, and Caelan slid his free hand around Abby's, holding it in a warm, strong grip while he reached for Michael's little paw with his other. Linked as the family they would be from now on, he and Michael and Abby went through the brief, unbearably moving ceremony.

Although her hand trembled when they exchanged wedding rings—identical bands of gold—she at last felt a kind of acceptance. It might not be the marriage she had longed for, but it would make Michael safe, and she'd find what comfort she could in that.

'You may kiss the bride,' the celebrant said.

Abby tensed. She didn't expect Caelan to kiss her with any sort of passion, but she was surprised when he stooped and picked up Michael before dropping a brief kiss on her lips. Michael hugged her and kissed her, burrowing his head into her shoulder, and then lifted his face and kissed Caelan on his cheek.

Caelan's face softened miraculously. It would be worth it, Abby repeated. It had to be...

Princess Lucia kissed her on the cheek. 'Welcome, dear Abby, to our family,' she said with every appearance of pleasure.

Hunt Radcliffe lifted her hand and dropped a kiss on the back of it. 'You'll get used to it,' he said cheerfully, watching her with cool, shrewd midnight-blue eyes. 'And once the official hullabaloo in Dacia is over, you can flee back to New Zealand where you won't have to deal with all that dull official protocol.'

His wife snorted in a most unladylike way. 'Don't listen to him, Abby—there's nothing to worry about.' Tawny eyes smiling at her husband, she added, 'Any time protocol reared its ugly head, Hunt dealt with it, and you will too.'

Although her husband's lean face gave little away, Abby sensed the strong, fierce love that linked them. A wave of bitter envy shocked her.

She wanted desperately to ask about the ceremony in Dacia, but it wasn't the time—her question would give too much away about their relationship. Clearly Caelan hadn't told his cousin and her husband why they were marrying; she didn't dare compromise the secret.

At all costs they had to behave like people in love, determined to make a good marriage that would last—at least until Michael grew up.

So when Caelan curved his arm around her, she leaned into his shoulder and tried to summon a radiant smile while the two men shook hands.

'Protocol isn't the sort of thing you have to worry about when you're growing up in a citrus orchard,' she said, while her body thrummed with delight at the strength that held her so lightly. He smelt so *good*, she thought, and flushed when she saw the princess's eyes twinkle.

But the other woman said calmly, 'It's not some deep, dark mystery; it's easy enough to learn—look at Alexa. She comes from a typical New Zealand background, and the Dacians adore her because she's everything a ruling princess should be, warm and gracious and deeply interested in them.' She flashed a reassuring smile at Abby. 'If you can seat a dinner party you'll do fine. And Caelan will help—he's an expert.'

Grateful to her for her attempt to give her confidence, Abby said, 'I know he will.'

Deep and completely confident, Caelan's voice reverberated through his chest, sending little shivers of pleasure through her. 'Abby won't have any difficulty,' he said. 'Now, how about some champagne?'

Looking back, Abby realised that he stage-managed the hour after the ceremony with consummate skill. They drank a glass of wine with the celebrant and the housekeeper and nanny, then the nanny whisked Michael off to their end of the house, and the helicopter removed the celebrant to the mainland. A delicious dinner was served on the terrace as the sun sank slowly, its fading brilliance casting a beguiling cloak of witchery and glamour over the bay.

Abby decided she liked cool, tough Hunt Radcliffe and his princess, especially when his wife produced photographs of her gorgeous little daughter.

'As her godfather,' she informed Caelan, 'you'll be interested to know that she now has four very sharp little teeth, but no sign of any others. And she adores blueberries.'

To Abby's surprise Caelan admired the photographs,

and from the subsequent conversation it was clear that he saw a lot of little Natalia Radcliffe.

Although Gemma had talked about her brother, she'd barely scratched the surface of his complex and intriguing character.

Hunt and Lucia—whom Caelan called Cia—left after dinner as the sun was setting. Watching the helicopter head straight into the glory of gold and apricot to the west, she said, 'Does everyone in your family fly their own private helicopter?'

'Quite a few,' he said calmly. 'You'll get used to it.'

It didn't seem likely. Trying to hide her stretched nerves with a calm, brisk tone, she said, 'I'll go and check on Michael.'

Caelan turned his head and surveyed her. What was she thinking? It was impossible to tell; her face was half turned away from him, but for all this interminable day her expression had been controlled and self-contained, the long, thick lashes over her almond-shaped eyes successfully hiding her emotions.

Quelling an undisciplined urge to smash through that self-contained barrier, he said, 'We'll both go.'

She stiffened, before saying colourlessly, 'Yes, of course.'

At first she'd resisted the idea of hiring the nanny to accompany them, but he'd insisted. While she'd chosen her wardrobe at the exclusive showing in the salon, Michael had been enjoying his stint in the hotel nursery with the friendly middle-aged woman, and had greeted her this morning with every appearance of pleasure.

It irritated Caelan that he still wasn't sure why he'd been so determined that the nanny should come. As they walked through the house, fragrant with the scent of the sea and the balsam of feathery kanuka trees, he accepted grimly that each day they spent together made him more aware of his wife.

His wife. A surge of elemental possessiveness startled him. So damned elusive, with the face of a sexy faerie woman and her slender, sensuous body, but he thought he was beginning to discern the lights and shadows of her personality. She kept her promises, at no matter what cost to herself. She loved Michael with the fierce, self-sacrificing adoration of a mother. She'd coped with Lucia and Hunt, and he'd been pleased by the way she took over the reins of the evening, sliding unconsciously into the role of hostess. Although he suspected she didn't real-ise it, she had a deep inner confidence that probably came from that life as the loved only child of two happy par-ents.

And she couldn't hide the fact that, although she re-sented the way he'd dragooned her into this marriage, she wanted him, he thought with a fierce, shockingly primitive satisfaction.

Michael was sound asleep. Abby kissed the boy's sat-iny cheek and watched as Caelan did the same.

On the way back, she asked something that had been bothering her. 'Do Lucia and Hunt know about Michael's parentage?'

'Yes, of course, but they don't know about the arrange-ment we have come to. They think we are marrying for real,' he said coolly.

Abby stared at his hard face, the afterglow emphasis-ing lines and planes sculpted by authority and a formi-dable will. That primal anticipation stirred within her, flexing claws.

Abby thought of Hunt Radcliffe, whose shrewd eyes had been backed by his intelligent conversation, and his wife, carefully not asking any questions. 'Do you really think they believe that?' she asked baldly.

'I don't care whether they do or not.' His voice took on an inflexible edge. 'I'm sure you'll agree that the fewer people who know that you lied to get Michael out of Palaweyo, the better.'

'Yes,' she admitted bleakly. 'Does *anyone* in your family know the real situation?'

'No. And if they have any inkling that all is not quite as straightforward as it seems, they'll keep quiet. We do secrets rather well in our family.' He dismissed the subject with a shrug. 'Don't worry, Abby.'

It said a lot for the effect he had on her, she thought warily, that she'd only just realised something he seemed to have missed. 'What if the writer you told me about— the one who's researching a book about Palaweyo—finds out?'

'I'll buy him off,' he said coolly. 'Yes, you can curl your lip, but most people have an asking price.'

Some note in his voice made her look up sharply. Was he implying that she'd married him for his money? His handsome face gave nothing away, and the ice-blue eyes were cool and translucent and completely unreadable.

By then they'd arrived back on the terrace. From somewhere inside came the low sound of music, and a glow in the east promised a moon. Caelan said abruptly, 'Would you like to dance?'

'What?' But her blood was picking up speed and her limbs felt weighted with sweet languor.

'It seems a pity to waste the music and the night, and the moon.' He held out his arm, and, although she knew she was dicing with danger, she placed the tips of her fingers on it, every sense taut with a feverish, forbidden anticipation.

His eyes gleamed in the gathering darkness, and when she moved into his embrace he steered her out of the light and into the shadows on the edge of the terrace, where a massive pohutukawa tree leaned over the railing. When summer came it would be blood-red with its strange, tasselled flowers...

The sultry, seductive singer's plaint wove a smoky veil of love lost and regretted. It hit too close to the bone. Too wary to relax, alarmed by the way her skin seemed to have thinned, Abby held herself stiffly.

Of course he was a terrific dancer. Their steps matched perfectly, so she willed herself to relax and enjoy this rare moment of peace in his arms.

Not that the peace lasted long. Too soon it was replaced by an insidious passion, a slow fever in the blood that blotted out everything but his presence, his touch on her hand, the faint, erotic fragrance that was his alone— male magnetism incarnate.

She bent her head so that he couldn't see her face, but that brought her forehead too close to his broad chest, and she had to fight the need to lean against him and let him take her wherever he wanted to.

The music slowed. Turning, he drew her closer with a strong arm across her back, and the simmering heat leaped into full blaze when she felt the strength of his thighs against hers and realised that he was aroused.

So was she, she thought with odd elation. These past few days had honed the forbidden attraction into mindless need, and if he wanted to take her to bed tonight she'd go with him, because hunger had eaten away her defences. The only concession she'd make to pride was not to suggest it herself, and that was getting harder by the minute.

He said quietly above her head, 'Relax. The worst is

over; tomorrow we'll sign the papers and have the first interview with the social worker assigned to our case. And once we get to Dacia you'll be fine; Michael will have little relatives to play with, and Cia and Hunt are familiar faces to you now.'

Another wedding, more princes and princesses, a life totally alien to anything she'd ever known. After a shallow breath Abby said tonelessly, 'Is that why you asked them here?'

His mouth curved in an enigmatic smile. 'To an extent—but I'm also dynastic enough to want some family at both our weddings.'

She straightened her shoulders. 'I'll make mistakes— I just hope they won't be glaring ones.'

'If you make mistakes,' he said coolly, the faint foreign intonation she'd noticed in his voice intensifying, 'it will be my fault for not taking care of you. Don't worry; my entire family are looking forward to meeting you, and, after your brilliant impersonation of a woman in love, Cia will tell them you hold my heart in your hand. As they've mostly succumbed to love, they'll be delighted to see someone else caught in its snare.'

His light, mocking tone hurt. And he was right—love was a snare, a dangerous, intoxicating blend of need and desire and the urge to give, all wrapped up in seductive hope and tied with the glorious promise of happiness.

If only we'd had time, she thought, and promptly chided herself for being so stupid. After all, Caelan had made a sacrifice too; instead of marrying a woman from his own world, a sophisticated, elegant woman who knew how to behave and what to say and the right sort of clothes to wear, he'd tied himself in marriage to a woman he despised.

For Michael.

Fighting back a swift, sharp ache of pain, she said brightly, 'I like your cousin. She's very kind.'

'She's a good woman,' he returned, easing her a little closer to his lean, strong body. 'She doesn't suffer fools gladly, but she's met her match in Hunt. Of course he's as besotted with her as she is with him, so they're happy.'

He sounded amused, as though he couldn't imagine what it would be like to love a woman as much as Hunt loved his wife.

Abby said, 'Their daughter sounds adorable.'

He laughed. 'She's a small package of charm hiding an implacable will. God help the world when she grows up!'

His arm tightened across her back. The music had sunk to a smoky, intensely personal whisper, backed by the ageless hush of the small waves on the beach. Every sense screwed to a pitch of intensity, Abby thought that she'd never forget these minutes spent in his arms. The singer's sultry voice lamenting a lost love, the subtle scent of salt mingling with the faint male essence that was Caelan's alone, the warmth of his hard body blasting through the silk that caressed her skin—all combined to release the lock she'd kept on her inhibitions.

Tonight, she thought dreamily, closing her eyes and resting her cheek lightly against the smooth material of his coat, she'd do what she wanted without thinking of anything but her own pleasure...

And Caelan's. Strange that after deciding as an adolescent that she'd wait for the sort of love her parents had before she committed herself to any man, she should fall for a man with a pirate's attitude towards life.

Except that they did have things in common; Michael, for example. She lifted her head and watched a white star wink into life just above the northern headland, and hang trembling in the darkening sky.

Star white, star bright...

The childish wishing game she'd played with her mother echoed through her mind. Of course she could be fooling herself, indulging in wishful thinking, hoping of the impossible. And not even to herself did she put into words what that impossible hope might be.

He said in a voice pitched so low she felt it reverberate through his strong chest rather than heard it, 'Are you tired?'

The anticipation that had been building caught fire, persuading her into recklessness. 'A little,' she murmured.

Barely moving, he swung her around in a slow, tight circle. The lean hand on her back slid lower, holding her hips against him. Feverish exaltation soared like sparks through her blood. She tilted her head, looking up into a dark, lean face. Starshine revealed narrowed eyes, a keen predatory look that should have terrified her instead of sending fiery little thrills along every nerve.

Then he smiled, and the heat inside her flared into a divine rashness. 'Perhaps we should go to bed,' he said.

She couldn't speak, but she managed to nod. Yet he didn't carry her off; instead, they danced on like lovers in a dream as his arms came around her, and his head lowered until their lips touched and their feet stilled.

His kiss was a seduction in itself, his mouth sure and gentle, so skilful that a flash of anger lit up her mind. She didn't want this practised, adept love-making; she wanted the half-angry kisses he'd given her before, because he'd barely been able to control them...

Yet she couldn't deny him. Heart to heart, bodies responding to the most elemental communication of all, they kissed until the perfume and sound of the sea permeated her emotions. His kisses lulled her with a honeyed enticement that masked her anger and wooed her into passionate response, so that when he picked her up and carried her into his bedroom she was ready for him, her whole body singing with arousal.

She didn't even look around the room, although she noticed that someone had lit candles there. Their warm, erratic light flickered across Caelan's face, dark, almost stern, its arrogant framework intensely pronounced as he set her on her feet beside a huge bed.

He looked down into her face and said, 'You make me drunk with desire.'

The words seemed torn from him, and were followed by kisses that closed each eye, more to the corners of her trembling mouth, one to the softly throbbing hollow in her throat. Her body became a stranger to her, drugged into heady passion, aching with a craving she'd never experienced before.

She felt his teeth close on an earlobe and shivered at the dart of desire that pierced her. 'You do the same to me,' she said in a voice she didn't recognise.

Delicious shudders of sensation arrowed through her, and she could only stare at him as he shrugged himself out of his coat and shirt.

Her mouth dried. He was magnificent, sleek and olive-tawny in the welcoming light of the candles, his powerful muscles hinting at his great strength as he said, 'Hold up your arms.'

Obediently she did so, and the camisole flowed over her in a susurration of amber silk, leaving her standing in the lace bra and briefs, bought, she realised on a sudden flash of insight, for just this moment.

Caelan's ice-cool eyes flamed the blue of the strongest

heat, and she had to quell an impulse to take an involuntary step back.

'You've always reminded me of some mythical, dangerous creature from a perilous land of faerie,' he said huskily. 'So beautiful, lovely enough to steal a man's courage and wit and sense from him until all he can think of is losing himself in you.'

She was shaking her head, her mouth soft and intensely vulnerable, her green-gold eyes filled with caution. '*La Belle Dame Sans Merci*?' she said, trying so hard to be sophisticated she sounded hard. 'I keep telling you, I'm just an ordinary woman, Caelan.'

His flash of white teeth revealed a smile that was humourless. 'Then why do my hands tremble when I touch you? Look!'

Fascinated, she watched as he stroked up one arm and the long line of her throat, closing her eyes when the delicate torture became unbearable. Her breath came sharply through her lips, and she couldn't bear this intense, tantalising temptation any more.

Yet she had to. Without thinking she mimicked him, smoothing over his sleek hide, her skin tingling at the slight roughness of the pattern of hair as her fingertips explored him. His heat blasted into her, and when he undid the scrap of material around her breasts she felt the rapid thud of his heart against her palms.

It gave her courage enough to let her hands slide down to the top of his trousers, courage enough to lay her cheek against his bare chest, the sound of his heart in her ear, and say, 'You've got too many clothes on.'

He laughed deeply. 'So what do you suggest we do about it?'

Turning her head slightly, she let her lips touch him.

She smiled, a small, secret smile that lingered when he lifted her face to his.

He said harshly, 'So much for any chance of a gentle wooing.'

His mouth closed on hers, and Abby gave herself exultantly, aware that there would be no turning back.

CHAPTER EIGHT

AFTER Abby had wrestled for several seconds with the fastenings of his trousers, Caelan laughed and covered her hands with his. 'I'll do it,' he said.

Was that a note of satisfaction in his voice?

But he didn't immediately strip. Instead he lifted his other hand into her hair, pulling out the clips that held it in place.

'Amber silk,' he murmured, sifting the brilliant sweep of it through his long fingers. 'Like a handful of flames, hot and glowing.' Laughter was a rough purr in the back of his throat and his eyes had glittered like ice-blue diamonds beneath thick black lashes. 'My own personal heat source...'

She thrilled to the raw note in his deep voice, the possessive caress of his hand as he cupped her breasts before bending to kiss each pleading centre, heating her eager body with the blatant aphrodisiac of his touch.

Although she struggled against it, she couldn't suppress a delicious shiver at the erotic contrast of his sleek, tanned body against her paler, more delicate skin. As for the hot, sensory pull of his ardent, skilful mouth and the light of passion that had burned in his eyes...

Then he lifted his head and started to undress.

Skin flushed and eyes dazed, Abby turned a little away, noting the wide, low bed, half covered in mosquito netting. The light coverings had been pushed back.

A moment of sanity made her wonder what on earth she was doing here. Making love with Caelan—with her husband, she thought with a primal frisson—would put her in such danger that she should call a halt right now.

Only she didn't want to.

She gasped when he nipped gently at the exquisitely tender place where her neck met her shoulder.

'Like that?' he murmured, and did it on the other side, sending tormenting rills of pleasure through her as her skin tightened.

'Too much,' she whispered, but he heard her.

'Good.' Again that raw, possessive note edged his tone. He picked her up and came down onto the bed with her, his big body fully aroused, gleaming and bronze and overwhelming.

Abby had little experience to base any expectations on, but she knew what she wanted—to pleasure him as much as he was pleasuring her, and she could only hope that desire would somehow compensate for the expertise he so clearly had in this most intimate of activities.

So, cocooned in his warmth, she touched his chest in shy exploration, her heart rejoicing when that familiar thunder of his heart deepened. Willingly, eagerly, she followed his lead, and lost her own way, falling deeper and deeper into a dark wonderland of the senses until all that mattered was his mouth on her breast, the fire that burned deep in the pit of her belly, and the sensuous glide of skin on skin, the heat of his touch and the glitter in his eyes, and her body's erotic awakening to his expert tuition.

She had no idea she could feel like this—every nerve alert and expectant, so highly strung that pleasure was poised precariously on the cusp between rapture and pain.

In the end she clenched her hands onto his sweat-damp shoulders and gasped incoherently, 'I can't—I don't— Caelan, please.'

He looked at her with smouldering eyes in a drawn, fiercely determined face. 'Yes,' he said thickly. 'It's time.'

Automatically she closed her eyes as he moved over her, then forced them open. This was the first time, and she'd make sure she remembered every second of it.

Candlelight gleamed in a warm patina across shoulders that shut out the rest of the room. Caelan slid his arms beneath her, lifting her slightly, and his mouth drifted down her breast. Fire scorched through her as she felt the full power and weight of his body. She had never, she thought wildly, not even in the hurricane that killed Gemma, felt so out of control, so helpless as she did now.

The erotic tug of his lips on the rosy centre of her breast banished the sad memories. Unable to stop herself, she arched up against him, and he laughed and lifted his head and slowly, steadily, eased his way into her, his eyes holding hers in a stare that held so many levels of meaning she couldn't separate them.

He filled her, and still he pressed on, and miraculously there was room, and with that overwhelming invasion came extreme pleasure, hot and heady and desperate.

Deep inside her a set of muscles she hadn't known she had clamped, holding tight to his long length. He said abruptly, 'Relax.'

'I can't,' she breathed, shocked and startled by her body's takeover of her will and mind.

He smiled, a swift feral movement of his beautiful mouth, and thrust home. Abby cried out, then soared, rocketed, raced into ecstasy, her whole body convulsing around him as sensations joined to send her to another universe where nothing but feeling existed, a transport of ecstasy so intense she thought she might die of it.

Slowly, so slowly she didn't know when it happened,

the delicious rapture faded into an equally delicious languor. But she fought it, finally opening her eyes.

Caelan was lying beside her, his expression so controlled he looked like a bronze mask against the creamy pillows. To her humiliation she couldn't remember him moving, but she knew one thing.

'You didn't,' she began, then closed her eyes in shame. What could she say? *What happened? What are we going to do now?*

'No, I didn't,' he said evenly, a slight note of humour in his voice. 'It's not important.'

'I thought—' She clamped her lips over the incautious words. Embarrassment made her cringe; she was, she thought miserably, the equivalent of those men who took their own satisfaction, then rolled over and went to sleep.

'Don't think,' he said coolly, echoing her thoughts. 'Go to sleep now.'

But she couldn't. Slowly, afraid of a rebuff, she turned into his arms, and kissed his shoulder, letting her lips linger on his skin. He tasted of salt and smoke and a faint musk that fanned her internal fires from a smoulder to an inferno, replacing physical satiation with eager anticipation.

His arms tightened around her and she felt every muscle in his strong body harden. Emboldened, she followed her own inclinations and licked the satiny skin against her lips, savouring the tastes and texture of his skin with unfeigned pleasure.

Shuddering, he said in a rough voice, 'You must be sore.'

She gave an experimental wriggle. 'I've never felt better,' she told him honestly.

He laughed and tilted her face, examining it with merciless, gleaming eyes that set her spine tingling. 'Sure?'

She stretched languorously, sliding against him in a shameless, openly seductive overture. 'Positive,' she said in a tone so demure it sounded smug.

'Then let's try again.'

This time it was slow and tantalising; he took her into realms of physical pleasure she'd never dreamed of until she sobbed for release, her body a taut, desperate bow against his hard, demanding one. This time, when at last she reached the heights they travelled together, tossed by the widening waves of sensation onto some unknown shore of satiation.

Locked in his arms, she fell headlong into sleep.

Michael's voice woke Abby with a start. She sat bolt upright in bed, only to slide hurriedly back under the covers when she realised she was naked. Caelan was gone; she heard his voice too, and realised that, far from standing in the doorway, Michael was some distance away, and that Caelan was with him.

On the beach, probably.

Colour burned up through her skin as she slid out of bed. At least she'd have clothes on when she met Caelan's ironic gaze. She picked up her pretty silk suit and the bra and briefs and scurried down the short hallway to the room she'd dressed in before that short, poignant wedding.

A long shower later, she walked into the wardrobe and examined the clothes there, still unable to believe that they were all hers.

Shopping with Caelan had been an odd experience. They'd stopped outside an empty salon, and she'd said, 'It looks as though they've closed.'

'For us,' he said with a shrug of his magnificent shoulders.

Sure enough, the door opened as soon as he'd rung the bell, and the owner, a very chic woman in her mid-forties, smiled at Caelan. She closed the door and with a murmured 'This way, Mr Bagaton,' escorted them into a private room with a fitting room at the other end.

Completely at home in such exotic surroundings, Caelan said, 'My fiancée wants clothes—casual ones for the summer.'

The owner nodded, surveying Abby with a measuring gaze that made her feel as though she were stripped of clothes. 'We have a new designer who should suit very well.'

Striving not to sound rude and abrupt, Abby produced a stiff smile for him. 'You might as well go—I'm sure you'll find this horribly boring.'

His smile was intimate and incredibly heady; only she could see the glint of mockery in his crystalline eyes. 'At the moment I can think of nothing more interesting than watching you parade for me.'

Abby heard a stifled sigh from the woman behind, but pride kept her head high and her face rigid. He was determined to make sure she bought what he considered a suitable wardrobe.

'I've never paraded before, but I'll do my best,' she said.

Driven by recklessness and that disturbing sense of being herded into a trap, she came out of the fitting room like a model on show, breasts jutting, hips swaying, flicking her hair carelessly when she turned after letting her eyes drift over Caelan in a parody of catwalk aloofness.

He lifted an ironic eyebrow, but the blue gleam in his gaze scared her into a return to common sense. The raw attraction between them was dangerous enough without her stoking it.

Surprisingly he and she had the same taste in clothes. And he had a good eye for the perfect accessory.

But then, she thought trenchantly, no doubt he'd had a lot of experience in buying clothes for his various lovers.

Had he really been celibate since they'd met all those years ago? It didn't seem possible—and it wasn't sensible to think about it.

Together, with minimal input from her, he and the forbiddingly discreet salon owner chose a wardrobe to see her through her sojourn in Dacia. Common sense muted any protest; Caelan knew what would be acceptable, and the salon owner certainly knew how to achieve results that transformed her client from an ordinary New Zealand woman to the faintly mysterious, exotic wife of a princely tycoon.

'Cosmetics,' Caelan said, getting to his feet. A faint smile crossed his face as he glanced at his watch before surveying Abby's face. 'Do you know what you want?'

'Yes, of course.'

He inclined his dark head. 'Then I'll pick you up in an hour.' He looked at the salon owner. 'You'll deliver?'

'Of course,' she said instantly, dropping a pen in her haste to take down the address of the apartment.

Of course, Abby thought cynically. With the lure of future sales, all things were possible. Caelan smiled and thanked her, and both women watched his tall, lean body move with a prowling, lethal grace out of the room.

The older woman was the first to pull herself together but a certain glow in her eyes revealed that the full impact of Caelan's potent masculinity wasn't lost on her. Flushing slightly, she said, 'I believe there is a wedding suit to choose. I have found what I think is the perfect one for you, but of course the decision must be yours.'

But there had been no decision to make; Abby had fallen in love with it at first sight.

And then the salon owner had said, 'Forgive me for saying this, but you need underclothes to wear those clothes as they should be worn. I'll get a fitter to bring in a selection for you.'

By now Abby had no pride left. 'Thank you.'

'And what brand of cosmetics do you prefer?'

The cheapest brand of generic moisturiser in the supermarket, Abby thought cynically, but she picked a name at random.

'An excellent line.'

Determined not to splash out, Abby stuck to basic underwear, although she allowed herself the sybaritic luxury of several silk camisoles and matching briefs. And when it came to cosmetics, the consultant persuaded her to indulge not only in a basic skin-care regime, but also a slick, gold-tinged lipstick and a seductive, subtle eyeshadow that turned her eyes to smoky green jewels.

Now, with the flight to Dacia only eight hours away, she was glad she'd let herself be talked into spending so much of Caelan's money. She needed, she thought mordantly, all the help she could get.

So she chose a sundress in smoky shades of green and gold, only to stare at her shoulders in shock. Theirs had been a long, sinfully gentle loving, but, even with Caelan tempering his great strength to her slender body, he had left faint marks on her. Hastily scrambling into a pair of trousers and a short-sleeved cotton shirt, she remembered biting his shoulder in a moment of ecstasy and thought with an odd twist of sensation that she'd branded him too.

For better or for worse, they were married. This, she thought as she closed the door behind herself, is going to be as good as it gets. The sex was a bonus; for her it had been frighteningly wonderful, but perhaps for Caelan it was simply more of the same.

It wasn't true happiness, but it had to be enough. Deliberately relaxing her facial muscles, she went out into the first day of her marriage.

It turned out to be so busy that after the first few moments she didn't have time to dwell on the future. Shortly before lunch they left in the helicopter for Auckland, and that afternoon all three Bagatons met the caseworker assigned to the adoption process.

Later in the day, when the private jet had reached cruising height, Abby said, 'What did you think of her?'

'Damned difficult to fool,' Caelan returned. 'And determined to make sure that Michael's rights are safeguarded.'

But for all her professionalism, the woman hadn't been immune to Caelan's cool masculinity. Was anyone? Abby wondered, smiling down at Michael's excited face. No woman, anyway. The caseworker noted that Michael seemed perfectly happy with both parents, but presumably she'd been looking for signs that would warn her all wasn't as it seemed in their picture-perfect family.

She yawned, a brief memory of making love to Caelan lighting treacherous embers in the pit of her stomach. Her body ached with a feverish languor that sapped her energy and summoned more vivid images of them together

She quelled it firmly. Ahead of them lay a long flight Although she'd made sure that the plane had everything necessary to keep Michael happy, she didn't fool herself that it would be easy.

In the end though, the journey went with remarkable ease. Keeping a lid on Michael's high spirits hadn't been nearly so difficult with Caelan as back-up. Abby looked down at Dacia, an emerald in an enamelled blue sea, and wondered whether she was dreaming. Only a week ago she'd been tense and edgy, bent on escaping from Nukuroa to a safer haven, yet aware that her life would be spent looking over her shoulder. And worrying whether by fulfilling Gemma's wishes she was depriving Michael of much that was important to him.

Now, half a world away, ears popping as the jet eased itself towards the runway, she was astonished at how much had changed in those short days.

A movement beside her brought her out of her reverie. 'Abby, my ears hurt,' Michael wailed.

'Swallow hard,' she told him. 'Have you finished your coffee? You could give a big yawn and see if that makes your ear feel better.'

After a prodigious gape, he screwed up his face and said earnestly, 'I think another toffee would make it better.'

From the corner of her eye Abby caught a flash of white as Caelan smiled. Her heart jumped in her chest.

No, she wasn't going to think of how her attitude had changed since he'd walked into her hall at Nukuroa.

Instead, she'd remember how unfailingly helpful he'd been during the long, often tedious flight. It warmed her heart to see the slow blossoming of his relationship with Michael.

He might not know much about children, but his tactics were working; Michael loved being treated as an equal. Once she'd looked up from her book to see them playing chess, both absorbed and intent as Caelan showed his nephew the moves.

She watched carefully, relaxing when she realised that Michael was thoroughly enjoying himself. Later, when he was asleep, she said, 'Thank you for entertaining him. I'd never have thought of playing chess with him.'

'It's a war game,' he said laconically, 'and most young boys enjoy it. My father taught me. Do you play?'

'Yes,' she said. 'My mother adored it, and she was a killer. I used to call her Attila the Hun.'

He looked a little startled at that. On a gleam of amusement she said, 'Enjoyment of tactical games isn't confined to the male sex, you know.'

'I'd like to have met your mother.'

But he didn't look convinced and Abby wondered whether he thought such pursuits were unfeminine.

She said, 'Tell me something about your family in Dacia. I mean, I know of your cousin the prince, because his wife is a New Zealander and their wedding got huge publicity at home. And of course I know Princess Lucia a little. But there's another cousin, Prince Guy—the computer man, who turns up in newspapers now and then.'

'He's married to Lauren, a charming Englishwoman.'

She said wistfully, 'I envy you these cousins. As far as I know, I don't have any relatives.'

'The word in Dacian has a much wider meaning than in English. We are all descended from a ruling prince—not the same one.'

Curiously she asked, 'So how did a Dacian prince end up a New Zealand citizen?'

'I have dual citizenship. My father came out to New Zealand and I grew up there.' He'd emigrated because his second much-younger wife had developed a crush on another man; instead of seeing her emotional unfaithfulness as an indication of her character, Caelan though cynically, his father had blamed her lover.

And the move hadn't worked. His stepmother had hated New Zealand, calling it a provincial little country on the edge of nowhere. But he'd learned to love it, and his dual nationality was a natural expression of his feelings.

He leaned back in the seat and surveyed her with narrowed eyes. 'You're scared.'

'Nervous,' she corrected smartly.

And still not convinced she'd done the right thing. There was a distance about her that piqued his hunter's instincts.

'Stop worrying. You liked Cia and Hunt, didn't you?'

'Yes,' she admitted.

'Then you'll like the rest of my family; they're just like any other.'

Three weeks later she understood what he meant. And how utterly wrong he'd been. Although the welcome from the prince and princess had warmed and comforted her, no other family she knew called a huge pile of honey-coloured stone the Little Palace, because the other one on the island, the Old Palace, was twice its size and built on the foundations of a Roman fortress.

No New Zealand family wore priceless jewels with such insouciance, or partied in immense salons lined with panelling and mirrors, fragrant with exquisite flowers and lit by candelabra in a timeless, romantic atmosphere of tradition and privilege.

No other New Zealand family drove to the accompaniment of smiles and toots and waves from every other road user. And none was related to every European royal family, those still in their thrones and those adjusting to lives as exiles.

She had been eased skilfully into Dacian social life, shocked when she realised that her name was appearing more and more in the Court Circular sent to the media by the royal household.

Caelan had kept his word. At every public function he was beside her, guiding her safely through parties and sailing trips, family picnics and the annual garden party, a glittering opera première for charity, the opening of an art exhibition in the Old Palace down by the harbour, dinners and receptions that ranged from formal to pleasantly casual.

Yet not the Caelan she'd known in New Zealand. Like her, he was playing a part, and perhaps only she could tell that whatever closeness had been forged by their wedding night had gone. He wasn't even staying in the palace; apparently he owned a house on the southern coast, and that was where he was living.

Tonight was their engagement ball; the official photographs taken the day after their arrival had been released with the announcement of their engagement that afternoon. Bells had rung across Dacia the moment the news was out, and fireworks were already flowering in the soft Mediterranean dusk.

Tomorrow there would be an interview with the only two journalists that Caelan had decided would be allowed near them.

And now, clad in a sensuous dress the exact green of her eyes, she watched the maid pin back her hair with five emerald stars while her stomach clamped tight in apprehension, because the extended family had arrived, and tonight she was officially on show. Her engagement ring, a glorious emerald flanked by two diamonds, glittered like another star on her hand.

Someone knocked on the door and the maid made an excuse and left the room.

Frozen with nervousness, Abby took several deep, grounding breaths, but when she recognised Alexa's voice she relaxed a little. Her hostess, Prince Luka's wife, was a lovely person; she'd been a staunch support, helping Abby tactfully through the intricacies of protocol and family dynamics.

The maid appeared in the door. 'Ma'am, the princess would like to see you.'

Abby got to her feet and dragged in another breath. 'Of course,' she said, and walked out into the bedroom.

The princess was radiant in satin, its tawny hue a contrast to the magnificent Dacian emeralds in her necklace and tiara.

'Oh, Abby,' she said, and came towards her with a smile. 'You look glorious! Maria's done a brilliant job with your hair.' The maid bobbed a little curtsey and withdrew. 'And your emeralds pick up the green in your eyes. How are you feeling?'

'Terrified.' Abby didn't mind telling her; although Alexa's grandfather had been the ruling prince of Illyria, another Mediterranean princedom, his love affair with her grandmother had finished before he'd known of her pregnancy, so Alexa had grown up in New Zealand with no idea of her heritage. Abby clung to the knowledge that if the princess could adjust to this whole splendid, glamorous ambience, so could she.

Except that the princess knew she was loved; although she and her husband didn't flaunt their feelings they ran deep and true, a powerful current between them that glorified their lives. For the first time in her life Abby understood envy.

The princess laughed. 'I know, believe me, the family *en masse* can look intimidating, but they're lovely people. Well, most of them.'

'How on earth can you fill a ballroom with relatives? Somehow I got the idea from Caelan that there weren't all that many.'

'Ah, he conveniently forgot to mention that even if the link is five hundred years back the family connection is kept.'

'He did indeed,' Abby said colourlessly.

Apart from a few rare moments, she hadn't been alone with Caelan since they'd arrived. When they weren't socialising he and Prince Luka had been secluded in various meetings while she and the rest of the royal family took the first tentative footsteps towards friendship.

Michael had been a great help there. The palace nursery was noisy with children—the two hearty boys who lived there and Princess Lucia's charming, strong-minded little daughter had welcomed Michael with enthusiasm and interest. All asleep now, tucked up after a glorious afternoon spent at a secluded bay surrounded by pine and olive trees.

Abby confessed, 'I'm scared of making Caelan look an idiot by forgetting who's who, or mispronouncing their names.'

'You couldn't make Caelan look an idiot however hard you tried,' Alexa said affectionately. 'He's idiot-proof. All the Bagaton men are. And remember, the family is quite accustomed to the Bagatons choosing the people they love and marry! Luka's poor parents were the last to be forced into a dynastic marriage, and he vowed that neither he nor anyone else in his family would have to do that.'

But that was exactly what Caelan was facing—a marriage of convenience established to safeguard his sister's son.

Perhaps the princess had caught a flash of Abby's misery. She said comfortingly, 'Caelan will look after you. If you don't already know it, he's an intensely protective man.' She gave a quick, far from regal, grin. 'And a possessive one—it's rather fun for all of us to see how carefully he watches over you! Now, come. And enjoy yourself tonight!'

CHAPTER NINE

THE last thing Abby expected from her own engagement ball was enjoyment, but it happened, mostly, she realised with an odd pang of fear, because Caelan was always there, supportive and reassuring and intensely compelling.

So during the first waltz, with everyone crowded around and clapping, she let herself relax against his lean, hard strength and gave herself over to the music, a Viennese tune she'd never thought to dance to with the man she resented and wanted in equal measure.

He murmured, 'I hear our son swam a whole ten metres by himself this afternoon.'

Startled, she looked up, and he smiled. Heart thumping, she said, 'He did, and you should have seen his face when he realised he'd done it! You've never referred to him as your son before.'

'From now on he's *our* son. I agree that he should know who his birth parents are, but he's lucky enough to have two sets.' And before she could reply to that, he went on, 'You look radiant. Every inch a princess.'

Somehow the raw edge to his voice gave life to his practised compliment; when he spoke like that, she foolishly wanted to believe that none of it was deliberate, that he really meant each word.

'I—thank you. So do you,' she returned automatically then flushed. 'Look like a prince, I mean. Champagne must have addled my brain.'

136

'One glass—and barely touched at that—shouldn't do that,' he responded on a dry, amused note.

Somehow she had to come to some accommodation with her unruly emotions, she thought desperately. They could do this, make a happy family for the child she loved; she mustn't let her feelings stand in the way of Michael's security. That was the whole reason for this glittering, elaborate farce.

Caelan was declaring to his family and the world that he valued her enough to make her his wife. The fact that it was based on a lie—that if it hadn't been for Michael there would have been no wedding, no future, no happy family—was their secret.

But she'd noticed a difference in him the moment they'd set foot on Dacia. Outwardly he'd been everything a woman would want in a lover—but instead of the forthright, formidable man she'd dealt with honestly in New Zealand, he'd retreated behind an impenetrable façade. In a week's time they'd be married according to Dacia's laws. They'd spend four days alone in a villa on the south coast of Dacia, then fly back to New Zealand.

And then what?

A life where superb sex and money replaced any communion of spirit and mind? A fierce pang of longing, of despair, ached through her. Defiantly she banished it. All right, so she'd always hoped for a marriage like her parents', but she was the one who'd made it impossible; her actions had brought Caelan to hunt her down like some dark nemesis.

And even knowing what she did now, she still couldn't work out whether she'd change a thing.

'Smile,' Caelan commanded, the word flicking her like a whip.

She looked up into a dark, absorbed face, into eyes that gleamed with hard mockery.

'Smile,' he said again, and lifted her hand to his mouth.

An anguished pleasure shot through her, setting her blood coursing, her thoughts tumbling endlessly. She was saved from melting by the glint of satisfaction in his gaze; he knew that he had only to touch her to let loose that bewildering passion.

Caelan wondered exactly what was going on in the brain behind those great, tilted eyes, shielded from his scrutiny by the heavy curtain of her lashes. Then, as he kissed her hand, defiance smouldered in their depths and she curved her hand against his mouth before moving it to his cheek, letting her fingertips linger as though she couldn't bear to break the contact.

Her smile, mysterious and a little taunting, made promises.

Every muscle in his body tightened. Without exception his mistresses had been experienced women, skilled in the arts of love, but none of them had been able to stir his blood like Abby.

'Why?' she breathed, and smiled, a slow, heady movement of her lush mouth.

Not only did she look like some mysterious woman out of myth, but she possessed a subtle sexuality that drew him as inexorably as though she'd put a spell on him.

He despised himself for that lack of self-control, so his voice was harsh when he said, 'We're meant to be in love.'

Abby barely heard the words, but her body sprang to life at the rough note of hunger in it.

The rest of the evening passed like a dream, a whirl

of good wishes and laughter and music, of colour and glitter and the perfume of flowers. And of Caelan, always there, coolly protective, letting that controlled sexual response stand in for the love everyone took for granted.

In the small hours of the morning they drove back through the scented night to the palace, where he kissed her hand in a formal salute and left. Exhausted, she went up to her bedroom. The maid stood up as she came in.

Summoning a smile, Abby said, 'I thought I told you not to wait up.'

The middle-aged woman said serenely, 'We Dacians are independent. We do what we want to, and I want to help you. Prince Caelan is much loved here, and it is a privilege to tend to his bride.'

They were all so kind, while she and Caelan were lying to them. Did the end ever justify the means? It had to— Michael's welfare was more important than any private emotions she and Caelan had to endure.

Abby crawled into bed, only to lie awake for hours. Her resolution never to let herself soften towards him was being sorely tested. Oh, she could cope with the fierce, wildfire passion that flared between them, but this reluctant appreciation was dangerous. It mined away at her independence. She'd been safer, her integrity less in jeopardy, when they'd been at daggers drawn.

'It's a matter of policy for him,' she said out loud, listening to the quiet sounds of a Mediterranean night.

As well as convincing the world—and the New Zealand social welfare system—that they were in love, Caelan would appreciate that a complaisant wife was much easier to live with than one who held aloof.

And her defiant attitude had been a mistake; his whole career proclaimed that he enjoyed a challenge. It would give him cynical satisfaction to turn her lovesick like his other mistresses.

So she wouldn't let it happen.

Eventually sleep claimed her, but only to inflict dreams on her, in which she ran endlessly from some hideous, terrifying being, only to force herself to turn and see that it was Caelan.

And she didn't have to search far to find a meaning to that! Once again she was being forced in a direction she didn't want to go, and the resentment she'd used to defend herself seemed a weak, futile emotion. Telling herself that his charm and wit and thoughtfulness were all false didn't help; each day that passed she felt the ground beneath her feet become more and more shaky.

Over the next week the tempo picked up. The wedding was to be held in a chapel at the Old Palace—'To give the people a chance to see you both,' Alexa said cheerfully. 'Dacians adore weddings.' She gave Abby a glance. 'All well?'

'Fine, thank you,' Abby said automatically, and summoned a smile. On an impulse she asked, 'How do you cope? You were brought up like me—ordinary. And so was Lauren, and Princess Ianthe of Illyria—another New Zealander. How on earth do you all deal with living in the public eye?'

They had retired to Alexa's private sitting room after a reception for local dignitaries. Alexa put her teacup and saucer down and said thoughtfully, 'Ianthe and I fell in love with men who made it perfectly clear that they came with a country attached. We had to choose whether or not to accept that.'

Ah, there was the source of her anguish in a nutshell. They had had a choice; Abby had none. But in spite of the questioning note in the princess's final sentence she couldn't admit that to this charming, warm woman.

Infusing her voice with a confidence she was far from feeling, she said, 'I'll get used to it. And at home it's not so—so different. We lead a much less structured life there.'

'From what Caelan said, you'll be travelling with him, at least until Michael goes to school. And there will always be formal occasions—which you seem to enjoy. You certainly don't show any sign of nerves.'

'Because Caelan's always there,' Abby said on a wry note.

'Of course he is. He wants you to be happy.' Alexa leaned forward. 'I think you're worrying unnecessarily. You have lovely manners, and it's only a matter of time before you become completely confident.'

'Actually,' Abby confided, 'everyone's been so nice that I'm not paranoid about that now. What really worries me is the thought of the media.'

The princess nodded, her face bleak. 'The wretched paparazzi! Only a couple of weeks ago Luka had one thrown off the island—he'd taken photos of our children.'

With a shiver, Abby muttered, 'I wish Caelan were just an ordinary man.'

'No, you don't,' Alexa said firmly. 'If you'd wanted an ordinary man you'd have fallen in love with one! As for the hounds of the press—yes, they're a nuisance and so is the constant attention, but love makes it all worthwhile.'

Uncomfortably Abby nodded. 'Yes,' she said simply, knowing that this was true, 'love makes anything worthwhile.'

But she wouldn't let herself love Caelan. She didn't dare.

The princess held her eyes for a few tense seconds, then gave a smile. 'Cling to that,' she advised. 'It does help. And remember that you're a New Zealander—infinitely adaptable!'

Abby kept those last words in her mind during the tumultuous week before the wedding, holding them close like a mantra as she walked up the aisle towards Caelan, magnificent in formal, superbly cut clothes, Prince Luka beside him.

For this wedding she wore a classically cut dress in cream silk that had been made by a Dacian couturier with magic in her fingers. The emerald stars held her veil in place above hair plaited in a formal French pleat at the nape of her neck. Behind her walked Michael and the royal children, the boys solemn in page-boys' satins, the two little Illyrian princesses in soft, summery clothes with flowers in their hair.

Hunt Radcliffe gave her away. Halfway up the aisle he murmured, 'How many nannies have you got posted around this chapel?'

'One for each child,' she whispered as the triumphal chorus swelled about her.

He said, 'With whips, I hope.'

So she was smiling when she reached the man who waited for her in front of the altar, his blue eyes hooded and gleaming beneath black lashes, his handsome face a bronze mask in the light of the candles.

Afterwards Abby couldn't remember much about the service beyond Caelan's deep tone as he made his vows, and the whisper and sigh of silk and satin as the congregation rose to greet them when they came back down the aisle.

Then the bells rang out across the city, mingling with the cheers of the Dacian crowds, and in the open carriage behind flower-decked white horses Caelan's hand closed around hers, warm and strong and firm as they drove back to the reception.

That and the wedding feast passed in a blur too, but at last it was over and she was kissing Michael goodbye, saying, 'We'll be back in four more sleeps, darling. Be good while we're gone, won't you, and have fun in the pool.'

He beamed at her. 'Uncle Caelan says I can go out on the boat with him when we get home.'

'That will be lovely.' She gave him a quick, hard hug and straightened. This was the first time they'd been separated, and she hated leaving him.

'But only if you keep practising that swimming,' Caelan said. He stooped and picked Michael up. 'Be good,' he said, and kissed his cheek.

Michael hugged him fiercely, clinging when Caelan went to put him down. He said in an unhappy little voice, 'I want to come with you.'

Abby hesitated, but before she had time to answer, Caelan said, 'You told your cousins you'd stay with them. A promise is a promise, Michael.'

His face crumpled, but he swallowed manfully, eyes wide and gathering tears.

'We won't be away long,' Abby said, heart contracting.

Caelan relinquished him into the care of his special nursemaid and said, 'We'll bring you a present when we come back.'

He nodded and Caelan took Abby's arm and steered her away, saying pleasantly, 'Don't look so tragic. People will wonder if we've had our first quarrel.'

'Little do they know,' she said, but her voice wobbled.

'He'll be fine. Would you like to bring his nursemaid back to New Zealand with us?'

She stared at him. 'Why a Dacian?'

He shrugged. 'Because he likes her. And so that she could teach him Dacian and Italian. I've checked Ilana's credentials—she's been trained in an excellent school, and, yes, she'd like to travel.'

Official goodbyes all said, they were on the way to the helicopter pad. Abby felt a chill at the thought of another woman in Michael's life, then chided herself. It was stupid to be jealous; soon he'd be going to school, and the words 'my teacher says' would ring in her ears with all the authority of holy writ!

As for the deeper, more shameful fear—Caelan had married her; he wouldn't be scheming to replace her with a nanny so that he could divorce her! A glance at his face wasn't exactly reassuring. Hard and forceful, it was the face of a man who, as Lucia had said, knew what he wanted and was utterly sure that he'd get it.

What have I done? she thought, on a swift kick of panic. This complex, tough, clever man is my husband!

She said, 'It's important for him to speak Dacian, isn't it?'

Caelan glanced at her. 'It's a common bond in the family,' he said after a moment. 'I'd like my children to be fluent in it.'

'Your *children*?' It emerged in an astounded squeak, but inside her some renegade emotion melted a hard knot of resentment.

Caelan's brows lifted. '*Our* children,' he amended smoothly.

And then they were ambushed by a laughing crowd of wedding guests, and escorted to the chopper pad amid a hail of sugar almonds and flowers. Once in the helicopter Abby picked rose petals off her skirt and thought of Caelan's smooth assumption that they'd be having other children.

Over the past weeks on Dacia she'd managed to push the memory of her wedding night in New Zealand to the back of her mind. Except late at night, she conceded. And in her dreams...

But clearly he meant it to be a full marriage in every way.

Well, why not? the cynical part of her mind asked unanswerably. He was a virile man with a great appetite for sex, and he'd promised faithfulness. Naturally he'd want to make love to the woman he'd forced into marriage.

And she, she knew with a painful twist of the heart, would enjoy it with rapture tinctured with bitterness. She recalled various women at the wedding—titled, elegant, exquisite, who navigated their way through society with a skill that came from being born to it. She'd noticed an occasional glance at her, slightly bewildered, even pitying; they still made her cringe.

Caelan could have married any one of the flock of princezas, marquesas, countesses and gräfins who'd decorated the occasion so suitably.

Yes, Alexa and Ianthe had made lives for themselves in this exclusive social milieu. But they had talents— Princess Ianthe of Illyria was a brilliant scientist, her work on the fresh-water dolphins of Illyria world-famous. Alexa was a superbly creative photographer. Of the other wives in the Dacian royal family, Princess Lucia was a Bagaton by birth, and Lauren, the exquisite Englishwoman married to Prince Guy, had carved her way through the financial world and now ran a charity she'd set up to help children in the third world achieve education.

And, that coolly logical part of her prompted, they love their husbands and they know their husbands love them.

It was simple as that. She'd always be the interloper with no glittering talent to offer, unloved and unloving; the best she could hope for was to settle into some sort of affection as the years went by and she became the mother of Caelan's children.

A wave of intense dejection shocked her. Summoning pride to her aid, she fought it grimly. At least this way she kept her self-respect. How humiliating it would be to have been like his previous mistresses and let herself fall in love with him, yearning pitiably for his love in return!

She wouldn't let it happen. But neither self-respect nor pride banished the lingering aftermath of pain.

Shocking her with its unexpectedness, strong tanned fingers closed over hers. Caelan leaned towards her and said, 'He'll be all right. He's having the time of his life with the other children, and Alexa has promised to tuck him up each night.'

She nodded, not daring to look at him in case he realised that she hadn't been worrying about Michael. The helicopter swooped low over a pine forest, and Caelan touched her shoulder and pointed. 'The villa. It's close enough so that if he gets too upset, we can be back in less than an hour.'

Don't be so thoughtful! she commanded silently, turning her head to stare through the window. His consideration undermined the defences she was struggling to keep intact.

Perched on a cliff overlooking the Mediterranean, the honeymoon villa gleamed white in the rapidly fading daylight. Abby made out a tennis court, a swimming pool still brilliantly blue, colonnades that would shade the walls against the midday heat, and enclosed courtyards where the silver gleam of water hinted at the music of fountains and rills. The sombre darkness of a pine forest crowded against an ancient wall on the landward side, and between them and the sea gardens stretched out, shadowy and inviting, with splashes of bold colour.

A path led from the landing pad through the pines. As they walked through the scented shade towards the mansion, Abby drew in a long breath. 'It's beautiful.'

'It began life as a fortress built by one of my more piratical ancestors to control the seaway,' Caelan told her drily. 'Whenever a sail was sighted ships would set off from the harbour and demand a toll, backed up by guns from the fortress. Everyone made a nice living for a couple of centuries.'

Fascinating facts that only served to underline the huge difference in their worlds. 'What happened?'

'Oh, things changed,' he said, not hiding the irony in his voice. 'Robber princes stopped being fashionable, so the then prince, a very practical man, set his mind to more respectable ways of earning a living.'

'What about the villagers?'

What did he plan for tonight? Did he expect to take her to bed? Heated anticipation roiled endlessly inside her, inextricably mingling with fear and tension.

He grinned. 'Trust you to worry about the villagers. They turned to fishing and tourism. Less exciting, but just as profitable in the long term.'

Abby tried to squelch a feverish thrill by reminding herself that he'd made no attempt to be alone with her during the past month; every kiss had been formal, every glance in public had been measured, calculated to convince anyone who watched them that they were truly in love.

Instead of wondering if they'd spend the night together, she should be refusing to consider making love—sex, she corrected herself bleakly. Passionate it might be—would be—but it would also be a soulless coupling, one of convenience; each cynically making use of the other's body for loveless pleasure.

The scent of the pines floated around them, clean and crisp, underlain with that particular fragrance she'd always remember when she thought of Dacia—a soft, fresh commingling of salt and lavender and flowers, sweet, earthy and intensely evocative.

'Welcome to our Dacian home,' Caelan said outside the huge panelled door that looked as though it had survived from the original fortress.

He picked her up, ignoring her shocked exclamation, and strode into the cool, candle-lit interior.

Heart jolting in forbidden expectation, she said unevenly, 'I didn't realise that carrying a bride over the threshold was a tradition in Dacia.'

He stopped and looked down at her, pale eyes glinting in his dark face. 'I make my own traditions,' he drawled, and bent his head and took her startled mouth in a frankly sensual kiss that told her exactly what he planned to do for the rest of the night.

And she, poor fool that she was, craved it just as much as he did.

'I've been wanting to do that for weeks,' he said, letting her slide down his body as he set her on her feet again. He touched her lips with a lean forefinger, the possessive light in his eyes still very pronounced, then said calmly, 'Come out and look at the view. By now there should be enough of a moon to set it off.'

With his scent in her nostrils and her heart jumping nervously, she was ushered through the villa, a magnificent building furnished in what she'd come to label the Dacian style—a skilful, serene combination of antiques and modern pieces, set off with flowers and stunning art. It reminded her of the apartment in Auckland.

He took her out onto a terrace, wide and shaded in part by a pergola covered in vines. Somewhere she could hear a Spanish guitar; it had been her mother's favourite instrument, and difficult tears stung her eyes as the mellow, oddly oriental timbre fell seductively on the night air.

Silently Abby walked across to the edge, and stopped, gasping; the villa seemed to be floating, with nothing but shimmering sea below and a moon as ripe and golden as an orange queening it over the sky.

'I think we should have a glass of champagne.' Caelan walked lithely over to a table where a bottle in a silver ice bucket waited. He poured two glasses, and brought them across to her, handing her one.

'To the future,' he said.

Thinly, her words falling into the quiet air, she repeated the words, and drank with him, taking the opportunity to move a few steps away on the pretext of looking out at the view.

He glanced down at her, his hard face challenging. 'What are you thinking?'

Her face clamped, thoughts and emotions locked behind a proud, sinfully sexy mask as she set the champagne flute onto a side table with a flick of her long, elegant fingers. His skin tightened when he remembered the erotic play of her hands over his body, the way she'd stroked him as though she adored the feel of him and the taste of him in her mouth...

Desire blasted through him like a neutron bomb, so

powerful he had to turn slightly to hide the betrayal of his body.

Abby said remotely, 'That this is an outrageously beautiful place with a fantastic view. How much time do you spend here?'

He swung around to meet her flat, empty gaze.

She was as stubborn as he'd often been accused of being; tough-minded and determined not to give an inch. Somewhere, a rather too-literal fate must be killing itself with mocking laughter, he thought cynically. Several times his conscience had made him break off a relationship because his current lover had fancied herself in love with him. He'd refused to use them like that. Now the woman he'd married flatly refused to do so.

Gemma would have said that it served him right.

His brows rose, but his voice was level, a lazy note of amusement more obvious when he returned, 'I come here as often as I can—usually three to four times a year.' His voice changed. 'Do you know what's really outrageous about this whole situation? It's outrageous that every time I look at you I want you.'

Her breath locked in her throat and her heart contracted into a hard ball in her chest. Torn by longing, she knew that love was the only sensible reason for taking that final step into surrender—and Caelan didn't love her.

He would never love her.

But you don't love him, some treacherous part of her murmured beguilingly, so that makes it fair enough to both of you. No lies, no false hopes.

She winced. 'It's not enough,' she said stonily.

His mouth hardening into a line she recognised, he came towards her. 'It's all we've got, Abby.'

'No,' she blurted, panicked into retreating behind a

elegant wrought-iron chair—a dead give-away to the emotions that were tearing at her.

All her pragmatism about their marriage, their future, was revealed as shoddy rationalisation, based on a cowardly desire for sex without commitment. She had promised herself to this man, to a future together, and that involved sex, so why the virginal flutterings and fears?

Caelan said impatiently, 'No? So you admit it's not all we've got.'

She chose words carefully, infusing each one with sombre conviction. 'I meant no, I refuse to let you bulldoze me into something I'm not ready for.' But one look at his face, cold and brutally determined, warned her she wasn't getting through to him.

'You were ready for it a month ago.'

Her instinct for self-defence, backed by a primitive fear, prompted her next defiant statement. 'I know. But sex is not enough to base a relationship on.'

'Do you want more than sex?' he asked, eyes glinting and keen.

Warning bells clanged. She'd known when she married him that she was taking a huge risk. After all, what did an ordinary woman have in common with a man descended from a line of autocratic princes? A man who'd been born rich, and built himself an even greater empire in the cut-throat world of international finance?

Nothing, she thought bleakly. But for Michael's sake he'd been forced to accept the challenge. Amazingly the resentment that had burned so brightly now flickered.

After a deep breath she said quietly, 'I—I don't know what I want. To be honest, I think.'

'I've been honest,' he said impatiently. 'You've known right from the start that I want you. Are you going to cower behind that chair all night? Grant me a little control; I don't intend to leap on you.'

'I'm tired.' Stung and shaken, she turned away.

She'd taken two steps when his hand on her shoulder froze her. 'Running away isn't going to help. We need to come to a decision.' His voice was cold and authoritative, for all the world as though she were a junior executive who'd admitted a mistake.

Abby swung around to confront him, eyes blazing green. 'When you say *we*, you mean that *you'll* make any decision,' she said, using contempt to cut the moment short. She was too vulnerable, every sense heightened, every nerve quivering. 'You can do that on your own. Let me go.'

The pupils in his pale eyes expanded until they were night-dark, surrounded by a thin circle of ice-blue. Her breath faltered, and she had to swallow to moisten her suddenly dry mouth. Get out of here, the last remnant of common sense warned. *Run!*

Caelan caught her flailing hand and lifted it to his mouth. Holding her startled gaze with his, he kissed the back. The heat of his mouth against her skin sent signals to every pleasure point in her body, curling her fingers in tormented need as she fought the swift expansion of hunger, the tightness in her breasts and their sensitive tips.

'Caelan, this isn't the way—'

Pulses jerking, she tried to wrench free, but he turned her hand over, and this time, instead of a brief brush of his lips against the skin, he bit the mount of Venus under her thumb, his teeth lightly closing on the fine, too receptive skin.

Lightning stabs of sensation rioted through her, setting her afire. And then he let her go.

'There, that wasn't so bad, was it?' His beautiful mouth curved in cold irony as he stepped back so she could pass him.

Seared by angry chagrin, she stiffened her shoulders and spine and stepped away. 'This is not going to work,' she snapped, 'if you keep mauling me all the time.'

He gave a sudden crack of mirthless laughter. 'You've led a very sheltered life if you thought that that was mauling,' he said cruelly. 'Perhaps I should show you the difference.'

'No!'

But it was too late. Caelan spun her round, deftly and ruthlessly blocking her blows before they reached his solar plexus. His fingers closed around each hand, pushing them behind her back while his head came down and he kissed her with a hard, driving urgency that sliced through her pathetic defences like a sword through satin.

Abby's wild response shocked her into a momentary stillness, just long enough for primeval emotions to shut down her resistance. Her mouth softened and opened under his, the magic of his kiss summoning an untamed heat that melted her into passionate surrender. Desperate, she tried to bring up her knee, only to be foiled by Caelan's strength.

He was aroused—as aroused as she was. And although she was sure he'd planned to teach her a lesson, she felt the abrupt change in him when the kiss transmuted to a potent assault on every sense she owned.

A shameless, risky delight purred through her; she angled herself into his body and lifted onto her toes the better to reach his mouth. Caelan smiled against her lips and let her hands go, pulling her even closer against his powerful body, his arms tightening across her back.

Sensuous anticipation sizzled like wildfire across her

nerve ends, pierced every cell, throbbed deliciously through her breasts as she instinctively pressed against him, silently demanding satisfaction for the craving that possessed her.

Eyes gleaming fire and ice, he lifted his head. Abby's heart blocked her throat when she saw the stain of colour across his stark cheekbones and the way his face had clamped into a drawn, predatory focus.

On her, she thought, thrilled even as she realised the danger. For once, the control that was so integral a part of him had been stripped away; he wanted her as violently as she desired him—and, although he was fighting it, he wasn't able to defeat the longing. This wild clamour of the senses was entirely mutual, and she was shamelessly, fiercely excited.

CHAPTER TEN

EYES gleaming, Caelan lifted his head. 'What the hell do you do to me?'

The abrasive note in his voice broke into Abby's trance, but only to increase her delicious, reckless response. She slid her hands up his back, relishing the way the muscles flexed beneath her questing palms, the sheer power and strength of his big body, both protective and intensely dangerous.

'It's entirely mutual.' Her husky voice startled her.

'I know.' He cupped her face, his lean fingers exquisitely gentle around the fine bones, his thumbs stroking across her lips to silence her. 'That it affects *you* so profoundly is the only thing that makes *my* weakness endurable,' he said roughly, and kissed her again, this time on the brow and then on each eyelid as it swept down.

Weakness? Oh, yes—divine weakness...

All coherent thought fled when he slid his hands the silken length of her throat. Abby shivered violently at the contrast between the heat of his hands and a rush of cool, salt-scented air across her skin when he undid the buttons of her jacket and pushed it down her arms. The fine material whispered in the silence as it slipped onto the floor.

Somewhere in the dimmest, furthest reaches of Abby's brain a small voice insisted she stop this before it went too far, but she was already lost to the sensuous magic of his nearness.

Everything about him—the subtle scent that was his alone, the way his breathing deepened when he was aroused, his taste in her mouth—alerted long-repressed responses. The bitter ache of loss was rapidly banished by the incandescent pleasure of being held close to his hardening body, of knowing that soon there would be greater pleasure, pleasure piling on pleasure until the final addictive ecstasy of union.

Everything—her heart, her head—disengaged; she forced up her weighted lashes and stared at him with huge, dazed eyes, darkly dilating as his fingers moved across the wisp of silken camisole beneath.

Her pulse stopped until a potent, dangerous excitement drove it into action again. Colour burned along the striking sweep of his arrogant cheekbones, and his eyes were flame-blue, so hot she thought they should burn the pale skin he was examining with all a conqueror's unwavering intentness.

Only who was the conqueror here, who the vanquished? Abby recognised the will-power it took for him to transfer that molten gaze to her face.

'If you really don't want this, tell me to stop. Another heartbeat will be too late,' he warned, for once without his usual crisp delivery.

A deep, insistent craving drove her answer. 'It's too late for me now,' she muttered hoarsely, and took his hand and put it on her breast. Immediately obvious, the pleading, demanding nipple thrust against his palm.

Eyes still locked with hers in a challenge, his hand closed around the soft mound, a thumb rubbing gently across the tip in erotic loveplay.

Arrows of delight pierced her, homing straight and true to the aching emptiness in the pit of her stomach, heating her into slick surrender. She had been lost and was found, safe again after long, lonely weeks. A soft sound, almost a moan, escaped her lips, and she slid her arms beneath his shirt and stood on tiptoe to kiss the tanned skin of his throat, her lips and tongue lingering so she could inhale his scent and taste him.

He froze, his face clamping into a mask of ferocious tension, and then his broad shoulders lifted as he dragged in a deep breath.

'Not here,' he muttered.

But when he lifted her he didn't carry her into the house. The heavily erotic perfume of unknown flowers filled her nostrils as he strode along the terrace, cradling her as though she was the most precious of burdens. When a fold of fabric brushed across her arm she opened her eyes and caught a glimpse of some sort of pavilion, open to the sea, closed by drifting curtains of white on the other three sides. From the corner of her eye she saw a wide couch.

And then Caelan eased her with erotic slowness down his aroused body.

After that nothing else mattered. He slid the filmy camisole over her head and unclipped the bra beneath. Her skin tightened; she should have felt vulnerable standing in front of him naked from the waist up, but enchantment lent her courage.

'You are so beautiful you unman me,' he said with such harsh emphasis her heart rejoiced.

With bold intentness she scrutinised him, and laughed deep in her throat. 'It doesn't look like it,' she said, and stroked lightly, delicately, over the evidence of the effect she had on him.

But when he caught her hand and held it away, her confidence fled, only to return with his words, delivered with tight restraint.

'Do that again and it will all be over,' he said, through clenched teeth. 'I might just be able to control myself if you undress me, but I'm not going to make it if you do any more.'

Excitement burgeoned into fever, summoning a heat that flashed through her like lightning, yet she was shivering and her hands trembled as she unbuttoned his shirt.

She hadn't forgotten how magnificent he was, how the sight of his wide chest and wider shoulders aroused her. She let herself stroke once across his sleek tanned skin, delighting in its warm exotic blend of bronze and gold, but stopped when his ragged intake of breath warned her she was too close to the sensitive nipple.

In a shaken, thick voice he said, 'I'll do the rest.'

Abby didn't trust herself to watch him undress. Instead, she fumbled with the fastener of her skirt, eventually getting herself out of it to stand in nothing but a sexy little suspender belt and the exquisite silk stockings the couturier had insisted on. Her body shook with such keen hunger that she thought she might not be able to stop herself from coming there and then at the sight of him.

So she kept her lashes lowered, only for them to fly up in startled shock when he dropped to his knees in front of her and slid his arms around her hips, kissing the soft indentation of her waist.

Her pulse pounded through her body. Unable to resist, she threaded her hands through the cool silk of his hair, holding him close until he said against her skin, 'If we're going to take these off I need to see what I'm doing.'

She held her breath as he unclipped the suspenders, but when he kissed the fine, satiny skin at the top of her thighs her knees buckled. Lips drawn back in a feral smile, he freed her from the wisp of satin suspender belt and stood up, magnificently naked and openly desirous.

Inside Abby, excitement transformed every nerve im

pulse into deep-seated craving; her hands clenched and she felt it beat up through her like a bushfire, beautiful beyond compare and ferociously dangerous.

For a few seconds he stood looking down at her, eyes smouldering crystals in his lean, tanned face. 'You're mine,' he said on a guttural note. 'Admit it.'

'Yes,' she conceded, unable to deny him this triumph.

His arms closed around her, clamping her against him so that they came down onto the couch in one smooth, powerful movement. He bent his head to rest his cheek against her breasts.

Abby's heart dissolved. 'And you are mine,' she claimed, her hand against his cheek, thrilling to the soft abrasion against her palm and the sensitive skin he was kissing.

He turned his face and his lips closed on the centre of her breast, and she cried out again, a ragged, wordless utterance of sexual hunger so powerful she couldn't think beyond her acute need for the heady satisfaction only Caelan could give her.

Primitively, she wanted to lie beneath him in complete surrender, to feel the hard thrust of his body as he entered her, to be driven up that slow, passionate rise towards the heights of rapture. And then, when the pleasure became unbearable she'd give him everything, and take from him too as the whole power of his big body clenched in release.

But not yet. Not for long minutes yet...

Slowly, as though every revisited caress, every newly minted sensation, every memory of how it had been for them a month before needed to be coaxed back into life, they explored each other's bodies. Abby could see how difficult it was for him; she knew how tense she was with frustrated desire, yet because this was special she let herself become as absorbed as he was in their journey of rediscovery.

And then, when at last neither could bear it any longer, he eased himself over and into her, watching her face so that he could see every nuance of emotion.

Her breath rasping her throat, Abby lifted her hips and locked her legs around his, pulling him into her as she tightened her arms around him. He gave a muffled groan and every bit of finesse went west. He thrust deeply into her, setting off an explosive release that rocketed her into orgasm. Panting, she felt waves of agonised pleasure catch her up and fling her into ecstasy.

He joined her there, and in that exhilarating final frenzy of physical passion she accepted that she would stay with him, not for all the reasons it made sense—not because he threatened her, not for Michael, but because she needed Caelan on some level that transcended everything else.

Love? She didn't know, and at that moment she didn't much care. It was enough.

And afterwards, it was poignantly sweet to lie in his arms, sweet to listen to the slow recovery of their mingled breaths and pulses, sweet to lie beneath him and feel his beloved weight on her once more. Yet a profound sadness overwhelmed her.

With all this, was she being greedy craving his love? Because that was what had happened. Somehow, in spite of everything, she'd done the unbearable—given him her heart.

Caelan rolled over onto his back and looped a long arm around her, pulling her to lie against him, her body lax and depleted, her face buried against his neck.

After a long time he said, 'Are you using any sort of birth control?'

'No,' she admitted in a voice that seemed to come from a huge distance away.

He said something blood-curdling beneath his breath in a language that had to be Dacian. 'And, idiot that I am, I didn't even think of it.' He tipped up her chin and examined her face, his own speculative. 'Why not?'

She searched for an answer, knowing that there was no good one. 'Like you, I didn't think of it,' she finally confessed. Only she'd had a month to consider it...

'So you might be pregnant right now.'

Oh, to carry Caelan's child under her heart...

Any child would be another chain binding them together to provide security for Michael, she reminded herself, a hostage to make sure she didn't leave this marriage. A child would simply give Caelan more leverage.

'I doubt it,' she said slowly, trying to pull away. His arms tightened around her, and into his neck she muttered, 'I believe it takes even the most virile sperm some time to actually get to the egg.'

But she couldn't suppress a tiny thrill at the thought of that most elemental of journeys happening inside her.

A note in his soft laughter told her that it excited him too. He stroked the curve of her breast, and that primal heat re-ignited in every cell.

Holding her gaze with his own, he said evenly, 'A child would convince everyone that we plan to stay together.'

Even though she'd thought exactly the same thing, to hear it put into words hurt in some obscure fashion. She snapped, 'I'll do a lot for Michael, but I'm damned if I'll have a child for him.'

Caelan said grimly, 'I hope that doesn't mean what it sounds like.'

'What?'

He was watching her, his face hard and purposeful. 'That you'll make sure no child eventuates.'

Abby felt sick. 'No, I won't do that,' she said quietly.

His gaze pierced her, searching into her very soul. 'I believe you.' He smiled when a sudden yawn took her completely by surprise. 'Bedtime, I think.'

He got up, perfectly unconcerned at his nudity, and scooped her up. When she realised he was going to leave the pavilion she blurted, 'What about servants?'

'Don't worry,' he drawled, 'there's nobody here but us.'

He carried her to a room filled with the slow music of the sea. Another bottle of champagne—or perhaps the same one—stood on a table in the window. A huge bed dominated the room.

What now? Abby thought frantically.

'Our clothes have been unpacked,' Caelan told her. He nodded towards a couple of doors. 'The one on the left is your bathroom; the other is mine.'

Two bathrooms? But clearly he intended them to sleep together, and some privacy might help her regain some self-possession. Relieved, she said thinly, 'I'll have a shower,' and escaped into a fantasy bathroom of marble and mirrors and exotic plants, the air heavily scented by the jasmine flowers that had been scattered in the huge, square bath.

Abby caught back a sob. Someone had gone to an enormous amount of trouble to set the scene for their honeymoon!

She welcomed the soothing hiss of cool water over her sensitised skin, then wrapped herself in the sensuous slither of satin she found hanging behind the door, a nightgown in palest green. Where had it come from?

It had to be Caelan; another example of his thoughtfulness—or his experience in romantic encounters. Frowning, she finished her preparations for the night, but before she'd removed the cosmetics from her face her speculation was replaced by pain.

Of course she'd fallen in love with him! Who was she to think she could succeed in keeping her heart inviolate when so many other women, sophisticated and worldly, had failed?

He must never know. All she had to cling to was her pride, and that would be shattered in humiliation if he knew she'd surrendered far more than her body to him.

The room was empty when she returned, but he came in shortly after her, devastating in a black wrap that emphasised the smooth, powerful flow of his body beneath the thin silk.

'Champagne?' he asked after a swift, keen glance that seemed to strip through the fragile protective skin she'd erected.

She shook her head. 'No, thank you. Caelan, who has gone to such trouble for us?'

'Trouble?'

Awkwardly she gestured at the exquisite garment she wore. 'This nightgown isn't mine,' she said, 'and my bath was scattered with flowers—some kind of jasmine, I think.'

'The gown is yours,' he said coolly. 'And the jasmine flowers would be the idea of the housekeeper. You can thank her tomorrow morning.'

'I'll do that,' she said, adding with stiff formality, 'And thank you for the gown.'

'You look like something wild from the woods,' he remarked, coming towards her.

Abby's heart started hammering in her chest. She couldn't move, couldn't do anything but let herself be captured by his dark sexuality. When he held out his hand she took it and let him draw her to the bed.

Later—much later—she listened to his breathing in the darkness and wondered wearily what was going to happen now. Exhaustion, physical and mental, dragged her down, yet she couldn't get to sleep.

Right from the start she'd known that his objective was—and a very fine one, too—to make Michael happy. She wasn't anything more than a necessary evil, albeit one he wanted.

Why couldn't she accept what he offered without longing for more?

She lay looking into an unbearable future until dawn; only then, to the sound of birds carolling, did she slide into exhausted sleep.

She woke to the scent of jasmine, and the sound of a telephone ringing at some distance.

'What the—?' she groaned, jackknifing upwards. She stared blankly at the curtains and pushed a tangle of hair back from her face. By the position of the sun it had to be mid-morning. God, she was making a habit of this!

Caelan's voice—deep and deliberate, textured in intimidating shades of authority—brought back the previous night. Erotic memories swamped her, so potent she had to fight back the instinct to cower under the bedclothes. If only it were that easy to hide! Last night she'd surrendered everything to the compulsion of passion, and been ruthlessly shown the limits of her will-power; now she had to face the consequences.

She pushed back the sheet and swung her feet onto the floor at the moment that Caelan walked in through a wall of shuttered glass doors. Fully dressed, he was carrying a tray.

Perched on the edge of the bed with the sleek satin nightgown rumpled around her thighs, she felt intensely vulnerable. She caught his raised brows as he took in her immodest covering, and, hot with embarrassment, swung her legs up onto the bed and hauled the sheet over them.

His smile told her she needn't have bothered, that he remembered everything of their fevered love-making the previous night.

'You didn't stir when I looked in earlier,' Caelan said, his voice amused and silkily reminiscent, 'so I decided to let you sleep as long as you could.'

Abby fought back another wave of humiliation. No doubt he thought he had her exactly where he wanted her—besotted! 'Thank you,' she said tonelessly. 'But I can be ready for breakfast in ten minutes.'

'It's all right,' he said with cool irony that made her feel stupid, and put the tray on the bedside table.

When she tensed, he smiled and bent to kiss her, his lips warm and seducing. In spite of everything, her mouth softened under his.

But when Caelan straightened, he looked down at her with burnished eyes as cold as a polar star.

'It's too late for second thoughts,' he said implacably. 'We've been married twice, and Michael is safe. I made vows; like you, I keep my promises.'

'I'm not having second thoughts.' Her voice was every bit as determined as his.

He held her gaze for several long moments, then nodded. 'Eat up. And then see if you can sleep some more. I'm afraid that I have work to do, but I'll see you in a couple of hours.'

Watching him go, Abby bit her lip. So much for last night's wild passion; today he was all business. Although the change hurt some newly sensitive part of herself, she forced down as much of the breakfast as she could, then hastily showered, skin scorching when she discovered the marks of their loving on it. No bruising—he had been exquisitely tender with her—but soft abrasions from his beard.

And her slow, deep tiredness wasn't all because of her lack of sleep—it went right down to her bones, and came from exhilarating sexual satiation.

She explored a little of the garden, but didn't like to go too far; it seemed an intrusion. When Caelan found her she was reading out on the terrace.

He gave her a narrow glance, then said, 'You forgot these,' and tossed her a handful of fire.

'What—*oh*!' She caught the rings automatically. Last night she'd taken them off and left them on the bedside cabinet.

'Put them on,' he said shortly.

Her heart heavy, she slid them onto her finger. They meant so much to her—and so little to Caelan. This, after all, was a sensible marriage, entered into for entirely practical reasons.

She looked up and caught Caelan's kindling glance; well, perhaps not entirely practical, she conceded. But what would happen when he was sated with her?

CHAPTER ELEVEN

'HOME again!' Michael announced, beaming with pleasure when the car drew up in the reserved parking slot beneath the hotel. He turned to the woman beside him and said, 'Here we are, Nanny! Home again!'

Relief warred with unease in Abby. She'd been ambivalent when Caelan suggested that Ilana accompany them back to New Zealand, but she had to admit that the nursemaid's help had made the plane trip back from Dacia less tiring. Between them all, Michael was kept busy and happy.

Perhaps it was a good thing the four days of their honeymoon, a jumble of vivid images that still brought the colour to her cheeks, a blur of sun and sea and passionate love-making, had been superseded by the long flight back to New Zealand.

Not love—*sex*, she reminded herself astringently. There'd been no love in Caelan's expertise, just a huge natural understanding of the pleasure points in a woman's body and a compelling masculinity that transformed her desire into a pulsing beat of reckless hunger.

And experience—lots and lots of experience. Put crudely, Caelan was a stud. He knew how to pleasure a woman, how to make her sob with longing and scream with ecstasy and eventually sate her of everything but the need to sleep in his arms.

The silence in the car recalled her to her surroundings. Caelan was looking down at her, his eyes gleaming and his mouth curved in a smile that sent a sensual shiver down her backbone. He couldn't know what she was thinking, but she'd better thrust those memories into the darkest recesses of her mind before she gave herself away.

It seemed incredible that she'd wondered when Caelan would get tired of her.

Early days yet, she thought cynically.

Not that she had much time to worry. Over breakfast the day after they arrived back in New Zealand he said, 'When is a good time for you to see a land agent?'

'Me? What for?'

'I'm feeling dynastic,' he said with a sardonic smile. 'We need a house, and you should choose it. I deal with one agent—my PA will make an appointment for her to call on you.'

'Any time.' She hid an odd pang of pleasure with her cool tone.

With a swift, unreadable glance he said, 'You'll manage.'

His assurance of her ability boosted her confidence, but she had to ask, 'What sort of house do you want?'

He leaned back and surveyed her. 'That's for you to decide. Do you want to live in Auckland, or would you rather be out in the country?'

They discussed it for some minutes, eventually deciding on a place with room for the pony Michael wanted, and then Caelan said, 'We have invitations to deal with. I've already accepted one—it's a dinner for a charity I'm interested in. White tie, so you'll need a suitable outfit.' He frowned. 'Your credit card should have arrived; I'll check the mail.'

She bit her lip. Common sense told her that she had to have some income, but she felt sullied, like a kept woman.

Of course he noticed. 'I've already paid your allowance into your account. We can discuss the rest of the invitations over tonight. Are you all right to stay with Cia and Hunt next weekend?'

'Yes.'

He gave her another keen, too-perceptive scrutiny. 'I thought you liked them.'

'I do, very much.'

'But?'

Of course he wouldn't let it go. She said diffidently, 'I'm not a huge party person, Caelan.'

'Nor I,' he returned promptly. 'Don't fret about our social life. You'll find your feet. Oh, by the way, I've been contacted by at least four magazines for interviews. Do you want to do them?'

Abby shuddered. 'No, thanks.'

He grinned, but said, 'I'd already refused, so even if you'd longed to adorn their pages your hard, dictatorial husband would have forbidden it. And the social welfare caseworker has been in touch. She'll call in to see us tomorrow afternoon.' His voice altered. 'Just be careful when you're out and about. There's been a lot of publicity, unfortunately, and it wouldn't surprise me if you're the target of photographers.'

She said gloomily, 'Three months ago I'd never have believed that I'd have to dodge paparazzi.'

Or kidnappers. That still didn't seem possible in New Zealand, but whenever she or Michael went out a man who doubled as chauffeur was close behind.

'The fuss will die down,' Caelan said coolly.

And indeed, after a couple of weeks of embarrassing attention, an All Black player was discovered to be having an affair with his brother's wife, and the media's interest switched abruptly.

The appointment with the caseworker—and the several subsequent ones—went well. Michael showed off on his jungle gym with every appearance of delight, introduced his nanny with pride, and chattered brightly about his new friends at the pre-school.

On the surface, she and Caelan settled easily into a life together, sharing Michael without too many significant silences. Occasionally their good humour stretched thin, but both made valiant efforts not to let underlying tension impinge on the third member of the family.

But although the sex remained wonderful and Caelan's support gave her the confidence to deal well with the various glittering social occasions they attended, a bleak sense of isolation robbed her days of delight and joy.

Nevertheless, she enjoyed the weekend with Lucia and Hunt on his huge cattle station. They weren't the only guests; she soon realised she'd been introduced to a tight-knit social circle that rarely appeared in the gossip columns. She and another woman, also from Auckland, discovered they had much in common.

After that she lunched with Peta McIntosh several times. Forthright and sensible and completely in love with her gorgeous husband, Peta had run her own farm. Abby hoped they were working their way towards friendship. It had been a long time since she'd had a good woman friend.

Soon the halcyon days in Dacia faded into a memory of pageantry and old-world fairy tale as Abby flung herself into the search for the perfect house. Michael blossomed, exercising every muscle in his sturdy, compact body on the gym bars, swimming, and teaching his nursemaid all the English nursery rhymes and stories he knew, while unconsciously absorbing Dacian from her.

Most afternoons his uncle came home early from work

to play with him, and their relationship prospered. But after dinner each night Caelan worked from the office in the apartment, and several times he flew to various places around the Pacific for meetings. He didn't ask Abby to go with him, but he did ring every evening.

Always he brought home gifts—amusing novelties for Michael, a New Zealand dictionary for Ilana.

For Abby there were golden pearls from Tahiti, an exquisite silk kimono from Japan, and after a trip to Australia he slipped a dress ring onto her finger, a glittering square-cut golden diamond surrounded by smaller ones.

'Yes, I thought it was the same colour as your eyes,' he said, and kissed her with controlled passion.

His thoughtfulness, his casual generosity, hurt her. Oddly, it seemed to emphasise that their relationship was a fake.

Forget about any meeting of minds, any emotional commitment. It wasn't love Caelan felt, merely its mindless brother, lust. She'd tried to trick it out in the panoply of love, but it was time to face the truth.

She'd stay safe if she didn't expect too much from this marriage or this man, she cautioned that romantic, hungry part of herself. But in spite of her attempts to grow a skin over her emotions, she couldn't stop herself from falling more and more in love with her husband each day.

Although he didn't want her love, his need for her body didn't fade; each night she surrendered to an ever-increasing hunger, flaming in his arms, but when it was over she wondered despairingly how she was going to keep her soul intact.

Previously she'd envied his iron control, preserved even when they'd made love. But that had been when she thought there must be something warmer behind it.

Now she was discovering in the most painful way possible that control was all he had.

Once, lying in his arms, she'd blurted, 'Have you ever been drunk?'

His brows rose. 'I admit to my fair share of the usual adolescent excesses,' he said blandly. 'Yes, I've been drunk. I didn't like it, and I don't plan to do it again.'

It figured, she thought savagely.

About a month after they arrived back he said casually just before he left for work, 'Are you busy today?'

Carefully composing her expression, Abby looked up from watching Michael do acrobatics on his gym bars. 'This morning I'm going out to Clevedon to look at a property the agent thinks might be suitable, but after that I'm free.'

'Meet me at the office and we'll have lunch together.'

Her foolish heart sped up. They'd never been on a date. 'I—well, yes, I'd love that.' And because the amused glint in his eyes made her self-conscious, she added primly, 'Thank you.'

He bent and dropped a swift, disturbing kiss on her mouth. 'I'll see you at one, then.'

At one she was in a private waiting room in his office reading a magazine when the skin between her shoulder blades tingled and her heartbeat sped up. Slowly she turned her head. Caelan stood in the doorway, tall and dark and dangerous in his superbly cut suit, examining her with narrowed eyes. He wasn't smiling.

'You look fantastic,' he said calmly. 'Hungry?'

'More than ready,' she admitted, pleased in spite of herself at the easy compliment. 'I've spent the morning tramping around a farm.'

'Any good?'

'I didn't like the house much—too heavily formal.' She frowned. 'Sometimes I think I'm too fussy.'

'Perhaps we should discuss building a house for ourselves. Forget about it for now, though.'

She'd expected to eat at a restaurant, but in the lift reserved for him he pressed a button and they shot upwards. 'Where are we going?' she asked.

'To a private dining room,' he told her calmly.

The lift slowed and stopped—only one floor up, she noted.

She gave him a startled glance. 'Why do we need privacy?'

His broad shoulders moved in the superbly tailored jacket and his eyes were bland and noncommittal. 'I have something to tell you. I don't want to risk being overheard.' He opened the door and ushered her into a small foyer.

Stomach clenching, she said, 'What?'

He looked down through his lashes, eyes gleaming like blue crystals, but silently opened a door and stepped back. 'Come in.'

'Said the spider to the fly.' Tension tightened her skin, but she made a show of looking around the large space he escorted her into, half sitting room, the other half occupied by an already-set table.

'A very beautiful fly,' Caelan returned smoothly.

It was another superficial, meaningless compliment; Abby knew very well that she wasn't beautiful. 'Thank you,' she said tonelessly.

Being Caelan, he didn't leave it at that. 'You don't believe me?' he drawled.

She shrugged. 'Striking is probably the most apt word for me—and then only because of my hair.' She didn't give him time to answer. Concentrating on shoring up her fragile façade, she asked, 'What is this place?'

'It's an apartment used by executives from overseas.' And by him when he needed privacy. He indicated the table, already set with silver and wineglasses and flowers. 'Come and sit down.'

'Where does the food come from?'

'The restaurant on the ground floor.' He held out a chair for her, and, once she sat down, pushed it in.

He was treating her like a guest. Yet in spite of her apprehension her body tingled and the low, subliminal throb of desire warmed her cheeks beneath the soft haze of blusher. His hands lingered on her shoulders, just long enough for the heat burning through her to turn feral.

'You forgot your skin,' he said calmly.

'What?'

It suddenly seemed very stupid for her to be here alone with him. Over the past weeks Michael and Ilana had acted as emotional chaperones, reminding them why they'd embarked on this masquerade marriage.

Here, on neutral ground, his fingers resting lightly on the silken skin of her neck, every sense quivering with the pleasure of his closeness, bold, consuming desire clamoured up through her like a summons, utterly elemental and reckless.

Was this planned?

Oh, almost certainly. Did she care?

Not at this minute, she thought, and thrilled to the knowledge.

Only to deflate when Caelan stepped back.

Shielding her dilating pupils with her lashes, she surveyed him as he sat down opposite her. The carnal need smouldering in her noted the stripped, fierce prominence of his facial structure, telling her he was as aware of her as she was of him. And his eyes were lit with blue fire, diamond-bright and intense.

'What did you mean—I forgot my skin?' Shocked and startled by the languid drift of the words, she folded her lips into a firm, straight line.

He let his gaze roam her face. 'You said it was your hair that makes you stand out. It helps, but you have skin like luminous gold silk. And your eyes are tilted enough to give you an air of mystery. Then you smile, and it's Circe all over again, an enchantress turning men into swine with that mocking smile.'

He spoke with cool detachment, and her heart froze in horror. Was that how he saw her—or himself? Did he despise himself for wanting her?

'Until I say something and reveal a perfectly ordinary woman,' she said, blundering along as best she could when her insides were churning.

Yet she was glad he'd said it. They'd never explored their deepest emotions and values. Oh, they'd discussed politics and music and art; they'd made love like tigers, fiercely and with such passion that it temporarily eased the ache in her heart, but love was founded on knowledge and understanding, not the primeval recklessness of sexual hunger.

He frowned. 'Ordinary? Far from it,' he said drily. '*Ordinary* women don't commit themselves to felony and poverty to keep a promise made to a woman who had no right to extract it.'

A subdued hum of activity through a door into the next room stopped her swift rebuttal, but when the waiter had left Abby said, 'Whether she had reason or not, Gemma was desperate. And I don't regret anything I did for Michael.' She looked down and added painfully, 'What I do regret is that you missed his first years. It's no excuse, but I truly didn't think you'd be interested in him. Gemma's fears influenced me, and I'd like to believe that the horror of what happened to her unhinged me temporarily. I should have done things differently.'

The silence that followed was almost too much to bear. In the end she glanced up, and met hooded eyes in a lean, arrested face.

She said hurriedly, 'You're so good with him, and he already loves you and trusts you. He's missed out on knowing you, and you've missed out too. I wish I'd contacted you—although I'd have fought you to a standstill when you tried to gain custody.'

Caelan said slowly, 'Actually, that's what I brought you here to talk about.'

She froze. 'What do you mean?'

'I've been contacted by the writer who was doing a book on tragedies of the South Pacific.'

Tender, delicious asparagus turned to ashes in her mouth. Eyes dilating, she stared at him as the colour drained from her face. 'And?' she managed.

'I've met him. He's done his research.' He spoke dispassionately. 'He knows that you claimed Michael for your own child.'

Her fork clattered onto the tablecloth. 'Oh, God!' But before he could speak, she said urgently, 'Caelan, it doesn't matter. In a way, I'll be glad to have it out in the open. And if I do get prosecuted and—and convicted, then I know you'll look after Michael.'

'Don't worry—he won't mention anything beyond the fact that Michael is now our son.'

'What?' She dragged in a jagged breath.

'You're my wife,' he said, as though that explained it. Shaken and sickened, she bit her lip. Of course he wouldn't want his wife—Michael's mother—to be sent to prison. 'I'm sorry.'

'You did what you felt was best for Michael.' His voice was cool, almost indifferent. 'And you were right; nursemaids don't have the same emotional investments in their charges as mothers. Michael is open and loving and happy, and he's secure in your love. He likes Ilana very much, but he runs to you when he hurts himself.'

Warmed though she was by his acceptance, she said miserably, 'But what's to stop this writer from blackmailing you again? Because I assume that's what he did.'

He said austerely, 'I don't blackmail easily. But he didn't even try; he simply wanted to make sure that he didn't make an enemy by revealing something I didn't want generally known. So, you see, that power and money and influence you so rightly despise have some advantages.' His smile was a masterpiece of sardonic acceptance. 'It appears I have a reputation for being a bad enemy.'

She could believe that. Choosing her words carefully, she said, 'I only despise power and influence and money that's used to harm people.'

Caelan said crisply, 'I'm glad to hear it. Forget about the writer; he's not going to spill the beans. When he contacted me I got in touch with my solicitor, who said it was highly unlikely you'd be prosecuted. And once Michael is legally our child you'll be safe, especially as you've shown yourself to be an excellent mother. So you've no reason to worry.'

'I'm not,' she said, and realised it was true. She picked up the glass of wine she hadn't touched, and sipped a small amount, then asked something that *had* been concerning her. 'Is it possible that Gemma's mother might want access to Michael?'

'She didn't want access to her own child,' he returned caustically, 'so why would she be interested in her grandson?' He gave her a shrewd glance. 'But if it eases that tender heart of yours, once the adoption is signed, sealed and delivered, we'll contact her and let her know.'

Abby looked at her plate, then back at him. 'I was never happy with the promise I made Gemma,' she said quietly, 'but I had to keep it.'

His brows lifted. 'I know that now. The woman I thought you were would have sold him to me. And as this is confession time, I'll admit that you were right to be scathing about my supposed plans for Michael when I arrived in Nukuroa.'

'*Supposed?*' she asked sharply.

'In reality I'd planned to set you and Michael up in a house in the suburbs in Auckland.' His mouth slanted in self-derision. 'I'd already bought a pleasant place with a garden in Titirangi. You'd have liked it—lots of trees for Michael to climb and lawns to run across. I intended to see him several times a week, have him sleep over with me when he got to know me—'

'And take him from me when he did know you!' she interrupted fiercely.

He shrugged, his mouth compressed. 'Yes. I didn't intend to let either him or you impinge on my life much.'

Something broke inside Abby. Panting, her voice low and furious, she snarled, 'You accused me of playing with Michael's life. Didn't it occur to you that you were doing exactly the same thing?'

'Yes.'

Scornfully she demanded, 'So what made you change your mind?'

His brows lifted. 'I told myself it was revenge.'

Silence followed the ugly word, dark as a storm with

unspoken thoughts and emotions. Every inchoate suspicion, every dark wondering moment, came back to haunt her.

In a dead voice she said, 'So you used the one thing I wanted, to stay with Michael, to force me into marriage.' Her chin came up and she stared at him accusingly, eyes wide and unblinking as a cat's. 'Is this where you tell me that you're going to divorce me?'

Blue eyes glittering, he demanded, 'Is that what you think?'

'What else can I think?' So angry and despairing she could barely articulate, she flung the words at him like bullets, knowing even as she spoke that it was useless. 'It would be the perfect revenge!'

His mirthless bark of laughter shocked her. He said between his teeth, 'Only if you loved me.'

She stared at him, and then closed her eyes, because of course he knew. Oh, the perfect revenge, she realised in bitter despair. Show a glimpse of paradise, and then snatch it away.

'Well?' he demanded.

She said thinly, 'What?'

'Damn it, Abby, I love you!' He spoke in a goaded voice that was unlike Caelan's confident tones.

Sometimes she'd dreamed of him saying that, and always she'd been ecstatic, filled with reciprocal delight and love. Now she felt empty, as though disillusion had ripped the heart from her body and left her with nothing but hollowness in its place.

A hollowness that wasn't filled when he said roughly, 'Of course I don't want a divorce.'

He couldn't have chosen a way to hurt her more. She longed with every atom in her body to give in, take what he could give and pretend to believe that they could somehow forge a life together. Forcing herself to look him in the eyes, she said brokenly, 'If you think I'm going to be like your father, so desperately in love that I'll put up with anything you want to dish out, you can think again. I'd rather die!'

His eyes glittered. 'Abby, listen to me! I love you.' And when she stared at him he said furiously, 'I can't live without you. I would die for you.'

Her throat locked. She could only stare at him with enormous eyes, her lips trembling. 'I don't believe it.'

'Believe it, if you believe nothing else.'

'Why?'

He paused, as though her question startled him. She saw self-control shutter his eyes against her, clamp his features into a ruthless mask. Panic kicked her in the stomach; she'd been an utter idiot! Far better to have said nothing, to shore up her defences and retain some tatters of pride.

Unable to stand it any longer, she scrambled to her feet. 'Everything you've just told me indicates that you'll never trust me. What sort of love is that? Useless.'

A muscle flicked above his angular jawbone and the white line around his lips made her realise that she'd gone too far. He covered the distance between them in a silent, predatory lunge that drove adrenalin through her in a desperate flood. She swung around, but he caught her by the wrist before she could take more than one step and pulled her to face him.

For the first time ever she looked at him and saw the man without the mask, his eyes narrowed slits of blue, glittering cold as diamonds between black lashes, his mouth compressed into a thin line, real emotion blazing through.

'And you love me,' he said, his lips barely moving,

and when she stared at him, colour firing up through her skin, he laughed deep in his throat and drew her into his arms in a movement that reminded her of the times she'd danced with him.

'No,' she whispered, shaking so much she thought she'd fall if it weren't for his strong arms around her.

'No what? No, you don't love me? Don't lie, Abby, you just admitted it when you said you'd rather die than live in an unequal relationship like my father.' He brushed her lips with his, tantalising her with the light pressure, so erotic she had to close her eyes against him.

But that only made things worse; she couldn't see, but she could smell the faint scent of their arousal and feel the hard strength of his body against hers. Her body clamoured for release and she had no idea what he'd just said, what she'd said, anything at all but the fact that she loved this man with everything she was, had loved him since the first time she'd set eyes on him.

And then she was free and above the chattering of her teeth she heard him say in a raw voice, 'Abby, don't cry. It's all right—you can do whatever you want to do. Just don't cry. I'm not worth it.'

She opened eyes magnified by brimming tears, and said on a sob, 'You're worth so much more, you idiot!'

A wry smile curved his mouth. He reached out a hand and slowly, knowing she was ceding much more than a simple handclasp, she put hers in it. He kissed her fingers, and then in a gesture that twisted her heart he held the palm to his face, and said, 'Is it too late to start again? Properly, this time?'

And this time she believed him. She'd glimpsed the vulnerability behind his intimidating authority, and it had shaken her to her heart. 'It's not too late,' she said softly, with trembling lips.

He held her eyes, his own gaze dark and intense, but not as intense as his voice when he said, 'Do you know when I realised that I loved you?'

Stunned delight shafted through her, rendering her mute. She shook her head.

'On Dacia, the night of our wedding, when you told me indignantly that, although you loved Michael, you wouldn't have a baby for him.' His voice deepened. 'That's when I wondered if it was possible you loved me, because you didn't say you wouldn't have a baby for me. I didn't think I could ever love anyone, but at that moment I felt as though someone had hit me in the heart.' His voice deepened. 'Talk about Cupid's arrows—it was as quick and unexpected as that. One second I didn't know that what I felt for you was love. The next I did. I realised that I wanted to wake up next to you all the mornings of my life.'

It sounded like a vow. She stared at him, then opened her mouth to speak.

A long forefinger closed her lips, signalling that he hadn't finished. Voice very low and sure, he said, 'I've loved you for all my life, it seems. Certainly since well before we were married. I wouldn't face it because I thought being in control of my life was more important than love.' His voice roughened. 'I was wrong.'

Abby gazed into his face, her eyes enormous and questing. What she saw there made sky-rockets go off inside her in mute, overwhelming joy. He gave her a wicked smile, and her last resistance melted, evaporated like rain on a hot summer's day, drifting away into nothingness. She kissed the finger across her mouth.

His eyes flared electric blue, but he shook his head. 'Let me say this now. Although I loved Gemma, and I grieved for her, you have no idea how I felt when I found out that you were still alive. But you'd stolen her child, and I hated you. It was simpler.'

Abby put her hand on his arm, feeling the muscles clench beneath her fingertips. 'She loved you too. Truly. Would you have tried to find me if I hadn't had Michael?'

'Yes,' he said simply. 'Even when I saw the first photograph of you imitating a mouse, your glorious hair straightened and dull, those appalling spectacles hiding your cat-shaped eyes, I must have suspected that it was only a matter of time before I'd love you.'

'You were an utter beast,' she said, believing at last.

'I was fighting a battle with myself,' he said quietly. 'You made a promise to Gemma, and you'd carried it out as best you could. Everything you've done you've done for Michael, and you had every reason to believe that he'd be far better off with you than with me.'

'I was wrong,' she said quietly, 'and so was Gemma. You love him already.'

He shrugged. 'He's a great little kid.'

'You told me he needed a man in his life and I was very scornful, but you were right. He's opened out— become much more of a little boy since we've been here.' She paused, then added, 'And he loves you too.'

A stain of colour emphasised his splendid cheekbones. 'He's a sunny-natured child.' He looked down at her and the passion that had been simmering beneath the surface while they talked flamed up into his eyes, heating them to crystalline fire. 'I'm sorry for hurting you; I'm sorry I was such an idiot that I couldn't recognise what I felt for you. I thought I'd made you resent me so much that the only way to bind you to me was with sex.'

She smiled at him, her almond eyes lazy and languorous, her mouth subtly beckoning. 'I enjoyed that immensely, but I loved you before we made love. I refused to admit it too, so let's not blame each other.'

Potent desire rushed through Caelan, a paradoxical mixture of fierce tenderness. Laughing, his eyes gleaming, he picked her up and held her high in his arms. 'Do you want to finish your lunch?' he asked.

'Somehow I'm not hungry for food any more,' she said demurely, adding with a fascinating upwards glance from beneath her lashes, 'Is there a bed close by?'

'A large, executive-size bed just through that door,' he told her. With the urgent hunger of a lover, he carried her into the adjoining room, and into the rest of their lives together, with complete confidence in their mutual love.

Robyn Donald brings you more royal romance
in Rich, Ruthless and Secretly Royal,
available September 2009,
in Mills & Boon® Modern™ romance.